# THE QUEEN'S ROAD

# THE QUEEN'S ROAD

## R.S. BELCHER

Charlotte, NC

FALSTAFF
BOOKS

WWW.FALSTAFFBOOKS.COM

*To my wonderful, loving, supportive children—Jon, Emily, and Stephanie.
I love you! Every story begins and ends with you.*

# THE QUEEN'S ROAD

BY

**R. S. Belcher**

# PART I

## INITIATION

# 1

_____

The asphalt ocean of the Bingo Truck Stop was finally giving up its heat at close to three in the morning. June in Texas was a sneak peek at Hell. Ray Cosa watched under the yellow, sodium haze of the gas pump awning and the lights as a hognose snake, sleepy and lazy from the heat, crawled its way across I-10. It was crushed under a big rig rolling into Bingo's rear lot.

Ray knew exactly how the snake felt.

In less than twelve hours, Juanita, his mom, would be dead if he didn't come up with two grand. Maybe him too, since he was the one who had made the promise to Mateo that he'd get the money and even up Juanita's debt. Two grand, no problem. Yeah, when he told his mom's drug dealer, he'd believed it too.

Mateo had driven up to Mom's house yesterday, in a tricked-out 1970 Chevy Nova, three of his Ciudad Azteca gang brothers riding along. He was blasting that *narcocorridos* shit. Ray hated it. It had the sound of traditional Mexican folk music, but the lyrics glorified drug dealers and murderers. He hated Mateo and his stupid, violent, swaggering *mara*. As much as he didn't want to admit it, he hated Juanita for once again getting herself in this deep.

Mateo was a ripped little *cholo* punk, skinny, with compact, tight muscles. He had tattoos all over his shaved head, face, neck, arms, and hands. He dressed in a floral western shirt, untucked to hide his piece, and baggy jeans, hanging low on his narrow ass. Ray and Mateo had gone to elementary school together and were the same age, but Mateo always treated Ray like he was still a child.

"Ramon," he said as he came up onto the porch. His eyes were dark and dead. "'Nita around?" Nita was around. She was high as a fucking kite in her bedroom, passed out. She had been so scared of what Mateo was going to do when she didn't have the money again. She ran into the only safe place she knew to hide, a drug-induced stupor. Ray had told her he'd talk to Mateo.

"Tuesday," she had whispered through the crack in her partially opened bedroom door. She was slurring her words. "Tell him I'll have some of it on Tuesday when the check comes in."

"That's for rent and power," Ray reminded her, but she was already fading out. Juanita had been beautiful before Pop passed away. He used to tell Ray and his brother the stories of how he had courted her while they were in high school and during his time in the Marines. How every *vato* wanted her and then wanted to be him when they were together. Now, Juanita's blonde hair was turning silver, and it was tangled. Her brown eyes were glazed over and bloodshot, and the dark circles underneath were like craters. If she weighed 90 pounds, it would be a miracle.

"Tuesday," she whispered and shut the door in Ray's face.

Ray stayed between the dealer and the front door. "She is, but she's not feeling too good right now."

Mateo snorted, "Yeah, I bet she ain't. She gonna be feeling a lot fucking worse if she don't have my money."

"I'm getting it together," Ray said. He didn't move, and he held Mateo's dead gaze. The gangster lifted his shirt to show the thick black butt of the pistol in the waistband of his jeans.

"I could kill you right now, go have some fun with that *puta* you call your mom, then blow her fucking head clean off. No one would say a word; no one would give a shit. You know I'm right, don't you, Ramon? You're ghosts already."

Ray swallowed hard. He never blinked. He wanted to punch this little bastard, but he knew he'd die and then Juanita would be left alone to deal with him, and she couldn't, not the way she was right now. "I know," he said. "Give me 'til tomorrow. I'll get your money."

Mateo shook his head and let out a huff of air. He took a few steps back and walked a short circle on the porch. "You got balls, Ray, always have. You can thank your old man and your brother for that. You should have joined the crew. You still could. I'd cut your old lady some slack."

"I can't. I promised Jess."

"Your woman's dead, man. You got to line up with the living, *ese*." Ray kept his mouth shut, but his jaw tightened; his eyes darkened. "Okay. *Cámara*," Mateo said. "You played the dead *papi*, dead *bro*, and dead girlfriend card. You get one time with that shit. Two thousand forty-eight dollars tomorrow or you're gonna have another sad story to tell."

Ray's friend, Lu, had picked him up after Mateo left, and they had spent the day selling stuff and trying to make deals, calling in any old debts that Ray or his late brother, Ben, hadn't collected on. He hit up his boss, Trevor, for an advance on his next paycheck. Trevor said he couldn't. It was official Chug-n-Lug corporate policy, but he did personally loan him a little money 'til payday. Ray got decent money for his and Ben's tools at 'Keem's pawn shop. By the evening, they had managed to come up with a little over five hundred dollars.

"It's enough gas to get the hell out of Port Arthur and keep going," Lu said. They were eating at the Jack in the Box next door to the Bingo Truck Stop as the brutal hundred-plus-degree June day sputtered out and made way for the sticky, humid, unforgiving night.

Pham Lu worked with Ray at the Chug-n-Lug. They had been friends since seventh grade. Lu was third-generation Vietnamese

American. His grandparents and their brothers and sisters had come over in the seventies and made a living first in Galveston, fishing, and now here in Port Arthur. Things had sucked pretty bad since Hurricane Harvey for the Phams. The town and the refinery industry had been virtually decimated. Lu's dad's and granddad's boats had suffered serious damage, and both men had taken jobs working with the cleanup and construction crews. It was still uncertain whether they would ever be able to get their boats back in the water again. All Lu had been able to contribute to the "Pay Off Juanita's Dealer Fund" was a ride and a cheap dinner.

"What are you going to do, man?" Lu asked around a mouthful of taco.

Ray shrugged.

"I can't run. No car, remember? Besides, that kind of money wouldn't get us very far, even if I could drag Juanita out of bed and convince her to do it. I donated plasma today already. Unless I can find a reputable organlegger to sell a kidney to, I'm shit out of luck."

"Go to the cops?" Lu suggested. Ray looked at him as if he had just said to call the Easter Bunny for the cash. "Okay, you're right, stupid idea. They *might* do something if they caught Mateo actually in the process of killing your mom."

"Maybe," Ray said.

"Look. You know I love your mom, but this really is her problem, not yours. You could just step back and let her handle it."

"And by 'handle it,' we both know that means she ends up dead or working on a mattress for Mateo for the rest of her short life. I can't do it, Lu. I can't."

"I know," Lu said, nodding. He offered Ray a fry, and Ray took it. "Too much of your dad and Ben in you. She's lucky to have you. If you had a decent ride, you could hustle up some race money quick. My Ford P-O-S couldn't outrun a drunk bumblebee, or I'd stake you." He saw the shadow cross Ray's face. "I know, you promised her no more after Ben died, but shit, man. She's the one that got her and you in this mess, and you've always been a damn good racer."

"Got that from my old man and Ben too." Ray sighed.

"It's getting late," Lu said. "Any place else you want to hit? I'll drive you all night if you need it."

Ray shook his head. A jagged thought was tumbling through his mind.

"It's okay. You roll. I'll talk to you tomorrow. I'm going to go hang out at Bingo's for a while."

"You're up to something. I know that look."

"Maybe a way to pull this out of the fire. If not, I can at least say that I tried everything."

Now, Ray stared out at the lifeless snake in the middle of the highway. Then he looked to the edge of the truck stop parking lot, to the car again, shrouded in shadows. It had been there the whole time he and Lu were at the Jack in the Box. It had been there since Lu had reluctantly driven away, making Ray promise to call him if he needed a ride.

The car was a 1964 Ford Galaxie 500. It was black and sleek. Its finish, like an obsidian mirror, caught the blades of light from the lot and reflected them like points of fake starlight. It was beautiful. Pop had told him many times about Abuelo having a ride just like it when Pop was a kid. Ray knew that Chuy, who worked at the auto parts store over on Gulfway, still ran a chop shop on the side. He could get five grand easy for the Galaxie, and it was a safe bet the guy who owned it and restored it hadn't put a computerized ignition system in it, so hot-wiring it shouldn't be a problem. Of course, it might have been sitting all day because it had crapped out, and the owner left it there until he could come back and fix it or get it towed. If that were the case, Chuy had a wrecker, and he could have it on the lift and gone in less than five minutes. It would still be worth enough money to placate Mateo, even if it wasn't running right now.

That just left the will to do it. When the idea of boosting a car had come to him, Ray had dismissed it as a desperate fantasy, but it kept coming back to him. He wondered, sitting at the table in the truck stop's diner, looking out into the sauna of the Texas night, how many people ended up criminals because of desperation, because they lost hope and didn't see a door they could walk through, only one they had to kick in.

Ray had stayed out of bad trouble, "toed the line" his pop had called it. There was the street racing, of course, but that wasn't like dealing drugs, robbing people, or joining a *mara*. Ben had started racing first at sixteen, and then Ray had tagged along at fourteen. Pretty soon, he was racing too. Nobody in Port Arthur, Groves, Nederland, or Vidor could beat the crazy Cosa brothers.

Stealing the Galaxie was crossing a line, but Ray didn't know what else to do, and he was out of time. He finished his Coke and sat at the table a few more minutes, just staring out into the parking lot. A wall of a trucker lumbered in, rumbling as he cleared his throat and looked at the roller grill of long-suffering hot dogs, sausages, and taquitos. Ray stood, dropped his empty cup into the trash can, and headed out the diner's door toward the Galaxie.

His legs felt like water as he walked toward the car, sitting all alone at the back of the massive parking lot. He had never been afraid when he had raced or even when staring down Mateo, but this seemed wrong to him on every level. It was like he was jamming himself into one of those Play-Doh Fun Factory molds that you pushed down on, and some shaped and formed creation oozed out. Maybe it was more like a meat grinder than Play-Doh. Ray felt himself ripping at some fundamental seam, and it made him sick and a little scared.

He approached the car. The Galaxie 500 was a two-door and a hardtop. Ray spotted the rear emblem still on the pristine, fifty-five-year-old car. More dollar signs popped into his head. The silver emblem announced that the car was the XL version, which meant it had more silver trim, bucket seats, and a console like a Chevy Corvair. It was the high-end, "sporty" version of the car and likely still had its big 289 cubic V8 engine, too. Whoever owned this car clearly loved it, based on the care and condition. That sent a sharp spear of guilt through Ray's chest. There was a weathered sticker on the back bumper. It had a faded purple background and a series of strange geometric symbols, one inside another, that made no sense to Ray.

The car had tinted, mirrored windows, rear window, and windshield. It looked like a 5 percent tint all the way up. It was illegal in Texas to have a tint less than 25 percent near the top of the window, so that some natural light could come in. That made Ray even more concerned. If he hot-wired the thing, he didn't want some trooper or local deputy pulling him over for the tint. Maybe that was why it had been sitting here all day; the owner got dinged for the tint and left it here rather than face any more tickets.

Ray walked around the car, trying to seem casual in the mostly empty lot. The car had Texas tags that were legal, and the silver plate holder that cradled them had something engraved on it in what Ray thought was Latin: *Honorem Reginae.* He thought about looking it up on his phone but decided against it.

Ray's eyes flicked back and forth to Bingo's store and diner, dreading the appearance of a white-and-blue Port Arthur police car, its prowl light on as it glided toward him. He cussed under his breath at his own stupid fear and tried to stay cool. *All you're doing is standing in a parking lot. They can't bust you for that, dumbass,* he told himself.

*Yeah, right, cops never fuck with people they can't arrest, and they can't just come up with a reason to drag your ass to jail.* It was his brother's voice, his pop's. His heart was a fist punching him in the rib cage; his blood felt like battery acid, burning in his veins. He wanted to puke, but he didn't. He stayed cool, tried to ignore the trembling of his legs and hands. He sucked at being a criminal.

He glanced back at the truck stop, thinking he had spotted someone watching him through the windows, but it was just his nerves. All right, damn it, either he needed to do this or walk away. He walked up to the driver's door and tried to peer inside, but the windows were too dark. Ray took a final, steadying breath and tried the door's handle. It wasn't locked. He opened the door and looked inside.

The stench of stale sweat and the coppery tang of blood stabbed Ray's nostrils. An old white guy was slumped in the passenger's seat, half-turned to face him. He held a nearly antique army forty-five pistol in his fist and aimed it at Ray. The old guy's pale-blue eyes were half-lidded. His skin was leathery, the way people who had worked out in the sun most of their lives looked, and he had a road map of creases and crags across his tanned face. He was wearing a torn army parka that was covered in dried blood. Three twisted, narrow black stakes, almost like arrows, jutted from the old man's chest and stomach. He had dried blood on his lips. "You took long enough to get some hair on your balls to do it," he said and then began a spasm of coughing. Ray's eyes were locked on the gun, which stayed steadily on him even at the worst of the fit. "Get in," the old man said. "Shut the door."

"Look." Ray started to back away. "I'm sorry. I'll just get out of here and . . ."

The old man cocked the hammer on the gun with a flip of his thumb.

"Get. In," he said. "Shut the door, or you'll whistle when you try to run away." He began to cough again, but the gun remained on Ray. Ray slid behind the narrow, horn-ring steering wheel and shut the driver's door. "Key's in the ignition. You wanted to drive her, now do it." Ray turned the key, and the Galaxie gave a throaty rumble as it came to life. Ray looked over at the old man. "Head onto I-10," he said, fighting back another coughing fit.

Ray slipped the car into gear, and they glided out of the parking lot and onto the street, toward the on-ramp. The dashboard glowed with green light that washed over Ray's gaunt face and the old man's slack, pained features. The Galaxie accelerated smoothly and more quickly than he had expected for such an old car.

Interstate 10 was the primary east-west artery for the southern United States. It stayed busy pretty much twenty-four-seven. Ray drifted between the traffic of eighteen-wheelers, pickups, and compact SUVs clustered near the ramp, even at three in the morning. The Galaxie drove like a dream. For a second, he forgot the old man's gun, Juanita's debt, and Mateo's threats. There was only the rushing darkness and the tight vibration of the powerful engine. Ray felt his whole body relax.

"Yeah," the old man said, a weird smile coming to his face, "you got it."

"What?"

"You love to drive her. Good. Perfect." He coughed again, this time almost doubling over. The old guy came back up and kept the gun on Ray.

"Hey, where are we going?" Ray asked. "I could take you to a hospital."

The old man's laugh turned into another hacking fit. He shook his head and caught his breath. "Too late for that. Their sap is in my blood by now."

"Sap?"

The old man looked down at one of the arrow-like sticks in his chest. "Yateveo spines. Their plumbing has this oily sap stuff instead of blood. It's toxic to most mammals. Even if I wasn't on this backwater, nobody has antitoxin for it. Only way to stay alive is to stay out of the way when they start spittin' them spines. Might do to remember that, kid."

Ray figured the old guy was losing it. It was clear he wasn't long for this world, but the gun remained stone-still, pointed at his stomach. "Listen, I'm sorry I tried to jack your car. I don't normally do things like that."

"Clearly," the old man said. "You're a shitty thief. No offense." He grinned the red-stained smile again. "Evan. Evan Welsh."

"Ray. Ray Cosa."

Evan choked a little for a bit. His cough was sounding wetter. He was choking on his blood. "So why did you turn to a life of crime, Ray Cosa?"

"Needed the money. Tried raising it honest, but I got more debt than an honest person can pay off."

"To paraphrase Bruce Springsteen, more or less," Evan said. "Ray, criminals don't give a damn about their debts unless the debt's gonna kill them, and we've already established you are the worst criminal ever. I figure you were getting ready to steal my beauty here to pay off someone else's debt. Am I right?"

Ray nodded. "My mom. She's a junkie."

"Well, that sucks. How long?"

"My pop died of pancreatic cancer about six years ago. Mom was just Mom up until then. After he died, she started taking his old pain meds, first to sleep, then to get by. Eventually, to do everything. When Pop's meds were gone, she started buying."

"Yeah, I get the rest of the story," Evan said. He was looking paler in the passing highway light. "Like I said, sucks." They drove along the highway for a few minutes. The only sound was Evan's labored breathing and the whoosh of the traffic moving past them. Ray finally broke the spell.

"Uh, look, Evan—Evan, right? Please let me get you to a hospital. Maybe they can help you with the whole sap thing."

Evan placed the pistol on his lap. For a second, Ray thought of swerving the car, trying to get the gun, but the traffic was still tight along the corridor, and it would be too easy to crash. Also, he no longer felt a threat from this old man; in fact, he really wanted to try to get him some help. Evan took hold of a ring on his left hand and gave it a tug. It slipped off his finger. "Ah, dammit," he muttered, "that . . . that ain't good." He picked up the gun and returned to leveling it at Ray, almost as an afterthought. "Thanks for the offer, kid. It's a rare person who wants to help the guy pointing a gun at him. Rare. You're going to do real good, Ray." His voice was getting weaker, a low rasp. "I can tell, real good." He groaned as he held out the ring, "Put this on."

Ray held out a hand and felt the heavy, cold metal of it drop into his palm. It occurred to his brain that it should be warm from Evan's finger, but it was cold. Too cold.

The ring was made of black metal, polished to a mirror finish; the band was encircled by small, round jeweled chips, eleven in total, each a different color. Ray glanced over at Evan. The old man was still holding the gun, but it was clear now he had no intention of shooting. "Put it on," the old man said, "please, Ray. It's important."

Ray balanced the car's steering wheel on the heels of his hands as he slipped the ring onto his left ring finger.

"Good choice," Evan said. "It's a hell of a lot like a wedding ring."

He started to laugh, but it turned into a coughing fit, the worst one yet. He shook violently, which set off a convulsion of pain from the wooden spines buried deep in him. Evan moaned and slumped back against the seat. He fought down the fit, the pain. He looked over to Ray; his eyes reminded the boy of the last time he had spoken to his pop in the hospital, eyes already seeing past this life.

"All right, listen up," Evan said, his lips wet with fresh blood. "I need you to go find Chain. That's what he goes by, Chain. He drives an old beat-to-shit wrecker. Most likely you'll find him at Nuurra's Station out on Bleeth, if he's not on a run."

"What? Chain? Bleeth? I don't know that street, Evan. You stay awake. You tell him! Is Bleeth even a street in Port Arthur? Another city?"

The old man raised a hand for silence as he fought for each word.

"The ring will get you there. Just think about finding Chain, focus on his name. Same with Bleeth. Visualization is the key. Easy-peasy. You're going to do good, Ray." He was fighting to stay conscious and he was losing. "Man who'll risk his own life, his freedom, everything for someone he loves—you got a good heart. A man with a good heart is better than an army at your back."

His eyes closed. His chest was still rising and falling, but he was wheezing hard. Ray began to panic. He recognized the rattle, both his grandfather and his father had done the same thing just before . . .

"Come on, Evan! Come on, man! Stay with me. We're going to get you some help!"

"The car . . ." the old man said, "don't ever sell her. She's got a good heart too. Tell Chain that the damned Yateveo did this to me, you understand? The Yateveo. He'll know what needs doing."

Ray looked around frantically. All he saw was an empty highway road, desolate wilderness, and the blazing cold firmament of stars. "Evan? Evan!" His breaths were getting further apart, the rattle getting heavier. Ray fumbled for his phone to call 911. The screen reported that he was in a no-service area.

"This . . . is how . . . we usually end up," Evan said with surprising clarity.

Ray heard the thump of something heavy hitting the rubber floor mat. It was the pistol. Ray looked over to the old man.

"Evan?"

The wheezing had stopped. Evan's chest was still.

He was dead.

## 2

Ray pulled over to the side of the highway in a screech of tires, opened his door, and climbed out. He looked back inside the car at the old man's body, felt his mind and heart race one another madly ahead of reason. Ray circled the still-idling car, rubbing his face and his hair, trying to calm down, trying to force his brain to think, not just react. He leaned against the Galaxie's trunk, his face illuminated in the red taillights.

Ray began fighting to get his breath under control as well as his mind. *All that crazy shit about poison sap and Chain the tow-truck driver was probably just his brain shutting down on him. So, you got a dead guy with a gun.*

"He said not to sell her—it." Ray said to the silent highway. "He expected you to go find this Chain. Maybe the only family he had?" Ray began to formulate a story in his skull where Evan Welsh was some kind of old war vet, who had grabbed his piece and his old fancy car and took off half out of his mind. Chain was probably his son, who looked after him, would be looking for him now. *So will the cops.* Shit.

Ray opened the passenger-side door with the same impulsive energy that had led to him walking out to steal the Galaxie. Evan sat in the seat, his eyes closed, three black gnarled branches jutting from his chest and belly. *How do those—what did he call them?—Yateveo spines, fit into your wandering old soldier story, genius?*

He slipped his hands under Evan's armpits and slid him as gently as he could onto the shoulder of the highway and then dragged him down the hill and into the tall grass. This, of course, would be when the Texas Highway Patrol would pull up and shine a bright light in his eyes. It looked like they were out way past Port Arthur, not quite to Hankamer or Wallisville but headed toward the big refinery complexes. There were trees and rutted fields and no lights from any nearby towns. There had been no traffic for too long a time on I-10. *This is crazy. Maybe I've lost my mind* . He looked down at Evan's body. *Maybe it's catching*. At any rate, no sense tempting fate. He walked back around to the open driver's door, switched off the engine, killed the car's light, and shut the door. The only lights now were the stars, the distant furnace of suns stretching from horizon to horizon, and the bright, drunken moon, low in the sky, stumbling its way home. It was plenty of light.

The key chain in his hands held the square key to the ignition and doors and a matching rounded key for the trunk and glove box. Both had the stylized V design of original Galaxie keys with "Ford" emblazoned above the V. No keys for houses or storage, no security dongle to arm a car alarm, nothing else. The two old keys were hanging on a loop of wire with a yellow-and-black rectangle of rubber that had several lines of weird symbols across it on both sides. Ray could read the symbols on the rubber tag as saying "Compliments of Zuto's Exotics," with an address that included someplace called Dorodan, wherever the hell that was. In smaller symbols, beneath the name of the business and the address, it said, "We proudly specialize in all manner of exotic vehicles! Let us get you back on the Queen's Road in no time!"

Ray let out a whoosh of breath and stuffed the keys into his jeans pocket. He paused for a second. *How the hell did I read those weird symbols and understand them?* The panic started to well up again. He wanted to call Lu and talk to him. He'd make sense out of all this. No, no, he wouldn't get his best friend and the most steady guy he knew mixed up with a stolen car and a dead body.

"Okay, okay. Be cool. Be. Cool," he muttered to himself. His phone's clock said it was almost four in the morning. He put the phone away and knelt by Evan's body. It felt wrong to go through his pockets, but Ray wanted very much to try to find someone who cared about this guy.

He searched Evan's jacket and pants pockets, careful to avoid the black wooden spines. Under his jacket, he had a leather shoulder holster for the forty-five that was on the floorboard. Then it struck Ray—*The gun is in plain sight*. He ran back to the car, retrieved the gun, and checked the slide to see if it had a bullet in the chamber. It didn't, but the clip was loaded. He made sure the safety was still on and tucked the gun into the waistband of his jeans at the small of his back.

Evan had no wallet, no ID, no cell phone. Ray found a purple cloth Crown Royal bag in the pocket of Evan's military parka. Ray pulled it free of the jacket with a loose metallic clink. The bag was frayed and thin with age and weight. Ray tugged on the gold drawstrings, and the bag yawned open. He upended it, and coins of all shapes and sizes rained down, some falling into Ray's outstretched hand, others spilling past and pooling on the ground among the high grass. "Oh, man," Ray muttered.

He picked up one coin; it was heavy, made of a greenish-blue metal, and stamped in the shape of an hourglass. The strange symbols laser-etched onto the coin's iridescent surface looked a little like Arabic or some other Middle Eastern language. Yet, again, Ray could understand it, read it. It said the coin was from the Aerie of Leefentitaar, and it was certified as one gram of pure Urichite. He could read it, but it made no sense, had no context.

Some of the coins looked and felt like gold. A small stack were white octagons that looked to Ray like they were made of some kind of plastic with a small gold computer chip in them. He gathered up the coins and put them back into the bag. Then he looked at the ring on his finger. The stones seemed real, and it was probably worth at least a grand. He tried to pull it off and add it to the bag, but it wouldn't budge. He struggled a little more and then gave up, standing and stuffing the heavy bag into his pants pocket.

Ray looked again at Evan's body. This was so wrong, just leaving him out here. What if some coyotes dragged him off or he sat out here for days, unfound? In a final act of desperation, Ray used the key to open the glove compartment. Inside were two transparent blocks that looked kind of like external hard drives. They twinkled with tiny firefly lights of red, green, and blue. Both blocks had narrow slits but no buttons or switches. Ray pushed on them to see if they had a touch control, but nothing happened. They seemed built into the car.

There was a large leather wallet with plastic sleeve pages that lay next to the two blocks and an opened, crumpled plastic bag of some kind of junk food. Ray took one of the candies out of the bag as he placed the wallet on his lap. He was starved, but he hadn't realized it 'til now.

The candy was about the size of a malted milk ball, but its color constantly shifted through the spectrum, and tiny little globes spun and orbited around the larger candy sphere. Holding the thing made his fingers feel tingly, especially when the orbiting bits passed right through his fingers like they weren't even there. He hesitated for a second before he popped the candy in his mouth. It reminded him of being a kid and eating the Pop Rocks his dad gave him. This time it felt different, like there was a rainstorm in his mouth made up of flavors, most of which he didn't have a reference for, but he loved them. Swallowing the candy was like swallowing delicious, flickering, flavor-lightning. The candy gave Ray the greatest sugar rush he'd ever had in his life. He wasn't tired at all, and he felt focused like Bruce Lee's one-inch punch. The label said they were called Psychic-Sprinkled Buppos!® Ray popped another Buppo in his mouth and then, reluctantly, returned the bag to the glove box and looked through the wallet.

The small book contained dozens of identity cards, driver's licenses, insurance cards, and vehicle registrations for multiple states, countries, and places Ray had never heard of before, written in a number of different languages and formats that Ray could now read, even if he had no clue what the languages were. There was no Texas license or registration, no address for Ray to locate.

He returned the wallet, swiped another Buppo, then added the pistol to the contents and shut the glove box. He exited the car and closed the passenger door behind him. He looked back down to Evan. "Couldn't make it easy, could you?"

The crazy old guy deserved better, but Ray's mind tumbled through each scenario, and they all led to cops, to questions, and probably to jail. In eight hours, Mateo was coming for his money, for Juanita. His only hope now was that Evan's coins were worth enough to pay the *mara* off. 'Keem's pawn shop opened at ten in the morning. That was cutting it close, but there was no other choice, not any more. The very least he could do for old Evan here was not to sell his Galaxie to a chop shop. No, that wasn't the least he could do.

"Thanks for the car," Ray said to the old man. "I'm going to use it to go find Chain for you. I wish I could do more than that. I'm sorry." There was silence; some hot breeze ruffled the grass. "Don't go nowhere." He walked back to the driver's door, got in, and turned the ignition. The Galaxie came to life, its angry carburetor growling like comeback Elvis. Eight hours. He'd find Chain by then or he'd cut and head for the pawn shop if he hadn't. For the first time in a really long time, Ray felt something other than uncertainty and fear, like he had control again. It felt good. He shifted the car into drive and spun loose gravel as he shot out onto the empty highway, a dead man behind him, a man named Chain somewhere in the darkness ahead.

# 3

The noise that shredded the air came from the direction of the highway overpass.

Ronnie Farmer looked up from the porn he had been watching on his phone in time to see the large dark shape buzz the lifeless silhouette of the condemned factory and drop from sight behind the boarded-up building. Was it a bus? A plane? Ronnie couldn't tell; all he knew was it was big.

There were still sections of Port Arthur that had not been resurrected after being swallowed whole by Hurricane Harvey. The Gould-Wright Nautical Engine Manufacturing Company was one of those places. Gould-Wright made engines for large freighters and one cruise-ship manufacturer. They had struggled to get a military contract for more than thirty years, but never got there. The families that started the company back in the late sixties had been bought out in the eighties, and the company continued making a fair profit, focusing mostly on older ships and their less-than-cutting-edge technology. It was a niche business, but most companies and countries that owned freighter fleets would rather tinker and repair than buy newer ships. Then Harvey had arrived, and close to sixty years of business vanished under his murky, churning waves.

Ronnie was a security officer for Paragon Security. His job from nine p.m. 'til eight a.m. was to watch over the water-damaged corpse of the Gould-Wright complex, which included a half dozen buildings spread over seven acres. Ronnie climbed out of the compact car with the Paragon Security logo on its doors. The June night was as hot and black as pitch. He clicked on his Maglite flashlight and headed toward the edge of the old central factory, behind which the whatever-it-was had disappeared from sight. Ronnie thought that maybe a trailer or something had come flying off the interstate and fallen down here, but the troubling part was, he hadn't heard a crash. In fact, he hadn't heard anything.

He reached the edge of the large building and scanned the deep darkness beyond. There was nothing but high grass and debris from the flooding. Ronnie wanted to go back to his car and the air-conditioning, but if something was back there when the sun came up in a few hours, he'd catch shit from his supervisor. Ronnie sighed and headed farther into the lot behind the factory. This was bullshit. There were snakes back here, and getting bit wasn't worth eight-fifty an hour. He slipped his pistol clear of its holster and tried to scan the ground ahead of him with the flashlight for anything slithering.

A hundred yards back, he found it, but he had no idea what the hell it was. The Maglite beam scattered over its featureless black surface. Ronnie slowly circled it. It was about the size of a large RV and was roughly the shape of a pill capsule. It was like someone had cut a section of starless night out of the sky. He holstered the pistol and ran his hand over the strange metal. He hissed in pain and pulled his hand back, looking at it. His skin was red and swollen, blackening a little, as if he had been burned, but the surface had felt unimaginably cold to him.

"Okay," Ronnie whispered, shaking his numb hand, "screw this shit, I'm calling the cops."

There was a rustling in the grass off to his right. Ronnie spun and swung the flashlight in the direction of the noise. He saw nothing but gently swaying grass and the hulk of an old tree, covered with tumorous-looking knots.

"Hey, who's there? I got a gun, and you're trespassing!" Ronnie tried to draw his nine with his hurt hand. The gun fell at his feet, and he crouched to retrieve it, still scanning around with the flashlight.

Something slithered through the grass by Ronnie's hand, but before he could snatch his hand back, it wrapped around his wrist and tightened. Something else, some kind of rope-like thing shot out and looped around his shoulder. Ronnie struggled against whatever had him. The beam of the flashlight jerked around as he was pulled off the ground and dangled ten feet in the air.

The Maglite beam bounced and thrashed. It settled on the tree. The tree was moving, lurching drunkenly, as it came closer to him. Its bark was black, weathered, and cracked; the sheen of a dark liquid in the cracks and dribbling from the knots glistened in the light. Rows of sharp, short branches ringed the trunk. The things that held him were like bark-covered vines that grew out of the massive central bulk of the thing. There were hundreds of the tendrils, whirring all about him. The sound reminded him of the thrumming chorus of cicadas. More of the vines entangled him, held him tight, and lifted him higher.

Ronnie pissed himself and struggled to try to reach his cell phone, to get help. This wasn't real; it *couldn't* be real. There was a sharp, crowded pain in his lower back, as if he were being stuffed. The pain numbed, and he felt a strange sense of euphoria diffuse through him like ink dropped into water. Something was inside him, under his skin, and it was crawling, climbing up through his back, up his spine.

From his altitude, he saw two more of the tree-things rise up out of the featureless black capsule. Even as his mind, his thoughts, began to feel crowded too, he wondered how that was possible. There was no hatch, no portal; they just rose up out of the solid, freezing hull. It also puzzled him how all three of these things could fit in the RV-sized craft; there simply wasn't room. There was no fear or panic with these associations. He no longer felt any pain, only pleasure. The flashlight slipped from his fingers and fell into the grass.

The three creatures entwined the thicker, stouter-looking branches near the crowns of their bulky trunk-like bodies. These "limbs" touched each other and warped together, forming a physical connection among the three. Ronnie could hear them in his mind. It was something like a singing river, full of colors, sounds, and ideas human beings didn't have words for. Ronnie's thoughts and memories were in the river too, struggling against the powerful, racing currents.

Whatever had entered him and crept up his spine, it was now expanding through the pathways of his brain, growing, snuggling into the deepest core of him. That was okay. He was learning all kinds of things now, like a second birth, like an extra brain was explaining everything to him. He wasn't really a person; he wasn't even technically alive. He was meat, and meat was for eating and for use as a tool —*slave*—no, tool, and for procreation. His name meant nothing; his existence before meant nothing. Only now, waiting to be given commands, mattered.

As he accepted his new role, Ronnie began to understand more of the thoughts of these beings—*monsters*—no beings, superior beings. They were here looking for someone, a Ranger, whatever that was. He had discovered them, and it was too soon for the other Rangers to be made aware of their return. The Ranger was dying, and they had tracked him here. They knew he was close.

Ronnie's first task would be to track and finish off this Ranger and make sure anyone he had told was killed as well. The meat robot that had been Ronnie Farmer felt pleasure when he focused on his goals, and pain when he did not. He still had access to his memories and could pretend to be his old self to fit in with the rest of the herd. His owners were pleased when they learned from his thoughts that two more meat creatures would be coming to relieve him after dawn. They would be harvested as well and sent with him on his task.

There was something else, something that the tiny, dying animal remains of Ronnie Farmer's awareness glimpsed in the thoughts of these beings who called themselves the Yateveo. He saw their plan for all the rest of his herd. His crumbling instincts screamed to fight or to flee, then they were silenced, devoured, by a claustrophobic darkness and the rustling of dry branches.

# 4

Ray turned the car around at Exit 812, leaving the old man's body in his rearview mirror. He headed back for Port Arthur along a nameless road that paralleled I-10. He drove the speed limit, and he kept checking his rearview mirror, expecting to see a cop's lights behind him. This was crazy, but what else was he going to do between now and when the pawn shop opened? Go home and sleep? No. He'd left a stranger on the side of the highway to rot, and all the guy had asked of him was to find his friend, give him one last message. That wasn't too much to ask, especially when he had a pocket full of his weird money and he'd given him the sweetest car he'd ever seen.

"So, where the hell are you, Chain?" he said to the empty car. He clicked on the car's antique-looking radio. There was a digital tone for a second, and then a female voice coming from some very good speakers asked him, "Please select local or global commosphere frequencies."

Ray smiled. "Shit, Evan, you didn't look the type to cough up for satellite radio or Alexa."

"I'm sorry, I don't understand your request."

"Play anything," Ray said. Then he remembered Pop telling him about riding in Abuelo's Galaxie and listening to a song as they shot down the freeway toward LA with the ragtop down. "Wait! Find a punk station, anywhere, playing the Minutemen." There was silence for a second, and then a song came on; it began with a few strums of an acoustic guitar, a simple, slightly disjointed chord phrase. Then it exploded into a rapid-fire, bare-bones punk song called "This Ain't No Picnic." Ray nodded and turned the volume up. He couldn't help his foot pressing down a little harder on the gas.

"All right," he said as the Galaxie barreled through the darkness. "Now, how to find Chain?"

He thought back to what Evan had said as he was dying. *He said the ring would help me? Okay, that was dying, delirious stuff. He also mentioned a name, a place, Chain hung out at . . . what was it? Bleeth. He called it Bleeth.*

Ray felt an odd sensation from his left hand, almost a pulse that came from the ring. He looked up and saw an on-ramp on the right coming up. He didn't recall any ramps on this road, but there it was, unmarked but dead ahead. The ring pulsed again. *Bleeth*, he thought. *I'm looking for Bleeth.* The ring throbbed more strongly, more insistently as they neared the exit ramp. His gut, his instinct, told him what to do, and he did it without thinking. It was like street racing again— no time for second-guessing, just do it. Ray accelerated onto the ramp, the ring pulsing almost continuously as he did.

He shot out of the loop onto a straightaway four-lane that looked to be running in both directions. There were no interstate signs or mile markers, just road and sky. The ring was still again, no pulses.

"Okay?" Ray muttered. The radio was now playing "Ángel Malvado" by Raymix. Ray nodded. "Good pick. I like this song."

"Thank you. I scanned your cellular communicator and downloaded the music you had been listening to most frequently," the female voice said over the music.

Ray smiled. "Thanks, Alexa."

"That is not my name," the voice said.

"Oh, okay, what is your name?"

"Cassandra."

"Nice to meet you. Keep the music coming?"

"Of course," Cassandra said. There was almost a smile in her voice.

The highway, whatever one it was, continued on. There were lights set on posts every few hundred yards, but not a single sign. Ray began to think that maybe he had driven onto some new construction, a part of a freeway still being built. He rolled down his window and looked up. The sky was awash in stars from horizon to horizon. The cool air rushing by kissed his face. He checked the time on his phone; it wasn't even five o'clock yet. He had plenty of time; he just wished he knew where the hell he was going and if he really was getting any closer to Bleeth and Chain.

About fifteen minutes later, he came across a cluster of off-ramps, still without signs. He was tempted to take one to get an idea of where he was, but there was no pulse from the ring. "Okay, this is stupid!" he said and turned onto one of the ramps.

The Galaxie spiraled down the long ramp and came out on an asphalt strip of a road with muddy ditches on either side, partly full of water. It was raining, and the cool, wet breeze felt good on Ray's face through his open window. He drove along the bumpy road for a time and then saw an interstate off to his left. He was on an access road beside it. He came to an intersection and was relieved to see a familiar green-and-white highway sign at the crossroads; then he read it.

The sign was written in what looked like Russian. What did they call it? Cyrillic? As crazy as that was, it was crazier still that he could read it, understand it. It listed a bunch of places he had never heard of before, and then at the end of the list, it said he was twenty-five kilometers from Belgrade, which was written as "Beograd."

The car sat idling at the intersection. Ray ran his rain-wet hand over his face. "Belgrade? Belgrade? That's *Serbia*! That's like, *Eastern Europe*? I thought maybe I was in Galveston! No way, no! What the hell is going on here?"

A car behind Ray laid on its horn. Ray gestured wildly with his arm out the window, "Okay, okay, I'm going!" He turned left at the intersection, figuring on U-turning and backtracking, but into the turn the ring pulsed again, so he followed through with the left. "Shit! Okay, fine! Scenic Belgrade it is."

Ray accelerated onto the ramp and merged into the stream of traffic. It was still night. The sky was hidden by clouds, and the rain was falling steadily. He was wondering how the hell he was going to get out of Serbia, let alone find Chain. The big old classic car was getting a lot of attention on the highway. Small compacts and SUVs beeped as they passed Ray. Any other time, it would have been cool, but right now, Ray was a little bit in shock. After about twenty minutes on the highway, the ring pulsed as they approached an unmarked off-ramp.

"Sure," Ray said to himself, "how much more messed up could this get? Why not?" He took the ramp, and it looped around and brought him back onto the unmarked four-lane highway. The rain lessened and then stopped, and he was back on the massive road without another car in sight. "This is crazy," he said, shaking his head. He passed another set of unmarked off-ramps but drove past them, afraid of where they might take him.

His cell phone rang with that annoyingly cheerful default ringtone, "Life's Good," that most people never bothered to change. It actually made him jump. He rolled up the window as he slipped his phone out of his jeans pocket. A picture of Lu, a Slurpee straw balanced on his nose, was on the screen, announcing his incoming call.

Ray answered. "You are not going to believe this!"

"You okay?" Lu asked. "I was just checking up on you, making sure you got home. What's up with your phone? The connection sucks." It *was* an awful connection. Lu sounded like he was at the bottom of a well during a blizzard.

"I . . . I may be in Serbia, man," Ray said, "I don't know. Hey, can you meet me at 'Keem's shop around ten?"

"What? Serbia?" Lu's voice was digitally slurring. He was shouting to be barely heard.

"'Keem's at ten!" Ray yelled, and the connection dropped. His phone told him that he was out of service. None of this made any sense. Ray looked down at the jeweled ring on his finger and felt a combination of fear and excitement.

He looked at the ring as he spoke, "Take me to Chain, to Bleeth."

He drove for an hour without seeing another car or an exit. He drove fast, suspecting he had no concern for cops out here, wherever here was. His cell said it should be a little after six o'clock, but there were still stars overhead and no sign of a sun or a moon. He did notice now a vast purple veil draped like a translucent silk scarf over the lower quarter of stars off to his left. Was that a nebula? He took a second and tried to look for any familiar constellations, but there were none. If he didn't find anything, find Chain, soon, he'd need to turn back to make it home in time. That was when a terrible realization occurred. How did he turn around if there were no exits? Did he dare just drive the wrong way on this thing?

As if in answer, a vehicle roared past him, headed the same direction he was. It looked like a double-decker bus, like the ones they had in London on TV. It had eight tires to a side and was bloused in garish fabric and fluttering flags, like a circus tent. The cloth puffed up and shivered with the wind, the flags snapping as it passed.

Ray accelerated to match the bus-tent's speed. He glanced over and got a quick glimpse of the driver. It had skin the color of dark wine, and three flattened faces stacked one on top of another, like pancakes. Six eyes, three noses, and, as it looked over to Ray's tinted window, it smiled. The divisions between the flattened faces widened, like an accordion's bellows, and showed Ray three mouths, each with rows of jagged yellow teeth that covered a 180-degree arc. Ray's foot dropped to the brake instinctively. The bus-tent roared ahead and was, in a moment, out of sight.

He pulled over to the shoulder of the highway and jumped out of the car. What was happening to him? Was he going crazy? Had Mateo dosed him somehow, had Evan? None of this could be real; none of this made any sense. He leaned his head against the driver's door and the roof of the car. It was still wet with rain from Serbia.

Nothing like any of this ever really happened, and if it did, it sure as hell didn't happen to somebody like him. He worked at a convenience store. He never made it past one year of community college. The only exciting things that had ever happened to him in his life had been Jess and illegal street racing with Ben. Jess was dead, and the racing got him arrested and his brother killed. The car, the old man, this highway, this was all too much, too much.

Ray got his breathing under control and turned around, leaned his head back and looked up at the endless sea of unknown stars above him. It was beautiful. In that moment, he knew he wasn't high, or crazy. The stars, the sky he didn't recognize, anchored him in a strange way that he couldn't fully explain to himself, but he understood all the same. He looked down at the ring on his finger, the jewels in it caught the starlight and seemed to flash.

He walked around the car and then he realized how badly he needed to pee. It had been hours, and he had drunk a lot of soda refills with Lu at the restaurant and then at Bingo's after Lu left. He looked around. There was a metallic rail, a barrier at the edge of the shoulder. Ray looked down the far side, past the rail, and saw thick rubbery trees and shrubs about ten yards back.

Ray made his way down the steep slope. There was a moment when his ears popped and he felt a tightness in his chest, but it passed. He looked behind him. The slope was still there, but the highway and the car were out of sight.

He took a few more steps toward the bushes. Their leaves were swollen and fleshy, like cactus. It was hard to see their color, but it was dark. As he unzipped and began to pee, Ray pressed the button on the side of his phone and illuminated the bush he was whizzing on. Its leaves were a deep blue; he'd never seen a plant like that before. Something big grumbled in the trees past the bush, as if the light from the phone had disturbed it. Ray hurried to finish, putting the phone away.

"Come on, come on."

The unhappy thing moved, and the big trees behind the shrubs swayed with its movement. Ray quickly zipped up and began to back toward the slope. The big thing was moving fast now; trees were not just swaying, some were flying as they were dislodged. Ray began to climb the slope, hurrying, looking over his shoulder as he ascended.

The thing erupted out of the tree line, bellowing like a wounded bear. It was loping on all fours and its forelegs had massive bone hooks, curved backward at the elbow joints. It had to be taller than two grown men at the crest of the sharp, leaf-shaped ridges which ran along its back. It was roughly twenty feet long, with strange glowing patches on its sides and belly. Veins the color of aqua glowed angrily down its long neck and flanks, pulsing brightly as it charged Ray. Its shovel-shaped head had rows of three-foot-long fangs ahead of its mouth, like the grill on a car. A cluster of eye tubes was arrayed behind the teeth on its leathery face.

Ray wished he had the gun as he reached the top of the slope and saw the safety of the highway and his car. The thing was nearly on top of him; those arm-sized fangs were close to Ray's back. He scrambled over the barrier rail. The beast roared and looked up at him. Then it stopped and seemed to scan around, as if it were searching. It snarled angrily, and swung its head around again.

*It can't see me*, Ray realized.

Ray slowly made his way to the driver's side door and climbed behind the wheel. He slid the key into the ignition, shut the door, and started the car. The beast's massive crane of a head had swung back toward the foliage at the bottom of the ridge, still scanning, still searching. Ray floored the Galaxie, the tires screeching and smoking as he pulled back onto the road.

"Okay," he said, still shaking, "rest stops. Only rest stops from here on out . . . or Bulbasaur will eat you."

About an hour later, the ring pulsed as he approached another exit. Ray slowed. A sign in several languages—all of which he could read—announced this was the exit for Bleeth. He took the off-ramp, the ring vibrating frantically as he did. The ramp ended at a series of roads, overpasses, and buildings. The signs announcing the businesses were a cacophony of symbols and letters that Ray could read, just like the road sign.

There was traffic, mostly vehicles, but also riders on the backs of beasts Ray had never seen on Earth. One of the creatures rumbled past the Galaxie. It looked like a salmon-colored brontosaurus with an arch of six eyes. The bronto looked down to Ray and smiled at him.

Carriages and wagons pulled by alien beasts were mixed in with the rest of the rush hour. The odd mixture of transports was driving into or out of a large lot off to Ray's left. It had gotten brighter too, coming off the ramp. It was now like a clear morning after a storm; however, everything had a strange orange-ish tint.

One of the signs announced that the large circular, multi-story building, and the vast, mostly full parking lot that surrounded it, was Nuurra's Station. That seemed to be the place most of the traffic was flowing about. *Nuurra's Station.* The name popped into Ray's memory. It was where Evan told him Chain hung out. The place looked like some kind of temple, but it felt more like a truck stop.

The Galaxie drifted into the lot and moved up and down the rows. Most of the vehicles in the lot looked like cars, but they weren't any make or model Ray had ever seen before, and they were in all manner of shapes and sizes, some with far more than four wheels. The colors of the vehicles were . . . odd too, hues and patterns that Ray seriously doubted Detroit released on factory models. There were some things he figured for motorcycles and others that looked like chariots and wagons driven by more bizarre beasts. Some of the vehicles had no wheels at all, hovering above the ground on some invisible field; others looked more like jets or UFOs than cars.

After a few minutes of looking, Ray found a beat-to-hell old tow truck that had "Aplyon-Jeed," whoever the hell that was, as its apparent manufacturer. The truck had a logo that Ray read as "Chain's Tow-A-Wreck." A line below announced, "Discounted Service for Vets and the Queen's Rangers."

Ray parked near the truck and climbed out of the car. He felt that tightness again in his chest, his lungs, for a moment, but then it passed. Ray stretched, looked up, and saw the sky for the first time since he got off the highway. It was a pale tangerine, and a massive moon filled a large part of it. Ray could see cities and roadways crossing the moon's cracked and cratered surface.

He didn't know what to say, to think. He had either completely lost his mind or this was actually happening, he was on another world. He didn't feel crazy, but—full disclosure—would he feel crazy if he *was* crazy? Until someone locked him up or stuck a needle in his arm, he was going to keep on assuming that this was real. "You . . . get really good gas mileage," he said, patting the car's hood. He locked the Galaxie and walked across the parking lot toward the circular building that was Nuurra's.

There were stairs that led up to the main entrances. Ray also saw ramps set between the stairs as he ascended them. Of the people going in and coming out, about a third looked vaguely human—arms, legs, a head. The rest were every shape, size, and configuration. Some flew; others looked like they were made of glass, or metal, or stone. One that floated past Ray was a talking cloud of asparagus-colored smoke. The cloud's companion was a hovering, scintillating column of brilliant light and distorted music.

Doors were set equidistant around the building. Ray entered through a pair that opened silently before him. The outer ring of Nuurra's was a marketplace. Hundreds of voices and an equal number of languages were all jostled against one another in joking, arguing, bantering, and bartering. Ray moved through the crowd and tried to stay out of everyone's way, especially the ones without faces.

"Don't stare," a three-foot-tall guy with orange feathers all over his body and brilliant blue plumage crowning his head said to his twin. They both looked like they just fell out of a Nick Park animated movie. His companion was gawking at Ray as they passed in the crowded bazaar. "It makes us look like tourists."

Ray paused in front of a table where a guy with light-blue skin and layers of thin black fins curved under his eyes and across his cheeks was selling some kind of fruit that looked like orange and yellow eggplants.

"Excuse me," Ray said. "Do you understand me?"

"Of course. You speak Yufari very well for a land dweller."

"I do? Uh, thanks. I'm looking for somebody."

"Aren't we all," the vendor said.

"His name is Chain. I heard that he . . ."

"Oh, Chain. You don't look the type. Second floor. I saw him drinking just outside the casino. I don't think he's fared well today."

"Thank you."

The vendor hefted one of the eggplants, offering it to Ray.

"Womb of Kotada? Its juice will transmute your awareness to the penultimate precinct of the Hyperspace Spirits, much better for your mind than Glass. What price can one put upon enlightenment?"

"Uh, thanks, man . . . but I get a rash," Ray said and hurried away.

He found his way to a bank of wide cylinders advertised as lifts to the casino level. Ray watched as people stepped into the tube, were caught in a pale-blue light, and floated upward. Ray followed them in. There was a moment when the beam caught him and his breath froze. He drifted skyward and relaxed after a moment, stepping off on the second floor.

There was a casino at the hub of the level, full of tables and all manner of gaming machines for those feeling lucky. There was no lack of gamblers milling about—laughing, cheering their victories, and cursing when they lost money. Ringing the casino were numerous bars, lounges, and restaurants.

He scanned the room for someone who looked like his name would be Chain, or someone who knew the place well enough to point him in the right direction. Ray felt eyes on him and turned. A man sat alone at a table, a crystal tumbler in his massive hand. He looked human to Ray, a dark-skinned black man, maybe in his late forties, it was hard to tell. He had long gray dreadlocks, thick twists that fell to his shoulders, and a full gray beard. He was looking straight at Ray.

"Lost?" the man said. "The little mammal's room is third on the left. Do not make the mistake of going into the silicon lifeforms' crapper."

"You"—Ray started walking toward the man—"You wouldn't happen to be Chain, by any chance, would you?"

"Depends on who's asking." Chain glanced down at the ring on Ray's finger and seemed to relax. "What can I do you for, Ranger?"

Ray didn't get the "ranger" part, but figured it must be local slang.

"We . . . have a mutual friend."

# 5

Before Ray could begin to tell his story, there was a commotion in the crowd moving around them. "Chain!" a booming voice called out. A human-shaped being pushed his way through the crowd to stand only a few feet away from Ray and the still-seated Chain.

The guy was big, over six feet, and his skin looked like uncooked pizza dough. One of his eyes and part of his lumpy skull had been replaced with some kind of machine that whirred and scanned them, and he had what looked to Ray like a flower grafted into and coiled around his shoulder, its black petals in bloom with glowing purple veins shot throughout. He wore a sleeveless tunic with a lot of zippers and . . . parachute pants? It would have been kind of funny except he had his hand resting on the butt of a huge gun holstered at his hip. The four guys that muscled through the crowd behind him were armed too, and seemed to be following dough-guy's lead.

"What?" Chain sounded more annoyed than concerned.

Dough-guy held out an empty palm with the hand that wasn't on his gun.

"The keys to that piece of *shoka* I own now."

"I gave you the keys, Gled." Chain drained his glass and refilled it from the nearly empty bottle. "At the table, when I lost. Remember? I know I'll never forget that magic moment." Chain raised a finger to Ray as if to say, "Give me a second."

"The *other* keys, asshole." Gled stepped forward menacingly. "The real ones."

"I *gave* you . . ."

"I had T'car's brother try them out in the lot a moment ago," Gled said, jerking a thumb in the direction of one of the guys backing him up. To Ray, T'car looked like a man-sized version of a critter Ray had seen on the Discovery Channel called an aye-aye, a wild yellow-eyed lemur-thing. He looked pissed at Chain. "He fits in the ashtray, now."

"Yeah, the security system can be a little touchy"—Chain looked over to the glaring T'car—"Did he jiggle the key a little?"

T'car went for Chain, but his buddies held him back.

"The real keys," Gled said, "you cheating, lying, murdering, double-dealing mammalian bastard."

"Hey!" Chain stood; he was taller than Gled. "I am *not* a bastard." Chain rummaged around in the pockets of his worn and dirty canvas work pants, the kind Ray had seen mechanics wear most of his life. "Tell you what, Gled. I'll buy the truck back off you . . . fair market value."

"I'm surprised your lingual flap doesn't burst into flames when you say the word 'fair,'" Gled observed as Chain searched all the pockets of his pants and then his jacket for money.

Chain glanced over to Ray, still searching. "You . . . ah . . . you help me out, partner?"

"Excuse me? What?" Ray asked, confused.

"Float me a little cash, chief? I'll pay you back, Ranger's honor."

"I . . . I got some money off your friend, Evan. But . . ."

"Evan!" Chain's face lightened a bit. "How is the old void rider?"

"Uh . . . he's dead. He sent me to find you. He wanted me to give you a message." Chain's smile dropped and the light dimmed in his eyes. It seemed legit to Ray. "Look, I'm sorry, man." Chain looked back at Ray's hand for a moment and seemed to see the ring again in a very different light.

35

"Damn it . . ." Chain was no longer patting himself down.

"Keys, Chain," Gled said. "Now."

"Give me a minute! How much to buy her back?" Chain asked and then snapped his head over to Ray. "How much you got on you?"

"What?" Ray shook his head. His hand instinctively went to his jeans pocket where the bag of coins resided. "No!"

"Oh, come on, man. One Ranger to another. Brothers in arms." He held his hand up so Ray could see an identical jeweled ring to the one Evan had given him. He placed the hand on Ray's shoulder "I need my wheels. Come on!"

"Look, I need that money to get my mom out of some very deep crap." Ray glanced between Chain and the growing-ever-angrier Gled.

"What's your name, kid?" Chain asked.

"Ray, Ray Cosa."

"Where you from, Ray? Same shithole as Evan? What's it called?"

"Uh, Port Arthur?"

"Planet, kid, planet? Galaxy?"

Gled looked over his shoulder to T'car and the boys. "Get me my keys." They raised their weapons and charged Ray and Chain.

"Shit!" was all Ray had time to exclaim before Chain, hand still on his shoulder, shoved him down to the floor and out of the way of T'car's wavering, water-like microwave blade. Chain punched T'car in his weird little primate face and Ray heard a sickening crunch. T'car fell, and Chain was already on to another of Gled's subordinates. Ray had time to note how absolutely filthy the floor of this intergalactic truck stop was and that T'car was in a heap on the floor beside him, either knocked cold or dead.

The black, seemingly polymer handle of T'car's knife was about the size and shape of a box cutter from back home. It was generating a barely visible, distorted "blade" about a foot long. Ray gingerly picked up the handle, careful to avoid the flickering edge.

Chain, meantime, had dispatched another of Gled's boys, this one fairly human-looking but with catfish-like tendrils encircling his sucker mouth. He had swung at Chain with his fist, but the bigger man had blocked his punch and lifted him up off the ground with a powerful hook to his gut. Catfish-guy made a burbling sound as he flew through the air and crashed into a crowded table of what looked to Ray like a group of little-old-lady-tour-bus aliens. The pack all had bluish-purple hair and elongated faces with ruddy, rubbery skin and wore silver padded housecoats. The old gals sounded pissed as their winnings were scattered everywhere, letting out a chorus of hissing like a rattlesnake ready to strike. They began to withdraw slender pistol-type weapons from out of their large straw-woven purses.

One of Gled's guys had drawn a pistol and had a bead on Chain. Ray scrambled to his feet and low-tackled Chain just as the gun shot a bloom of green fire from the barrel. It missed Chain and blew a glowing green plasma crater in one of the angry gambling ladies' chests, sending her flying back to the ground. The other ladies all fired on the gunman, their pistols whistling as a dark mass escaped the barrels. The shooter dropped to the floor, his body resembling a bloody pincushion filled with hundreds of black glass-like shards.

Chain looked around and grabbed Ray by his coat. "Thanks. C'mon, the sisters will keep Gled pinned down for a second."

"Sisters?"

"The Sisters of Lakasia." Chain jerked a thumb back in the direction of the frothing tour-bus-lady aliens. "They're clones from a matriarchy in the Hodan Galaxy. They take their little gambling junkets very seriously." There was a nearby explosion of plasma. "Run!" the big man shouted, staying low and trying to use the tables for cover.

Gled and his remaining soldier were tied up in the firefight with the sisters while Chain and Ray crawled their way back toward the lift tubes. Ray paused for a second and fumbled with the microwave knife, trying to find a way to switch it off. Chain reached over and took it, pushing down on a section of the hilt, and the ghost-like blade faded away. He showed the trigger to Ray as he handed it back to him.

"Look, I really need to get back home! I'm on kind of a deadline!" Ray said over the cacophony of weapons fire, angry shouts, and screams of agony. Before Chain could respond, the table he was under and the people around it were blasted in all directions. "Evan wanted me to tell you . . ." There was another blast, closer and louder. It threw Ray and Chain in opposite directions.

"You go!" Chain shouted as one of Gled's men grabbed him by his sleeveless leather jacket. Chain popped up from the floor and sucker-punched him, grabbing at his gun. "Go on! I'll catch up!"

Ray paused for a second, debating if he should stay and try to help. He suddenly had an image of Mateo kicking in the door to Juanita's bedroom. "Whatever!" he shouted to Chain. He looked back to see the gunman—whose skin was a patchwork of transparent glass with firefly lights under it and raw, exposed fiber optic muscles—wrestling with Chain for control of the gun.

Ray sprinted the rest of the way to the lift and was relieved that no one seemed to be chasing him. The beam caught him and lowered him gently to the first floor and the marketplace again. It was hard to tell if the fight upstairs was adding to the chaos of the market, or if this was all just business as usual.

Outside, in the orange light of the lot, Ray found his Galaxie, still parked near Chain's tow truck, which now had a scorch mark beside it and a pile of dust Ray assumed was roughly T'car's-brother-shaped. He closed his eyes and tried to shake off all of this insanity. But it was still all there when he opened his eyes.

"Well, I tried," he said to himself. His voice sounded a little distorted, kind of muffled. He had never talked this much out loud to himself, but since last night, it was kind of a test, like he was hoping to verify to his other senses what was happening by narrating it out loud.

If any of this was real, and he was pretty sure it was, Chain didn't seem the type to be too concerned if he never got his friend's last message. Ray had seen real pain in the big guy's face when he'd told him Evan had died, but he seemed to mourn in the span of seconds. Ray had done as right by the old man as he could. Now, he had to take care of his own problems.

"Get me back home, back to Port Arthur," he said, holding up his hand and addressing the ring. He felt stupid doing it, but he'd played enough video games to know sometimes you had to do everything in a proper sequence for the game to let you keep going. "Uh . . . Earth, Milky Way, I think." The ring throbbed against his finger and Ray shook his head as he unlocked the driver's side door of the car and climbed inside. He started up the engine, and the Galaxie growled to life.

He edged through the parking lot of Nuurra's Station toward the road he had come in on. Traffic was more snarled now, and Ray assumed it was morning rush, or maybe afternoon . . . who fucking knew? A red straw with a row of angry, blinking eyes and two stick-like arms honked its car's horn at Ray as he merged out onto the street and headed toward the unmarked on-ramp he was certain had not been there when he had arrived. The ring pulsed for him to take it.

The red-straw guy shook a tiny, outraged fist from the cockpit of his vehicle, which was vaguely shaped like a hot dog. Ray gave a dismissive wave to the guy, and muttered under his breath, "I'm in a goddamned Richard Scarry acid trip." He pulled onto the ramp he figured was just there for him and floored the gas before some worm in an apple-car showed up.

# 6

Pham Lu woke up in a tangle of sheets and blankets to shouting in Vietnamese and rapid, powerful beating on his door. It scared the crap out of him until he realized it was just Grandma.

"Get up! Lazy! Up, Lu! It's already eight o'clock!"

"Grandma!" Lu shouted back in Vietnamese from under his pillow, "I don't go into work until four today!"

The beating on his bedroom door paused for a moment. Then it resumed at a greater intensity. "Plenty of time then to get up and look for a second job!" his grandmother barked back. Lu groaned and rolled over.

"Okay, Okay! I'm up!" he finally called back, this time in English.

"I'll be back in ten minutes if I don't hear you moving around in there," Grandma said menacingly. Lu forced his eyes open and saw his phone lying among his blankets. He half remembered the phone call in the middle of the night to Ray. Something about . . . Serbia? He checked his phone to see if Ray had called back or messaged him. Nothing.

The walls of Lu's room were covered in gaming and anime posters. His floor was a sea of discarded dirty clothes. His TV was still on, a dead, black screen connected to his yellow Pikachu Switch system. Lu groaned a little as he recovered a few-days-old pair of jeans, some less-dirty socks, and a not-too-bad-smelling T-shirt that declared him a "Weeaboo" in Japanese kanji. He recovered the wrinkled polyester bright-red-and-blue shirt that he had to wear to work at the Chug-n-Lug later today from the floor where he had discarded it—sniffed it, approved, and turned it right-side-out and hung it over his desk chair.

Lu checked his phone again. Still nothing from Ray. What had he said last night? Meet him at 'Keem's later . . . at . . . ten? He messaged Ray to confirm that and to ask if everything was okay. There was no response.

Lu slipped on his Vans, grabbed his keys and wallet, and unlocked his door. He glanced around furtively. He heard the talking heads on *Fox and Friends* yammering on the TV in the den and thought he heard Grandma agreeing loudly with whatever they were going on about. After a quick bathroom pit stop, Lu made his way quickly to the kitchen, opened a box of blueberry Pop Tarts, and retrieved one of the foil packets inside. He opened the kitchen door as quietly as he could.

"Come back with a second job!" Grandma bellowed over a commercial for buying gold as a stopgap to the inevitable collapse of all currency.

"You got it, Grandma! Will do," Lu called back and shut the door behind him.

He had a while before 'Keem's opened, and there was still no reply from Ray. He tried calling him a few times, and each time it rolled immediately to voice mail. As much as he didn't want to do it, Lu decided the best thing he could do was swing by Ray's house and see if he was home, maybe asleep after his long night touring Eastern Europe. Lu started up his battered, old blue 2001 Ford Focus and headed for Ray's on Fifteenth Street, eating his foil-entombed breakfast on the way.

Fifteenth Street was a working-class hood that had seen better days. Lu and Ray had been friends forever, and Ray's house was pretty much Lu's second home. He had watched the neighborhood diminish piecemeal by the time Ben, Ray's brother, had graduated high school, and Lu and Ray had started. Lu drifted down the street, knowing by six or seven the driveways and curbs would be lined with work trucks and vans, their weary occupants working on the six-pack they had picked up at the end of a long day that most likely started at five a.m.

That had been Ray's father's life, until the cancer ate him up. Lu winced inside at the pain of that. Ray Cosa was a genuinely good guy —Boy Scout good—and he had been through so much shit in his life in such a short time, beginning with his dad.

Mr. Cosa—Hugo—had been a legendary figure in Lu's life as much as in Ben's and Ray's. Hugo had married their mom right out of high school and then gone into the Marines. He'd fought in Desert Storm and then came home to raise a family and make a living. He busted his ass for his family. Lu recalled when Hugo would arrive home—tired, not always in the best mood. He'd unlace his work boots, usually groaning with the day's accumulated aches and pains, and drop them by the front door, per Mrs. Cosa's demand. He'd always make time to wrestle with Ray, Ben, Lu, and any other kids that were hanging out there that particular day. Lu grinned at the memory. Hugo always called him "Fruit Lu-oop" and tried to pick him up by his rather prominent ears. It always made Lu giggle uncontrollably.

Hugo Cosa was a hero, and he raised two sons who were stand-up guys just as much as he was. It had been so hard to see him near the end, frail, in bed with tubes up his nose and in his arms. Even the fierce light in his eyes had dimmed. In a way, Hugo had been Lu's dad too, and it had killed a part of him to see him die like that. He couldn't imagine what it had felt like to Ben, Ray, or Juanita. He had been the stable, immutable core of their world.

Lu pulled up to the empty curb in front of Ray's house. The heat-choked grass of the small front lawn needed a mow. Lu climbed out of the car and avoided the broken wooden porch step. Hugo would have stopped and fixed it as soon as he pulled up from work, but Hugo was long, long gone.

There were a few plastic yard chairs and folding camping chairs on the porch. The seat of one of the camping chairs was filled with old, rusty-looking rain water. Mosquitoes danced and flitted above their tiny breeding pool.

Lu knew the doorbell was busted, so he knocked on the front door. He waited. No response. He knocked again, louder and longer. He checked his phone and sent Ray another text. Nothing. Finally, Lu knelt down close to the porch's floor and found the two bricks with the gap in the mortar between them. The emergency house key was still there. He wiggled it free, unlocked the door, and returned it, making sure to look about to see if anyone might be watching him. The street seemed deserted.

Lu stepped inside and closed the door behind him. "Hello!" he called out. There was no response.

Everywhere, there were islands of boxes, clothes baskets, and general clutter. It looked like someone had been packing and then just stopped. He caught the stench of rotten, decomposing food and made his way toward the kitchen, passing a teetering column of plastic storage tubs marked *Navidad* in black Sharpie.

At the entrance to the kitchen, Lu saw the fridge was still covered with magnets made from old family photos and certificates of awards and achievements, mostly Ray's. His own family would never do this; they'd consider it "clutter." He knew they were proud of him, though, and that each ribbon, each certificate and perfect report card had been carefully packed away and preserved. Lu always liked the messy chaos of Ray's fridge door. It seemed more like genuine love and pride to him, something that demanded to be shouted out and expressed. Lu knew his family loved him; they were just very reserved in how they showed it. It was one of the many things he had envied about Ray and his family . . . at least until everything began to unravel. Now the festooned door seemed like a memorial to a time and a people long dead, long gone.

The smell was coming from the kitchen sink. It was half-full of dirty dishes. Lu could tell that someone had been making an effort to winnow the contents down. There was also a box of plastic trash bags and a bottle of Pine-Sol on the cluttered kitchen table. A bucket was on the floor near the table next to a propped-up mop and broom. Lu knew that it was Ray, that he was trying to battle the chaos. He also knew that Ray was fighting his own battle inside, to not lay down, to not sleep and slowly die. It had only been six months since Jess had died. The pain was still a fresh wound for Lu; he couldn't imagine what it was doing to Ray.

"Hi, Lu."

He started and turned. Mrs. Cosa, Juanita, was standing in the hallway behind him.

"Ray's not here."

When Lu had been younger, every friend of Ben's and Ray's had had a crush on Mrs. Cosa. She was cool and never turned away one of Ray's buddies for dinner or a sleepover or to give them a ride home or pick them up. She actually listened to them. She was beautiful.

Now, she looked like a horror-movie-zombie-apocalypse version of herself. Her skin was dead, almost gray. There was no life behind her eyes and no expression on her lined, haggard face. Her blonde hair was greasy and had a lot more white in it than he ever remembered. She clutched her dirty bathrobe closed. Under it, she wore a T-shirt with dried vomit stains on the collar and baggy sweat pants. She was trembling, like someone with the flu who was running a fever, but Lu knew the shakes had nothing to do with a virus.

"I hope you don't mind; I let myself in. I'm looking for Ray. Did he come home last night?" Juanita struggled to focus on the words. Lu suspected the second he was gone she'd be back to bed.

"I . . . I don't know." Her words shook as much as her body. "I think so. I've been sick." Lu said nothing. "He runs around so much . . . I don't know where he is. He . . . he doesn't tell me anything, anymore."

Lu tried to stay cool, but some panic was building in him and frustration, too. "Yesterday, he was running all over trying to get money together to pay Mateo Morales off."

"Oh," she said, as if she had completely forgotten her debt to the drug dealer. Lu felt anger bubbling up in him.

"Yeah, so last night he said he had an idea of how to pick up some more money." Lu's voice was a little sharper now. "He sent me home. I talked to him in the middle of the night, and he sounded kinda crazy."

"Do you know if he got the money?" Juanita asked, fighting to stay upright.

Lu lost it.

"You know, I'm really sorry for everything your family's had to go through," Lu said, moving past Juanita as he headed for the front door, "but your son, your only living kid, lost his girlfriend a few months ago, and he's hurting bad."

"I know," Juanita muttered, bumping into the wall to avoid Lu as he passed. She almost fell over. "I've been . . . I've been sick."

"Would it hurt you to at least pretend you give a damn about him, about anything other than your own . . . problems?"

"My problems? *My* problems! Get the hell out of my house, *el cabrón*!" Juanita snarled, trying to turn to face Lu and swat at him. Lu was already past her and to the front door. She slipped and slid down the wall, ending with her back to it. "You have no idea what we've been through! Get out! You call yourself his friend? You talk to me like that? Get the fuck out!"

Lu opened the door. "If you see him, tell him to call me." He shut the door, but not before he heard Juanita beginning to sob and wail.

*Damn*, he thought as he got back into his car. *How the fuck is Ray even staying sane, functioning, with that shit-show to deal with?*

He looked at the time: 9:35. He tried calling Ray again and got another shunt direct to the message that his voice mail was not set up and to try again later. By now, he felt bad for saying anything to Mrs. Cosa. She had lost people too, and everyone didn't deal with pain the same way. But right now, he was much more concerned with Ray and where he was.

As he looked up from his phone, he saw an old-school Chevy Nova prowl by Ray's house and then drift past his car. It was Mateo, dressed in black and silver, looking like death incarnate. The gang leader scanned Lu for a second, and Lu felt ice water pool in his guts. He froze, like a rabbit suddenly confronted with a snake. Mateo sized him up and then looked back to the road, accelerating away. Lu looked down at his phone and messaged Ray again: *Ray, where are you, man?*

## 7

R ay's car pulled into the parking lot of City Pawn at 10:23. Most of the locals who had need of the services of the store had come to call it "'Keem's," after its sole owner and operator.

In the aftermath of Harvey, 'Keem's had ended up being a lot like George Bailey's Building & Loan from *It's a Wonderful Life*, providing much-needed cash to keep people going who had just lost everything. While there was still some suspicion of 'Keem because of his nationality, most folks in Port Arthur liked and respected the former Afghan soldier, and even the ones who distrusted and hated him owed him a little money.

Ray saw that Lu was waiting for him, sitting in his own car, on his phone. The only other vehicle in the lot was 'Keem's old beat-to-shit Toyota truck. Ray parked and got out, stretching as far as his aching arms would allow.

"Where the hell have you been?" Lu said as he climbed out of the Focus. "I've been trying to find you all morning!" He paused for a moment in mid-fret and looked at the Galaxie, its black-mirrored surface flashing in the already-hot morning sun. "Oh my god, you boosted that car that was at the truck stop last night!"

"Keep it down!" Ray hissed, walking up to Lu. The two fist bumped. "At first . . . yeah, I did try to steal it, but the old guy who owned it—Evan—he ended up giving it to me. It's legit mine." In the back of his mind, Ray had been worrying about one troubling scenario. The cops find Evan, they run him through the system and find out he owned the Galaxie. They start looking for the Galaxie, and they pull him over and decide he killed the old man for the car.

Lu saw the worry behind Ray's dark, tired eyes. "Okay," he said, dropping it for now. They walked toward the pawn shop's steel-barred front door. "You . . . you planning to try to see if 'Keem will buy it?"

"No. I'm keeping her. I got something better to sell him."

Lu had a million questions for Ray, but his friend seemed more than a little weirded-out and clearly on a mission to get the money for his mom. His questions would keep. He followed Ray inside.

City Pawn was pretty typical for its kind of business. An electronic tone announced his entrance. There were cheap steel shelves covered in hand and power tools that greeted him as he came in. A gas-powered soil tiller was hunched in front of the tool shelves next to unfolded work horses and a stack of battered construction helmets on a table with worn leather tool belts and work lamps. A glass shop counter ran along the wall to the left of the door, filled with jewelry—everything from wedding rings to Rolex watches. Ray didn't know why, but the jewelry counter of a pawn shop always felt very sad to him, like he was walking past a gallery of lost dreams, surrendered happiness. There were big flat-screen TVs on the walls, most connected to DVD players or the graveyard of old video game systems.

"Oh man!" Lu exclaimed. "He's got an old-school Neo Geo! Still in the box!"

"Don't drool on anything," Ray said with a wan smile, "you'll have to buy it."

The games themselves were in locked glass display cabinets, next to laptops and tablets. There were seemingly endless rows of DVD movies, even cardboard boxes squatting on the floor, overflowing with VHS tapes, three for a dollar. The sign on the wall by the front door was impossible to miss—that was the idea. It said in large, menacing block print: YOU ARE UNDER CONSTANT VIDEO SURVEILLANCE. SHOPLIFTERS WILL NOT MAKE IT PAST THE DOOR ALIVE. The grim message was repeated in Spanish as well.

Behind the raised wooden counter at the back of the store were cages filled with guns of every imaginable type from AR-15s to one-shot derringers. Between the buyer and the artillery was the man himself, Khan Hakeem. 'Keem was tall and fit, which silently spoke to his military past. He kept his still-mostly black hair cut very short, but he had maintained a long, traditional beard that was shot through with a little gray. He wore a black T-shirt and old jeans.

"Ramon, Lu." 'Keem nodded as they approached. 'Keem's oldest—his son Aarash—had gone to school with Ben, and the two had been friends. Aarash was in the army now, overseas, back in his father's homeland. 'Keem's whole family, including Aarash, had come out for Pop's and Ben's funerals. "How can I help you?"

Ray fished the bag of coins out of his jeans and placed it on the wooden counter. Lu crowded in to look at what his friend had acquired.

"I'm in a bind. A guy I met gave me these weird old coins. I'm pretty sure some of them are gold . . ."

"Gold?" Lu said, looking incredulously at Ray. Ray gave him a dirty look and then emptied the coins out on to the counter.

"I really need the money, 'Keem. It's for my mom." 'Keem frowned as he examined the strange coins.

"I've never seen coins like this from anywhere in the world, Ramon." He turned the small plastic square bits over. "You may have been lied to by this man. These may be some kind of . . . tokens. Perhaps for a Chuck E. Cheese in Sumatra?"

He took one of the heavier gold-looking coins to the back counter, where he picked up a large metal block and held it several inches above the coin. When nothing happened, he nodded and put the block down. "It's not magnetic. That's good." He scraped the corner of a square of unglazed ceramic plate over the coin.

"The old guy gave you a bag of weird money *and* his sweet ride?" Lu said in a hushed voice to Ray. "You just trusted this guy?"

"I didn't have a choice, at least not at first," Ray hissed back. "Shut up, I'll tell you later." 'Keem was examining the coin now through a jeweler's loop. "This looks like solid gold, Ray. I'll need to check the others. It will take a while."

"I have to . . . meet someone by noon with the money." 'Keem took the loop away from his eye and looked at the young man, who was obviously exhausted and stressed. "I'll see what I can do." The pawn shop owner got to work on the other coins.

Lu and Ray bought sodas from a small fridge-cooler in the corner and wandered the store. Lu flipped through row after row of DVDs. He looked up to see Ray staring out the glass door to the now-bright day outside. His brain was clearly somewhere else. Lu felt sorry for his friend. The weight of all his responsibilities and his grief were on top of him like bags of lead. He decided to say nothing about his confrontation with Juanita. Most likely, she had already forgotten it too. Ray had enough to worry about without Lu adding another rock to his back.

Ray checked his phone. It was getting close to eleven, and his guts were twisting in pain. His phone was still at close to 100 percent. Apparently, it charged automatically inside the Galaxie. Of course it did.

A text message popped up on the screen. It was Mateo: *You got the money?*

Ray looked back at 'Keem, who was diligently at work on the other coins. What the fuck. He was too tired and too sick to care anymore. He swiped in his reply: *Yeah. Meet me at the Run at noon.*

If the coins were a bust, if 'Keem didn't have the money to pay him, he'd give Mateo every cent he had and a promise to sell the car and get him the rest as quick as he could. The thought of losing the Galaxie made him angry. Then he closed his eyes and thought about what Pop would do, what Ben would do, and he pushed the anger away in a deep sigh.

"Okay, Ramon," 'Keem said, "Let's talk."

49

Ray and Lu returned to the counter. 'Keem laid the coins back on the bag.

"The big coins are pure gold and not legal, I'm pretty sure. These coins here are nearly pure silver, and there are microscopic gold threads in the plastic chits. These coins . . . I have no idea what they are made of. I don't have a mass spectrometer laying around in the back next to the taxidermied bear. I searched the internet and the dark web for them, for the markings. Nothing. I even took a peek in a few databases I can access, but shouldn't be able to—not a thing. So I will buy the gold and silver ones, and I'll give you the current weight per ounce, but I have to tell you I think I will have to melt them down to get my money back on them. These are not legal tender anywhere in this world I have been able to search. They are worth, all told, ten thousand dollars. I can give you eight, and that is because it's you, and I know you are not a criminal. If you say you need this money for an emergency, for your mother, then I believe you."

The remark about not being a criminal stung a bit, but Ray nodded. "Thanks." Relief washed through him, but it didn't wash away the stress or the exhaustion.

"Very well"—'Keem slid the other coins back over to Ray—"I will need to go down to the safe to . . ." He paused when he noticed Ray's hands, putting the other coins back in the purple bag that were on the counter. He looked up at Ray, shocked. It was the first time in their lives Lu or Ray had ever seen 'Keem anything but stoic and cool. "That ring . . . where did you get that from?"

Ray froze.

"Oh, yeah," Lu said looking down at Ray's hand, "Where'd that come from? The old man give you that too?"

"Old man?" 'Keem said. "What old man, Ramon?" 'Keem could tell the boy was exhausted and afraid. He kept glancing up at the clock on the wall.

"I just . . . look, I just have to get this money to someone by noon."

"How much do you want for the ring?" 'Keem asked.

Ray's hand dropped to the black steel band with its tiny jeweled chips.

"It's . . . not for sale," Ray said, and wondered why he felt like that. What did he care about it? In the bright light of day, under the harsh fluorescence of the pawn shop light, did he really think this was some kind of magic ring that went with his magic muscle car and led him to secret roads that existed only for him? That was way past crazy and into insane. "Why do you want it, 'Keem?"

"This old man, did he drive an old military-style truck? A deuce-and-a-half, painted in desert camo?"

"No. Why? What's so important about that ring?" 'Keem stepped back from the counter, as if he were suddenly flooded with too many memories, too many emotions, to be still.

"A man wearing a ring exactly like that one saved my life back in Afghanistan, back when you were in kindergarten, I imagine." The former soldier got over his initial surprise. "Did the man who gave you this ring give you the bag of coins too?"

"Yeah."

"Okay, I'll buy the whole bag. I'll give you ten thousand."

"Eight's fine." Ray glanced over to Lu for a moment. "Can you throw in the Neo Geo system too?" Lu's face lit up.

"Sure. Let me get the money from the safe." 'Keem disappeared through the door behind the counter.

Lou's face erupted into a grin, "My dude! You didn't have to get me the console!"

"Who said I did?" Lu mouthed a vulgarity and they both laughed. "I've never seen 'Keem like that before." Ray held up his hand with the ring. "I know this thing is weird, but . . ."

"Hey, can I see it?" Lu asked.

"Yeah." Ray tugged on the ring, but it didn't budge. He pulled harder, and nothing moved, but he felt like he was pulling his finger out of joint. Ray stopped, flexed his fingers and shook them a little. "It's stuck." The electronic tone announced the arrival of a new customer.

"You can stop trying," Chain said as he entered the pawn shop. "It ain't coming off anytime soon."

Lu watched Ray's face go through a gymnastic routine as this big guy walked in. The stranger looked a little like a young George Clinton from Parliament Funkadelic if he were swole as hell and dressed like he was an extra in a *Mad Max* movie.

"What are you . . . how are you?" Ray asked.

"I told you I'd catch up." Chain walked up to the counter. He looked over at Lu and offered his hand. "Chain. Nice to meet you . . ."

"Lu." He shook Chain's hand. "You the guy who gave Ray the car and the coins, and the weird ring?"

"Lu," Ray said, trying to shut his friend up.

Chain gave Ray a dismissive wave and answered Lu. "No, but the guy who did was a friend of mine. A late friend."

"Late?" Lu said louder than he should have as he looked over to Ray. "You never said this guy was dead."

"I . . . wait," Ray stammered. Everything was going to crap. "He wasn't . . . but then . . . he was."

"You said Evan had a message for me?" Chain was unperturbed by Ray's anxiety.

"Evan?" Lu said, "That the old guy that gave you the . . ."

"Yes!" Ray said, shutting him down. He glanced up at the clock and saw time speeding away from him. 'Keem stepped out of the back room, a small brown paper bag in his hand. "Is there a problem here?" the former soldier asked, his eyes falling squarely on Chain.

Chain gestured, his palms open, and smiled. "No problem here, friend. Certainly no reason you'd need that gun tucked away at the small of your back." 'Keem's glance fell on Chain's ring. "Another one," he muttered. He handed the paper bag to Ray, while keeping his eyes on Chain. "This man is not the cause of your . . . emergency, is he Ramon?"

"No, no." Ray took the bag and checked its contents. It was full of money. Ray knew he had no need to count it. "Look, I've got to run, to get this . . . where it needs to go. Lu will take the game console. Thanks, 'Keem."

"I would very much like to hear the story behind that ring," 'Keem said.

Ray glanced over to Chain, who was amusing himself by

rummaging through the VHS tapes. "Yeah, me too. I'll come by and tell you everything, I promise. I'd like to hear your story too, if you don't mind." 'Keem nodded, tersely, then went to help Lu get the Neo Geo out of the display cabinet.

"I got to go," Ray said to Chain as he headed for the door. "I can catch up with you later. You got a phone number? How'd you find me, anyway?"

Chain held up his hand with the ring on it.

Lu called out, "Hey, don't be late for your shift today! We're on at four!"

"Shift?" Chain asked.

"Yeah," Ray said, "my job."

"Look, I didn't come all the way over here to wait around." Chain sounded more than a little irritated. "Just tell me what Evan said, and I'll be on my way."

Ray looked up at the clock again.

"Listen, I'm sorry, but if I don't meet this guy in a very little while, my mom's in a lot of trouble." Chain wound up to complain, but Ray shut him down. "Look, I drove all damn night to tell you, and you ended up trying to shake me down for money and almost got me killed. So, you can meet me at work later—Lu can tell you how to get there—or you can take off."

Ray pushed out the door into the late-morning heat. Chain watched him get into Evan's old Galaxie and pull out of the parking lot.

# 8

The interior of the Yateveo's capsule was vast, filled with twisting dark mazes of corridors that opened into junctions of portals to other dimensional pockets on the ship and lifts to various levels in this particular dimension. The small craft held worlds' worth of space inside itself; it would be frighteningly easy to become lost within it.

One of the eldest of the Yateveo remained in what had once been a sprawling garden park in the capsule. Originally filled with all manner of flora from the Tribanni home world of Triban, the Yateveo's presence had devoured the park's plant and animal life, transforming it into an exact replica of the biosphere on their long-dead planet of origin.

The elder's "name"—a specific vibrational pattern made by the whipping of the medium-sized upper tendrils on its trunk-like body—sounded roughly like "Hooruuul." It had been Hooruuul who nearly killed the Queen's Ranger during the invasion of Triban. Now, the eldest of their kind had sent him to this savage little planet to finish the job. The younger ones among the hunt party were given the task of locating the accursed spy, ensuring he was dead, and ascertaining whether he had gotten word of the Yateveo's return to any of his comrades.

Now, two members of the expedition—Yateveo named Wuuuyun and Sshraaash—entered the park, the air dark and thick with olive clouds of pollen. The dead Tribanni trees were swollen with tumorous, pulsating seed pods, out of which some young Yateveo had already emerged and taken root in the soil, a thick mud rich in food-animal blood.

They addressed the elder; their language was one of vibration, spores, and the Morse code of osmotic pressure.

"Elder Hooruuul," Sshraaash said, "the food animals we modified to serve us will depart shortly to search out the Ranger."

"It is well. Make sure they kill any who encountered the Ranger as well. There must be no mistakes this time. We will let the Royals know of our presence when it is far too late for even them to stop us."

"Will the others of the Nemesis return and join us again?" Wuuuyun asked. "The N'kbrd? The Hira'Firma? The Twisting Mirror?" It paused, as if afraid to voice the next name, "The . . . Lytch? All the others?"

"As we were freed from the prison by the Pilgrim of Chaos, then the others will be as well," Hooruuul said. "Our joined purpose—the crumbling, frozen degradation of the damned essence of viability—will finally be realized."

"Praise be to the Stillness!" the youngsters proclaimed.

"Go now to your tasks," Hooruuul said. "This primitive little planet will soon know the glory of unmaking."

The youngsters departed, and the elder was once again left to his meditations upon the Stillness and the war to come. He paid no attention to the gutted food animals left buried in the blood-soaked mud to pump more fresh, hot blood into the soil and suckle the children.

"Please . . ." one of the food animals sobbed as the feeding tubes of the young pierced their flesh and drained their succulent juices. "Please, kill me."

## 9

When Ray arrived at the Run, Mateo was waiting, leaning against his Nova, wearing a silver-and-black cowboy shirt, a black Stetson, black jeans, and his rattlesnake boots.

The place hadn't changed very much in the year and a half since Ben died. The Run was the winding access road to one of the factories that had been put underwater by Hurricane Harvey, and had never come back. The local street racers had started using it as a track, since it was easy to spot cops heading from the main road a quarter mile off, and it was paved, always empty, and had some wicked turns. The property owners and the Port Arthur cops had all tried to lock it down, but the racers kept finding a way around the fences, the locks, and the barriers.

Ray had some amazing memories of racing along the dark, unlit road at night, the wind like perfume in his face, Ben laughing and whooping. The speed, the freedom, the sweet taste of pushing life to its crumbling edge and sailing through to victory. Ray had one horrible nightmare of a memory from here too—Ben's crash and death. He pulled to a stop beside Mateo's car, closed his eyes for a second, and pushed the pain away as far as he was able. It was a dull ache in his chest and mind.

"Cherry ride," Mateo said. "You win the lottery or something, Ramon?"

"Something like that." Ray climbed out of the Galaxie and shut the door. He handed Mateo the money. "Here, three thousand. The extra is to cover any 'interest' you tacked on since yesterday. We're clear now, right?" Mateo took out the wad of cash and began to flip through it as he counted. He looked up at Ray and nodded.

"For now, 'til the next time your mom gives the doctor a call to come visit."

Ray held up another wad of cash.

"Here's another thousand. You never sell to Juanita again, and neither does any of your crew. Ever. Deal?"

"You know if it's not me, not my people, it will be somebody else, *ese*. Maybe someone who doesn't know you and your family the way I do."

"Yeah, you've been a big help. I'm getting her clean." Ray was still holding the cash. "You want this or not?"

Mateo took the grand and added it to the other pile of cash. "She in on this intervention?" he asked as he tucked the money in his pocket, "'Cause she's been blowing up my phone all morning, looking to score."

Ray said nothing.

Mateo saw how tired he was, how desperate. There was a hardness behind his eyes that reminded him of Ray's brother and father. The dealer nodded slowly and shrugged. "I'll put the word out Juanita's money ain't no good." He nodded toward the Galaxie. "It won't do much for very long, but maybe you can ship her off to Passages Malibu or wherever with all this money you've come up on."

"Thanks." Ray walked away from Mateo and back to his car.

"Hey, you know you and Benno, you two were, like, unstoppable out here." Mateo gestured to the road. "The fucking crazy-ass Cosa brothers." He laughed. "Nobody could beat either one of you. I am sorry for how it went down with Benno, y'know. He went out the way he would have wanted to. I guess that's something, huh?"

"Yeah, I guess." Ray started up the Galaxie with a low rumble and drifted down the access road, taking the turns as he accelerated as easy as taking a breath.

It was after nine p.m. when Ray, dressed in his red-and-blue uniform shirt unbuttoned over a black T-shirt, entered the Chug-n-Lug.

Lu, wearing the same shirt—albeit a tad more wrinkled—shot from behind the counter to meet him.

"Are you okay? I've been trying to call you! I thought maybe Mateo went all Ted Bundy on you or something!"

"I'm okay."

"Yeah, if 'okay' means you didn't get any sleep and you look like crap," Lu said.

"Do I still have a job?"

Lu nodded as he ducked back behind the counter to ring up a customer. "Trevor said it was cool, you could cover for him some this weekend." He scanned and bagged the man's purchases. "You've worked here since you were seventeen, that's like ninety-four in convenience-store-clerk-years. I'm pretty sure you could axe-murder a customer, and you'd still have a job." The customer looked up, a little shaken. Lu smiled and shrugged, "That'll be four twenty-seven." The man paid and scuttled out of the store as quickly as he could, with a few concerned glances back at Lu and Ray.

"Thanks for covering for me." Ray walked over and started making himself a big cup of coffee.

"What happened?" Lu asked.

Ray sighed as he poured.

"I went home to check on Juanita, and she was sick, really sick. Withdrawal, big-time. I managed to get her up and to the hospital. It took hours, but they finally admitted her."

"Shit. I'm so sorry, Ray."

Ray shrugged and sipped the lukewarm coffee. "I'll get a new pot going,"

The doors to the store swung open and Chain strode in, saying, "You're late."

"I'm sorry." Ray's voice was sharp and a little rusty as he dumped the old coffee out into a sink. "I make you late for a hot craps game you got no money for?"

Chain smiled and held up his hands in surrender. "Sorry. Just not much to do around here to kill time."

"Try living here," Lu offered as he straightened the candy bars.

"No." Chain glanced over to the two small circular plastic tables wedged between the I-SCREAM! cooler and several standing metal spinners full of a variety of phone cases, chargers, and earbuds. "Got time to have a seat and finally talk?"

"They're for paying customers," Ray said, sliding a clean, empty pot under the well of one of the industrial coffee-makers. Chain frowned and looked around. He grabbed a fistful of spiced meat sticks and a large can of energy drink from the displays around him and brought them to the counter.

Lu rang him up. "An excellent choice."

Chain fished around in his pants pocket and recovered a wad of damp, greasy American currency. "Keep the change."

"Where'd you get . . . Earth money?" Ray asked.

Chain gestured dismissively. "You really don't want to know." He nodded to the bum-wad Lu was carefully unfolding. "You may want to decontaminate your hands after handling that."

Ray looked over to Lu. "You mind?"

Lu, now using two pens like chopsticks to manipulate the cash, shook his head. "Go ahead."

Ray joined the tow-truck driver at one of the small tables. He sipped his bad coffee while Chain figured out how to peel away the packaging of one of the meat sticks. He ate half of it in a single bite and washed it down with energy drink.

"This tastes like the rations the Lambogodians feed their soldiers," Chain said, holding up the gnawed-on meat treat.

"Lot of high cholesterol on Lambogodia?" Ray asked as Chain finished the stick and unwrapped another.

"So, what did Evan say to you that got you to drive all the way to Bleeth to find me?"

"Bleeth." Ray shook his head. "No, you first. What the hell is Bleeth? How did I get there? It was another planet, right? How did I drive to another planet?" Ray held up his hand with the black jeweled ring. "What is this? How did I find you with this, just knowing your nickname and that you were on Bleeth? As soon as I tell you what Evan said, I know you're gone—I know that. I think I deserve a few answers too, don't you?"

Chain burped and leaned back in his chair, a tangled, greasy pile of meat-stick wrappers in front of him. "Okay, I'll tell you. You do deserve to know, given you're wearing that now."

"What's the deal with the ring? Evan had one, you have one, and 'Keem apparently ran into somebody wearing one too."

Chain leaned forward. He looked at his own ring for moment, then raised his gaze to Ray. "I guess to explain the ring, I need to start with the war."

"War?"

Chain nodded.

"It began thousands of years ago. An elder race, the Lytch, started it, appearing out of nowhere, laying waste to whole cultures, whole worlds. They worshiped entropy—you know about entropy right?"

"Vaguely, from science class. Uh . . . disorder, systems breaking, everything winding down, ending."

"Close enough. At the end of the day, you're talking death, death on a cosmic scale. The Lytch found other like-minded fanatics. What can I tell you? It's a big universe; it takes all kinds. They wouldn't have amounted to much, but somehow they found a way to manipulate the road and travel it with impunity."

"The road? You mean that highway I took to get to you and then get home?"

"Exactly. It's called the Queen's Road. It connects the entire universe and makes civilization possible across vast, unimaginable distances."

"Who's the Queen?"

"The Queen of the Universe, of course."

"Oh," Ray said. "I . . . didn't know . . . that was a thing."

"She and her children built the road at the beginning of the universe. It's a predictive, fluid, hyperspatial overlay, a tunnel, a pocket reality, that connects every point to every other point."

"And the rings let you navigate it?" Ray recalled the ring pulsing as it directed him which exits to take and which roads to remain on.

"Exactly. The royal family created keys that would allow limited access to the Queen's Road, so you could travel specific paths to specific destinations but nowhere else. Those keys are called tokens, and they facilitate trade and limited alliances. They also created keys called guidestones that give you unlimited access to the road."

"These bad guys, the Lynch . . ."

"Lytch," Chain corrected.

"OK, the Lytch. They figured out a way to move around like they had a guidestone?"

Chain looked impressed.

"Yes. They were moving their armies and their allies' forces through the universe on a crusade to tear everything down, ending civilization, wiping out life on a scale no one had ever conceived of before. They wanted to burn down creation. Their alliance came to be known as the Nemesis. The Nemesis somehow found a way to move vast armies very quickly over long distances along the Queen's Road."

"How'd they do it?" Ray asked. "Steal a bunch of guidestones?"

"No." Chain paused to chug his energy drink. "This is really good. I might take some of these with me. No, a guidestone wouldn't let you take that many vehicles and people through—not even a lot of guidestones. They moved quicker than they should have been able to, as well. They bypassed defenses, outmaneuvered armies, avoided blockades, even reached worlds that they shouldn't have been able to reach with a guidestone. No one ever figured out how they did it, not even the Royals when they finally got involved in the war. However they did it, it gave them a huge advantage over the Shield Pact."

"The good guys, right?" Ray offered. He began to take a sip of the now-cold-and-nasty coffee and thought better of it.

"You know, you're handling all this unusually well."

Ray shrugged.

"In the last five years, I've lost my dad, my brother, and the girl I loved; I've watched my mother kill herself a little every day. I haven't slept more than a few hours a night in over six months. Last night, I drove across the world and then off into space in a car I stole from a guy who wanted me to have it, who gave me this weird ring that seems kind of alive. I almost got eaten by a dinosaur-thing while trying to take a leak and was nearly shot to death by something that looked like a fallen souffle. I have some kind of invisible-light-saber-knife-thing in my pocket. You telling me about intergalactic highways and space wars and queens of the universe . . . that's pretty much not going to raise the bar at this point."

"Fair enough," Chain said. "If it matters, I'm sorry for your losses. I've never been that close to my family. Truth be told, I think most of them are assholes, and don't even get me going on my mom." He chuckled. "But even with all that, I hated losing some of them. I know you don't want to hear this, but pain and loss, it toughens you up, shows you how much you can handle; it usually surprises you, really, how much you can take." Ray looked at the table and said nothing. "You've got a good attitude, and it will help you a lot with what's coming,"

At that, Ray looked up. "What's that supposed to mean? *What's coming?*" Chain seemed to be trying to find some words to move forward a little more delicately. Ray shut him down. "No, don't you fucking dare. Don't candy-coat it after all that locker-room bullshit about toughening up. Just tell me. It's too late for you to try to dance around shit, Chain."

"You're right." Chain nodded and pointed to the ring on Ray's finger. "It ain't coming off your finger, ever. Well, until the day you die. You're married now, like it or not."

"What are you saying?" Ray tugged at the ring, but it didn't budge. "Married? Evan said something like that too, right before he died." Ray paused, remembering. "Right after he took the ring off and asked me to put it on."

"You're a Ranger now. One of the Queen's. 'Til the day you die."

Ray was silent, looking at the ring, then at Chain. "That like being a soldier?" he asked. "Fight in this war you were talking about? I can't do that. My mom's sick; she's in the hospital. Trying to get her better, that's the only fight I can do right now, Chain."

The big tow-truck driver waved his hand, shook his head.

"War's over, Ray, going on five hundred years. We won. The bad guys are gone. You don't have to do anything; you don't got to fight. It's okay."

Ray looked at the tiny jewel chips and the mirror-black metal of the ring on his finger flashing in the harsh florescent light of the store. "Then what am I *supposed* to do?"

"Relax, for starters. Rangers got only one boss—that's the Queen. You got no one to report to, no routine. We come and go as we please. So, take a breath, okay? Why don't you tell me about Evan? What did he say to you exactly that he wanted me to hear?"

Ray tried to shake off the stress and fear that he was feeling. *A Ranger? Like fucking Aragorn?* He cleared his thoughts and nodded to Chain. "Yeah, okay. He wanted me to tell you the name of the guy who killed him. He said for me to make sure I told you that somebody named Yateveo did it."

Chain sat up a little straighter. He looked like he had just got punched in the face. "He said *Yateveo*? You're sure? You must have misheard him, Ray." Ray was a little pissed off at the inference. "No. He said Yateveo. I heard it clear. I remember, because I thought it was a weird name. In Spanish, it means, 'I already see you.' So, no. It was Yateveo. Why?"

"He must have been out of his mind, then." Chain sounded like he was trying to convince himself. "Nearly dead, hallucinating."

"He wasn't." Ray was starting to feel himself catch a little of Chain's sudden aura of panic. "The man was dying, but he was clear. He fought to get every one of those words out so I would get them to you. Chain, what's going on, man?"

The older Ranger leaned across the table and grabbed Ray's arm. "How did he die, exactly? Tell me."

"He had these . . . wooden arrows, sticks in his chest. He was bleeding out from them but also said they were . . ."

They both said "poisoned" as one. Chain stood up, almost knocking his chair over.

"How did you know . . . ?" Ray began to ask.

Chain cut him off. "I need to see the body," he said, already heading for the door. "Come on."

"The body?" Ray followed him to the door. "Chain, I left him on the side of I-10. I'm sure the cops have found him by now. He's probably in Beaumont for the autopsy."

"Great, let's go."

"You don't need me. The ring will get you there."

"It will, but this isn't my world. I can't navigate the social stuff, the legal system. I need you, Ray. I'm sorry, but I do, and it's vital. We don't have much time. Your world's in danger."

"Wha . . . the *world*? What the hell is going on? Why are you in such a big hurry now? What's a Yateveo?"

Two drunk guys, one in a Misfits T-shirt and combat boots, the other in a Dierks Bentley concert shirt and cowboy hat, pushed through the doors and wobbled their way around Chain and Ray.

"I'll explain, but we have to go, now. If Evan was right in what he said, every living thing on Earth is going to die."

Ray looked past Chain to the hot night, the evening traffic on Sixteenth Street. *Everybody . . . dead.* He glanced back to Lu. "I'm . . . I got to go."

"It's cool," Lu said, starting to ring up the two drunk guys. "Go. Save the world or whatever. I'll cover the beer rush."

Ray waved to his friend and pulled off his unbuttoned work shirt as he followed Chain out the door.

# 10

---

The Galaxie drove south on US 96, headed for Beaumont. Ray was playing "Rosa Pastel" by Belanova on the car radio. He was driving about five miles over the limit, but he desperately wanted to floor it. The windows were down, and the night wind cooled the oppressive summer air.

"I like this," Chain said from the passenger seat, nodding to the radio. He was searching his jacket pockets for something.

"You speak Spanish?"

Chain shook his head.

"No"—he held up the ring, wiggling his fingers—"but this does. Lets you understand most languages and transmits the translation to you telepathically with no lag. One of the Queen's gifts. Ah, here we go." He pulled a device out of his pocket that looked a bit like a tire-pressure gauge with a small keypad built into the cylinder. Chain carefully punched a button on the keypad with his thick finger and spoke to the device, "Yateveo spore count, parts per million, maximum range." After a moment the device made a sound a bit like an electronic burp. Chain worriedly read the tiny screen, and then relief spread across his broad face. "We're clean. No spores detected and this little sniffer has a very good range."

"And that means?"

"That hopefully Evan was wrong, or confused, or tripping. Worst case scenario, it means that the Yateveo haven't been on Earth long enough to contaminate it yet."

"He was in his right mind. It's a little over twenty minutes to Beaumont, can't we jump on the Queen's Road, or whatever, and get there quicker?"

Chain started to answer as he put the atmosphere scanner away, but stopped himself. "You try, with the ring." Ray focused on getting to Beaumont, on getting to Evan's body. The ring was silent, no vibration, no pulsing. Ray looked over to Chain.

"The Queen's Road doesn't deal well with distances as small as we're traveling. We have to do it the good old-fashioned way. Why don't you just go faster?"

"Because we have speed limits here . . . and police. Getting stopped by the cops for speeding or getting into a chase with them wouldn't help anything right now."

"Sounds like it wouldn't be your first time outrunning the law," Chain said. Ray laughed in spite of himself.

"Yeah. I used to race with my brother, Ben. We got caught in speed traps a few times." He looked over to Chain; it was the first light Chain had seen in the young man's eyes since they'd met. "We'd smoke them every time." They both laughed. "It was usually a car we'd won racing, so we'd ditch it somewhere and walk home."

"It's one of the things you're known for. Earth, that is."

"We're . . . Earth's known about . . . out there?" Ray gestured through the open window to the night sky and the stars.

Chain nodded. "Yeah, for your cars."

"That's it?" Ray said incredulously. "When the universe hears the name Earth, they think of cars?"

"Some of the best in all the Known Galaxies. Oh, and your music too."

"Not Einstein, or Hawking, or Marquez, or Shakespeare?"

"Who?" Chain asked earnestly.

"Never mind."

. . .

The Forensic Medical Management building was near the Jefferson County Correctional Facility, the county jail. The parking lot was mostly empty. Ray drove by the building on the US 69 access road.

"Okay, your planet. How do we go in?" Chain asked.

"We pull off the road about a half-mile up." Ray did, and the two of them left the car and crossed the highway toward the giant white cylindrical fuel tanks, illuminated in the seemingly endless dark fields. They stuck to the shadows and slowly, carefully made their way toward the rear of the forensics building. They both stopped and crouched low as the headlights of an oil company pickup appeared. The truck drove past them on a narrow asphalt access road between the tanks and one of the pump complexes. They waited a few moments after it passed and then continued on.

A sloping grass hill divided the properties. Ray and Chain watched the rear parking lot. There were several hearses parked next to a small loading dock. Some of them looked to be official; others probably belonged to local funeral homes. Two white work trucks with "Forensics" stenciled in black were parked nearby. A few cars, which most likely belonged to late-night employees, were parked in a far corner of the back lot.

"So now what?" Chain asked.

"Wait a sec."

After about fifteen minutes, a metal door opened, and a young man in a lab coat with long, black hair and a neatly trimmed goatee stepped out onto the empty loading dock and started vaping.

"Smoke 'em if you got 'em," Ray said.

Ray and Chain exchanged glances and kept watching. When the guy was done checking his phone and blowing massive clouds, he opened the steel door without a key; he just swung it open and disappeared back inside. The two Rangers cleared the distance between the hill and the parking lot quickly.

"They might have surveillance cameras," Ray said as they ducked behind one of the parked cars.

"I think I got something for that," Chain said. It took him a moment to find it among his pockets. It was a plastic sealed tube like the ones that held cigars. Inside it were a number of small orange and green lights flitting about that reminded Ray of fireflies. Chain unplugged the tube, and the small lights flew out and seemed to multiply as they danced around the lot. "Okay, go!" The two sprinted to the loading dock, and climbed up on to it.

"What are these things?" Ray asked as they headed to the metal door.

"Engineered spectrumvores. They eat the invisible EM frequencies that most non-picotech electronics operate through. When they're full, they shut down. Communication and surveillance devices all around us should be having some trouble right now."

They reached the door. Chain opened it with no problem, and they disappeared inside.

"Is this how all your dead are treated?" Chain asked as they walked down featureless corridors under wan, shuddering fluorescent light. Ray searched for any signs or directions that would let them know whether they were going the right way.

"No. Just the ones where the death is suspicious or possibly a crime. They're released back to their families afterward." A sharp memory stabbed him. "They brought Ben here after the wreck." Chain started to say something but held his tongue. Ray noticed but didn't call him on it. "How do you guys deal with death?"

"We, ah, we don't," Chain said, "at least not very often, and then, pretty badly."

A nicked and partly torn piece of paper had been taped to the wall at the meeting of three hallways in a Y intersection. Printed on it was an arrow pointing left that said "Admin," and another arrow pointing right that said "Morgue."

"This way," Ray said, taking the right. That led to a set of stairs that went down; another paper sign over the stairwell announced this was the way to the morgue and cold rooms. They both heard a door opening behind them, then footsteps. They quickly descended the stairs and took a corridor that led them left. The sounds of the other person were lost once they hit the lower level.

"Are you, your people, immortal?" Ray asked quietly as he scanned the doors on the hallway for any indicators of what they were looking for.

"I don't think there is such a thing. Maybe the data-spirits, the temporal elementals, and some of the NOIs . . ."

"NOIs?"

"Non-organic intelligence. They used to call them AIs, but that's no longer considered polite—I have a hard time keeping up with that. Not to mention there's plenty of naturally occurring non-organic intelligences out in the universe. Even with the NOIs, you could make an argument they're not immortal. They just live an extremely long time. There's a bunch of races like that."

"Your people one of them?"

"My folks can get pretty damn old, but we can die same as anyone else, same as you. Let me ask you something, why did you leave Evan on the side of the road?"

Ray felt a blush of shame run through him. "I hated doing it. He did threaten me with a gun, but I knew he didn't intend to use it. I . . . was . . . scared. I figured the cops would assume I had carjacked him or something like that if I brought him to a hospital, and it would be worse if he was lying in the backseat. I *was* going to steal his car. Who would believe he actually wanted me to have it?" He paused in the hall and turned to Chain. "I'm sorry I didn't treat Evan more respectfully. It sounds like he deserved it. I was just . . ."

"You did right by him." Chain urged the boy to keep moving. "He wouldn't be the first Ranger to end up in a ditch or on the side of a road. It's not an easy life. Sometimes, it's not a long one. Part of our job is to act as messengers, harbingers of great and terrible events. We warn of what's coming, usually stand against it until the bitter end. Evan gave you his last mission to carry out, and you did. There's no higher honor for a Ranger than to die with your mission fulfilled."

"Now that's *my* life," Ray said, but he didn't feel fear right now. He should have, breaking into a government building with an alien to mess around with a corpse. Instead, he felt calm, the same way he felt in a race. There was adrenaline and a hint of fear hovering at the periphery of his awareness, something bright and sharp.

"He was from here, from Earth," Chain said. "I think he liked the idea of passing the ring along to a local boy. He wouldn't have given you the ring if he thought you were a thief or a coward. He gave you the ring because he saw a Ranger already in you. Now, come on, let's see if he was right or not about the Yateveo."

Another hallway and they found the morgue. There was a radio playing somewhere. The signal was laced with static, probably from a combination of Chain's fireflies outside and the reception sucking in the basement of the building. The double doors were open. Ray slid his hand to his space-knife in his pocket, reassured by the feel of the handle. Chain followed him in.

The morgue was a series of interconnected rooms. One held large industrial sinks, a computer terminal, and shelves of supplies and equipment. Another room contained a large steel examination table with gutters running along the sides and surgical suction and water irrigation systems built in. The harsh light of the large lamp overhead reflected off the dull steel of its surface. There was also a podium next to the table with a microphone, recording equipment, and a mounted video camera for documenting procedures. Someone's notes and a cold cup of coffee were resting on the podium. There were drains in the floors of both rooms.

The oversized door to the last room was closed, and there was a rubber seal around it. A plastic plaque declared it "Cold Storage." Chain began looking through the file cabinets that lined one wall of the sink room, but Ray stopped him and pointed to a series of brown file folders in pocket-like shelves in the examination room.

"It will be a current case, so I'd check those first. He'll most likely be listed as a John Doe, since they don't have his name."

"Who's John Doe?"

"What?"

"Why would they give Evan the name John Doe?"

"I . . . never bothered to wonder about that." Ray joined Chain in looking through the files. "It's like a nickname, like 'Chain.' Why do they call you that, anyway? Is it the chains on your tow truck?"

"Not exactly." Chain paused and handed the file he was scanning over to Ray. "John Doe Number 2. This sounds right, yes?"

Ray looked over the file.

"'Caucasian male in his late sixties. Cause of death: blood loss and poisoning by an unknown substance caused by puncture wounds from three wooden projectiles. Wrongful Death.' This sounds like him. They removed the projectiles from his chest. They're in Bin 00813. His body is in Drawer 14."

"You find him. I need to see these 'projectiles.'" Chain walked over to a set of metal shelves holding plain cardboard storage boxes, each with a case and file number on them as well as a last name. Ray opened the door to the cold room and entered.

The room lived up to its name. It was as cold as a walk-in cooler, which it basically was. The walls were ceramic tile like you might find in a school locker room shower. Again, there was a drain in the floor. The opposite wall was filled with small metal doors, about twenty of them. Ray was suddenly back in the hospital with Pop, back at the funeral home with Mom when they brought Ben's clothing for the viewing. He was running up the stairs in Jess's house, throwing open the door to her bedroom and seeing her . . .

Ray blinked; he shook it off as best he could and opened Drawer 14. Evan's body was inside, secured in a zipped-up body bag so dark green it almost looked black. Ray took another breath and saw his exhalation swirl about his face. "I found him," he called through the open door. There was no response.

Ray prepared himself and unzipped the bag. Evan's bluish face greeted him. Every time Ray had seen the dead, they always looked fake. You take the animation, the spark, out of a human body and you take something fundamentally connected to identity. He knew that Evan's nose was the exact same number of millimeters from his eyes as it had been when they had talked in the car; none of the math had changed, but the face looked fake, wrong, a mask that something unnamable had departed from behind. Evan was here, but he wasn't.

Ray left the drawer and bag open and walked out of the cold room to see how Chain wanted to proceed. "Okay, I found him," he repeated, turning back into the exam room. "Now wha—?"

He froze.

Two men and a woman stood in the sink room by the double doors. They wore dirty, stained security guard uniforms. Their faces were blank. All three had their pistols out and leveled at Chain, who was holding one of the cardboard boxes off the shelf. The lead guard, whose name tag on his jacket said "Farmer," moved his gun off Chain and onto Ray.

"Thank you," Ronnie Farmer said, "for finding him for us."

# 11

nto the other room," Farmer instructed Chain. "Bring that box with you." Chain complied, placing the cardboard container on the steel examination table. He joined Ray on the other side of the table from the guards. Ray noticed the security guards' filthy uniforms were wet with fresh blood.

"Look, officers," Ray said, "We had a friend of ours pass away, and we were just down here trying to say goodbye." Farmer and the female guard stood on the other side of the table. Their guns didn't waver an inch. The third guard dropped back to the morgue doors. He closed them and stood by them. Chain made a strange whistling, clicking sound. Ray blinked uncontrollably.

Neither guard seem to notice the odd whistle. Ray looked over at the tow-truck driver. "You okay?"

"Fine," Chain said, not taking his eyes off the guards. Farmer opened the cardboard box and removed several sealed and bagged items from inside, setting them on the table as he examined each one. Most of them contained Evan's clothing. Ray recognized some of the contents of Evan's pockets as well. Finally, Farmer withdrew a clear plastic bin from the box that contained three black, twisted wooden stakes. The security guard lifted one of the sticks to his lips and licked it.

"You don't want to do that!" Ray called out. "There's poison on those things!"

Farmer ignored him.

"Don't waste your time talking to them," Chain said. "They've been converted. They might as well be dead."

"What are you talking about?" Ray asked as Farmer returned the stick to the plastic bin with the others.

"Evan was right. I don't know how—it should be impossible—but the Yateveo have returned."

"Take these," Farmer said to the guard by the doors, "and bring me the gas." The guard complied, taking the plastic bin from Farmer and handing him a small red plastic gas can. Farmer holstered his pistol.

"Returned? Returned from where?" Ray asked, eyeing the gas can and feeling his stomach twist. "And what was that weird sound you made?"

"It's a test we came up with during the war. The tone's specific. It's supposed to produce a measurable neurological effect in mammals. It didn't in them. Their nervous systems, their brains, are pumped full of Yateveo nerve-vines now. They're meat-puppets—robots—until the toxins in the vines turn their insides to mush."

"Shut up," Farmer said as he walked into the cold room, "both of you. You wouldn't understand the glory, the pleasure of serving our masters . . . and you never will."

The female guard on the other side of the surgical table kept them both covered. Farmer walked to the open drawer, and looked down on Evan's body. He opened the gas can, poured the fuel and let it pool inside the body bag. Ray glanced over to Chain. His face was stone. A terrible force, something more than anger, radiated from his eyes as he watched Farmer use a lighter to set his friend's body on fire. Farmer slid the shelf back into its alcove and closed the small door. "Shoot them," Farmer said.

Faster than Ray could react, Chain raised his leg and kicked the steel examination table with enough force to send it flying across the room, smashing into the female guard. The table kept going and crashed into the wall by the morgue doors, catching the second guard as well and crushing him against the far wall.

Farmer was moving to draw his gun. Chain hurled himself toward him. He shouted to Ray as he crossed into the cold room, "Take them out. Shoot them in the head or the back of the neck!" Ray reacted, he didn't think. He found the female guard's pistol, a nine millimeter, on the floor. He scooped it up and ran toward the overturned table.

Farmer's gun had cleared his holster and was coming up to take a bead on Chain. As the Ranger charged, his metal gauntlet began to unravel on its own, unwrapping into a large, dull-silver metal chain, uncoiling from his wrist. The end of the chain dropped into his palm, while the rest of it expanded and hurtled toward the possessed guard. Farmer fired just as the chain snapped his wrist, crushing the bones.

The bullet whined as it bounced off the tile wall beside Chain and ricocheted off the steel drawers on the opposite wall. Chain closed the gap and drove a hard hook into Farmer's head. The guard staggered, but his face remained calm. The two circled one another, each searching for an opening. Chain's weapon and namesake hovered and circled in the air, acting more like a serpent than an inanimate object.

Ray peered over the crashed autopsy table. His head whipped around when the shot rang out in the cold room. He looked back to see the female guard, her face a smear of greenish-black blood, scrambling over the table toward him, wielding a wicked-looking bone saw. Ray raised the gun and fired. The round hit the woman square in the forehead. Her expression didn't change. She fell backward and lay still near the morgue doors, more of the black-green blood spreading from the back of her skull across the tiled floor.

Ray was shaking. He felt cold, dizzy. He wanted to throw up. There was a thunderous blast that cut through the humming cotton that his ears felt stuffed with. Sparks flew as a bullet hit the edge of the overturned examination table, narrowly missing him. The third guard, his back to one of the doors, was shooting. Ray ducked low behind the steel table as another round smashed into it.

Chain heard the shots and drove the heel of his palm into Farmer's nose, shattering it. A normal man would have died from the splinters of bone the strike buried in his brain, but Farmer kept going. He jammed his stun gun into Chain's side and thumbed the trigger. Numbing fire and aching pressure filled the Ranger's body. Even as his muscles seized and he fell to one knee, he clutched his animated chain tighter, then willed a command to his weapon. The chain, coiled and floating, shot out straight and blasted its way through the front and out the back of Farmer's throat, severing his spine in the process. Farmer tumbled to the ground and lay still. Chain fought to get his muscles to listen to him again. He thought to his chain, and the weapon slithered free of his hand and out the open door of the cold room.

Ray knew to hide back here was to die. He had to act, to keep moving. He popped out from the side of the table, not over the top, and caught the injured guard, struggling to his feet, by surprise. Ray fired an instant before the guard did, and the shot Ray intended for his head caught him in the throat. The guard slid back to the floor. It took Ray a second to figure out that the man was dead; his expression remained the same.

Ray, trembling in shock, blinked and took a breath. There was a smooth metallic rattling sound behind him, near the floor. Ray spun, the adrenaline screaming in his veins. A chain, undulating across the floor like a serpent, raised itself up as Ray fired on it again and again, wildly missing.

Chain rushed out of the cold room, Farmer's pistol in his hand. "It's okay! It's okay!" he shouted to Ray. "He's with me!" Ray felt like he was genuinely going to pass out. Chain closed the distance to him; the animated chain coiled itself around his right forearm and solidified again into the metal gauntlet.

"You okay, kid? You look pale. You get hit?"

"Wha . . . what was that thing?"

"NOI picochain," Chain said, as if that answered everything. "Keyed to my telepathic print, follows my orders. I told it to come out here and give you a hand." He looked over at the two guards, their lifeless eyes staring back at him. "But, obviously, you didn't need the help."

"I . . . killed those people," Ray said. The voice didn't even sound like his. "I've never . . . fired a gun at anything other than some beer cans."

Chain placed a hand gently on his shoulder.

"Look at me. I know you feel sick, and I really do understand. I remember the first time I had to kill someone. I still see it sometimes when I shut my eyes. At the end of the day, you have to decide if you want to live more than they do. Your instincts do the rest. Besides, you did them a favor. They were already dead. They were dead the moment the Yateveo stuck their damn shoots into them, re-wrote their genetic code."

"All those gunshots." Ray shook himself free of the fog he was in. "We're right next door to the jail. If we don't get out of here, every cop and state trooper for a hundred miles is going to be on us. You got what you need?"

"Yeah." Chain picked up the pistol Ray had dropped and stuffed it in the waistband of his pants. Smoke was beginning to fill the autopsy room. "Yeah, unfortunately I did. Help me drag these bodies closer to the fire, and we can get going."


In the back parking lot, the jamming fireflies were still flitting about, but there were fewer of them now. Ray and Chain found the car Farmer and his associates had arrived in. It was a white compact car with "Paragon Security" stenciled on the doors and trunk, and a yellow roller light system on the roof.

"You drive us over to the Galaxie," Chain said, struggling to fit in the passenger seat. "There may be some intel in here about the Yateveo and how they crossed those poor bastards' paths. You know how not to attract attention more than me."

"I hope you're right." The keys were still in the ignition, and he turned the engine over and pulled out to the back lot. Chain looked at the console and then flipped on the yellow flashing LED rollers as they pulled out onto the access road that led directly to the highway. The wail of sirens filled the air, and Ray already saw strobing blue and red lights coming down the highway. He grabbed a Paragon Security baseball cap that was in the back seat and put it on. Ray maintained a few miles over the speed limit and kept going as half a dozen cop cars came right at them from the opposite lane. He felt the old calm he had experienced in races fill him, taking away all the shock and the panic. The cops shot past them without a second look. Ray glanced over to Chain, who was already reexamining the atmospheric sniffer he had used earlier.

"Still clear. The Yateveo evolved to aggressively dominate any biosphere they encounter. To that end, they destroy the existing biosphere and make it suit their biology. Within a very short time of being in an alien environment, they begin to release spores into the atmosphere. Once that happens, the planet, as it currently exists, is doomed. Every kind of life on it dies or is changed to serve the Yateveo."

The detector made the rude electronic sound again, and Chain nodded and put it away.

"No spores detected yet, so we can assume that they haven't been on planet very long. If they're being cagey and trying to cover their tracks, it means it's an expeditionary force, not a full-scale invasion. And that means we might have a slim chance to stop them. We don't have long, though. Best case scenario, we have 'til dawn."

"What do we have to do?" Ray asked, shutting down the rollers as they U-turned to make it back to the Galaxie.

Chain glanced over to Ray. "Wipe them out. Destroy every last one of them on your world."

# 12

Ray and Chain arrived back at the Chug-n-Lug around two a.m. They found Lu listening to anime soundtracks over his phone and mopping the floor near the Slime-ee frozen drink machine.

"Hey," he said, slipping off his buds, "planet out of danger?" He saw the grim look on both of their faces and stopped mopping. "Oh, shit . . ." He looked pleadingly at Chain. "Please tell me you're some delusional homeless psycho? Please."

"He really is a tow-truck driver from space," Ray said glumly. "There really are alien monsters out there, running around Port Arthur, who are about to turn the whole world uninhabitable in about . . . four hours?" He glanced to Chain for confirmation; Chain nodded. "And we are all going to die—us, our friends, our families . . ." Ray hopped up on the sales counter to get off his feet. For a second, he remembered that was against store policy and then he realized how ridiculous it was to be worried about something like that right now. "Unless we track them to their lair and go all Ripley on them before then."

Lu looked to Chain.

"A little on the fatalistic side but essentially accurate. Who's 'Ripley,' by the way?"

"Oh, my god," Lu said to Ray. "He really is from outer space."

"Can't we call in more Rangers?" Ray asked. "Don't you have like an emergency-space-radio-signal thingie?"

"'Fraid not. The Queen didn't see fit to develop an instantaneous communication system contiguous with her road."

"Why not?" Ray shook his head. "If you can transport cars and trucks across time and space, radio signals should be easy."

A hint of a grim smile crossed Chain's face.

"True enough." He nodded in agreement. "Why not portals that spaceships could fly through, or why not make it so you could simply step through a doorway and be on another world? All good questions. I have my own theories on the whys, but right now we need to focus on the current problem at hand. Communication between the countless worlds of the universe goes no faster than the fastest engine. We Rangers are scattered everywhere, and there are places known to us where our kind gather often. We can seek out a specific Ranger with the rings, and if I had more time, there are a few I've worked with before that I'd go find, but we have no time. First rule of being a Ranger, you are usually on your own."

"'One riot, one Ranger,'" Ray said.

"What?"

"A story my pop told me when I was a kid. They used to send one Texas Ranger in alone to clean up a town or take on a whole gang of criminals."

"Sound like my kind of people."

"So, we're on our own," Ray said.

"You got me," Lu added, clutching his mop. He was obviously afraid but trying hard not to be.

Ray smiled at his oldest friend.

"Thanks, man. Right now, we need all the help we can get."

"These chemical-powered projectile weapons won't even phase the Yateveo," Chain said. "We need flamers or plasma weapons."

"Good thing you landed in Texas," Lu offered. "They're probably legal here."

"We don't have access to weapons like that," Ray said.

"I guess nuclear explosives are right out, then?" Chain asked.

Ray and Lu looked at each other in horror.

"We got those," Ray said, "but they are, y'know, weapons of mass destruction—really bad. They kill a lot of people and fuck up the environment."

"So do the Yateveo. But nukes do it on a smaller scale if you use them accurately."

"Well, we don't sell those," Lu said, "and there's no Nukes-R-Us around. Only the military has the kind of weapons you're talking about. Hey! Why don't we just call the cops and the military?"

"We do often work with the local authorities, but usually on worlds that are aware of the Queen's Road and the Rangers."

"By the time we convinced anyone with actual authority we weren't mental patients, it'd be too late." Ray thought of Juanita, of Mom—how long had it been since he had thought of her as Mom?— sleeping fitfully in some hospital ward.

"So we need an army loaded up with military weapons in less than four hours," Lu summarized.

"Essentially, yes," Chain said. "Perhaps we can make some improvised explosives from civilian materials."

"I got a PDF of *The Anarchist's Cookbook* on my phone," Lu offered, "for entertainment purposes only."

Something was tumbling in Ray's mind. He hopped off the counter, already searching on his smartphone.

"We still need enough firepower to get close enough to place the charges. Yateveo are damned hard to kill," Chain said.

"I got an idea. It's crazy, but then so is the rest of this." Ray found the number he was looking for and dialed it. After a moment, someone answered. "Hey, it's Ray . . . Ray Cosa. I need you to meet me right now at 'Keem's. Yeah, I know you got shit going on. Cancel it; this is more important. I'll explain when you get there." Ray hung up the phone and began to search his contacts list for another number.

He looked up before he dialed. "Lu, hold down the store." He looked at Chain, "I need you to convince some people."

"Who?"

"Our army."

Mateo Morales opened the unlocked door to City Pawn and walked in. His eyes were red and glazed, and he looked pissed. Five of his fellow brothers in the Ciudad Azteca followed him into 'Keem's shop. They, too, looked fucked up and unhappy. 'Keem had an AA-12 military automatic shotgun up from behind the counter the moment the gang members strode in. Mateo and his crew followed suit, almost instantly bringing up pistols, shotguns, and fully automatic rifles.

"Wait, wait! Hold it!" Ray stepped between the two armed factions. "Take it easy! *Frío!* Nobody shoot, okay?"

Mateo and 'Keem locked stares for a moment, and then the pawnshop owner and the gang leader both lowered their weapons. Mateo's men followed his lead.

"Why have you brought criminals here, Ramon?" 'Keem asked.

"I was kinda wondering that myself," Mateo said, looking to Ray. "You confuse me saying 'I'm sorry for how fucked up your family is' with us being *amigos*? 'Cause there ain't anything that gives you the right to call my ass up in the middle of the night, be disrespectful to me, and hang up."

"I needed you here, and I knew that would do it. I need you to listen now."

Mateo walked up to Ray, jammed the barrel of the pistol under his chin, and thumbed the hammer back. Ray could smell the weed coming off him and the booze on his breath. "What you need is to ask forgiveness for interrupting my night and my business."

Ray's legs felt wobbly. His throat tightened, but he managed to summon his words.

"It doesn't matter if you shoot me." He swallowed hard. "If you don't listen to what this man has to tell you" —he nodded in Chain's direction—"right now, we will all be dead in less than three hours. *All* of us, Mateo. You, me, your mom, your sister, Elena, your *vieja*, your little girl, my mom . . . *everyone* will die unless you calm the fuck down and listen. Please. We need you."

Ray held Mateo's eyes, and the anxiety began to leave him, replaced by a numb calm. He wasn't sure if that was good or bad, but it was true. Mateo lowered the hammer on the gun carefully and then took the weapon away from Ray's throat.

"Where did these newfound balls of yours come from, Ramon?" Mateo looked over to Chain, who had watched the whole exchange leaning against a counter, his massive arms crossed. A small duffle bag rested against the front of the counter beside him. "I think maybe from you?"

Chain shrugged and smiled.

"I think he's doing just fine on his own," the Ranger said. "He told me you were smarter than you look. Smart enough to listen. I'm glad he's right. I'm Chain."

"That your nasty-looking tow truck out there, old man?" Chain nodded. "So, what you got to say, tow-truck driver?"

Chain looked to Ray, and Ray nodded.

"Lay it down," Ray said. "Everything."

Chain told 'Keem, Mateo, and his boys the story: The eons-long war against the entropy-loving Nemesis, the Queen of the Universe and her cosmos-spanning highway, and the Rangers and their duty to preserve the Queen's justice on the endless worlds they wandered. Finally, he told them of the Yateveo, of their recent arrival on Earth and how they would soon introduce their biological toxins to the atmosphere and begin to make Earth a lifeless breeding ground, a dark garden for their kind.

Mateo laughed. His squad laughed. "And I thought I was high!" he finally managed to say.

'Keem had listened intently. He was not laughing. "Your people, these Rangers, they all wear the rings?"

Chain nodded. "Its official name is 'the Ranger's signet.' Yes, we each wear the ring until the day we die."

"Wait, wait!" Mateo said, wiping tears away. "What if the guy's like a big pile of space shit, y'know, like a big Jabba-slug or something? It ain't got no arms or fingers, right?" His fellow *mara* members burst out laughing again, but Mateo struggled to keep a straight face. "How's that work?"

"The signet adapts to a form suited to each Ranger. It looks like this for most of the humanoid species."

Mateo let out a sound like a whoopee cushion venting and nearly doubled over laughing from Chain's response. "Humanoid!" Mateo managed to get out.

Ray was tired, and his stomach churned. He kept his cool, but he wanted to punch Mateo in his contorted, laughing face.

"I have met one of these Rangers," 'Keem said calmly. "What he's saying . . . I believe him."

"Shit, 'Keem," Mateo said, "I always thought you were a pretty chill guy. Don't tell me you're buying this bullshit."

"Back in Afghanistan, in the summer of 2010, I was what the Americans called a 'Terp,' a battlefield translator. I was supposedly only there to interpret for the soldiers." He chuckled at the memory. "But that . . . was not how it was. I fought beside them. Me, my two brothers, and my father, we all did. Some of them were my friends." Mateo and his men had stopped laughing. They were listening to 'Keem's calm, powerful voice. "We found a town in the western provinces. There had been a slaughter. There was blood, damage, but no bodies, no people. We tracked the attackers for three days and on the way, found a small village; it didn't even have a name. Again, signs of violence everywhere but not a single body.

"On the third night of hunting them, they ambushed us. They came out of the darkness like, like *daeva*. They . . . they weren't . . . human. We lost a third of our people in the surprise. Their weapons were like ordinance—heavy artillery—but handheld, and horribly accurate! Between all of us, we had over a century of combat experience, and it was like nothing any of us had ever seen." 'Keem's voice sounded different, more gravelly. Ray recognized the pain leaking out of him, thrashing pain he was trying to hold tight. "When it was over, my brothers were dead, and there were only eight of us alive out of twenty, including me and my father. Most of us who survived were wounded. All our vehicles, most of our equipment, were lost."

"Are you for real?" one of Mateo's men asked. Now, they all looked to 'Keem like kids listening to a ghost story around a campfire.

"Shut up," Mateo said to his man, and then looked to 'Keem. "Go ahead."

"We knew it would be days before a contact patrol would hook up with us. The next day, one of your Rangers showed up, Chain. He looked like a man. He had a ring, like the one you and Ramon wear. He drove a desert-camouflaged old deuce-and-a-half truck. He told us his name was Utaru. He said he had been tracking the things that attacked us, too, and had picked up our trail a day ago. The few of us left all agreed to go with him, to avenge our fallen. He had a cream that, when applied, healed wounds that there was no way we knew of could be healed. He had weapons that worked like our attackers', and he showed us how to use them. He said the things had murdered many people across a very large distance. We all assumed other countries; now, I think he was talking about other worlds.

"We found them, with the Ranger's help, the following day. We set up in the entrance of a cave he tracked them to, and this time, we surprised them. It was the longest, bloodiest firefight I've ever been in." He looked from Chain to Mateo and his men. "You know that feeling—freefall—you fire, reload, and your friend a few feet from you dies. It's like a fever dream, the blood thudding in your ears, screaming to you you're still alive. You're holding your breath, waiting for the shot that ends you. Angry, numb, terrified, you almost dare it, like a child taunting, to finish you if it can. Even with all the training, all the experience, it's like you're trapped in a loop, in a nightmare. It went on forever.

"At the end of it, the only ones who walked out of that cave alive were me, the second lieutenant who commanded the unit, and Utaru. I lost my father that day. We all should have died."

The Ciudad Azteca members were silent. So was Mateo. 'Keem walked into the back room for a moment and returned with two black plastic rifle cases, one in each hand. He sat them on the floor of the pawnshop in front of Mateo and the others.

"What's this?" Mateo asked. 'Keem knelt and began to open the cases. "The US military came in very quickly. They cleaned up the scene, took the creatures' bodies away, and gathered up all the technology they could find. We were all debriefed and thoroughly examined in isolation for weeks. The whole incident was designated SCI by the Department of Defense—something more secure than Top Secret." He flipped open the cases. "I managed to hide a few pieces of the monsters' technology, and after a few months, I went back and retrieved them. I had a friend in the Air Force who helped me get them out when my wife, my children, and I were granted visas to the US."

He lifted something that looked like a badly assembled rifle from the cut-foam cradle inside the case. It looked like a patchwork monstrosity. Parts had been poorly welded together and the barrel was short and wide—wider than a shotgun's barrel—with a rubber adjustment ring on it. The weapon looked to have more switches than it should have, and all in the wrong places. It retained a pitted, worn wooden stock and a stained and frayed nylon rifle sling. In the place of an ammunition magazine on the underside of the rifle was a small metal box with a toggle switch on the back and an ill-fitting hinged access door on the side.

"What the hell is that thing?" one of Mateo's boys asked. "It looks like it might have been an AK-47, but it got chopped hard!" The gang member looked to his leader. "Mateo, man, you buying this *mierda*?"

'Keem stepped away from the cases, the odd gun in hand. Ray noticed Chain was a bit more engaged, suddenly, and he could almost see something going on behind the Ranger's eyes as he looked at the weapon and its similar, but unique, companion in the one gun case and the two equally piecemeal handguns in the second case.

"What's it do besides look ugly?" Mateo asked 'Keem. The pawn shop owner flipped the toggle on the attached box and stepped back. He brought the rifle to his shoulder and took aim at an old black iron safe with an orange clearance tag on it that was squatting between other merchandise. His hand flipped what was probably a fire selector switch and then another switch that was most likely a safety. He put his hand on the rubber adjustment ring on the barrel and slowly twisted it as he placed his finger on the trigger.

"Step back, everyone," 'Keem said. He gave everyone a chance to comply and then squeezed the trigger. A bolt of crimson energy howled from the barrel, sounding as if it were shredding the very air before it. It struck the old safe. The safe was engulfed in a compact explosion of blue-white radiance, which smelled and looked like lightning to Ray. The flash of light faded, and the safe was gone, save for some charred, smoking shards of metal in a pile. Little white energy particles drifted downward lazily, like snowflakes, and faded to nothing before they hit the floor.

"*Santa Madre!*" one of Mateo's men cried out and crossed himself. Others went with the more secular "Holy shit!," and one just nodded. "Niiiiiice."

Ray, having seen what he had already seen, was still impressed, but he stayed cool. He liked feeling more in control of the situation than the gang guys right now. What surprised Ray the most was Chain's reaction to the weapon demonstration. The Ranger shot forward to stand beside 'Keem and looked at the weapon and the store owner with newfound regard.

"That's a sacred Archain bond destabilizer!"

"Is that what it's called?" 'Keem asked coolly.

"The slang for them around the universal gun club is 'abolishers.' They destabilize the electron and proton charges of matter." Chain saw the confused looks on the faces around him. "They tear things apart from within and make them go away."

Ray and the others stepped closer to Chain and 'Keem, who flipped the safety on and toggled off the power switch on the lower attached box.

"May I?" Chain nodded to the rifle. 'Keem hesitated for a moment and then handed the abolisher to Chain.

Chain flipped open the small hinged door on the mounted box. Crimson light poured out from within, emanating from a prominent mounted strand that looked a bit to Ray like a piece of glowing vein. It looked organic—as opposed to the wires it was connected to on either end, and the other components of the cramped compartment. "Yeah, it's Archain all right." He looked at 'Keem again, smiled, and shook his head. "I'm impressed. The Archa view murder as the most holy of undertakings. There's a whole tourist industry built around their morbid religious fetish. Part of the rite they undertake, if they really want to be old school about it, is to make their first kills unarmed and then build a ritual weapon from the weapons of their victims. They actually sacrifice part of their own essence core to power it."

"That's messed up," Ray said at the exact same time Mateo said, "*Pinche Chido!*"

Ray gave Mateo a disapproving look and shook his head. Mateo returned Ray's shade with a dismissive wave. "Hey . . . *that* is badass."

Chain closed the compartment and handed the abolisher back to 'Keem, "You survived an Archain Communion. Not many, in all the known galaxies, can say that. We could really use you with us tonight." He looked over to Mateo. "And you and your soldiers too."

Mateo gave his men a nod, and they drew weapons, leveling them at 'Keem and Chain primarily. 'Keem was holding the abolisher in an awkward way, and he'd probably get a few bullets in him before he could make cover or swing the gun around to fire. "And what keeps me from saying 'fuck you' to all of that, smoking your asses, taking the Star Wars guns, and going?"

Chain sighed and looked to Ray.

"Not a damn thing," Ray said. He was past exhausted and done with all this *mara* bullshit. "Enjoy them. You'll have about"—he glanced up at the clock on the wall—"three hours to play, and then your stupid asses will be dead, like everyone else on Earth. It's real, and it's happening, and we *need* you." He looked past Mateo to his men. "All of you. For once in your lives, do something that really matters." Ray stepped closer to the gang leader; only a few inches separated them now. "For once, do the right thing." He stepped back away from all of them. He held his arms out to his side. "But, if you're determined to be the stupid *pendejo* that kills everyone on Earth, then start with me. Right now."

Chain looked like he was going to do something, but he stopped himself and looked at Ray with an odd expression.

Mateo searched Ray's eyes, and Ray felt nothing inside—no fear, nothing. He would have liked to have seen Juanita one last time before the end. He wished he could have saved her; he wished he could have saved everyone. Mateo looked back at his men and gave them a sign. They nodded and lowered their guns, looking a little surprised and maybe a little relieved.

"I seen that look a hundred times a day, Ramon," Mateo said. "You think you got nothing left to lose. I'm here to tell you right now, boy, that will get your ass killed and killed quick. You ever talk to me like that again, I'll close your eyes myself."

Mateo turned to Chain.

"Okay, what you need?"

# 13

The rotting corpse of the Gould-Wright Nautical Engine Manufacturing Company facility was a dark blot of shadow between the land and Sabine Lake to those who sped by on the highway overpass above. No one had noticed the odd mirrored black capsule that had sat in the overgrown field since last night. If anyone had seen it in the light of day, they most likely dismissed it as a mobile home or large trailer.

Ray, in the Galaxie, pulled off Levee Road onto the wide private-access road to the seven-acre abandoned complex. He came to a stop in front of the empty guard shack and high chain-link gates that kept him from going any farther up the road.

The gates had several "No Trespassing" signs affixed to them, as well as a sign that announced the property was protected by Paragon Security, the same company the now-dead guards who attacked them at the morgue had worked for. When they had taken the Paragon Security car to flee the scene ahead of the cops, they had found a clip-board with a duty roster on it and listed job sites. Farmer, the apparent leader of the possessed guards, had been working at Gould-Wright.

Chain had been checking the atmospheric scanner every few

minutes, and so far, the results were in the planet's favor. Ray looked at his phone, knew there was still time, but he felt the velocity of anxiety building inside him all the same. He hit the call button for the messenger service on his phone, and after a second, Mateo answered.

"I'm in position," Ray said.

"Okay." Mateo was whispering. Ray knew the gang leader was hooked up to a set of ear buds and a microphone. "We're over the fence and heading across the field toward the back of the factory, toward the ship. Chain says give us one minute and then start the show."

They had formulated a plan in a hurry. While Mateo gathered his soldiers and 'Keem gathered weapons, Ray and Chain had taken off in the Galaxie to scout out Gould-Wright. While driving their second time across the overpass, Chain had spotted the capsule.

"Damn," he muttered.

"What?" Ray asked, trying to both look and keep his eyes on the road. The morning traffic was starting to come out. All the folks who had to be up this early for work were making their way onto the roads.

"Nothing. I hope I'm wrong. Let's deal with what's in front of us for now. Their ship is down there. So we know where we have to go, and after another pass, I'll have a pretty good idea of the layout of the place. I wish we'd grabbed the guard's keys, not just their guns."

When they got back to City Pawn, the plan was set by Chain with some good input from 'Keem. Ray had called Lu to update him. "You need me to come over? I can close up the shop," Lu offered.

Ray smiled.

"I wish you were with me, man, but right now, you just keep everything going there." There was no need to tell him how dangerous and possibly futile this whole mission was. "I'm sorry I sucked at work tonight." They both laughed.

"No worries," Lu said, "Next week, when I blow you off to save the universe, I know you got me."

There was a long silence. Finally, Ray broke it. "I'll call you on the other side of this. Breakfast is on me."

"Holding you to that. Good luck, man."

They hung up.

The plan was pretty simple; it had to be. They didn't have time for something complicated, and they had a bunch of stoned and coked-up gang bangers to implement it. Ray would come in alone, down the main road, to draw attention and possibly fire. Hakeem and his five-man fire team of Aztecas would come in from the eastern side of the property and be support for any trouble Ray found himself in. Chain, Mateo, and the remaining fifteen gang members that Mateo could reach and could count on would come in through the half acre of forest to the west of the property fence and make their way straight toward the Yateveo's ship in the overgrown field behind the ruins of the main factory.

"You want to know why you got the decoy detail?" Chain asked Ray as gang members were loading the weapons and gear out of 'Keem's shop and into his pickup truck. The parking lot was full of the Ciudad Aztecas' muscle cars, tricked-out compacts, and motorcycles. "It's because Mateo is right. You don't care if you live or die, and that does get people killed in combat. If you're out there on your own, you can only do so much damage."

Ray's eyes darkened. "Don't worry. I'm getting through this. I won't screw up the plan. I got stuff to live for. You think you know everything—you don't know shit about me."

"Good," Chain said with a genuine smile. "Stay pissed. At least it shows me you're still alive down in there."

Now, at the gate, Ray checked his phone's clock as the last seconds of the minute slipped away. "All right, old man," Ray said as he set the timer on his phone to alarm in fifteen minutes. That was Mateo's best guess on the cops' response time to all the noise. Part of the plan also included some Ciudad Azteca members making trouble far away from here to draw off responding units. It was also near the end of shift for many officers; Ray knew that from working at the Chug-n-Lug. Cops often came in to grab a cup of coffee and sit out in the parking lot in their cruisers to catch up on their paperwork. They might have twenty minutes, tops, before patrol cars rolled in. He wondered if he'd still be alive in twenty minutes.

He slipped an alien abolisher pistol out of the waistband of his jeans. The gun had been cobbled together from parts of an old Soviet Makarov pistol. Ray racked the gun's slide back, which now worked to activate the living Archain power source inside.

"Here's your distraction."

Ray pulled the trigger. A bolt of red energy screamed from the gun and enveloped both gates in a blinding, bluish-lightning-like explosion that boomed and echoed across the property and beyond. Ray jumped into the idling Galaxie and hit the gas, blasting through the drifting motes of white energy and the few sparking, charred, and tangled fragments of the gates. "Hey, Cassandra," Ray called out to the car's smart speaker, "play me some Los Monjo, loud, and keep it coming." A second later, the speakers were spilling "Cobardes" by the Mexican punk band through the car. The music loudly announced his approach through his open driver's side window. The Galaxie was a rocket headed straight down the complex's main road, toward the factory.


Chain, Mateo, and the others paused when the explosion from the gates lit up the front of the property and counterfeit thunder rolled across the sky. A second later, they heard the snarl of the Galaxie's engine, growing louder and . . . music?

Chain smiled. "Right on time. Good job, kid."

They had reached the edge of the thickly wooded lot and cut through the chain-link fence into the field. Chain turned and quickly addressed the gang members. "I know basic training for most of you was the ride over, but try to remember; one man advances, the men on either side cover him, and then the next man advances. Don't shoot until Mateo or I tell you to, and keep your asses down. You have the cover of the tall grass. See you all at the ship. May the Mother protect you."

Many of the Ciudad Azteca crossed themselves and whispered a prayer, and then the advance began.

Ray turned hard right onto the access road, toward the large empty front parking lot of the main factory building, drawing attention away from Chain's assault. In the distance, he saw the emerging form of an old fixed harbor crane jutting skyward near the collapsing structures of the company's dry dock at the edge of the water. His attention was pulled back by the crack and whine of gunfire. Sparks jumped near his door and on the hood of the Galaxie. "Shit!" he called out. He drifted the car into the parking lot and then swung the wheel tight to the left.

"Hostiles detected on the roof of the structure to the left," Cassandra said blandly. "Would you like to deploy defensive counter-measures?"

"You can do that?" Ray nearly screamed, as more gunfire rained down around him. He swerved again as another round sparked off the pavement near a tire. "I thought you just did the music and gave me time and temp?"

"It's not my fault you believe stereotypes. Perhaps you should read the owner's manual, even if that is a racist name for it. Would you like counter-measures?"

A bullet spark flashed against the wide hood.

"Yes! Please!" Ray shouted as he figure-eighted the dark light poles in the parking lot, trying to use them as meager cover. Bullets struck the poles and their concrete bases as the Galaxie swung wide and made another run.

"Magnetically reinforcing biotic metal chassis. Activating nutrient-restorative packets. Polymer tire integrity at 100 percent, internal restoration compressors online. Tracking and analysis stealth UV-LADAR activated. No weapon locks detected."

"Thanks," Ray said, turning the wheel hard again. Coming out of the turn, he fired out his open window with the abolisher. Part of the upper level of the factory vaporized in a plume of lightning. "How long we been at this, Cassandra?"

"One minute, twenty-seven seconds since blowing the gate."

Suddenly, twenty minutes didn't seem like such a short time after all.


"Ray's taking fire," Chain said, unslinging the abolisher rifle he was carrying. "The Yateveo must have gotten a hold of more people. Okay, we need to hustle up!" The team advanced, getting closer and closer to the black-hulled ship, the moonlight reflecting off it. Chain pulled the atmospheric analyzer out of his jacket.

Mateo watched him read the device's tiny screen and saw him put it away. "We still good?"

"Still time." They were bent low and moving as quickly as they could.

"Okay, these Yateveo, these big, evil, space-vampire tree things . . ."

"Yes?"

"If they are so badass and built to just take over everything, why can't they just . . . nut, spore, whatever the fuck it is they're doing, whenever they want?"

"Tell me, can you urinate on command? Defecate when ordered?"

Mateo looked confused.

"Sorry. Piss. Shit," Chain clarified. "This is part of their biological process. It takes some time for their bodies to analyze the new world and its biosphere and develop specific spores to rewrite it. It's possible that the Queen influenced their evolution to work that process in as a stopgap. It's hard to say how much she could have done, given the intervention of the Stillness . . ." Chain saw he had completely lost Mateo. "The lag is the only break the other lifeforms in the universe got; otherwise it would just be Yateveo everywhere . . . and maybe the Lytch."

"What's a Lytch?"

95

"Pray you never find out." There was a scream and an angry stutter of machine-gun fire ahead of them. "Damn it!" Chain called out.

Mateo looked in time to see three of his men die.

The black shadow of a twisted tree towered over them. The Yateveo had stepped out from the stand of other trees. Three of its limbs had shot out like whips, impaled two of the Aztecas, and decapitated the third. Shouts and curses went up from the other gang members.

Mateo's eyes were wide with rage, "Cruzito! Bonafide! Oso!" he called out to his fallen men. He drew his abolisher pistol and snapped back the activating slide as he shouted to his troops, "Light that motherfucker up!"

All the Aztecas opened fire, a rain of machine gun bullets that struck the Yateveo and seemed to do nothing but chip at its bark-like hide. Then Chain and Mateo fired with their abolishers. The beams hit the creature, and parts of it exploded, raining down debris and greenish-black sap. The Yateveo struggled to remain upright, looking as if some massive maw had taken huge burning bites out of it. Its upper tentacle-branches flailed and howled as if in a hurricane.

One of Mateo's most trusted lieutenants, Mumpy, opened up on the damaged alien with another gift from 'Keem's basement vault, an M240B machine gun. The massive crew-support weapon cut through the Yateveo like a chainsaw. The monster stumbled and crashed to the ground. Mumpy grinned at Mateo in the pre-dawn light, and then died as he was shot through by a hail of foot-long wooden spears. The air was full of the sounds of the screaming and dying as the hail of spines shot out from a second Yateveo which was climbing out of the impossibly small capsule ship through the seamless black hull.

Chain managed to block one of the spears heading straight at Mateo's face with his gauntlet, even as he shouted for someone to advance and get the machine gun from Mumpy's body. There were dead and dying Aztecas everywhere. Chain shouted to Mateo, "We've got to tighten up and advance now! We don't close the gap to that ship, we're all going to die!"

Mateo screamed and fired on the new threat, willing his hatred through the scarlet bolt of energy. If he heard Chain, he didn't act like he gave a damn.


Ray fired again on the rooftop, and another section of the roof vanished. "Hey, Cassandra, how many people you think are up there?" He had broken pattern again, and was strafing the now-burning factory. He heard explosions and gunfire behind the building where Chain and Mateo were and hoped they were okay.

"From trajectory and rate of fire analysis, approximately six to eight. It's difficult to be more accurate as they no longer register as lifeforms."

"Have I hit any of them?"

"Your damage to the roof structure has effectively eliminated approximately two to three of the attackers."

"Thanks! I just got an idea." He spun the Galaxie closer to the building and accelerated as he reached the driveway directly in front of the structure. He reached out the window, the air whipping at his arm and face as he pulled the trigger again and again and again at the ground level of the massive building. Clearing the building and running out of driveway, he swerved hard to the right, back into the parking lot.

The ground floor looked as if it had been lifted off the ground in blue-white fire, like a rocket ship leaving the launch pad. A massive plume rose up to the third floor, and then the whole building began to fold in and collapse on itself. Ray came to a screeching stop at the far edge of the parking lot and watched the factory fall. The gunfire had stopped. Ray let a whoosh of a sigh escape his lips as he eased back in the seat.

"Proximity alert!" Cassandra called out. "New threat detected!"

The whole car shook as if there had been an earthquake. Ray's eyes snapped open. A Yateveo had moved right beside the car and was grabbing at it with a half dozen of its large, powerful branches, beginning to lift it off the ground. Ray gasped and tried to floor the engine to get away from the monster, but he couldn't get traction.

Ray scrambled across the seat to the passenger side, even as the Galaxie began to flip as it rose. "Cassandra, drop the passenger window!" he shouted. Gravity pulled him back toward the wheel, but he scampered to climb up even as the window rolled down. The car was a few feet off the ground now and being turned completely sideways. A swarm of tentacles from the Yateveo wriggled through the car's window, lashing and grabbing at Ray. The abolisher was slapped from his hand and fell clattering against the driver's door below him. Ray pulled the microwave knife from his jeans and snapped it on. The wavering, intangible blade hummed to life, and Ray slashed at one of the tentacles, the blade passing through it. The tentacle's chitinous bark darkened and smoked as it quickly withdrew the limb, but others wriggled in to take its place. Ray slashed and yelled as a claustrophobic panic began to set in. Some of the flailing feelers began to slip behind him, and his mind filled with dread recalling the transformation of Farmer and the other guards.

There was a whoosh outside the car. Ray saw streams of flame run up the back side of the Yateveo in a brilliant glow of orange light. The alien's upper tentacles thrashed wildly, making a mournful sound that reminded Ray a little of a didgeridoo. The rope-like appendages grabbing Ray quickly withdrew, releasing him and the Galaxie. They both fell back toward earth, the car landing on all four wheels with a suspension-testing boom, and Ray ending up wedged sideways between the car door and the steering wheel.

'Keem and his fire team of five Ciudad Aztecas advanced on the burning Yateveo. 'Keem fired another burst from the old Vietnam-era M9-7 flamethrower he had slung over his back, and more of the monster burned. "Down!" 'Keem shouted to the team a second before the spray of poisonous spines flew from the Yateveo's body toward them. He heard one of the men, Martin, get hit, groan, and fall.

Tendrils from the Yateveo lashed out toward the group, even as they fired on the alien with guns which didn't slow it at all. 'Keem came up and fired the flamethrower again. At the same time, Ray tumbled out of the driver's door of the car and leveled the abolisher at the Yateveo, bracing his aim on the roof of the Galaxie. The blast from

Ray's pistol annihilated a large section of the creature that wasn't already burning. Ray ducked to avoid the fragments of debris that pelted the Galaxie. The Yateveo took a few stumbling steps and then collapsed in an unmoving bonfire in the parking lot.

"Thanks," Ray called out to 'Keem as he stood up again after the blast. 'Keem said nothing, kneeling beside Martin's dead body. He closed the boy's unseeing eyes.

"Pour it on!" Mateo shouted to his surviving soldiers as he fired again on the second Yateveo to climb out of the alien ship. The first monster, the one who had killed Mumpy and the others, was now a burning husk nearby. Chain had gone alone to flank the new threat, and Mateo suddenly saw the rapidly fading night illuminated by a blast of red energy from the other side of the creature.

One of the handful of surviving Ciudad Aztecas was chopping away at the Yateveo with the M240B, and greenish-black "blood" was pouring from the alien's mangled base. The machine gunner, a young man whose gang name was Spyder, was the third man to retrieve the heavy weapon from the still-warm body of one of his gang brethren and advance toward the ship. Venomous spines thudded into the earth all around Spyder as he screamed at the nightmare before him and held the trigger down. Hot brass shells flew by his face.

Chain dived as a new burst of Yateveo spines hissed, barely missing him. He rolled and came up a few yards away from his last position. Kneeling, he fired again and opened the barrel aperture wider with a twist of the rubber ring on the barrel. The blast sheared off a good section of the Yateveo's upper body. The thing finally crashed to the ground near the ship, dead.

There was anxious silence for a moment from the few Ciudad Aztecas remaining, then a raucous cheer went up. Mateo, bathed in the light from the burning alien bodies and the inferno of the collapsed factory, slumped a little, the tension escaping his body. He looked over to Chain, who was walking toward him, atmospheric analyzer in hand.

"Still good?" Mateo asked.

Chain nodded. "Now, we got to get into that thing." As the words were leaving his lips, the black capsule silently lifted up off the ground a few feet and began to rocket across the field toward the rest of the complex. "They're making a run for it!" he shouted. "Get Ray on the phone!"

Ray's cell rang, and he answered it. "You guys okay?"

"The alien ship's on the move, headed toward the water!" It was Chain's voice; he sounded as if he was running. "You got to cut it off, stop it."

Ray nodded to 'Keem as he slid into the Galaxie, slammed the door, and peeled out of the parking lot.

"On it. I'll blast it . . ."

"No!" Chain cut him off, almost frantic. "That thing is a Tribanni transport. It's multi-dimensional. You destabilize its molecular structure with an abolisher, and you create an implosion that will take out everything within fifty miles!"

Ray saw the black pill-shaped craft suddenly veer onto the access road ahead of him. It was moving fast, headed for the dry docks and the water. "Great! So what do I do?"

"I don't know. You're there. I'm not. Improvise."

"Helpful." Ray was closing on the capsule, but at this speed, it was getting harder to take the curves in the road. "Gotta go. I'll get back to you." He tossed the phone on the seat beside him next to the abolisher and the still-humming microwave knife and took the wheel with both hands. He was almost up on the thing's back bumper . . . if it had a bumper. For all its otherworldly looks, it seemed to handle a bit like a truck or an RV.

*What to do? Ram it? Try to get ahead of it and cut it off? What if it's armored or can just plow right through me? And what the hell is a Tribanni?*

Ray glanced up to see a shadow eclipsing part of the dawn sky. Time was almost up. Then, the answer came to Ray in an instant. He jammed on his brakes and let the alien craft accelerate away from him. He came to a full stop and climbed out of the car, abolisher in hand. He asked Cassandra to do a quick calculation for him and tell him exactly when he'd need to fire. Ray took careful aim, waited, waited . . .

"Now," Cassandra said, and he fired.

The Tribanni craft was nearly to the water when the massive arm of the dock crane came crashing down on top of it with a terrible sound like the world itself were sundering. A moment later, Ray pulled the Galaxie to a stop near the huge debris pile. He saw the black capsule wedged among the twisted and broken girders, like an insect caught in some great metal web. He picked up his phone to hear Chain still on it.

"I got it," Ray said. "Just follow the cloud of dust."

"Time check?" Chain asked.

All the survivors of the raid were gathered by the crane wreckage. 'Keem and four of his team were alive, as were Mateo and five of his. Of the twenty men who had agreed to come and fight, eleven were dead.

"Less than four minutes to cops," Ray said, "if we're lucky. All those fires and explosions—plenty of people saw all that from the overpass."

Chain grabbed a steel girder that probably weighed four hundred pounds and, with a grunt, tossed it ten feet to clear a way to squeeze through and reach the hull of the alien craft. 'Keem and Ray looked at each other as he did it. Mateo was looking at nothing. His eyes were dark wells of anger and sadness.

"You all need to start clearing out and then regroup at 'Keem's," Chain said.

"Where are you going?" 'Keem asked.

The Ranger nodded to the alien craft. "I need to go in there. There's likely more Yateveo inside, and I need to get some answers to how they got here and what they're up to."

"We should all go," 'Keem said.

"Yeah," Mateo said, breaking his silence.

Chain shook his head. "The atmosphere inside there may already be compromised by their spores. It would kill you all in minutes."

"Why not you?" Mateo asked.

Chain held up his hand with the ring. "One of the Queen's gifts. Besides translation, it also protects us from lethal environmental conditions."

"I'll go in with him," Ray said to the group. Before Chain could argue, Ray held up his own hand and signet. "Hey, 'Keem, you mind driving the Galaxie back? I'll catch a ride with Chain."

"Good luck," 'Keem said, "and don't tarry."

Chain and Ray struggled over and under the wreckage until they were next to the craft. The sky had lightened, and dawn was on the cusp of arrival. Chain removed a small pyramid-shaped object from his jacket. It was about the size of a grape.

"What's that?" Ray asked.

"Cipher decrypter. It's a fluid programmable supercrystal matrix with a clairsentient picotech NOI built into it."

"Oh, one of those. I see those on late-night TV."

"Long story, short: it will get you into anything from a computer net to the most advanced locks. Never tried it on Tribanni technology before, though." Chain placed the base of the pyramid against the black, mirrored hull.

"Where do you get this stuff?" Ray looked on as the decrypter stayed affixed to the metal once Chain took his hand away.

"Odds and ends I've picked up along the way. This was a gift, made just for me by the best damn thief I ever met." Blue lights now winked on all the sides of the pyramid. Chain pulled it off the hull with a smile and put it away. "We're in."

They stepped through the solid hull as if it were air. Chain led them through the seemingly endless dim corridors, sweeping ahead with the abolisher rifle.

"This place is huge," Ray said.

"The Tribanni are dimensional engineers." Chain paused to make sure a hallway was clear. "Stick close. You do not want to get lost in here."

"Can we shoot in here?" Ray whispered.

"Just don't miss what you're aiming at."

They moved quickly, but even then the ship seemed to go on forever. Eventually, they cleared a junction of about a dozen corridors, and Chain led them down one that opened into a large circular arboretum. A Yateveo, larger than any Ray had seen, stood at the center of the room. Both Rangers leveled their weapons on the creature. Its upper tendrils whistled and snapped.

"I'm surprised to see you, Lord of Iron and Fire," Hooruuul said.

The Yateveo's "voice" came from a small koala-like animal with large dead eyes that crouched at the crook of one of his clusters of branches. One of Hooruuul's smaller tendrils was buried into its skull. The creature, once part of a race called the Axolli, had the ability to translate any language it heard, comprehend it, and transmit back a reply in the speaker's tongue with flawless inflection. The Axolli's world had been subsumed by the Yateveo during the Lytch War. Those who did not die in the resistance or the horrific transformation of their planet were converted into useful organic devices.

"Not as surprised as I am to see you," Chain said. "Neat trick, that —still being alive and all. How'd you pull it off?"

Hooruuul ignored the question. "I had expected you to have skittered back to the shadows after you assumed your pathetic Queen destroyed us."

"I'm not the skittering type, unlike you guys. You were banished, all of you, all of the Nemesis, to the tiniest sliver of space-time by the lady who helped build the universe. So how'd you do it?"

"Faith. Our faith is that of inevitable fate. Heat dies, life dies. Your kind cling to the warm fantasy of hope. In the end, we always win."

"So, that's a 'no' on telling me how you came back. Too bad, that's what was keeping you alive."

"I am prepared to embrace the Stillness. You Rangers will fail to stop us. All will return to the Still—"

Chain opened fire. Ray joined him, and the Yateveo vanished in an expanding cloud of brilliant light.

"After you," Chain said.

. . .

Chain led Ray through the seemingly endless hallways to a room that looked like a multi-tiered cockpit combined with a museum. He searched from bank to bank of instruments and finally removed a piece from something . . . Ray couldn't determine if it was artwork or a control panel. The small object looked like a piece of ever-shifting origami that hovered just above Chain's palm. He examined and shut off one touch-screen bank of buttons and lights. Then they stepped through the wall of the bridge and were outside again in the cool morning air.

There was a symphony of sirens all around them by the time they sprinted back to Chain's tow truck and slowly drove away.

The sun was up. Ray watched from the highway as they passed numerous condemned and abandoned warehouses and factories along the river's edge. The water flashed and glittered in the light of the ascending sun.

"I've hated this place for a long time," Ray said, looking out his open window. "I blamed all the awful stuff that was happening to me, in my life, to my family, on *here*. The whole place reminded me of death. Everywhere there were abandoned buildings, empty decaying houses, and endless refineries. So many people left, and so many more had nowhere to go. I didn't want to look at it, so I kept looking down. This place is a waterlogged dump."

Chain drove on. "So tell me," he said, "how's it looking today?"

"It's the most beautiful sight I've ever seen."

# 14

By the time Ray and Chain arrived back at the pawn shop, Mateo and his crew had departed.

"He had to let the families of his people know what happened to them," 'Keem explained. "He also suspected quite a bit of scrutiny from the police once the bodies were discovered at the scene."

"I heard something about it on the radio coming over," Lu said. "They're calling it some kind of gang fight."

"He also told me to emphasize to you," 'Keem said to Chain, "not to 'fly off' or anything, until he had a chance to speak with you. He also said you owe him."

"I do, and you too." 'Keem shrugged. "Anyone would fight for their world, their loved ones. You owe me nothing."

"Thank you, all the same." Chain handed his abolisher over to the pawn shop owner. Ray did the same. "We couldn't have done it without your help."

"If I can be of any further service, you have but to call on me. Now, if you will excuse me," he said, shutting off the store lights, "I need to put these items away and I want very much to see my family before they head off to work and school."

"Thanks, 'Keem," Ray said as he, Lu, and Chain headed out the door of City Pawn.

"You owe me breakfast," Lu said with a grin. He looked around at the early-morning traffic, the blue sky, the sun, and let out a "Woo-hoo" of pure joy. "It's all still here! Man, saving the world is great!" He caught himself and backpedaled quickly. "Not that *I* saved anything!" Ray and Chain were both grinning. "You guys! *You* saved the world . . . man, that's weird to actually say!"

"Every army I've ever been in depended on its support personnel to keep working," Chain said. "They're vital, Lu."

Lu smiled. He reached into his jacket pocket and handed the big Ranger a fresh can of the energy drink he had enjoyed so much the night before.

"See? Thank you. I need this."

"You helped, buddy," Ray said, "more than I can tell you. Come on, let's get that breakfast."

"Details," Lu said as they walked to the Galaxie. "I want every laser blast, every Jerry Bruckheimer explosion!"

Ray paused as he opened the driver's side door. He looked back at Chain. "Hey, you coming? It's on me."

Chain was climbing into his truck. "Go ahead. I got a few things to follow up on."

"Hey!" Ray said, trying to do his best Mateo impression, "don't fly away or nothin'."

Chain smiled. "I'll meet up with you at your house. Get some rest. You deserve it."

Ray watched him start up the truck and pull out of the parking lot into early-morning traffic. He sensed something was bothering Chain and he knew it had to do with what they had discovered on the Trib-anni ship. He shook off the ominous feeling. The Earth was still here. Ray climbed in the car and looked over to Lu.

"Awful House?" Lu asked.

Ray smiled. *Waffle House is still here*, he thought. "You bet."

· · ·

After breakfast with Lu, Ray dropped him back off at his car and then drove to the hospital. He asked the nurses on the unit if he could visit with his mom, and after about fifteen minutes, they let him go into her room. Someone was snoring over the sounds of *The Price is Right* on the other side of the curtain separating the room. Juanita was sleeping, an IV in her arm giving her fluids. She looked pale and sunken, with dark circles under her eyes. For a second, Ray recalled his pop in his hospital bed, but he quickly brushed that image away. His mom was still beautiful, even with all she had been through.

Sitting in the little plastic chair next to her bed, it suddenly occurred to him how long he had been up, how long since he had showered or slept. He slumped back in the most uncomfortable chair in the world and watched her sleep. "You're going to be okay," he said softly, his voice a dry rasp. "It's all going to be okay."

He fell asleep at some point and awoke when a nurse came in to check on Juanita.

"You look *really* tired," the nurse said. "Go home. You can visit her again tomorrow. You both need sleep."

Ray vaguely recalled the drive home and searching for his old keys in his pocket next to the microwave knife, for which Lu had offered his graded near-mint copy of Dell Comics' *Dracula*, Issue One, in trade. He unlocked the front door, stumbled in, slipped off his high tops, and fell deeply asleep on the couch.


Ray awoke well after dark. He didn't recall dreaming anything. He sat up on the couch, and it took him a second to remember where he was —he was home. He felt odd and out of sync with the rest of the world.

He got up, found his way to the bathroom and then the kitchen, snapping on lights in the dark house as he went. The lights reminded him that he needed to pay the power before they shut it off again. He still had a few days, and then it hit him. He had thousands of dollars from selling golden space coins. Was that all real? He checked his wallet, saw that it *was* real, then looked around the messy kitchen and recalled the sparse and past-sell-by-date contents of the fridge and

R.S. BELCHER

cabinets and ordered himself a pizza. *You save the world, you probably deserve a pizza.*

About ten minutes after the pie arrived from Crown Pizza, there was a knock at the door. Ray, a slice in hand, opened it when he looked through the window and saw it was Chain. "Hey, come on in. You hungry?"

Chain walked in. "You look better." He nodded toward the slice. "What's that?"

"You have got to be kidding me. It's pizza. You guys don't have pizza out in the 'Known Galaxies'?"

"I . . . don't . . . think so." Chain sniffed the air. "It smells good."

Ray gestured for him to sit on the couch. The pizza box was on the cluttered coffee table in front of it. He had the TV on in the corner, tuned to a show about the Daytona 500.

"Okay, we are fixing this right now." Ray handed him a fresh slice, the cheese oozing down. "Eat."

Chain took a bite of the slice and the focus of his eyes softened. He made a deep murmuring sound of pleasure and smiled after he swallowed. "This is . . . art. So many flavors and textures, brought together so . . . simply." He took another bite, and then another. "Magnificent. How could they not add this to the list along with cars and music?"

"Exactly!" Ray finished his slice and grabbed another. He had a six-pack of Coronas, and he offered one to Chain, then raised his bottle. "To saving the Earth for the preservation of pizza." They clinked and each took a long drink.

"I've had something like this before." Chain looked at the bottle. "Fermented grain. Very nice. You need to try a glass of Smarka sometime." He took another drink and burped softly. "Your world's safe, but I have to leave tomorrow."

"You're not done with the Yateveo yet, are you?"

"No." Chain took another bite of pizza and chased it with the beer. "They've invaded the Tribanni's home world, a place called Triban."

"Damn," Ray said.

"That world gives them access to dozens of jumping off routes to hundreds of other inhabited worlds. Once they have enough Yateveo

108

matured and ready to fight, there will be no stopping them. They'll transform those worlds the way they almost did Earth. We have to contain them, and then destroy them."

Ray drained his beer. He and Ben and Pop had sat on this couch and watched races for as far back as he could remember. "So . . . Earth's not really safe, is it?"

"You're pretty far off the beaten path. The only reason they were here was because they were chasing Evan. He was on Triban when the Yateveo invasion started. He made it out, but he got wounded in the process. He made it as far as Earth before he had to stop. He knew he was dying, and he needed to find someone who could get the warning through. Luckily, he found you." Ray smiled grimly. "They had to make sure he was dead and that he hadn't warned the Rangers yet. That was why they were after his body. That also means they know they are not ready to launch a full-scale invasion on the Shield Pact worlds yet."

"How'd you find all this out?"

Chain pulled the small, ever-shifting device he had removed from the control gallery on the Yateveo's craft. "I've been reviewing the records on here. We have a little bit of time to stop them but not very long."

"They really worship death?" Ray shook his head. "Goth space-trees."

"Not just individual death, universal decay—entropy. The Yateveo and the other members of the Nemesis want to destroy all progress, all civilization, all life, all hope, everywhere."

"Can't you guys like nuke the Tribanni home world, if they've already killed everybody by now?"

"I wish we could. The Tribanni are . . . were multi-spatial engineers. Their whole world is honeycombed with dimensional adjuncts, worlds within worlds. Imagine the problem we had with shooting the transport with the abolisher but on a cosmic scale."

They were both silent for a moment. The sound of the race on the TV filled the room.

"So, what *are* you going to do?" Ray opened two more beers and handed one to Chain.

"First I'm going to eat more pizza and drink more . . . beer, is it?" Ray smiled and nodded. "Then tomorrow, I'm going to head off Earth, alert the leaders of the Shield Pact that the Yateveo have returned, and then . . . I don't know what else to do, but I have to do something."

"One riot," Ray began, raising his bottle.

"One Ranger," Chain finished. They both drank.

"I want in," Ray said. "I know I'm not much help, but . . ."

"Actually, I was hoping you would come. I do need you, and you did a hell of a job today."

"Thanks. Surprised me too, actually."

Chain laughed. "I need to take care of a few things tomorrow before we head out."

"You have a place to sleep?"

Chain shrugged. "I figured I'd bunk in my truck."

"No. You can sleep up in my parents' room," Ray said. "After the last few days, you should get to sleep in a real bed."

"Pizza, beer, and a real bed to sleep in. You Earth folks know how to treat your heroes, I'll give you that."

Ray returned to the hospital early the next morning. Sunlight filtered through the big plastic blinds of Juanita's room. When she eventually opened her eyes and saw Ray, she muttered, "You look tired, *mi cielito.*" She'd called him that since he was a baby.

"How are you feeling?" Ray reached for a Styrofoam cup of water with a bendy straw on the table next to her bed.

"Pretty awful, but I know it will pass. It has before."

Ray was silent. This was her third, fourth try at cleaning up? Next up were the promises.

"This time, it's going to stick, Ramon."

Ray summoned up a smile even as a war raged inside him. He wanted to believe her, wanted to believe that his mom was still in there, that she truly wanted to fight the thing that was trying to wipe her from existence. The other part of him was angry, and cold, and done with the bullshit promises. Both parts knew what he was about to say would hurt her, maybe sabotage her before she even began.

"It will," he said, holding the water cup for her while she eagerly drank. "Look, I have to go . . . out of town for a few days, maybe a week."

"Out of town?" Juanita sat up in the bed; she looked confused, and the fringes of panic were in her voice. "What's wrong, why?"

"Nothing." Fake smile to the rescue again. "Trevor, my manager at the store, he asked me if I could help out. ChugCo lost half a store crew over in Houston. They were stealing lotto tickets and trying to hide it on the inventory counts. Regional fired everyone, so they want me and some other guys to fill in 'til they rehire. They're going to put us up in a motel and give us money for food and everything." He saw the concern behind her eyes, and he knew what she was thinking —*what about me?* The warring factions inside him understood and hated her for it. To her credit, she tried to summon her own fake smile. It was a little shaky, but she managed.

"That's great, Ramon! I'll get myself home when they discharge me and . . ." She was thinking of coming home penniless and sober to a dark, powerless house. The resolve was already crumbling in her, and he could see it.

"I got some good news about that too," he said quickly. "I got you into a residential treatment program!"

"What?" she said, confused and maybe a little excited. "Ramon, those things cost a lot of money."

"I took care of it. There's a new government program, it's called . . . CHAIN, or something like that. They're covering everything. It's thirty days, and I'll be back before you even get home."

He'd paid up all the house bills and a little ahead. The rest of the money from the coins had gone to paying for Juanita's stay at the rehab program. It was no wonder why only rich people seemed to go to rehab. The administrator at the rehab had looked at Ray with thinly veiled suspicion when he had paid for Juanita's whole stay in cash.

"You . . . set all that up for me, Ramon?" Her eyes were glassy and wet.

Ray felt something very old and battered stir inside him. "Yeah. I love you."

She took his hand and he held hers. He saw a little strength and light appear in her wet gaze, and he had to admit, he felt better too. They sat and said nothing for a long time.

"You look after her, Lu," Ray said. They were in the parking lot of the Bingo Truck Stop. It was around one in the afternoon, and Ray was getting ready to leave with Chain. They had agreed to meet here, and the tow-truck driver was a little late. Lu, in his Chug-n-Lug uniform, was standing with Ray beside the now-pristine-looking Galaxie.

Ray had asked Cassandra what had happened to all the damage from the other night.

"The vehicle has repair capabilities as long as the nutrient-restorative packets remain at optimum levels," she had replied matter of factly. "Of course, you could get a girl a car wash now and then . . ."

"I'll check in on Juanita every day," Lu said. "I don't think I'm her favorite person, but I promise I will. You put me on her visiting list, right?"

Ray nodded. "Thanks."

Chain's truck pulled into the parking lot.

"I really appreciate it, Lu. Thanks for smoothing everything out with Trevor. I'm sorry I'm slacking so much these days."

"Got you covered, and don't worry one bit about that," Lu said with a chuckle. "Focus on staying alive and remembering everything you see out there. I wish I could come with you."

"Me too. After this crap is over with, I owe you a long road trip."

"I'll hold you to it, like the breakfast."

The two old friends hugged and then stepped away.

"You ready?" Chain asked from his lowered driver's window. Ray nodded and opened the Galaxie's door.

"Lu, thank you again. I touched base with 'Keem and Mateo, and they will both be ready if we need them . . . for what comes next. You need to be ready too."

Lu nodded and gave Chain and Ray a thumbs up. Chain looked over to Ray. "Follow me, focus on me, on my truck, just like you did when you found me on Bleeth."

"Got it. Where we headed?"

"A world called Norama. Even if you lose sight of me, keep focusing, and we'll end up at the same place." Ray nodded. Chain pulled away, toward the road and the interstate ramps.

"I'll see you soon," Lu said. "Be careful, Ray."

Ray nodded and drove off, tailing the old, beat-up tow truck. The two cars headed up one of the ramps to I-10.

A moment later, Lu had lost sight of them. He wondered if he'd ever see Ray Cosa again.

# PART II

JOURNEYMAN

## 15

I t turned out that there were three days of hard driving between Earth and Norama. It was always night on the Queen's Road, and the sky above was a slowly shifting starscape of constellations, luminous nebulas, spinning galaxies, and void. Thinking about the Nemesis and their nihilistic religions made the wastelands between the stars take on a much more ominous tone for Ray.

When he looked to the side of the Queen's Road, sometimes he saw blurry landscapes whipping by. Most of the time he saw stars and emptiness. At one point in the journey, Ray put his brakes on when he saw a figure trudging along the shoulder of the highway, using a staff as a walking stick.

At the next stop, Ray asked Chain about the figure.

"Most call them Fordolon. They're travelers who seldom stay in one place very long. They made their way onto the Queen's Road by riding as a passenger or a stowaway on a transport. Others own or have stolen tokens or guidestones that give them access onto the road, and then they simply walk it and live on it."

"Hitchhikers," Ray said. "We call them hitchhikers back home."

"Be very wary of these 'hitchhikers.'" Chain got serious. "Most are harmless. They have their own cultures, their own ways; they can even be excellent company on a long trip. But they are very insular. They look on most outsiders as potential marks or threats. There are other Fordolon who *are* dangerous. They're brigands, murderers, and worse—cultists, cannibals, madmen. Some worship the Stillness. Sometimes it's very hard to tell the difference between the good ones and the bad."

Ray laughed.

"What's so funny?"

"That is almost exactly what my folks told me about hitchhikers when I started driving."

Ray kept Chain's truck in sight for most of the trip. He could tell when they got closer to more populated areas, because more traffic would appear on the Queen's Road. It was a bewildering array of vehicles and technology: everything from steam-powered juggernauts and animal-driven wagons to spinning-top-like things the size of houses awash in flashing iridescent colors. Huge alien beasts, larger than dinosaurs, had structures and other seeming lifeforms growing out of them. There were plenty of cars too. Some hovered, like the Tribanni ship had; others had tires, or treads like tanks, or mechanical legs, like insects. He was pleased to see his Galaxie getting plenty of admiring looks as he passed. It was weird and wondrous, and yet it felt familiar.

When they got hungry or needed a break from driving, either he or Chain would visualize what they needed and find an exit. It turned out that most places in the universe had very little knowledge of the Rangers, of the cosmic war against the Nemesis, or that they had a Queen. The place they stopped at on the second day was an exception.

It was off an old pothole-riddled road right off the highway. The sun was a lucent, but distant, pinprick of light, like a bright LED. The air was heavy and damp. The "exit" was a fork in the road where several signs announced nearby places to stay for the night and get food or feed your Julgrra, whatever the hell that was. The inn they settled on was a medieval-looking affair. It was a cross between a mansion and a fortress, and it must have had a hundred rooms, easy. There were about twenty vehicles out front from probably as many different worlds. There was also a large number of rat-like things that were the size of Earth horses, tethered to posts with iron rings. Ray assumed that these were the aforementioned Julgrra.

Chain was already climbing out of the truck as Ray parked. The song of countless birds filled the air. It felt odd to Ray, because their song didn't sound similar to what he was used to back home.

"Lots of traffic," Chain said. "Usually means good food." He opened the door and gestured for Ray to enter.

"Do . . . do we need money?" Ray asked. Chain shrugged with a smile and followed him in.

The locals were vaguely humanoid, with long flexible necks and bodies covered in orange and black feathers. Tube-like antennae were positioned above their golden eyes—which had black irises—and below their short curved beaks.

Their server came over and looked at both of them, "What can I get you soulless monsters today?"

Ray looked up from the menu; Chain didn't bother. "Give us two of the number fours with water and . . . choli juice, you preening zealot," the elder Ranger replied.

The server walked away without another word.

"Why did you do that?" Ray asked.

"What, the number four? It sounded safe, and I thought you'd like it."

"Not the number four. Why did you insult him . . . her . . . our waiter? And why'd they say that about us?"

"Some cultures place a premium on straightforwardness." Chain scanned the crowded dining room as if it were a habit. "'Better to speak your truth than stain your lips and heart with a lie.' Plus, humanoids that look like us kind of run the show at the galactic and universal levels."

"Really?"

Chain nodded. "The members of the royal family are humanoid. The Queen is humanoid. There are species scattered everywhere across creation that you or I could blend right into. The prevailing theory is that at the dawn of the universe, the Queen stacked the evolutionary deck in favor of species like her own. 'Made them in her own image' and all that."

"So all of us on Earth . . ."

Ray paused as the server returned with a tray of their food and drinks. The "number four" was a large bowl full of something that looked a bit like pinkish rice and vegetables. A platter was set down between them laden with plentiful chunks of some white meat that smelled spicy and good. There was also a paste made of something like vegetables and beans. Unleavened bread in rectangular sheets was stacked on the platter too, along with a half dozen small cups of sauces. After setting everything down, the server made a gesture with both hands and bowed slightly, then whispered something Ray thought might be a prayer.

"May this food nourish your body and spirit and fortify you for the trials you may face," the server said at a regular volume.

"Thank you," both Chain and Ray said. The server departed. There were no utensils, so Chain grabbed a piece of the bread and used it as a scoop. Ray followed suit. They dug in and ate heartily for a while in silence.

"This is really good!" Ray said. Chain smiled and nodded as he took another bite. "So, Earth-folk may be related to the Queen of the Universe."

"Most likely." Chain wiped his beard with the back of his hand. There were no napkins. "Most of the humanoids are. Sadly, there are whole religions that worship the Royals and proclaim our form the 'divine form.' Which of course precipitated religions among the non-humanoid races that say humanoids are soulless demons created by an evil goddess and her spawn. I think our current hosts subscribe to some interpretation of that orthodoxy."

"Wow, space racism and humanoid privilege." Ray sipped his water. "I feel like I'm home."

"In my experience," Chain said, "people are people, no matter the galaxy or world, no matter how they look. And most of them are assholes."

"Now I definitely feel at home."

They ate some more. One of the natives came up onto a small stage near the edge of the dining room, did a brief ritual that looked to Ray a lot like another prayer, and then began to sing a cappella. It was beautiful, and it sounded like a chorus of voices and instruments were all coming out of the singer's mouth. That was when Ray noticed that the singer looked to have multiple voice boxes running along their long throat, almost like vertebrae in a spine.

"You're a Ranger; you work for the Queen, right?" Chain grunted in the affirmative. "So why don't we just go see the Queen. If the Yateveo being back is such a big deal, she'd want to know, right? Then she can call in all the armies and troops we need."

Chain paused in devouring his meal and looked a little uncomfortable.

"First off, you're a Ranger now too. Don't forget that. Second . . . The royal family . . . the Queen . . . they're assholes too, maybe the biggest assholes of them all."

"What?" Ray said. "You're kidding me."

Chain took a sip of the choli juice, made a face, and set it back down, chasing it with water.

"For most of the history of the universe, the Royals have all hidden away. The Queen set everything in motion and meddled when it suited her, but otherwise she was content to let the developing races fend for themselves. Her kids followed suit, wandering the galaxies, doing as they pleased, treating the races they encountered like playthings for their amusement, and leaving messes and mythologies in their wake."

"But you said they fought beside the Shield Pact in the war." Ray felt very uneasy with what Chain was saying and was trying to make some sense out of it.

"Eventually, they did. After thousands of years of fighting, after whole galaxies were snuffed out like candles, after quintillions of sentient beings were slaughtered. Finally, when the Nemesis actually hurt the Royals, then they decided to step in and do something." There was genuine anger in Chain's voice. "How fucking noble."

"Do you know what happened? You said you were there at the end of the war."

"I was. The prevailing story is that the Nemesis destroyed a world very important to the Royals, a world called Binah. No one knows exactly where it was. It was a mythological world, like the throne world of the Queen, Malkuth. Knights of the Shield Pact had taken oaths and quested for millennia, searching for Malkuth to entreat the Queen to join the fight. None of them was ever seen again.

"When Binah fell, Prince Micah fell with it. That was the turning point. That was when the demigods decided to pitch in with regular folk and try to stop the worshipers of entropy. It took the death of one of their own to rouse them to give a damn."

"If you hate them so much, why do you serve them?" Ray didn't feel much like eating anymore.

"A hurricane may destroy your home, but you don't hate the sea or wind for that. The Royals are selfish, and petty, and arrogant, but they are saints compared to the Nemesis. For all their faults, they like creation, they made it themselves—and they don't want to see it destroyed. It was a royal who founded the Rangers, who fought beside us."

"Can we go to *them* for help?"

A strange expression crossed Chain's face at Ray's question, a painful mixture of sadness and regret.

"That royal died in the war." Chain shook his head. "And after the Queen herself took to the battlefield on Yesod and wiped the Nemesis out of existence . . . the Royals left. They disappeared again to become even greater figures of mythology and religion. Worshiped, venerated, but too damn good to stick around and help clean up the mess."

They were both silent. Ray picked at another morsel of food, and Chain took a second go at the choli juice.

"Well, that's disappointing," Ray finally said. "You hear 'Queen of the Universe' and you figure that's somebody who has their shit together."

"You'd think. Don't worry though. The Rangers have been holding things together ever since, saving whatever needs saving, doing the dirty work the royal family won't deign to do. We got this."

"And doing it all in the Queen's name."

Chain laughed. "People need something to believe in, even if the reality is . . . disappointing."

The singer finished and Ray clapped loudly and enthusiastically. He was the only one. Chain motioned for him to stop, and he did. Their server was over in a flash.

"How dare you insult my brood fledgling with your mammalian ritual noises!" The server's face tubes were up and vibrating angrily, "I should call the temple wardens to—" Their host stopped cold when they spotted the ring on Ray's finger, then glanced to Chain and saw his too. "Oh! Oh, my apologies, noble Rangers! I did not know . . ."

"It's okay," Ray said, trying to calm the alien. "My apologies. I didn't mean to insult you or your kid." He gestured toward the table. "The food was wonderful, and I've never heard anyone sing as beautifully as your child did."

The server bowed, deeply. "You honor my brood, mighty Ranger. Please, there will be no tithe necessary for your nutritional communion." Ray looked to Chain, confused.

"The meal's on the house," he said. "Come on."

Ray thanked the server again and followed the elder Ranger back to the cars. It was drizzling outside now, and the birds were all silent. "My first free meal as a Ranger." He smiled. "Pretty cool."

"Like I said"—Chain opened the door to his truck—"people need something to believe in."

Ray looked at the signet on his finger and then climbed into the Galaxie. Soon, they were back on the Queen's Road, bound for Norama.

# 16

It was night as they came off the exit from the Queen's Road into the beating, burning heart of Norama's capital city, which bore the same name. Ray had never seen anything to compare it to. His mind struggled to comprehend the scale, the scope. There were buildings that were mountains of glass, steel, and light that pushed skyward past the upper atmosphere. Canyons of shadow between the giants, punctuated by rivers of slowly moving traffic on levels upon levels upon levels of ramps, overpasses, and streets. Colors of every possible hue lit the buildings and the windows, reflecting off the hulls of aircraft of every size and shape, which swarmed the city skyline like gnats.

They pulled over into a parking deck.

"How . . . many . . . people live here?" Ray craned his neck, turning as he looked all around.

Chain was enjoying the young man's reaction. "About a billion, give or take. Lots of tourist and trade traffic too, not to mention that this is the seat of government for the Shield Pact. Eight hundred and thirty-nine governments spread across three hundred galaxies. It's one of the largest social experiments in the history of the Known

Galaxies, all started by a handful of beings seeking to stop the Nemesis."

"This is all . . . wow," Ray managed to say.

Chain crossed his arms, leaned against his truck, and tried to recall the first time he'd come here, the last time anything had made him say "Wow." He envied Ray his unjaded eyes.

"It sure is." Chain walked over to a cube of soft white light hovering about four feet off the ground.

"Your vehicle is occupying space 1173-adjunct, observation deck 431," the cube said in a pleasant voice. "Please provide your account information to confirm payment, or insert 280 bars for one cycle of housing."

Chain held his hand in front of the cube. "Ranger override. Official business."

"Confirmed, Ranger. No charge. Welcome to Norama. We honor your service. Would you like hard copy, comm receipt, or data chit?" Chain asked for a hard copy, and a small sheet of paper floated out of the apparently seamless cube. He took it.

"We can hop a transport or find a flash box after you're finished. This city is a nightmare to drive through."

Chain had retrieved a bracelet from his seemingly endless pockets and clipped it on. He placed his finger on the narrow band of bronze-colored metal and a vein-work of thin, glowing lines sprang up all over the bracelet. He glanced to Ray as he kept his finger on the device.

"I know most folks prefer the injections now, but I'm old school. Our ride will be here"—a bubble-shaped craft drifted down next to them—"now."

The hatches on either side faded away, offering entry to the luxurious interior. Chain squeezed himself in, and Ray got in on the other side. There were thick, leather-seeming seats, but Ray saw no pilot, no controls, no machinery of any kind. Once they were in, the doors rematerialized, and the bubble lifted off from the parking area and took them skyward very quickly.

"Destination?" the bubble asked in a soothingly modulated voice that sounded a lot like the cube's.

"Central Administration," Chain said. "Take us to a secure access deck. Ranger override. Official business."

"Ranger signets confirmed," the voice said as the bubble banked left. "We thank you for your service, Rangers."

Ray was mesmerized. The bubble was translucent, and it seemed to become more so once it was in the sky. He looked down at the dizzying distance to what he figured was the ground below and then all around.

"This place is . . ."

"Yeah, I know, 'Wow.' I just hope they'll listen to reason and give us a hand."

"Why wouldn't they?"

"The Nora are very proud of their culture, their traditions, and their place in universal history, especially their role of leadership throughout the Lytch War. They can be a little . . . rigid . . . in their thinking. They don't like change, they don't care for surprises, and they hate to be wrong—sometimes to the point of denial."

"Again, sounds pretty familiar to me."

"Enjoy the view." Chain pointed toward a colossal ziggurat whose apex was lost to view at the edge of space. "We're almost there."


"This way, step lively," the young woman said to Ray and Chain as she led them through the maze of the Central Administration building.

"This is worse than the DMV," Ray whispered. "This place goes on forever!"

"Probably a little Tribanni engineering, and a lot of boredom."

The woman who had met them at the landing deck said her name was Ratari Pana Goss.

Chain explained, "The Nora are really big on titles and social status. Our friend here is a Ratari, a Knight of the Shield Pact."

Pana looked completely human to Ray. She had blonde hair that fell to her neck. Her skin was ivory with a faint silver undertone. She wore a long-sleeved black tunic that fell to her knees with loose trousers of dull silver beneath it and knee-high boots. A silver-and-black sash belt was wrapped around her waist. The clothing reminded Ray of Middle Eastern attire back home or maybe Indian. Her outfit was the same style and color as those of the others who had been on watch at the platform when they arrived. Ray figured it was some kind of uniform. She didn't appear to carry any weapons or gadgets that Ray could see, except for a silver disc, about the size of a half-dollar coin, on her forehead.

"What's with the silver disc?" he asked Chain.

"It's a weapon. They're called 'wards.' It's part of the reason you do not mess with a Ratari . . . if you're smart."

Pana led them to a central hub of corridors. There were ten closed metal doors set up equidistantly around the corridor hallways. Pana walked toward one of them, and it opened automatically, revealing a small chamber inside that reminded Ray of an elevator car. "Inside," she said curtly. Ray and Chain complied.

"Take a few deep breaths," Chain said. "And close your eyes. It will help your body."

Ray looked at the older Ranger, confused, as Pana entered and the door closed behind her. Ray noticed that rows of narrow rectangular brass panels encircled the small room. There were similar arrays on the floor and ceiling. There was a blinding flash of light, and Ray blinked reflexively. When he opened his eyes, it was the same chamber. Then the door slid open, and beyond it was a completely different hallway. Pana and Chain walked out, seemingly unfazed by the change in scenery. Ray followed, looking all around. His body was trembling a little, and he caught himself holding his breath. He took a few deep breaths and felt better.

"Did we just get beamed?"

"Flash booth," Chain said, following Pana down the long, narrow hallway. "Teleporter network. It lets you get around quickly."

"We got those on Earth." Chain looked over to him incredulously. "On TV."

The hallway was lined with flags and an elaborate mural of ever-shifting light and shadow. It gave the silent impression of a night battle, the shadows of soldiers advancing, dying, falling back, fighting forward, with the occasional flare of an energy weapon or an explosion. The other side of the hallway was lined with windows providing a breathtaking view of the surrounding city and the night sky. They were so far up now that the light pollution no longer blocked out the canopy of stars that seemed closer than the counterfeit firmament of the city below.

Couches and chairs were lined along the wall, and several beings, mostly humanoids, were sitting on the furniture chatting or locked in intense conversations in hushed whispers. There were two more Ratari, dressed like Pana, standing on either side of the large closed double doors. The doors looked to be made of beautiful real wood, and bore a circular mandala seal made of metal that looked like silver.

Pana nodded to her fellow knights and the doors swung open, revealing an immense office. Pana gestured for them to enter, and they did, Chain taking the lead, striding toward the distant stone desk. Ray noticed Pana seemed annoyed with Chain's boldness. She hurried to catch up to him, announcing them as she did.

"Exalted High Marshal Thierry of the Blood of Thierry, Master Ranger, I am Ratari Pana Goss of the Blood of Goss, Knight of the Shield Pact worlds. May I introduce . . ."

"I'm Chain," the Ranger said, interrupting Pana. He had reached the desk by now and met Thero's gaze. "My blood has been spilled and no longer carries a name. I am a Master Ranger of the Fourth Circlet, initiated at Grozec."

Pana and Ray were beside Chain now. She stepped between Chain and Thero. "This is Master Ranger Ray . . . of the . . . Blood of Earth. They have come under the seal of signet to receive your counsel. They say it is most urgent, High Marshal."

Pana gave Chain a look of contempt that would melt steel and stepped back, clasping her hands behind her. Chain held Thero's eyes, crossed his right arm across his broad chest and gave a deep bow at the waist. Ray followed Chain's lead. Thero responded in kind, but his bow was nowhere near as deep, little more than a slight dip.

"Welcome, Master Rangers," Thero said. He gestured for them to take two of the seats arrayed before his desk. Pana stood watch, her face once again serene. Thero looked at Chain, "Initiate of the Fourth Circlet? I didn't know any of you were still left."

"I'm the last, High Marshal." Chain nodded to Thero's signet. "Where were you initiated?"

Thero mustered a fake smile. "I'm afraid at my father's death bed. This ring has been passed from eldest Thierry to eldest Thierry for over a thousand years. The first to wear it, Oban Thierry, was initiated as a Ranger by the late Prince Chango himself, at the founding." He held up the signet so Ray and Chain could see it better. "It's one of the originals created. Second Circlet."

"I hope you will forgive our breach of protocols, and accept our apologies, High Marshal, but this is information that simply cannot wait," Chain said. "It deals with the security of the whole Shield Pact, and far beyond that."

"Tell me."

Chain told the story, from Ray finding him on Bleeth, to the discovery of Evan's body on Earth, and the battle with the Yateveo who had pursued Evan.

"The Yateveo have returned, as impossible as that sounds. It is a fact. They occupy the Tribanni home world, and they mean to use it as a staging ground for an invasion of the Shield Pact, for starters."

Thero frowned. "Forgive me, Master Chain, but is there proof of any of this?"

Chain placed something on Thero's desk. It was the small white ever-folding Tribanni data core he had recovered from the transport the Yateveo were using on Earth. The tiny device hovered an inch or so above the stone surface.

"All the information and proof you need is here, High Marshal. If I'm correct, we have less than a decacycle before they have replenished enough of their kind to attack."

Thero sized up Chain with a long look. "You, Master Ranger, know your way around a sales pitch." He looked over to Ray. "What do you say, Master . . . Ray, is it?"

"Huh, me?" Ray said. He sat up a little taller in the chair. "Uh . . . well, sir. I'm pretty much playing catch-up minute by minute here. My home is . . . nothing like what you guys have out here. We don't know about any of this stuff. But I can tell you the Yateveo are still around, and they nearly wiped out Earth. I think you might want to take this seriously and get all the help you can get, quick . . . sir."

Thero smiled in spite of himself. This skinny, dark-haired, dark-garbed boy was a primitive, a cave dweller, but he was sincerely telling the truth. It was refreshing after being surrounded by polished, practiced liars.

"Very well," the High Marshal said, standing, the Tribanni core in his hand, "I'll summon my cabinet at once. Ratari Pana will find you some accommodations. I'm sure you're both weary from your trip. We'll get to the bottom of this, gentlebeings, I assure you."

As the knight led the Rangers away, Thero was faced with the disturbing prospect that an old and terrible enemy had returned from the dead.

## 17

Pana took them to suites in another section of Central Administration. She said they were diplomatic quarters. They dropped off Chain first at a room across the hall from Ray's. Pana didn't say a word to the elder Ranger. Chain gave Ray a nod and disappeared into his quarters, shutting the door.

Pana opened the door to Ray's rooms with only a thought. Ray had never experienced such luxury in his life. She followed him in and waited near the door as Ray looked around. "The door is now bio-synced with you, as is the comfort station."

"The comfort station?"

"Yes, where you ah . . . bathe and . . . such. The water temperature and the biometric configuration of the fixtures have now been set to serve your particular biology. It usually only takes the suite a few moments to do that after it scans you. The media devices, lights, and other utilities will now respond to verbal, comm, or telepathic requests." She paused, watching Ray stare out the window at the city far below. "Do you have anything like this on Earth?"

"We're starting to. Smart houses, smart speakers, stuff like that. Nothing like *this*." Pana smiled in spite of herself. Ray smiled back. "You seem really serious, Ratari . . ."

"Pana's fine. You don't have to call me by my title."

"Thank you. Chain said titles are really important here. I just didn't want to make you mad, like you are at him."

"I have to admit, he did anger me. Your friend knows there is a protocol, but he breaks it and clearly enjoys doing so. It puts me in a compromising social situation as your escort and the one introducing you."

"It seems like an awful complicated way to live."

"We do honor to our ancestors by adhering to the codes of society. We know no other way."

"I'm sorry Chain didn't follow the codes. I haven't known him long, but he's pretty direct."

"I've heard that about Rangers. For all their heroics, they have a reputation for being . . . unorthodox."

Ray laughed.

"Yeah, I guess. I haven't met too many Rangers, yet, but they don't seem to have a lot of rules. I suppose knights have a lot more. How did you become one?"

"There is only one way. Any lowborn Nora who wishes to rise in station has to join the military and hope to distinguish themselves. I fought in the war with the Leth. I . . . distinguished myself." She sounded a little sad when she said that. "I was granted a commission, and then, in time, an appointment to the Academy of Valor. Even highborn have to attend the academy to gain admittance into the military orders. I graduated and was given the title of Ratari."

"Oh, that easy?" Ray grinned.

Pana shrugged, but her smile remained. "I've served here ever since graduation and taking the oath. That was five comps ago."

"Comp like a year?" Ray asked. Pana thought for a moment, accessing data through her comm, and then nodded.

"That's a long time to be a . . . security guard. No offense."

"None taken. Garrison and guard duty is . . . tedious, I agree, but necessary to the protection of the Shield Pact. I do wish for a more engaging assignment. That's hard to come by. There are social standings, even within the militant orders. Regardless of my title, to many I will always be seen as lowborn." She was silent for a moment; the smile had faded.

"Hey, if it helps any, where I'm from, a lot of jerks think me and my family are 'lowborn.' They're morons. My dad was in the military and he told me and my brother no one, *no one*, can take the things you accomplish away from you."

The smile came back. "My mother said something very similar to me."

"You sound like you've accomplished a lot. I bet most 'highborn' couldn't hack what you've been through."

Pana laughed. "You're right. If you need anything else—food, drink, clothing, or information—ask the room. If you need to summon me, ask it to do that. It's nice to meet you, Ray."

"You too, Pana. Good night."

She departed. Ray kicked off his shoes and lay back on the bed. He wondered how Juanita was doing in rehab. Was she suffering, was she afraid? How was Lu holding up at the Chug-n-Lug? He even hoped the cops hadn't busted Mateo's *huevos* too much over the firefight with the Yateveo.

The weariness of the long day pounced on him, and Ray fell asleep. He dreamed of sitting on the front steps of his family's house on Fifteenth Street with Jess. Her hair was blue and green this month, and she looked pale and perfect. Her eyes were sad, and she was holding his hand tight. All night long, he struggled to hear her voice, to understand what she was saying to him, but his dream thwarted him.

The next morning, Ray quickly showered and asked the room to make him fresh clothes that looked like the ones he had been wearing since they'd left Earth. The gym bag that he had thrown a few T-shirts and jeans into, along with a fresh pair of socks and boxers, deodorant, and a toothbrush, was back at the Galaxie. The room provided him with all of that.

Pana arrived to take them to the meeting shortly thereafter. "Have you been outfitted with a comm yet?" she asked as he tied his high tops.

"That like a cell phone? No, and I can't get any bars out here with mine."

Pana looked confused. "I'm . . . sorry about your 'bars,' but I'll see if I can get you set up with service. You want a bloc or a ject?"

"Whatever is . . . easier? Thanks."

Chain walked out of his room and Ray did a double-take. Chain was dressed in a white collarless shirt, a gold-and-brown vest, and dark brown trousers. He still wore his gauntlet. "You, uh, you clean up pretty good without the post-apocalypse starter pack," Ray said as Pana led them to the flash booths.

"Dress to impress." Chain then looked Ray up and down. "All the fashions in the Known Galaxies to choose from and you go with black jeans, black T-shirt, black shoes, and a black jacket. Daring."

"If it's good enough for my boys G-Eazy and Johnny Cash," Ray said as they entered the flash booth, "it's good enough for me."

"Johnny Cash," Chain said just before the flash. "Now him, I've heard of."

The window behind High Marshal Thierry's desk showed that dawn had arrived. The sky was a pale violet, bleeding away into the edge of space. Several dozen beings were seated around the Marshal's desk. They were reviewing an image hovering in the air before them. It showed roadways burning, mangled vehicles, and the bodies of black-and-silver-garbed soldiers scattered like discarded toys.

"Master Rangers," Thierry announced as they approached, with Pana leading the way this time. "Welcome. I wish I could tell you your mission here had been one of unnecessary concern, but it was not. The data you provided us, as well as the reports we received from the surviving reconnaissance units, confirm the Yateveo have indeed taken Triban."

"Surviving units?" Pana said, stepping closer to look at the images playing in the floating window.

"The damn teevs have mined all the access ways in by the Queen's Road," said a humanoid in a crisp black-and-silver military uniform with a wall of ribbons on his chest, "and they already have troops manning barricades at most of them."

"General, I don't see how racial slurs make this situation any more palatable," another humanoid said, this one was dressed in a very impressive pale-green suit with a bright-yellow cravat. He looked to Thero. "It certainly does not play well with the media."

"Minister, these monsters nearly wiped out all existence five centuries ago. They don't need you as their press agent," the general replied.

"Still," another being said. This one looked to Ray's eyes like a cloud of polychromatic smoke. "Are we so certain that a diplomatic solution is not possible here?"

That began a heated debate. Many voices rose, stepping on one another. Ray was lost in the noise of it. He looked to the High Marshal to see what he was going to do and saw him observing keenly, measuring and analyzing each being's reaction, like a lion looking for the weakest prey. An image of Mateo suddenly crossed his mind, a term from the Discovery Channel with it—*apex predator.*

Thero let the shouting match go on just long enough to gauge the mood of his cabinet and the assembly members present, and then he stood up behind his stone desk.

"Gentlebeings."

His voice was perfect in its modulation, a hint of impatience, a shade of anger, but the overall impression was one of control and direction. He didn't even need to use the available amplification or subsonic modifications to silence the room. He had clearly practiced this voice since he was a child.

"The matter at hand is that an ally of the Shield Pact has been invaded by a known hostile power. What are our options for response?"

The general nodded to the window, and the image vanished, replaced with detailed images of a black-mirrored orb Ray assumed was the Tribanni home world. Numerous animations showed dozens of red lines leading into the orb with streams of data scrolling beside each line.

"We can blockade Triban at each route on the Queen's Road that the Yateveo could use to break out, effectively pinning them down there indefinitely, Marshal."

"Aren't you forgetting something, General?" Chain said. All eyes fell on him, and he didn't seem to notice. "Your military history? The Nemesis were infamous for somehow appearing and retreating along the Queen's Road with seeming impunity. They easily bypassed ambushes, forced engagements, *and* planetary blockades through most of the war. Their unexplainable ability to do that was one of the primary reasons the Rangers were formed. We never did discover how they did that, remember?"

The general's eyes darkened a little, but he retained his cool.

"Ogillvin wrote an excellent book on the subject. However, we're not dealing with the Nemesis as a whole, not even the Yateveo species as a whole. This is obviously some lost band of teevs . . . Yateveos that were . . . overlooked by Her Majesty."

"Overlooked." Chain looked at Thero. "Is that how this is getting played?" He turned back to the general. "I read the book. Ogillvin is an idiot."

"Master Ranger," Yellow Ascot said, "we see no reason to alarm the good citizens of the Shield Pact with the notion that the Nemesis has returned. We don't want a panic, do we?"

"Obviously, we want a slaughter." Chain shook his head. "We need to hit that planet with as many Pact troops as you can muster. We need to do it now."

The general and Yellow Ascot looked to Thero. Thero addressed Chain.

"Master Ranger, you may not be aware, but the Shield Pact is currently in the process of reducing the size and scope of our military operations. We have been for more than a century now. The war with the Xavin and then, recently, with the Leth were not popular with the public. They want us using those resources for other things. We've maintained a wartime military for more than three centuries, but now ... now we're at peace."

"It wouldn't be good optics to see wave after wave of Pact troops getting slaughtered trying to take back Triban," Yellow Ascot said. "It wouldn't play well."

"I see," Chain said. "So the only option on the table is a blockade?"

"That, or driving drone vehicles in with nuclear weapons," the general added. "Even the minefields wouldn't stop them."

"You detonate nuclear weapons inside a world with multiple layers of spatial architecture, and you end up with a singularity that would suck in star systems for thousands of light years," Chain said. "Long term, it could wreck a large portion of that galaxy. It's madness."

"I must concur with the Ranger," a voice said from the back of the crowd of bureaucrats and politicians. "Such a course of action would be disastrous. For all my people, everywhere."

Ray looked in the direction of the voice. It seemed to be coming from the vicinity of a gushing, tumbling, frothing fountain of quicksilver in the High Marshal's office. It wasn't until the "fountain" moved toward them that Ray realized the voice had come *from* it.

"Master Rangers Chain and Ray, Ratari Pana," Thero said, "this is Senior Ambassador Excellency Neste Maji of the Tribanni Encompassment." Ray now saw that there was no base to the "fountain" that was the ambassador, merely a five-foot-high column of constantly churning silver liquid.

"A pleasure to meet you Rangers, Ratari," the ambassador said. "I wish it were not under such dire circumstances. High Marshal, I cannot in good conscience condone the use of nuclear weapons on my people's home world, even to stop the Yateveo. The price is too high."

"I agree," Thero said.

"So as I was saying, that leaves us with a blockade that probably won't work or a massive, bloody invasion that the Shield Pact won't condone," Chain continued. "I wouldn't be surprised if the Yateveo chose Triban because they knew they could hole up there and we couldn't dig them out easily."

"There's an alternative," the ambassador said grimly. "Though it is a drastic and disastrous option, but it would stop the Yateveo. It may be possible to unlock the spatial stabilizer network on my home world. The stabilizers anchor our planet to this dimension and allow us to layer dimensional architecture on our world. If freed of that tether, Triban would simply drift out of phase with this space-time and fall into a dimensional limbo, gone forever."

"You can do that?" Thero asked.

"It is theoretically possible."

"What would that do to your people on the planet?" Ray asked, all eyes turning to him.

"Kill them. I hope, I pray, we can find another way, but if not, the Yateveo must be stopped and stopped now." The ambassador looked at the assembled politicians, officers, and bureaucrats in the room. "For me to attempt this at all I would need to go to Triban to access the systems myself."

"You?" Chain asked.

"Yes. I was a professor of spatial mechanics at Lukinnar University back home prior to accepting my current position. I would say, modesty aside, that I'm as qualified as any other Tribanni engineer you'll find and more so than most, given our current predicament."

"Impossible," the general said. "We've seen the footage. Not a single recon team could get past the Yateveo defenses. Nobody can."

"We, the Rangers, can," Chain said. "I can put a team together in five days or less that can get the ambassador in there and keep him safe until he gets the job done."

A murmur of disbelief and even some dry chuckles met Chain's words.

"Master Ranger," Thero said, "you have no idea what's in there or how many Yateveo there might be. It sounds like reckless bravado and suicide. I can't sanction such an operation."

"With all due respect, Marshal, I don't need your sanction. I take my orders from Her Royal Majesty, not you. If I say we can do this, we can." Chain looked over to the Tribanni. "Provided you're willing to go, Ambassador. It will be dangerous."

"Please, call me Neste. If we're going to be dying together, I feel we should be on a first-name basis." Pana quickly stepped forward. "High Marshal, I would like to volunteer to accompany the Rangers to act as Ambassador Maji's personal security and to be liaison between the Pact Worlds and the Ranger team."

Thero sighed and looked over to his general, who rolled his eyes.

"Ratari Pana, you know that there are numerous members of the orders with significantly more . . . experience than you, who should get first crack at this assignment," the general said.

"Yes, Flag General Fulry, but they're not here, and if this is a suicide run, better to sacrifice someone of my . . . experience, than one of them, yes?"

Fulry almost laughed. "Keep your eye on this one, Thero. She's ambitious."

"It would be an honor to die in the service of the Pact worlds, sir."

General Fulry shook his head. "We have a rather sizable invest-ment of time, training, and equipment in you, Ratari. Let's try to keep you alive for the Pact worlds, shall we?"

"Yes, sir."

"If it's all the same," Neste said, "I'd be just fine not dying for the Pact worlds. For the record, I hope we can find a way to stop the Yateveo other than destroying my home."

"Permission granted to accompany the ambassador," the general said to Pana.

Ray glanced to Pana and winked. He saw her stone face almost crack, but she retained her soldier's demeanor.

"We will implement the blockades at once," Thero said to those assembled. "How do you plan to start, Master Ranger?" he asked Chain.

"I have some old colleagues to locate. The best Rangers I've ever worked with. I find them, I find our way in."

# 18

T ell me," Kreesh—eldest of the surviving Yateveo race—asked the two Tribanni engineers. "With your knowledge of time and space, is there room within your philosophy for the mystic?"

"Yes," the engineer named Rolc replied, "without question."

"Don't help these psychopaths," the other engineer, whose name was Ginh, snapped. "They've conquered our world, they hold our children hostage! They want to drag the universe back into another dark age!"

"None of which precludes a discussion of mysticism," Rolc said. "Forgive my colleague. He is one of the greatest minds of our culture, but he allows his passions to overwhelm him at times."

"You're a fuzzy-minded fool," Ginh said. "Fine, waste the damned Yateveo's time with your nonsense. Means he's not off killing someone."

"I take it there is some controversy to your theories?" Kreesh said. His "voice" came from one of the converted Axolli creatures. "You are here because your own records indicate you are two of the three greatest minds of your people."

"Who, pray tell, is the third?" Ginh asked.

"Ambassador Neste."

Ginh made a sound akin to a snort. "Please, Neste is no serious scientist. He spends too much time amusing himself with the childish novelties of other cultures. He hasn't done serious work for ages."

"Your commosphere seems to credit him with making extraordinary breakthroughs in spatial anchoring technology."

"Lucky amateur," Ginh said, but Rolc heard the pride slip into the old man's voice.

"I'm curious why you brought us here," Rolc said. "While I'm happy to discuss my theories and beliefs with you, I will do nothing to harm my people or strengthen your position."

"We'll see. Tell me why you, a scientist with an intimate knowledge of the workings of the universe, entertains the notion that one may gain a greater understanding of truth by methods other than pure intellect?"

"Her assembly was faulty," Ginh remarked. "A maker's defect."

"Hush, you bitter old thing," Rolc said. "My studies have shown me that there are fundamental elements of the universe that our conventional knowledge does not explain."

"Yet!" Ginh said. "Doesn't explain *yet*. Just because it might take a while to suss out doesn't mean we start thinking that giant balls of gravity and plasma control our future actions or begin praying to id constructs."

Rolc ignored her colleague and continued.

"Our kind predicated much of our spatial engineering disciplines on the discovery that sections of this universe's space-time have . . . 'divots' in them, scattered across the whole of creation."

"Divots?" the Yateveo elder asked.

"Weak spots, gouges. We have found it is much easier to build multi-spatial constructs in these weak points, and they also seem to be places where psychic powers, like telepathy, work much more effectively."

"That is anecdotal," Ginh said. "There has never been a convincing finding as to any quantifiable improvement in psi talents near these anomalies, or that they appreciably improve the speed or quality of spatial architecture. Junk science, Rolc."

"Aren't you the one who just said to be patient waiting for answers to unanswered questions?" Rolc snapped back.

"Do these weak points affect the overall cohesion of the space-time?" Kreesh asked.

The Yateveo heard the smile in Rolc's voice.

"I'm sure you wish that were true, given your teleology toward entropy. The fact is, it might very well. However, as my colleague here would be eager to jump in and point out, we don't have enough data from enough sample points to see if the phenomenon is truly universal or if it has any impact on entropy as a cosmic force. Sorry to disappoint."

"Besides, even if it does," Ginh said with a mocking tone, "there are mitigating agencies working against entropy, aren't there, Rolc, old girl!" The scientist laughed. "Tell him about the dark matter, oh please tell him."

"Take your own advice, you windbag," Rolc said, "and shut up."

"What about the dark matter?" Kreesh spotted one of his aides, making his way past the guards at the door. Rolc remained silent. "Tell me, or I'll have the 'windbag' here shot and then I'll ask you again."

"It's nothing, a theory. I believe some agency, long ago, seeded the universe with subatomic machines, something far smaller and more advanced than the picotech we commonly use today . . . attotechnology perhaps, maybe even plancktech. These devices . . . their mass and energy density could have been sown as a method of slowing the entropic decay of the universe."

"Why does your colleague scoff at your theory? Why do you wish to not speak of it?"

Silence. Kreesh leveled a rip gun at Ginh.

"Because the theory requires an advanced species in existence *prior* to the great cosmic expansion that jump-started the universe as we know it," Ginh blurted out. "Which seems impossible."

"You're both holding something back from me. Tell me or thousands of your children will suffer and die."

"No, please. The background radiation," Rolc said, defeated. "It may be a form of microwave networking."

"What? What are you saying?"

"If this hypothetical advanced species existed . . . they may have linked these subatomic dark matter machines to a universal network. It would require localized use, you understand, given relativity, but . . ."

"Eldest." It was Kreesh's aide. "I have news, most urgent."

"It had best be," Kreesh said, irritated.

"Shield Pact forces have taken positions on the Queen's Road. They blockade all the passages off Triban."

"Unfortunate," Kreesh rumbled, "but not unexpected."

"The mighty, the legendary Yateveo," Ginh sneered.

"Ginh . . ." Rolc said. "Don't."

"Apparently, not as superior as data demonstrates." Ginh laughed. "You tyrants always . . ."

Kreesh fired the rip gun. Ginh's brief gasp of pain as the beam crushed and crumpled him into a clear puddle of fluid soothed a touch of the anger that churned in the elder. Rolc sobbed and rushed to his dead friend's remains.

"I'm afraid our chat about philosophy and theoretical science will have to wait, Professor Rolc. Rest assured you will make great strides in your research for the glory of the Nemesis. Excuse me." He paused at the doorway and whispered to the guard. "I want this Tribanni opened up. I want its mind intact and its personality . . . dissolved. Make sure it doesn't try to end its existence."

Egath Rolc—one of the greatest minds of her people—mourned her old, cranky, disagreeable friend. She hoped, for the first time in her centuries of existence, that she was wrong, that her theory was junk science. Because Rolc didn't just believe in mysticism. If she was right, she believed in magic.

They were ready to set out from Norama that afternoon. Chain made sure to oversee stocking the Galaxie and his truck with supplies, and the High Marshal and general provided them with plenty of military-grade equipment and weapons. Pana brought Ray two small clear cubes. Each had a unique symbol on it. "This"—she held one up—"is your comm ject, and this is a standard military-issue plaser ject."

"Oh . . . okay. Thanks. What does any of that mean?"

"This one is like a 'cell phone,'" she said, holding up one of the cubes. "This one is a weapon augment. They both last about an xtent." She saw Ray's confused look. "A month?" He nodded. "Put this side here against your skin and touch the symbol. It doesn't hurt. You'll see a display come up before your eyes, and you'll be able to summon it or dismiss it with a thought. You can also set your own preferences on it. The plaser augment display will appear when you think of it. It has the discharge properties of a light pistol, and there are inhibitors to keep you safe until you know how to use it. It's simple—point and fire. I'll teach you."

"I think I'm going to have a lot of questions."

"If you need help, comm me." She walked off to check on Ambassador Neste.

Chain looked at the ject cubes when Ray walked over. "Going native?"

"Are these things okay?"

"They are. Picotech, tiny little bio-organic constructs. They set up shop in your body and brain. Eventually, they degrade and are flushed out. It usually takes about a month."

"An xtent!" Ray proudly added.

Chain's amused smirk widened.

"You *are* going native. Me, personally, I don't care for a bunch of junk that interfaces in my skull, and Mother help you if you get one with a ton of eye ads built into it."

Ray looked apprehensively at the cube and placed the first one to his wrist. A cold chill went through his body, and the cube darkened. The symbol went red. "Now the gun one," he said and applied the second cube with similar results.

Chain handed Ray a large, white polymer pistol holstered in a nylon-looking shoulder rig. "Here, Plan B. Those augments draw off your body's energy, especially the plaser. That's why I always say carry a hardware backup."

"Plaser?" Ray looked down at the pistol.

"Uh huh. Heavier version of that ject you just took. They call them 'sun guns.' Thing fires a beam of amplified, coherent, jacketed light. It charges the ions along the channel until it hits an object of significant mass, then *boom!*—it converts that mass into super-heated plasma. You get the punch of a fusion gun without all the collateral damage, and the accuracy of a smart laser. A pistol like this one can generate a fireball about the size of a humanoid's head on impact. Standard Shield Pact military issue."

Ray took the rig and the holstered gun.

"Okay, I'm packed now. We ready?" Chain nodded. "Where we headed first?"

"Rudian."

"That a planet? A galaxy?"

"No. A guy. The Chosen One."

Chain's truck led the way again as they took to the Queen's Road. The violet day was torn away by the cold darkness of the infinite highway. Ray tailed the tow truck in the Galaxie, with Pana and Neste as his passengers.

This time, the trip took about six hours. As they approached an exit, Ray saw fire. It was a dancing, flickering sheet of red-and-orange flame. In the fire there were words, shouting out to passersby in loud fonts, in a dozen different languages. Ray could read them, thanks to the ring. They said, "Revival! Come hear the word!"

Chain's truck took the exit and Ray followed him. They were on a narrow, winding dirt road. The only lights besides their headlights were the shimmering band of stars that crossed the heavens—the belt of this galaxy—and the bluish light of a perfectly shaped octagonal moon, low and large in the early evening sky. Fields with rows of some kind of tall, saw-leafed plant flashed by the cars as they sped on. Ray felt a strange pressure in his lungs, then it eased.

"Their atmosphere is a bit off from humanoid-standard," Pana said from the shotgun seat beside Ray. "My environmental web aug just kicked in."

"I think my ring did too," Ray said.

"Are you all right, Your Excellency?" Pana asked Neste.

"Yes. Just fine, thank you. There are some very . . . interesting spatial field patterns up ahead. I've never seen anything like them."

"What does that mean?" Ray asked, glancing back at the Tribanni professor for just a moment.

"This region of space impinges on a dimensional weak point. They exist all over the universe—places where, for some unknown reason, something punched through from another dimension and left a scar, for lack of a better term. Spatial engineers use these points, as do many psychics and thaumaturgists."

"*Thaumaturgists?*" Ray said.

"Yes, wizards. You don't have those on Earth? At any rate, someone is playing with that local weak point to manipulate dimensional energy."

Ray decided to try out his new toy. He concentrated on reaching Chain, and he suddenly felt a tingle down his spine. A window appeared at the corner of his field of vision, and Chain was in it, obviously in the cab of his truck. "Hey," Ray said out loud.

"Just think it," Pana, Neste, and Chain all told him at the same time.

"*Hey,*" Ray thought, "*Neste said somebody's messing around with space around here or something.*"

"Yeah," Chain said into his comm bracelet. "That's our destination. Rudi likes to put on a flashy show."

"*What world is this?*"

"Not a clue. I guess we can ask one of the locals when we meet them."

"*Okay, out,*" Ray thought. He turned back to focusing on the rear bumper of Chain's truck, bouncing on the rutted road. He saw a swarm of something that looked like bats the size of small airplanes cross the lustrous sapphire glow of the strange moon. He thought,

*Great. I hope the locals are friendlier than the thing that wanted to kill me when I was trying to take a leak.*

"You need to hang up the damn comm," Chain blurted out. Ray blushed and directed a thought to his comm to close the connection. Ray suddenly understood how his late grandmother must have felt trying to get the hang of a cell phone.

The dirt road and the crossing spotlights led them to a field half-full of cars and trucks in various states of disrepair and maintenance. Most of them were splattered with thick mud. There was an expansive tent set up in the middle of the field. The tent had pennants fluttering all about it, and it reminded Ray of an old-time circus. The powerful spotlights in the sky were being generated from what looked like dinner-plate-sized discs on the ground. There was one on either side of the entrance flaps.

When they got out of the cars, they heard singing—loud, boisterous, joyful singing from a multitude of voices.

"Good," Chain said, "We didn't miss the show."

They approached the entrance. A four-foot-tall being with no discernible neck and pebbly, mustard-colored overlapping plates for skin sat on a stool next to the door. A battered-looking rifle was propped against the stool.

"A love donation of five grabthars is encouraged," the doorman said.

"Oh, this should be delightful," Neste said. "I've heard of these but never experienced one." Pana looked like she was about to dive into a grove of Yateveo. "Be at peace, Ratari. We're safe here."

"They're all with me. You take commcash?" Chain asked, showing his bracelet.

The doorman smiled, revealing a single golden fang implant among his rows of sharp teeth. "The Opened Scroll says all things are of one thing." He held up a small device about the size of a pack of cigarettes and scanned Chain's bracelet. "Welcome, seekers. May the Word fill you."

Inside the tent, there were more than a hundred beings. The majority of them looked like they were of the same species as the doorman. However, scattered about were other species as well. The whole audience was singing. Some were wildly dancing in the rows and the aisles, jumping, flipping, shaking their bodies, and in general having a good time. The music was contagious, Ray had to admit. To his ears, it was a weird cross of blues and techno, but he really liked it. The lyrics were simple and repetitive and encouraged you to join in, and even those not dancing were on their feet singing.

Near the DJ, standing at the end of the central aisle, was a humanoid with a wide, enraptured grin on his face. He had his arms raised to the heavens as he swayed to the music. He looked to Ray like a guy pushing sixty. His face was florid, craggy, and lined. A blotch of what looked like sea-green fungus resided on his left cheek. He had the nose of an old drunk who had gotten in a few bar fights. His hair was a sandy mop of tight curls that made you think of a kid's mussed hair —messy, but in a cute way—or maybe an old guy hitting the disco with his brand new perm.

He was tall, close to seven feet, and stocky. He had an impressive solid and perfectly oval beer-gut. The belly was restrained by a loose V-collared tunic with wide bell sleeves and equally comfortable bell-bottom pants. The whole ensemble appeared to be made of sparkly gold satin and looked vaguely like really expensive pajamas. The man saw Chain and his party and winked at the Ranger. That was when Ray noticed that this man wore a Ranger's signet among numerous other bits of ostentatious bling on his fingers.

The music rose to a crescendo, teasing, stringing on the crowd, bringing them to a near frenzy.

"I've never seen this before," Neste said over a party-comm call to the others. "The crowd's emotional state is actually affecting the local spatial-time cohesion. And that being seems to be the nexus of all the activity."

"That," Chain said, "is Rudian. Keep watching; it gets better."

The DJ held the high as long as he could and then brought the music to a sudden end. The crowd erupted in cheers, screams, shouts of praise, and laughter. They were good and warmed up.

"Thank you, dear Oskar"—Rudian gestured to the DJ—"for starting out this night by bringing our spirits to joy through your wonderful music! Doesn't he kick ass, everybody?" The crowd went wild again with cheers, applause and hoots. "Yes, he does, yes, he does."

Rudian began walking from one side of the tent to the other, making and holding eye contact with individuals all throughout the audience. His voice was naturally strong, reassuring, and booming, needing no amplifier. "It does my hearts good to see so many of you here tonight, willing, eager, aching to know the Word, to hear the Truth."

There was a murmur of agreement and encouragement throughout the tent.

"Now, I know many of you are here because you heard 'that crazy preacher down the road puts on a good show.'"

Laughter rolled across the audience.

"I *do* put on a damn good show!" Rudian paused for a perfect beat and looked around the crowd before he picked up again. "I was once a seeker, like many of you. I grew up on Illgear. I was inducted into the mysteries of the Fellowship of the Whispered Word as a child, yes, I was."

A tremor of something moved through the crowd—fear, nervousness. Rudian smiled brightly and waved a dismissive hand. "Have no fear, my people! I know, oh I know, you have heard the stories of the Fellowship, of their secret cults, of their forbidden texts, of the terrible sacrifices, and their other . . . unnatural ways."

Chain tried to keep the smile off his face. He and Rudian exchanged glances but the preacher stayed in character and looked away. He was telling a ghost story now, stitching it seamlessly into his pitch.

His voice boomed like thunder, bolstering their courage. "I do not fear the Whispered Word, for we have the Proclaimed Word! I do not worry about the secrets of the universe they hide, for I have opened and seen their scrolls, and I . . . know . . . the Truth!"

The crowd's mood churned, going from apprehension to titillation.

"I learned their ways, all their secrets, all their vast wisdom and hidden powers and then"—he held aloft a tattered cloth scroll—"I liberated the first scroll of their teachings from their jealous grasp! Behold, my people, the Opened Scroll of the Proclaimed Word!"

Rudian nodded toward Oskar, who slowly began to bring up some deep, somber music. Rudian waved the scroll around, pointing from attentive face to attentive face.

"Lo, these many years, have I sought to bring its powerful wisdom, its supernatural powers to those thirsting for truth, aching for soul-deep understanding of the infinite. Tonight, my dear, dear people, I give you . . . the Word!"

Oskar broke into another powerful moody number as the crowd surged to their feet in praise and applause. A beautiful woman—dressed in a glittering golden gown—came from the front row and joined the DJ. She began to wail and sing powerfully along with the music. The song built in force and tempo, bringing the crowd back to a near frenzy yet again.

"This . . . is . . . remarkable!" Neste said through the comm link. "Somehow, this Rudian has tapped into vast amounts of cross-planar energy, and he's doing it through his handling of the crowd. There are no signs of him possessing any augments that would allow this. Is it part of his biology? How is he doing this?"

"He's always told me," Chain replied, "that he has to believe so they can believe. He said that's how it works."

There was more singing, more raucous dancing. It built to a cathartic conclusion that left the performers and the audience sweating, smiling, and humming with drive. Rudian preached and Ray found himself nodding in agreement with a lot of the message.

Rudian spoke of fixing your perceptions to bring about positive change. Making your focus your reality. He wasn't telling these people to depend on a god or a church or a government to make their lives more livable, but to count on themselves. It reminded Ray of stuff his pop and mom had said to him. He wanted to believe; in a lot of ways, he already did. The preacher used anecdotes from his time as a Ranger and as a disciple of the Whispered Word—whatever that was, exactly—to demonstrate how terrible times in one's life could be overcome, could become a victory.

"Somewhere along the line, the word 'faith' got a bad rap." Rudian's voice was still strong, his face, hair, and tunic all wet with sweat. "It became childish, naive in a universe where technology can make normal people into gods, where the idea of a higher power is so easily dismissed, mocked, and cast down. Miracles exist everywhere, but we no longer see them.

"My people, I *have* seen, and I have lived how far down you can fall. I have seen returns, recoveries, from that dark prison, as epic as any fable or myth." He paused and scanned the crowd, seeming to connect with each and every face, every heart. Ray thought of Juanita. "The only power you'll ever need in your darkest hours is within you, my beloved. If you believe . . . if . . . you . . . believe."

Rudian paused as if he had heard something. He scanned the crowd. "I can feel your suffering, your pain. I can show you the power of faith, the power of absolute belief. If you are broken, come unto me. If you are sick, or beset by darkness, come unto me. Come and see the power that resides within you!"

Oskar and the singer began to perform again; their music low, subdued, so as to add, not distract, from Rudian's call.

Slowly, shyly at first, they began to come forward. The first was a local, a child who was missing his arm at the elbow.

"We don't have the money or a way to take him to a world where they could repair the damage or replace his arm, minister," the father said, his head low. "Can you help him, please?!"

Rudian knelt by the child and spoke to him quietly for a moment.

The preacher stood. He placed his hand on the child's head, closed his eyes, and looked skyward. At first, nothing happened, then an audible gasp went up as the audience caught sight of the boy's arm regrowing before their eyes.

"He's a biokinetic!" Neste exclaimed out loud. Several attendees near the Tribanni shushed him. He switched back to the private comm chat as he spoke to Chain. "I've never heard of a documented one able to perform cellular regeneration to this level."

"Rudi's talent pretty much goes off the scale. It's based in large part on the size of the crowd he can rile up."

"Of course, he's using that spatial energy he's somehow cooking up with the crowd to power the regeneration. Ingenious!"

The child's arm was completely regrown. The audience went wild, crying, shouting out praise, and wildly applauding. The boy's mother was hugging him tightly and weeping. The father fell to his knees before Rudian.

"Get up, friend." He helped the farmer to his feet. "I didn't do this. Your son's faith did."

A few more people came up: the lame, the dying, the sick of body and of spirit, and one by one, they were healed. The work did seem to take a toll on Rudian. He looked pale, and he sweat profusely. Once, he almost fell over, but someone caught him.

Then came one final sales pitch, the commercial that went along with such an excellent night of entertainment.

"My people, my beloved," Rudian began. "The power is within each and every one of you. *You* are the Proclaimed Word, you are your own salvation. As we depart tonight and go our separate ways, know that we are *not* separated. All things are one thing."

He held aloft a scroll. It looked much newer and nicer than the one he had begun the evening with—a bit cheaper too.

"If you would like to study the mysteries that opened my eyes to the true power of the self, the secrets of how the universe works . . . then I want to give each of you a gift."

"Here we go," Chain whispered to Ray. "Here comes the hook."

"This is a painstaking recreation of the Opened Scroll of the Proclaimed Word—the text that I liberated at great personal peril from the Silent Archive of Illgear, and that, in turn, liberated me. Within its transcendental words you will discover truth, wealth, and power. Now, if I could, my dear friends, I would give these high-quality reproductions to you for free. However, necessity demands that to continue my crusade, and to support my acolytes and myself, I must ask a love offering of at least twenty grabthars, which will go toward us spreading the Proclaimed Word to every corner of this dark and conflicted universe. Please, beloved, give. Give if you can. Thank you so much. Good night, and have a safe journey home!"

With that, prerecorded music came on, and Rudian, Oskar, and the young singer departed through a tent flap. A group of ushers, most of them locals—including the guy who had been covering the front door—moved among the crowd with baskets, collecting donations and passing out copies of the scroll. Neste purchased one.

They walked around the tent while car engines roared to life and headlights snapped on in the field as the audience began to depart. They found Rudian, Oskar, and the girl passing a slender wand-pipe back and forth among themselves, wreathed in a cloud of pungent smoke.

"A little post-show communing?" Chain asked with a grin.

"Chain!" Rudian nearly shouted. The preacher lumbered over and hugged the tow-truck driver. "You crusty old bastard! How are you?"

"That stuff legal?"

"We don't intend to hang around long enough to find out. What brings you out to this backwater spiral arm?" Rudian paused when he saw Pana; his smile widened, and a light came on behind his eyes. "Hello, and good knight," he said to her, his eyebrows rising. Chain put his arm around Rudian's wide shoulders and shook his head. Pana's expression was one of restrained disgust.

"Down, killer. This is Pana; she's with us. Ray, Neste, this is Rudian Thop, the absolute best bullshitter in the Known Galaxies."

Rudian walked over to Pana, bowed, and took her hand. Her eyes widened at the gesture and then narrowed. The preacher struggled to lift her hand to kiss it. He quickly stopped trying.

"Pleasure," he said to her, none of the honey leaving his voice. Ray gave a casual nod from the back. Rudian returned it, jovially.

Neste approached Rudian. "I wanted to thank you, minister. That was the most impressive and effective display of interpersonal manipulation and biokinesis I have ever witnessed."

"Thanks," Rudian said, a wry twinkle in his eyes. "That means a lot coming from someone of your status, Ambassador."

There was a pause for a second. "Chain said nothing about my position. Have we met before?"

"Never, just the way you speak. You're used to being treated a certain way, and you know your way around a polite conversation. You have a silver tongue, Neste."

Neste chuckled. "I haven't had a tongue for close to four hundred years, but if I did manifest one now, it would be silver, I assure you."

"This is Oskar"—Rudian gestured to the DJ—"and his bonded, Kerri." The singer smiled.

"You guys were great." Chain took Rudian by the arm and walked him away from the group. "You know why I'm here."

Rudian nodded. "Yeah, you need me for something. Chain, I'm out of the Ranger business, brother. There's no liquidity in it."

"You and I both know you ain't out 'til that ring comes off your finger. This is important, Rudi. I need you. Nobody else can pull it off."

"Chain, baby!" Rudian shrugged off Chain's arm. "I got a good gig going here. The money's not bad . . . getting better. You see my fungus?" He pointed to the green phosphorescent patch on his cheek. "It's a Narworly, cultured just for me! You know how much those go for in the populous sectors, in the cores? I'm making fungus money now, Chain!"

"What are they talking about?" Ray asked. He was standing with the others by the tent and the ramshackle fleet of trucks and vans that made up the transportation for the revival's staff. Already, the local workers were breaking down the site. They saw Rudian gesticulating widely and pointing to himself, to his face.

"I think he's telling him about the fungus," Kerri said.

"Oh no," Oskar sighed.

"I'm getting the word out to the people who need to hear it," Rudian said. "Folks out here don't have many prospects, not much hope. The Gatterack Coalition, the Shield Pact . . . those guys don't give a damn about these folks. This is drive-by country to them."

"Yeah, and hiding out here keeps the Whispering Monks off your ass too, right? Little added bonus?"

Rudian stopped but kept his back to Chain.

"I am out. O-U-T."

They were both silent. The sound of the last car leaving the field faded and was gone.

"You planning to run forever?"

"Running beats lying in the dirt. If that whack-job-cult-turned-major-universal-religion catches up to me, I'll be lucky if they just kill me for stealing their damn scroll. No thanks."

Chain started to walk back to the others. Rudian turned back to Chain.

"Why did you say nobody else could pull it off? What is *it*?"

"What do you care?" Chain said. "I'm sure Windrah can do it when we find her. Sorry to have troubled you, old friend."

"You are very, very bad at trying to bait and switch. You did good with the walkaway—perfect, almost—but then you reached too far too fast. You're about as subtle as a plasma enema. I'm curious, that's all. What near-death experience am I turning down?"

"Lera is locked up at Balisk. We're breaking her out."

Rudian roared in laughter. It echoed across the dark field and made Ray and the others, who were talking quietly near the tent, turn.

"I think he just asked him," Ray said.

"I know that laugh," Oskar said. "That's his 'hell no' laugh."

"I need her," Chain said to Rudian. "She can get us into where we need to go. No one else can, and no one but you can talk us in and out of that prison."

"Balisk isn't a prison." Rudian wiped a tear from his eye. "It's what lies beyond death. They put her there because it's the one place in the whole of creation that can hold that deranged, narcissistic misanthrope."

"You sound frightened."

"I am, and I already told you, you are *terrible* at trying to play someone. It's . . . it's just cringe-inducing."

"Okay, no games then. The Yateveo are back."

"What are you talking about? That's nonsense, children's stories." He paused and looked Chain over. "You're telling the truth. At least, you think it's the truth."

"It is. I have less than a week to stop them, or a lot of people are going to die. Worlds are going to die, Rudi. Eventually, it will spread out to worlds like this, to people like this. War always does."

Rudian scratched his head, put his hands on his hips, and looked up at the galaxy's stars. He let air slip past his lips, and it sounded a bit like a whoopee cushion deflating. He looked back to Chain. "That last bit . . . that was good." He turned back toward the tent and began to walk to the others. The tent was collapsing like a souffle as the workers did their job. "Okay," he said, walking past Chain. "I'm in. You're right, no one else could do it. But, whoever sent you out here with a Shield Pact knight and a Tribanni ambassador, they are going to make a very, very large love offering for this."

"The biggest." Chain smiled as he followed the preacher back to the others.

# 19

After Rudian joined them, the party split up. Chain said they needed to cover more ground. So he, Pana, and Rudian headed off to pick up someone named Lera Trade on a world called Balisk. Everyone said "Balisk" like they had poison in their mouths.

Ray and Neste were sent off after another Ranger, a man named Skein. "He doesn't go by that name anymore," Chain had told them, "but if you seek him under his true name, you'll find him quicker."

"What is he called now?" Neste asked.

"Skye Salvo," Chain said.

"Oh, my!" Neste exclaimed. "Master Ranger, you never said you knew famous people."

"What's a Skye Salvo?" Ray asked.

"One of the most popular performers in the Known Galaxies," Neste said. "I had no idea he's a Ranger."

"You keep up with intergalactic pop culture?" Ray asked the Tribanni.

"My children adore him. My daughter saw him on Chammer two comps ago."

"You'll find him easy enough," Chain said. "Tell him what we're up against. Tell him we need his help with Ajeet."

"Who's—?"

"I'll tell you later," Chain interrupted.

He had a long, private discussion with Neste about something and then saw the ambassador and Ray off.

"Get moving. Head for a world called Onao once you get Skein on board." He slapped Ray on the shoulder. "Be careful."

"*You* be careful. You don't turn up, I'm coming to look for you."


They were on the Queen's Road in less than an hour, the Galaxie purring along, the stars streaming by them. Ray asked Cassandra to play him some Skye Salvo. The music wasn't bad, a little discordant, like early punk, but layered with some complex melodies and lyrics that were pretty deep. Cassandra played one of his more popular songs, a ballad of sorts called "Maven in Red Snow." It was a song of a woman who had lost everything—her family, her loves, her history, and her heart—and who sought revenge for her loss. It was haunting as well as good music. Ray decided he liked Skye Salvo.

"I hope I am wrong about who 'Ajeet' is," Neste said.

"You know them?" Ray asked.

"The only Ajeet I am aware of is . . ."

"What?"

"'Ajeet' is the only known name of the most prolific and dangerous serial killer in the Known Galaxies. She's never been caught, and her victims are legion."

"Wow. You guys have those too. Well, if Chain is planning to go hunting for her . . . that sounds . . . pretty awful."

"I hope that I am mistaken. I don't see a way such a being could help us reach the goal of liberating my home world in any way."

"Yeah. I haven't known Chain long. I do trust him, but I don't understand him at all."

"It seems sometimes we can know the soul of a person and not truly know a thing about them."

"You guys believe in souls?"

"Some of us do, some don't. Our beliefs vary as much as any other peoples'. As for me, I think I began to believe in more than the mere physicality of life when my children were born."

"My mom used to say to my brother and me, when we were little, that she saw God's face in our eyes when we were born." That seemed like another life now.

"Children can turn the crassest of us into philosophers," Neste said. Some sadness leaked through his voice as he said it.

They drove on, past flaring suns and icy wastelands of vacuum. "Can I ask you a question, Neste?" Ray asked after they had been driving a few hours.

"Of course, Ray, anything."

"Your daughter likes this music, this Skye guy?"

"Yes, very much."

"Are your kids . . . like smaller versions of you? Are they . . . built? Born? You said 'born' before. I'm not trying to offend you. We just don't have anything like . . . you on Earth. I just want to understand."

Neste chuckled. "No offense at all. Our bodies are different, but in many ways, we are the same. We were humanoids once, long ago, very much like you."

"No kidding?" Ray kept his eyes on the road.

"No kidding. As our understanding of technology increased, we made choices about our specie's development. We evolved slowly into this form over hundreds of thousands of years. We have no biological tissue or systems anymore. Our senses and our ability to manipulate the world around us are much more adaptable than in our organic forms.

"My current brain, for example, is a virtual simulation of my organic brain that I had four hundred years ago. The only difference is that, with spatial information technology engineering, I have a virtually unlimited number of brains to access, process, network, and deploy as circumstances demand."

"I can't even imagine that."

"Have you ever wished you had multiple yous to deal with all the things you had to attend to in a day?"

"Yeah, sure."

"It's kind of like that. You can give your undivided attention to pretty much everything at once. You can construct a full or partial brain almost instantly to deal with what you must at the moment. For example, I've had several brains formulating spatial calculations to unphase Triban since the meeting in the High Marshal's office. Still working on it."

"So you guys just kind of make your bodies now from the beginning of your life 'til the end?"

"No. We saw the danger in that, in losing ourselves to . . . over-engineering. Our solution is that, when we decide to have children, we use the virtual simulation of our old biological genetic code. Our genetic blueprints are reproduced chemically. Some of us choose partners, and we combine our genetic templates with single or multiple partners. Others prefer to become parents alone. Our children are born fully organic, humanoid. We let them grow, let them experience life as we used to do so long ago, as you do now."

"That's really cool." Ray smiled.

"Do you have any children, Ray?"

Jess was there, her warm, pale arms tangled around his neck, her soft lips at his ear. Ray pushed her memory away, focused on the road. "Thought about it a few times . . . it didn't work out. How old are your kids?"

"My son, Tion, is in his forties. He's an advocate on a world in the Aquillia Domain. He has a wonderful family. I am a grandfather!" Both Neste and Ray laughed at that. "He will most likely remain humanoid and eventually pass, but I hold out hope he will change his mind. We don't force the transition on any of our children. If they remain humanoid, they are still Tribanni. My daughter, Veme, is fifteen . . . a very . . . volatile age."

Ray chuckled. "Yeah, I bet. Mom used to say when we hit our teens is when me and Ben started giving her gray hairs. Veme lives with you back on Norama?"

"She did. She's back on Triban, right now."

Ray looked over, eyes widening at the revelation.

"I'm . . . I'm so sorry, Neste. You must be going crazy right now. How are you staying so calm?"

"The 'me' you're talking to now, the one I've been maintaining since this started, is an iteration of all those brains I told you about. It's at the forefront. I assure you, Ray, deep inside, I am going crazy. I'm scared and angry, and desperate to get to her, to make sure she's okay. I'm afraid my little girl is already dead."

"No, she's not." Ray clutched the wheel tighter. "Chain's got a plan, and it's going to work."

"I hope our faith in your fellow Ranger is not misplaced. His mysterious plan looks to be based on putting ourselves in the hands of holy men and criminals, singers and serial killers."

"Chain will get us in. Your daughter, Veme, she's going to be okay. She's going to be fine."

The frantic, wild-fire thoughts, the same hollow words spilling out of his mouth now. Ray had said them like a prayer, to Jess as she lay unresponsive in the ambulance, the paramedics fighting to pull her back. *Do you know what she took, do you know what she took?*

"Everything will be okay. You're going to see your daughter again, and it's all going to be good, okay? We'll get her out of there, don't worry."

Neste was silent for a long time.

The exit off the Queen's Road took them deep below dark waters. The off-ramp and the roads were all inside sealed, transparent tunnels. Ray felt a little like a hamster in a giant Habitrail. The city, what he could see of it through the murk and distortion of the water, was built into and around towering rainbow mountain ranges of coral. The buildings' architecture was all based on curves, not straight lines—ovals, stacked one on top of the next, domes, and bubbles, drifting free, tethered by gently swaying tunnel-roads. Lights, as in any other major city, burned everywhere, and Ray saw schools of small underwater craft speeding along lanes established by light buoys.

"I think . . . this is . . . Durco," Neste said. "It's an independent republic . . . at least in name."

The tubeway that was bringing them in widened, and several lanes all began to merge into a long, immobile snarl of traffic.

"There an accident up ahead?" Ray asked.

"More likely a checkpoint. Durco is a police state. A very shiny police state, but still a police state."

They made slow, stop-and-start progress as they crawled ahead. "We going to have trouble with these guys? Should I flash the ring?"

"I doubt it would do much good. Let me talk to them, if you don't mind."

"Knock yourself out."

After almost an hour of slowly advancing, the Galaxie arrived at a series of distorted, wavering energy barriers blocking the road. Humanoids in dark-green coveralls wearing body armor and helmets, cradled rifles with vertical, rectangular barrels. The guards were clustered near a series of small booth-like structures that divided each lane. Ray became very aware of some creatures that looked a lot like larger Komodo Dragons on leashes held by some of the troopers. He assumed they were the local equivalent of drug-sniffing dogs. A trooper armed with a tablet-looking sheet of polymer instead of a rifle walked up and tapped on Ray's window. He rolled it down.

"State your business in the republic," the trooper said.

"Need to see my green card?" Ray said with a smile. He couldn't tell the trooper's response behind the tinted visor of his helmet, but he was guessing pissed. Ray's smile dropped. "That's a joke . . . where I come from . . . I don't even have a green card." He did his best Texas accent, "Born in the USA." Still no response. He looked over to Neste. "Yeah, you handle this."

"I am Ambassador Neste Maji, of the Tribanni Encompassment. I am transmitting my official credentials to your comm right now. This is my diplomatic driver. This vehicle is my official transport. We are here to see the Skye Salvo concert and hopefully to speak with your secretary of foreign affairs."

The troopers looked from one to another. The one with the tablet-comm stepped away to make a call.

"Nice transport," one of the troopers said to Ray. "Earth?"

"Yeah," Ray said with more than a little pride in his voice.

"Ford?"

"Yeah." Ray was amazed. "'64 Galaxie 500."

"Everyone out," the trooper said. "We must inspect the vehicle."

"This is a sovereign state transport of the Tribanni Encompassment," Neste said. "Section 461 of the Multi-Lateral Civilization Accords clearly states that . . ."The trooper waved his rifle. "Out." Ray and Neste reluctantly climbed out.

*Should I deploy intruder counter-measures?* Cassandra asked silently, directly to Ray's internal comm channel.

*No,* Ray thought back. *Not now, but don't let them hurt you.*

*I didn't know you cared.*

The troopers motioned Ray and Neste to stand aside. They remained covered by two troopers while the others looked through the trunk and lifted the hood to admire and comment on the engine. Ray spotted a few troopers carrying off boxes of their supplies.

"Hey! That's our stuff!"

The troops covering them moved threateningly close, their weapons humming to life.

"Let them take it," Neste said softly. "That's how things are done in places like this. Regardless of how opulent it may seem around here, there are shortages of everything for all but the ruling class—medicine, food, any luxury items. Think of it as the price of admission."

They found Evan's old forty-five in the glove compartment along with the nine millimeter Ray had taken off the Paragon Security guards back on Earth. They uncovered all the weapons stored in the trunk and carted them off with the supplies. Ray still had the plaser pistol under his jacket, but there was no way he'd stand a chance against this firepower with just that gun.

The trooper with the tablet returned.

"Welcome to the Republic of Durco, Ambassador. Please proceed. The secretary of state has asked you to be his guest this evening for the concert. He has also arranged rooms for you in the city's finest hotel. The details have been sent to your comm. You can move along. We will be required to keep the weapons you have brought with you. They are illegal here. Including the one your driver has on him."

Rifles were again pointed at Ray. He carefully pulled aside his jacket and let one of the soldiers remove it from the holster.

"I see. And what of our other cargo?" Neste asked.

"What other cargo?" the trooper asked, coolly.

"I see. Well, thank you."

The two walked back to the car. Ray paused to glare at one of the troopers who was holding Evan's pistol.

"Hey. Hey, you. I better get that back, you hear me? Or we're going to have a problem."

"Ray, please," Neste said, "get in the car."

The force-barrier was lifted from in front of the car and they drove past the guard booths. Immediately, Ray received a notification from his comm that many of its functions had been disabled by the central commosphere. His plaser augmentation announced it had also been remotely disabled.

"I hate this place already."

"Welcome to Durco," Neste said. "I'm pretty sure 'I hate this place' is its tourism slogan."

# 20

The prison planet Balisk was perched precariously on the lips of a monster.

Region 8171-P was nestled between the fringes of the Ement Triumphate, a backwater galactic government of a few hundred systems, and the Noffen Freehold, one of the many far-flung governments that made up the Shield Pact. Neither government claimed 8171-P and for good reason. A thousand -solar-mass black hole squatted in the center of the dead, curdled space.

A single world—a massive, solid planet roughly twenty times the size of a gas giant—hung at the edge of the place where light could still exist, at the fringe of the event horizon. The planet was made of two-hundred-fold, flexible-reinforced graphene. Twelve-hundred Tribanni-manufactured spatial anchors held the planet fast against the relentless, insistent hunger of the singularity.

The planet and the project to build it had been named Balisk back when it was on the production drawing board of the Kouvri Security Corporation more than a century ago. Kouvri was a well-known brand respected across the Known Galaxies. The company did everything from producing restraint systems and personal protection for law enforcement, to training and deploying prison personnel, to constructing and managing prison facilities on planets and building prison space stations.

Balisk was Kouvri Corp.'s most ambitious project in its five-century history. The concept was to create the most secure, inescapable prison facility in existence, tailored for the worst of the worst of intergalactic criminals. It took twenty-five years to build and required intensive Tribanni spatial engineering to allow the prison planet to exist at the very knife's edge of annihilation. After five years of shakedown to ensure everything was working as it should, Balisk had opened for business and found plenty of clients among the nearly infinite number of stellar governments within the Known Galaxies.

For the last seventy years, every hardened criminal knew that there was a place beyond the hell of prison, a place from which no one ever returned, crouching at the very edge of existence, of normal time and space. Death was better than to be sentenced to Balisk, and many convicts had taken their lives before they could be transferred.

A gleaming, armored luxury transport, a Histron LXE 1000, made its way toward the prison planet on the single route along the Queen's Highway that led there. The transport's sharp angles and metallic green hull gave it an almost insectile appearance as it sped along on the best hover suspensors money could buy.

Chain piloted the luxury craft dressed in a dark and expensive corporate suit. Pana, out of her knightly vestments, was also dressed in steel-gray, first-class corporate couture and sat in the cockpit beside Chain. She had removed her ward, the silver disc on her forehead.

In the back, Rudian sat, sipping a drink. The revival preacher was now wearing a shimmering, custom-made suit of psi-silk, which made Chain's and Pana's costly clothing look off-the-rack. The silk was what the Arachnid super-telepaths—who had conquered and feasted upon the Soundless Galaxy—used to spin their interplanetary soul-webs. The silk had to be stolen from the Soundless Galaxy, at great danger and expense. The material amplified, sweetened, and projected the emotional and telepathic energy of the suit's wearer.

Only a few such suits could be made each year because of the scarcity of the silk.

Sitting across from Rudian was a humanoid with lemon-colored skin and a small island of black hair at the top of his elongated head. A ring of black pupil-less eyes circled like a crown above a star-shaped mouth full of tiny pebble-like teeth and suction cups. Small pairs of pits sat in between the eyes and provided the being with the senses of smell and hearing. The humanoid wore a high-collared tan shirt with a pale-beige jacket and pants, all of which looked amazingly expensive.

"Maybe you can explain this to me since you're a Ranger," Pana said to Chain in a low voice. "Balisk Ultra-Max Prison has been around, what? A century, correct?"

"Give or take." Chain nodded.

"Her Majesty, the Queen, and her children, built her Road at the dawn of the universe."

"Correct."

"How could they have had the foresight to put in a route that would lead directly to an artificial planet that wouldn't be built until countless eons later, which was balanced at the edge of a massive black hole? How could they know all that way back then?"

"Simple," Chain said. "The Royals are gods. They see everything, know everything." He glanced over to see her reaction and broke into a wry smile when she looked less than happy with his summation.

"A simple 'I don't know' would have been fine," she said.

"The way it was explained to me was that the Road is . . . aware, to a certain degree. It senses changes in the universe outside its hyper-space tunnels and makes tweaks and adjustments as needed."

"A road driving up to the edge of a black hole is quite the tweak," Pana said.

"Routes that led to worlds where the star goes nova or burns out, things like that, those routes are blocked as hazards—roads to nowhere. New space stations, rehabilitated worlds, artificial planets—the Queen's Road constantly scans for new connection points like those and builds itself new routes and exits as needed. It's the greatest feat of engineering in the history of the universe."

"I don't know of any NOI life form or disembodied intelligence, not even the Ghosts of Yet to Come, capable of that kind of predictive capability. It boggles the mind."

"Call it the Royals' magic if it makes you feel any better," Chain said.

"It does not," Pana said.

In the back seat, Rudian drained his tumbler, letting the ice spheres tinkle as the last of the burning, smoky alcohol slid down his throat. His companion looked on a little disapprovingly.

"How did I get here, again?" the yellow man asked.

"Don't you recall the discussion in your office?" Rudian asked smoothly, setting the empty glass in the cup holder built into the leather armrest of the couch-like back seat. "You insisted, Mr. Vice President . . . on accompanying us." The vice president looked bewildered, but he was trying to hide his confusion. "The inspection . . . of the prisoners?"

"Oh yes, of course," the vice president said. He turned to address Chain, "You there, how long until we reach Balisk?"

"Exit's coming up," Chain said. There was a large window hovering ahead of the exit. The screen announced in numerous languages: BALISK ULTRA-MAX PRISON. RESTRICTED. NO ADMITTANCE BY UNAUTHORIZED PERSONNEL.

"It is," Pana muttered as she nodded to the sky above the exit. A dark maw snarled at them as they drove closer toward it. Light struggled at the edges of the beast's mouth to no avail and then was gone. "May Shylah protect us."

"You are staring into the face of the enemy," Rudian said. "Entropy in its purest form. It exists only to chew things up, devour them, end them. It's very efficient at what it does. At the end of all things, only our friend there and his kin will remain."

"We built the prison here as much for psychological reasons as logistics," the vice president explained. "A prisoner sees they are approaching that . . . thing, they give up all hope."

"An understandable feeling," Pana said.

Chain took the limo down the ramp, and they found themselves in a dimly lit, winding steel corridor. Chain snapped on the limo's lights and noticed that they were being tracked by a multitude of weapon emplacements built into the ceiling, floor, and walls. Their comms all received a curt message: "You are entering a restricted area. Prepare to stop and be searched. Have your identification ready."

"Nice touch," Rudian said to the vice president with a nod of approval, "the tonal architecture and the underlying telepathic flavoring puts the listener right on the defensive."

"Thank you. We've tried to anticipate any contingency, any threat, and address it. We wanted Balisk to be a prison no one would ever dare try to escape from or attempt to break someone out of."

"Yes," Rudian said, fixing himself another drink, "so I've heard."

Ahead of them, a force screen that could repel battlefield-weapons fire lowered and revealed a reinforced hatch that could endure a massive explosive force. It slid open, and the limo pulled inside. The hatch slid shut, and the chamber was filled with blinding light. Seemingly out of nowhere, cylindrical, seven-foot-tall war-constructs—non-organic life forms—appeared. They were bristling with weapons and sensors and completely surrounded the car. "Out . . . now!" barked the one whose hovering holographic ident-code designated him as a commander.

Rudian drained his new drink in a single swallow, tossed the glass to the floor, and then fanned his hands out in front of him, in a manic wave, as if he were presenting them. "Showtime!"

They all stepped out of the transport. A hovering eye, about the size of a basketball, flew out of the limo and took up position between Chain and Pana. Its glowing green iris and dark pupil scanned back and forth, moving completely around the sphere, taking in everything. Everyone's comms reported that all non-essential functionality was being shut down, and all non-essential augmentations were also being blocked.

"Project your identification," the construct commander said. Chain had seen many constructs built to fight in conflicts over his lifetime;

these were the most impressive. He recognized some of their arma-
ments and knew if the guards wanted to, he and the others would all
be hot clouds of ash in an instant. He projected his ID.

"You," the commander addressed the vice president, "your identification matches that of Kouvri Security Executive Cire Mocsnarb, vice
president in charge of the Balisk program."

"Yes, I am. I'm personally escorting these people for an inspection
of the facility, on my authority."

"Please stand by, Mr. Mocsnarb," the commander said, his tone
changing to something more obsequious. "Genetic scan confirms
identity. No counterfeit alleles detected, no genetic inconsistencies
with physical form detected. Identity confirmed. ID documents
confirmed. No weapons, no aggressive or camouflaged augmentations
detected. Welcome to Balisk, Vice President Mocsnarb."

"Thank you. This"—he gestured to Rudian—"is Syndian Poole with
Amnesty Universal. And this is Jolan Kep"—he gestured to Pana—"and
Trosillius XX131," nodding to Chain. "They're with Courier Media
Complex. They are our guests, commander." Mocsnarb's voice carried
within it the tone of someone used to being obeyed without question.

"Yes, sir. Genetic scans confirm identity. No counterfeit alleles
detected, no genetic inconsistencies with physical forms detected.
Identities confirmed. ID documents confirmed. No weapons, no
aggressive or camouflaged augmentations detected. However," the
construct pointed to the hovering eye, "no unauthorized image
capture of any kind is allowed on Balisk."

"Well, I am making it authorized in this case," Mocsnarb said.

The commander scanned the orb and found nothing but a standard organomech full-immersion recording device with no aggressive
or camouflaged programs, mounted on a gravity suspension system.
The Ranger signets that Rudian and Chain wore never set off security
scans, reading only as normal jewelry, another bit of the Queen's
"magic."

"We need to see the warden," Rudian said. "Right away."

. . .

Warden Octavio Gollosan was in mid-shed. His scales were chalky and peeling in places, giving him a somewhat ghoulish appearance. His burning, slitted, crimson eyes still glowed with menace, however. His lids had already fallen off, revealing deep, dark olive beneath the dead skin. The warden made no excuses for his appearance. His desk was empty, and he had no screen in front of him, preferring to review his visitors' information on his comm display behind his eyes. He looked up and addressed Mocsnarb. "Such impromptu visits are frowned upon, Vice President. You know that. I have no correspondence to request this visit, nor anything from corporate to explain it."

Mocsnarb glanced to Rudian and smiled. The smile dropped as soon as he looked back at the warden. "Nor will you, Warden Gollosan . . ."

"Octavio," the Warden corrected. "Gollosan is my species name. It is only used in formal presentations of title where my species and our superiority require recognition."

"Of course." Mocsnarb was getting angrier by the moment. "Warden Octavio, there is to be no legal documentation, no data trail of this . . . tour. My words are the words of the president of our division. He'd be here himself, but he wants to have . . . plausible deniability in this matter."

"And what exactly is 'this matter?'" Octavio asked. "The president obviously expects you to fall on your blade for him, Vice President, and you expect the same from me. I want to know what is being asked of me and why."

Rudian stepped forward. "Warden Octavio, several complaints have reached my organization from stellar governments that house prisoners here. These reports are of abuse and unethical treatment, in violation of basic sentient rights. As you know, Amnesty Universal is a watchdog organization for such abuses. I and these reporters from CMC with whom I have a long and satisfactory working relationship, approached Kouvri Security, and were directed to Vice President Mocsnarb."

Mocsnarb took over at this point. "We are going to show these good beings that the rumors they heard are nonsense, that Balisk is run in full accordance with the sentient rights laws of all the galactic nations who bring inmates to us."

"I see." Octavio turned his gaze on Rudian and the others. "And the secrecy?"

"Because if this gets out, even internally, the executives from other divisions will jump on this, the ones always whining about how much Balisk Division cost as a startup, how much our operating budget is now. If there are internal memos and reports, the next thing you know we'll have this coming up at a Board of Directors meeting or, Mother forbid, a shareholders meeting!"

"Then why reporters and a recording device?" Octavio gestured toward the floating eye.

"I'm afraid the vice president had no option there," Rudian said, a small seasoning of threat in his voice, just enough to imply something going on between him and Mocsnarb that the warden didn't need to know about. "Whether the stories are true or not, we need independent verification."

Octavio almost took the bait and was about to suggest to this pompous idiot that they could easily arrange for an "accident" to occur on the tour. None of them would ever leave Balisk alive . . . and their little eye too. Instead, he narrowed his glowing gaze, seeming to scan Mocsnarb as the prison's sensors already had.

"Do we understand each other, Warden?" asked Rudian.

Octavio leaned back in his chair and peeled away a big strip of dead scales from his face, dropping it in the suddenly summoned waste portal.

"Perfectly, Mr. Poole. I'll summon a guard unit to accompany you. Eighty-five percent of our guard staff is constructs. Would you prefer organic?"

"Yes, please," Rudian piped up. Mocsnarb nodded in agreement. Octavio took note of his eagerness.

"Very well, they will meet you in my office lobby. Would you like me to join you?"

"Oh, no need for that," Mocsnarb said after a quick glance to

Rudian. "I'm sure you have important peeling to do. Now, if you'll excuse us."

Mocsnarb gestured for Rudian and the others to precede him through the door, and then he gave the warden a look usually reserved for discovering animal waste on your shoe and departed himself. The door slid shut behind him. Octavio looked at the door for a moment and then ordered his comm to access all the security data on the visitors.

Chain had to admit that, so far, part one of Rudian's plan was working without a hitch. Even the warden's responses were what they had planned for. When the preacher told him and Pana what he had in mind —described as a "brilliant mash-up of the 'find the Queen,' the 'big store,' and the 'Altarian Prince' cons"—Chain had his doubts. The detour to Ampho he had insisted on had taken a whole extra day of driving, but Rudian said they had to go there to see a man who was on the cutting edge of identity theft. That turned out to not be hyperbole in the least.

Ampho was a dumpy little low-tech world, less advanced than even Ray's Earth. However, there were enclaves everywhere, whole makeshift cities full of every kind of shill, con artist, criminal, and black marketeer you'd ever care to meet. Rudian was a legend, practically a god, there.

He introduced them to a humanoid named Krayto. Krayto had russet fur and a white mane full of multi-colored nano-lights that mimicked the movement of constellations. He had a short, pointed snout and small pointed ears that peeked out of his mane near the top. "Krayto here is a pioneer," Rudian had explained. Rudian transferred a data packet from his comm to Krayto's. "Here's the particulars. We're in a rush."

"Aren't they all," Krayto had said laconically. He quoted a price. Pana balked.

"Are you serious?" She looked to Rudian. "What's he doing for us, sending an army in there? In antimatter-armored tanks?"

"An army would fail; you already know that. This won't. He's the best; in fact, he's the only."

Krayto examined the data for a moment, blinked as he broke the connection, and looked to Rudian. "Where's the protein, Rudi? There's no genetic data in here for me to trawl with."

"Trawl?" Chain asked. Krayto ignored him.

"Didn't have time to scare it up," Rudian said.

"Well, that puts you in the seventieth percentile. Fine for a play-thing dop but shaky for anything involving finesse."

"And how much would it cost to get us up to the nineties, m'boy?"

Krayto quoted another price.

Chain chuckled. "We're approaching planet-buying money now."

"And at least three days' time," Krayto added, staring right at Chain.

"Ninety percent in two days, at the most," Rudian said. "You're milking us now, m'boy. Might I remind you of that little service I extended to you back when you had that trouble on Liltuh?"

Krayto came back with a figure at once.

Chain took Rudian by the arm. "We need a minute," he said, leading the preacher away. "Where are we supposed to get this kind of money from, exactly?"

"Did you or did you not tell me that the Shield Pact is footing the bill for this little outing? If they can tax so many sentients across so many galaxies, I'm sure they can afford something that costs as much as one itty-bitty planet."

Chain accessed the credit account the High Marshal had given him for any mission-related expenses. "I had better not be paying off the interest on your gambling debts, Rudi."

"Perish the thought," Rudian said, returning to Krayto and Pana. He clasped his hands together tightly with a loud clap. "Excellent, we have a deal."

The squad of prison guards encircled Chain, Rudian, Pana, and Mocsnarb as they directed them through mazes of featureless corridors and seemingly endless flash booths. "A great deal of the interior of the sphere is taken up with super-strong, flexible architecture." The vice president sounded a bit like a tour guide. "The cores of the support cradles are made of 100 percent pure flaked Durrallyium . . ."

"Diallium, sir," one of the guards corrected. "We use Diallium for the support struts. What's Durrallyium? Never heard of it."

Mocsnarb frowned and seemed confused, but he brushed it off quickly. "Right, Diallium. You sure about that . . . ? I've never heard of that."

The guard began to speak again, but Rudian seamlessly slid into the conversation before he could.

"This is all very fascinating, if you're a stockholder, but we're not. The prisoners?"

Mocsnarb nodded and snapped at the guard. "Never mind. You're not paid to lecture. Take us to the prisoners." The guard quickly ushered the executive and his guests down the hallway. Chain and Pana gave each other a worried glance but continued.


They had spent their second day on Ampho securing counterfeit identities through some more of Rudian's friends. They bought DNA overlays that, when injected into them, would temporarily give them the right genetic data to match the fake identities crafted for them. They were given a complete social footprint from fake money accounts to job credentials and social backgrounds.

They each purchased two identities to layer over their own, and Rudian made a request of the gene fixer which gave the criminal scientist pause. "You *want* a flaw in one of the protein sheaths?" the genetic counterfeiter asked to make sure he had heard correctly.

"Exactly. Nothing too obvious, mind you. I need it to stand up to scrutiny for, say, four to six hours after injection and then a very slight decay. I want it to look like a shoddier job than it actually is."

"Okay . . ." the fixer said with some apprehension. "You want that on both layers of the IDs?"

"Oh, no. Just this one." He pointed to the data and the rotating helix on one of the windows floating before them. "Make the other ID as solid and long-lasting as you can, my good fellow."

"This is going to be expensive, Rudi. Multi-layering is tricky. You want to avoid any mutations, not to mention smudges on the gene scans. Some of the new models of genetic sniffers are more sensitive than a Selkit newborn."

"Money is no object." Rudian jerked a thumb in Chain's direction. "Send him the bill."

"This must be one beauty of a con, Rudi," the fixer said, getting back to his job. "I'm sure as hell confused."

Krayto commed them later that day and told them to meet him at his workshop. It was tucked away in a sub-level of a condemned block of tenements, home to hundreds of squatters. Krayto's security people ushered them through after an intense screening with lots of multi-lasers aimed at them.

The lab was a masterpiece of clutter and jury-rigging. Portals cracking with dark motes of dimensional energy—known as Kirby discharges—flashed and snarled. Tank upon tank of vat-grown neural processors lined the walls in seemingly endless rows.

Hovering naked in the expansive lab, dripping with some clear gelatinous slime, was an unconscious Cire Mocsnarb in all his middle-aged glory.

"Magnificent!" Rudian said. "Another triumph, Krayto, my lad."

"Magnificent is not the word that jumps to mind," Pana said looking at the pale, pasty exec. "We paid all that money for a clone? Really? They'll be able to detect the accelerated growth in the gene print, and any decent telepath can . . ."

"He's not a clone," Krayto said. "He's a dop."

"Dop?" Pana said.

"Doppelganger," Rudian said. "An exact match for Cire Mocsnarb, the vice president in charge of the Balisk Division of the Kouvri Corporation, because he *is* Cire Mocsnarb, just from a parallel universe. There will be no inconsistencies in his genetic print or his neural scans. Krayto here skims alternate universes looking for matches to specific criteria. When he finds a high-percentage match, he extracts them from that universe and brings them to ours."

"Impressive." Chain nodded to Krayto. "I'd heard rumors, but I thought they were just that. How'd you finance all this?"

"I have investors with deep pockets."

"So, what you're saying," Pana said as she circled the hovering body, "is that you pulled this being out of another universe where he was doing the exact same thing we want him to do for us, and he was interacting with us as our fake personas . . . who looked like us. Correct?"

"He's a ninety-percent match for the criteria Rudian gave me. Right down to the hidden agenda and the genoprints I had to go digging for myself, thank you very much. He'll pass any conventional scanner, memory, or medical examination."

"Ninety percent of the time," Pana added.

Krayto shrugged. "Yeah, ninety percent."

The knight gave Rudian a less-than-congratulatory look, and then asked Chain, "Why didn't we just have this man cook us up an alternative-universe Lera Trade and be on our way? She'd be ninety percent as good as the original."

Rudian and Chain looked at each other and then to Krayto. "Tell her," Chain said.

"You couldn't pay me enough to try," Krayto said. "Lera paid me out of the haul she made off that Sarreene job she pulled. She had me eliminate all her dops from the proximate parallel lines all the way out to the distal lines. You might still find a Lera out in the far parallels, maybe a twenty-percent match, if you're lucky. But someone else is going to have to trawl her for you; I sure won't. Anyone paranoid enough to kill themselves off in every alternate universe they could find won't give a damn about canceling me if I cross them."

Pana looked to Chain incredulously. "We're breaking this person out of a jail?"

"She's a ranger," Chain said. "One of the best to ever wear the ring."

. . .

Stepping out of another flash booth, the visitors found themselves at the edge of a catwalk that encircled an expansive, featureless, spherical chamber. "Here we are." Mocsnarb led the party along an extension of the walk that ended in a circular platform at the center of the sphere. "Ultra-secure population. The worst of the worst. The universe's most dangerous criminals are locked away here, safe and sound."

"It's the manner in which they are being secured we need to verify, Vice President," Rudian said with a sniff. "We have the names of several prisoners for whom we received complaints about their treatment. We'd like to check on them first, please."

Mocsnarb gestured to a guard, who stepped toward the center of the platform. He motioned, sending his encrypted comm ident. A dedicated window and hovering panel wavered into existence in front of him, a pedestal of force fields and energy projections. "Name of the inmate, please?"

"First one is Kotor Nol," Rudian said.

"Nol, Kotor," the guard repeated as he entered another code into the panel. This code was changed every six hours and required a full confirmed bio and telepathic scan of the being entering it to accept the code. The terminal chirped its approval, and a glowing square of pale gold light appeared along part of the sphere's interior. The gold square detached itself from the sphere wall and floated free. It zoomed downward to come to a sudden stop at eye level with the party on the platform. Beyond a scintillating golden force field was an empty chamber occupied by a being who looked like a floating wall of cubist art. The being moved toward the golden force field and examined its visitors.

"The cells are spatial constructs," Mocsnarb said, "providing the prisoners plenty of room and legally fulfilling any requirements for exercise that the sponsoring government may have."

"What about furniture, recreation, sustenance?" Rudian asked.

"Each tailored to the being's species. Our terrorist friend here is a non-humanoid form with very few physical requirements. He receives three nutrient sprays per standard cycle and has access to our limited telepathic entertainment gallery."

"Everything seems in order to me." Rudian looked over to Chain and Pana. They both nodded as the eye recorder documented the examination. "Next prisoner."

The reviews went on for the next few hours without a hitch.

"Finally," Rudian said, "Lera Trade."

A nervous energy, like a current, went through the guards. The guard who had been accessing the terminal to summon and return the prisoner's cells looked over to Mocsnarb for confirmation. The vice president nodded in approval.

"I'll need a second," said the guard at the control pedestal. Another guard stepped forward and they both manipulated the panel, entered their codes, and had their identities scanned and confirmed. "Commander," the guard addressed his superior, "I'll need your command authorization now, sir." The guard leader was stepping forward to the pedestal when the bank of flash booths all opened and the warden and a contingent of guard-constructs hurried out.

"Belay that!" Octavio shouted, striding down the catwalk to the central platform. The heavily armed constructs drifted along behind him, a wall of death. Rudian's smile dropped, and fear widened his pupils. Chain and Pana looked at one another quickly, their faces stern.

"What's the meaning of this, Octavio?" Mocsnarb bellowed.

"These people are not who they claim to be. And they are under arrest."

# 21

The eldest of the Yateveo, the one called Kreesh, regarded the information being sent to the photo sensors covering his body from the Tribanni data windows. It showed the vehicles and troops of the accursed Shield Pact worlds amassed at every exit off the Queen's Road onto the Tribanni home world, Triban.

Kreesh had hoped for more time to build up defenses, but he had made sure that the entry roadways were already packed with Tribanni singularity mines. He knew his people didn't have the numbers yet to guard against an external invasion and control the local population if they decided to revolt.

"You smell worried," a voice said from the dim recesses of the terrace Kreesh was using as a command center. "I've taken you this far, haven't I?" A humanoid dressed in a Stygian tunic and pants, with an open doublet decorated in a black-and-jade diamond pattern, revealed himself. He had emerald eyes and an unruly mop of sable hair.

"How did you get here?" Kreesh asked.

"The same way I get everywhere. The same way I got you to this world. The same way I brought you and the others back from oblivion. I know the secret routes." He walked to the edge of the terrace and looked around.

Triban's sky was a patchwork of a million different worlds. Clouds of every imaginable shape, color, and composition drifted among a chandelier of spinning galaxies. Full, bright, swollen moons—some with rings, others glittering, drifting gemstones the size of continents —shared the night sky with burning silver sickles, shadowed mirrors of reflected light. Dawn was far away, but when it came, the moons would slip from view to make room for the coming of boiling sunrises and simmering sunsets, smearing the air with rose, amethyst, ocher, olive, teal, cinder, and fire.

The city, if such a word applied on this planet, reached to the horizon and beyond. The architecture was as piecemeal and as varied as the sky, taking in influences from hundreds of galaxies and thousands of cultures.

The man in jet and jade took it all in. "It's lovely, just lovely. A masterpiece."

"Surely the Pilgrim of Chaos himself has not been seduced by the existent? Has not forgotten the holy work we undertake?" Kreesh said.

"No," the Pilgrim said with a sigh as he turned from the view and toward the towering elder. "That *you* undertake. Let me remind you of something. It was you, you and the others, who made our cause into some ridiculous religion, not me! I'm a pragmatist, a scientist, and a cosmic naturalist. Unlike you zealots, I can appreciate the beauty of all this"—he spread his arms skyward to encompass the Tribanni night —"and still understand that it must eventually be destroyed."

"You, who have directly communed with the Stillness, you do not believe?" the Yateveo said. While he had one of the tiny Axolli translators, he never needed to use the food animal with the Pilgrim. They simply understood one another.

"Let's just say you and I have very different opinions on what the 'Stillness' is. Enough of the theology debate. I'm here to tell you that when your forces are ready, I want you to use the Tribanni transports and weapons and prepare your people to assault the dozen inhabited worlds we discussed. Once you have a foothold there, the Shield Pact will have to fully commit to war to dislodge you, and their politicians have no stomach for war. Our allies have seen to that."

"And what of the accursed Rangers?"

"Scattered, leaderless, ignored. They're a joke of their former selves. During the war, the Shield Pact, the Rangers, they were all so focused, so desperate to keep the Nemesis from achieving its goal. Letting a foe think they have won takes the fight out of them more quickly than letting them think they lost. Still, one irritating Ranger showed your hand sooner than we would like. Have your people stay vigilant for any small unit incursions. The Rangers do have an annoying habit of showing up where they're not invited and getting into places they shouldn't. See to it."

"Of course. You will get us past the blockades, as you did back in the war?"

"Yes." The Pilgrim looked out across the city again.

"Praise be to the prophet of the Stillness."

"Prophet, please. I detest your religion, but I have the same broad goal as you. This universe, all that is, has outlived its proper time . . . again. All thanks to *her*. No more. Be ready for me."

"We shall be. Three to five cycles at the most, and we'll be strong enough to advance on the worlds and begin the holy war again. This time, no one will stop us. The universe will burn."

Silence. No reply.

The Pilgrim of Chaos was gone, without a trace or a sound.

# 22

Durcoian troopers, two of them, sat in the back seat of the Galaxie, accompanying Ray and Neste to the luxury hotel in which the secretary of state had set them up. Neste assured Ray on the way there that their rooms would be bugged. The troopers acted as if they hadn't heard what the ambassador said.

They drove through the downtown district, a clean, glittering jewel of progress and affluence. Smiling, healthy, happy-seeming people wandered the streets carrying shopping bags from the endless boutiques that lined the central business district. Others snacked on food from street vendors.

The interior surface of the dome that held the dark-green waters at bay was awash in lights, advertising, scrolling state news posts, and slogans of encouragement for the populace. Ray noted that one of the more prominent advertisements mentioned a ration reward for any information that led to the arrest of criminals of the Republic. It was next to a looping, quarter-mile-long video image of the president of the Republic of Durco, waving to his adoring public. His teeth were white as a blizzard and stood out in his jowly, mint-colored face. Beyond the lights of the city, the neighborhoods were in darkness.

"Power rationing," Neste said. "Since the Shield Pact embargo, they've had trouble getting perpetual energy technology or even fuel for the energy systems they do have."

Ray looked around at the dizzying, fluid display of lights. "Really?"

"Oh, this, this is all for us, for the tourists. The only locals allowed to wander around here are high-ranking government officials, bureaucrats, military commanders. For them, the party never stops. For everyone else . . . lights out."

Ray glanced back at the troopers. "Is it a good idea to say all that in front of . . . ?"

"Oh, don't worry. They have sedition filters built into their helmets to keep them from hearing anything that might be 'ear crime.' They get a redacted version of all conversations instantly, with any non-'politically-positive' words, thoughts, or ideas edited out. It's all recorded and piped real-time to their secret police handlers for intelligence and threat analysis."

"That is . . . fucked up."

"A civilization so distrustful of its own people, so afraid of words, ideas, ideologies, as to make them illegal, grinds itself to a halt, and sentences itself to a slow death."

"This place sucks."

Neste chuckled. "Yes, yes it does. I've never heard that phrase before, but it is very apt. This place does suck."

The suites were lovely, perfect even. Both of them were introduced to their 'cultural liaisons,' locals who would accompany them everywhere and help them navigate Durcoian society. Ray thought they looked more like cops than tour guides.

Once they were alone in Neste's room, the ambassador extruded a slender tendril from his fountain-like body and slid it into Ray's ear. Ray hadn't seen the line and jumped back when he felt it. "Whoa! What was that?"

"Be still," Neste said. His voice was tinny but audible in Ray's ear. "And quiet."

Ray tried to be cool as the thread-like wire slid deeper into his ear canal.

"They can't monitor this nanowire. It's not coming over a

frequency, and their microphones and cameras aren't that sensitive. They can't see the line. I doubt we will be able to lose our secret-police liaisons before the concert tonight. We need to talk privately with Skye Salvo. I'm making a request of the secretary of state to let us go backstage and see him before the show."

"Mmhm," Ray mumbled.

"Just swallow," Neste said. "Once for yes, twice for no. We'll need to reach out to him as best we can with a room full of spies and recording equipment all around us. We need to let him know that Chain sent us, that Chain needs him, and I suppose we should mention this Ajeet. I think you should talk to him."

Ray swallowed twice.

"You're a Ranger, Ray. He'll trust you and you can send him non-verbal cues and body language that I cannot."

Ray sighed. "So I guess we just watch whatever's on the screen until showtime tonight."

"Don't watch too much screen here," Neste cautioned, still through the ear-line. "It will mess with your brain."

They were picked up at the hotel by a government limo and taken, along with their escorts, to the center of the business district of the central dome. Ray spotted several posts on the ever-changing collage of the dome's surface that announced that all citizens would be able to view the Skye Salvo concert tonight on Republic Channel 4, and that the normal lights-out and data closure would be suspended for the night to allow citizens to enjoy the whole show.

They approached a bubble that looked to Ray like it was a hundred stories tall and stretched over thousands of acres of land. The bubble was semi-translucent, and within he could see, even from his vantage point miles away, the endless rows of seating. Whatever material the bubble was made of, it shifted through a sequence of colors and patterns, like some giant snow globe in the center of the city. Spotlights swept back and forth all around the concert stadium. Holograms orbiting the massive sphere announced that for one night, tonight only, Skye Salvo and the World-Breakers were playing.

The limo drifted through the thousands of fans swarming around the base of the stadium. Other limos were also being let through the barricades guarded by more visor-faced troopers. The limos pulled into a queue and, one by one, drove up to a red carpet to allow their passengers to exit. Crowds of state media and fans from the upper echelons of Durco society swarmed behind narrow force-beam rope lines. Dark-suited state security men hung near the back, like grim statues.

Ray hadn't bothered to dress up, still wearing his basic black attire. He and Neste made their way through the cheering, applauding crowds. Their escorts stepped out of the limo and peeled off, replaced as soon as they reached the stage entrance doors by a large local with pistachio-colored skin who introduced himself as Trannixx, their backstage facilitator. Different title, but this guy struck Ray as a Fed, not as a local cop.

Trannixx led them through the stage doors and hustled them into a bustling corridor full of technicians, more security, and what Ray would call "roadies." There were more than a few "groupies" haunting the doors to the green room and dressing rooms. The beings guarding the way to the kingdom were not locals. They were each around seven feet tall, with brick-colored skin and a triangle of six eyes at the center of their faces. They had four large, well-muscled arms, all crossed—the universal symbol for "no way."

Trannixx flashed his credentials—a glowing hologram that materialized above his raised palm—and then nodded toward Neste and Ray to inform the giants that they were cool. Several of the groupies reached out to Ray as he was led inside.

"Aw, come on, sweet-ped," a glass serpent the size of a motorcycle whined, playing with Ray's hair with a crystalline tendril-arm, "take me in with youuu!"

The doors shut, and they were in yet another reality. It was quiet, almost muted, with a smell like cloves mixed with some kind of cleaning product thick in the air. There were tables full of food and snacks. A few dozen well-dressed and mostly beautiful beings were scattered about, chatting and laughing softly. Ray felt that he and Neste were being analyzed by the beautiful people and it seemed more intrusive and intense than any search he'd been exposed to yet here on Durco.

"Ambassador!" A tall, handsome Durcoian in a suit, with creases that could cut covalent bonds, approached Neste. He gave a slight bow at the waist. "I'm Juthcar Ronnz, secretary of state for the Free and Democratic Republic of Durco. It is an immense pleasure to finally meet you in person, your Excellency."

"The pleasure is mine, Secretary Ronnz. This is my diplomatic driver and personal assistant, Ray Cosa of Earth."

"Yes," Ronnz said bowing again to Ray. Ray waved and nodded. "Your Earth car has been making quite the stir with the Ministry of Security, Mr. Cosa. I understand the president himself is considering making you an offer to buy it." Ronnz and Neste laughed. A few lurking sycophants laughed as well. Ray gave a weak smile and forced out a chuckle.

"Thank you for your invitation tonight," Neste said. "I'm looking forward to talking with you after the concert."

"I must admit, I was rather surprised when I was told you were here, Excellency. After all, you were one of the loudest voices urging the Shield Pact Assembly to enact the current sanctions against Durco."

"Yes, well," Neste said, ushering Ronnz over to a quiet corner. Trannixx followed the two senior officials over and stood at a discreet but protective distance. "That was some time ago, and it has been encouraged by some of your supporters close to the assembly that I might want to reconsider my position." Ronnz smiled, but it was guarded. "I think, now, that it may be mutually . . . beneficial for me to throw my support to lifting the sanctions on your government . . ."

While Neste kept the secretary and their handler busy, Ray wandered over to the other side of the green room. Several humanoids dressed in flamboyant finery—a mix of old and new styles —joked, smoked, and drank among themselves, while hangers-on kept a worshipful distance. Ray assumed these were the World-Breakers.

Standing alone, apart from the band, was a slight, striking humanoid. His hair was trimmed down to a thin black fur, nearly shaved. He wore tight black leather pants, boots, and an open leather vest with no shirt. His skin was a warm, dark beige. His chest, arms, and head were etched in prismatic neon-inked tattoos. The tattoos flickered a few inches above his skin, moving, changing, cycling through patterns. His face was veiled in thorns of flame and then ice. His ears were larger than a human's, curved and pointed on both sides, like crescent moons. He wore numerous hoops and stud earrings along their edges and a pair of large-gauge plugs. His eyes were fitted with enhancements that made them look like molten diamonds.

Ray spotted the Ranger ring on his finger. He wore many other rings on his right hand but only the signet on his left.

"Excuse me, you must be Skye Salvo."

"Uh, yeah." Skye looked uncomfortable and was already trying to figure a way out of the conversation.

"Hey, nice to meet you. I'm Ray. I only heard a little of your music, but I really liked it."

"Thanks. Look, I got to get ready to go on."

"Yeah, well, here's the thing. A mutual friend of ours sent me to find you. A Ranger named Chain."

Skye stopped. He looked at Ray, really looked at him, and then saw his signet.

"Really? He tell you that the last time I saw him, I told him to forget he ever knew me?"

"He, uh . . . he left that out." Ray glanced over to see Neste and Ronnz still conspiring. "Listen, Chain needs you. The Yateveo are back, and they're going to kill a whole lot of people. He's pulling a crew together to stop them. He asked me and the ambassador there to come get you."

"I can't just drop everything. I got my own thing going on right now."

"Yeah, I guess the rock star gig is a lot sexier than keeping people from dying."

"Space you," Skye said with a snarl. "You don't know shit about me, and I can already tell you don't know shit about Chain, either." The words were echoes of what Ray himself had said to Chain not too long ago. He suddenly felt bad for being such a dick to Chain.

"Space yourself." Ray stepped up to the singer. "I know your name is really Skein . . ."

"Keep your voice down," Skye said.

"I know you got a ring, same as mine, and that means you're supposed to help people."

Skye chuckled. It was a dry sound, and Ray got the impression he didn't do it too often.

"So, you're green as well as rude. Let me tell you something, recruitment boy, you lose as many people to this damn signet as I have, and then, then we can have a conversation."

Something snapped in Ray. A wall he had built, brick by icy brick, for so long he couldn't remember it not being inside him, exploded. His voice stayed low, but the fire in it, in his eyes, struck Skye like a slap.

"You go straight to hell, you fucking *farsante*. It must be rough to be rich and famous and spoiled, and so, so, so fucking sad. I made the mistake of thinking that music you wrote, those lyrics, that that was actually you. I'm a whole lot closer to the ground than you are, asshole, and I'm still trying. I don't want to most days. Most of the time I want to curl up and fucking die. So go on and pretend to be some kind of damaged artist. We're better off without you."

Ray was shaking, pale, and sweating. He felt exhausted.

Skye was looking at him differently now, like he was fully engaged in seeing him. It gave him an odd sensation.

"You have lost a lot. The wounds are still bleeding. Why the hell did Chain drag you into this?"

"He didn't. I dragged him in."

The performer nodded. "Something to keep you busy, right?"

"Yeah, something like that."

"I'm sorry. I have to keep myself shut off, for my sake and the sake of everyone around me. I used to do it with drugs, but that . . . didn't go well. It took your emotions to knock my guard down a little. Did Chain say why he was looking for me?"

"Something to do with someone named Ajeet."

Skye's orbiting tattoos all shut down for a second. His eyes widened. All the swagger was gone from him. "'Jeet? He's going after *her*? This must be bad."

"It is. Sorry. I know you don't know me, and I really don't know you, but this is serious. He needs you. I guess this Ajeet needs you too."

Skye ran his hand through his buzz cut. "Ray, right? Ray, I *have* to do this show, and then after that I'll go with you, okay? This is a really important night. We've been working up to it for a really long time. It has to happen tonight. Then, I'll go with you to Chain . . . and Ajeet."

Ronnz and Neste joined them, with security in tow. Another local, dressed in expensive clothes designed to look casual, and wearing a disturbingly unreal smile, came with them.

"Ah, Skye! You've already met Mr. Cosa, I see."

Skye bowed slightly to the secretary of state. "Yes, a very passionate fan."

"This is Ambassador Neste, of the Tribanni Encompassment. And this"—he gestured toward the smiling man—"is Secretary Trough."

Skye bowed, and Ray followed suit.

"Ournel Trough," the smiling man said. "Secretary of Cultural Hygiene. A *true* pleasure."

"Hi," Ray said, getting a super villain kind of vibe off Secretary Trough.

Trough turned to Skye. "I am a *huge* fan of your work. *Huge.* This really is a life-defining moment for me, for all of us. The president is so glad we could finally arrange to have you perform on Durco."

"Pleasure's all mine. I've wanted to play here for a very long time."

Trough leaned in a bit closer, trying to instill a sense of cama-raderie with the performer. "Listen, Skye, we need to make sure you understand the ground rules before you and the band go on. There are some pretty disturbing rumors out there about some of your past shows."

Skye gave him a disarming smile. "I know, I know! We get this all the time, Ournel. May I call you Ournel?"

"Of course," the secretary said. Trough felt so much more at ease already.

"One of the greatest tragedies of intergalactic civilization is that information can only be disseminated as quickly as a courier can deliver it along the Queen's Road. It's led to so much gossip, misinformation, and speculation with no basis in fact. We're famous; we get blamed for everything." Skye laughed, and Trough did too.

"Of course, of course. We deal with that as well here on Durco. The things that get said about our government, our president, by these media companies—it's criminal!"

"I absolutely agree," Skye said. "Criminal. That's why we wanted to play here so badly. We hope we can do something to change that perception."

"Wonderful, excellent!" Trough said, laughing and patting Skye on the back. "I'm so glad you understand and are on board. I just sent a list to your and your mates' comms. It's the songs that can't be played tonight. They're currently banned by the Department of Cultural Hygiene—no offense, you understand?"

"Of course. We've had such requests by governments before. Perfectly understandable, given your circumstances."

"It's so refreshing to work with professionals," Trough said. "Thank you. I'm really looking forward to the show!"

"Not as much as I am." Skye gave his bandmates a nod and they returned it. The World-Breakers began to stand and grab their instruments, kiss their current partners, and down their final pre-show drinks.

"I do have a request, if you don't mind," Skye said to Ronnz and Trough. "I was talking with Ray here, and I'd like to have him and Ambassador Neste be guests in my box tonight for the show."

"Certainly!" Trough said, looking at his counterpart.

Ronnz nodded and said, "We can continue our promising conversation after the show, your Excellency."

"Very good," Neste said. "Thank you, Mr. Salvo for the invitation. You are very kind."

Skye strode toward the door that would lead to the corridor and then to the ramp onto the stage. Ray noted that the rock star was back, walking like he owned everything, everyone. He turned back to Ray and the others and with a wink said, "We're on."

## 23

Restrain them," Warden Octavio commanded. "If they resist, kill them."

"You're up," Chain said to Pana. With a gesture, the knight summoned her ward to her hand. The small silver disc, which had been acting as the anti-gravity generator in the base of the floating eye-camera, flew across the room on gravitic micro-pulses and grafted itself to her palm. As the eye fell, Chain grabbed it in mid-air, completing the circuit between the harmless and inactive pico-implants in his hands and the also-seemingly-harmless circuitry in the surface of the camera. Rudian had thrown himself to the floor, pulling Mocsnarb with him. The preacher covered his head with his arms and curled up like a shrimp.

The circle of guards around them were in motion by now, raising their hands to fire their plaser augmentations. The beams flashed from their hands toward Chain and Pana. Pana gestured, and the destructive light bent inward to a point of micro-singularity and exploded harmlessly between the guards and their targets. The flash of the detonating plasma blinded the guards for a second. That was all the time Pana needed.

She cleared the distance to the guards, who were standing at the control pedestal, in a single micro-gravity jump over the violent, flashing cloud of plasma, increasing her gravity as she came down, driving a knee into one guard's face and striking another with a punch, both with around fifty g's behind them. The guards crumpled to the catwalk floor as her feet touched down again. They were badly injured but clung to life.

The eye orb in Chain's hands spilled brilliant blue-white light out of it as he spun toward the remaining guards. A humming, continuous beam of ravening energy erupted from the orb and burned through the remaining organic guards, cutting them in half before burning itself out and growing dark. Chain tossed the smoldering, charred orb as he and Pana stared down the warden and his inorganic contingent of construct soldiers, who were not advancing.

"Damn it, Octavio!" Mocsnarb shouted as he clamored to his feet. "You've ruined everything!"

"Explain that to me," the warden said coolly. "You are who you claim to be, but this one"—he pointed to Rudian—"scrimped on his genetic masking. When I had a new scan done on all of you a few hours ago, a decaying protein sheath showed up on his." He looked at the preacher. "You get what you pay for. He is not who he claims to be, Mocsnarb. And I can safely assume these two who just wiped out a full guard contingent in a few seconds are not media."

Rudian made sure to seem a little hesitant to reveal the truth. This was a very important part of the performance; it had to be played just right. He sighed and looked to Mocsnarb. "I don't know. Maybe better just to kill him. He game to play?"

"Play what?" the warden asked.

Rudian nodded to Chain. "Show him." Chain made a complex gesture with his arms and hands while muttering a mantra in a deep, guttural voice. Wavering into existence before him was a glowing neon-violet flower, with wide, drooping petals like an orchid. The flower opened in a languid fashion as the warden's mouth fell open.

"The UV Bloom," Octavio said. "That's the psychic projection taught to initiated members of the Samtok." He looked from a smiling

Rudian to a glowering Chain and Pana. "You brought mobsters into the prison?"

"Seemed as good a place as any for them, don't you agree?" Rudian said, shifting his inflection and body language to one of calm, casual power. "Don't call us mobsters again, or I'll have my associate here" — he nodded to Pana—"turn you into a hundred-G rug."

"I didn't have a choice, Octavio," Mocsnarb said. "They had something over me, and they threatened my family unless I got them in here."

"Yes, and if you"—Rudian started walking toward the warden —"hadn't tried for Employee of the Month, we'd most likely be on our way out now with no bloodshed, no complications. Those dead guards are on you, Warden."

"What do you want here?" Octavio asked.

"Before I tell you, I need you to answer a question for me. Would you rather be rich beyond your wildest dreams or dead?"

"The answer seems obvious."

Rudian circled the warden and the construct guards whirred defensively, but Octavio waved them off. "Perhaps not as much as you think. A smart man, an ambitious man, may see his way to power and position by confounding his employer's enemies. Like taking the initiative to run a second gene scan on suspicious guests, even those with the approval of one of his superiors in the corporation. If you are that kind of man, then I'll tell you what we require. Then, you'll die."

Rudian saw the warden swallow hard. His Gollosanian physiology made it impossible for him to sweat, but he was giving off all the tells for his species that he was nervous. They had picked the Samtok for two reasons. One was that both Chain and Rudian knew a good deal about their customs and secret ways and could fake them, and the second was that they were the most feared of all the secret criminal brotherhoods that haunted the galaxies.

"However," Rudian continued, stopping directly in front of the warden now, "a smart man, an ambitious man might also see his way to power and prestige through more money than a thousand kings could ever dream of. If you are that kind of man, then I will tell you, and you will live and prosper."

Rudian nodded toward Chain. He was up. "Have you ever heard of the Sarreene Hegemony?" Chain asked.

"Of course," Octavio said. "They used to be a major intergalactic power. They nearly collapsed after an economic correction comps ago, fell into chaos, anarchy, for a time. They've never fully recovered."

"The reason that all happened was because Lera Trade stole the Hegemony's treasury—the entire wealth of 17,386 worlds—every last credit. She took the job on a drunken bet, and she pulled it off . . . alone." Chain had delivered his lines perfectly. It was easy, because that part was completely true.

Rudian stepped in, not missing a beat. "Our organization had numerous enterprises in the Hegemony. *Numerous.* Good Lady Trade cost us a lot of money. We intend to get it back from her, with interest."

As if on cue, the holographic pedestal-panel chirped a reminder that it was waiting for confirmation from a third party to proceed in bringing Lera's cell to the fore. Octavio glanced at it and then back to Rudian and Mocsnarb.

"My executive clearance won't unlock interior systems here," the vice president said, "and the guard commander who was about to give us clearance is . . . well . . . nearly dead right now. We need you to unlock it, Octavio."

"So," the warden began, "you talk to her, and you get the codes she used to hide the money. Then what? You write me an IOU?"

Rudian laughed.

"That's funny. No. That amount of money takes a lot of time and care to launder to avoid every intergalactic government in the Known Galaxies sniffing it out and coming after a piece of it. That's why she hid most of it away in a sub-quantum-encrypted shadow-bank account out near the Dark Eye in the Galaxy of Tears. Vice President Mocsnarb, here, is going to retrieve the money for us. You may accompany him to ensure that your interests are represented. He will use his position with the Kouvri Security Corporation to hide and filter the funds back to us. He'll be taking a . . . 'processing fee' for his troubles. You help us get to Lera Trade and get the code, and you can expect a similar accommodation."

"It's enough money to buy worlds," Mocsnarb said. "Don't be a fool, Octavio."

The warden seemed to be thinking, balancing the risk and the reward. Rudian stayed silent and let his body language tell the Gollosan all he needed to know.

"I have a quarter-million security forces on Balisk," Octavio finally said. "That's just the organics. I have over a million and a half constructs here as well, all with the firepower to lay waste to a city. I say a word, and they all come down on you, right now."

"And we die," Rudian said. "And you can never, ever leave this little kingdom of yours again, Warden, without looking over your shoulder, wondering when one of our brethren will come to claim you. Time to call or fold."

This was the moment. In this moment, Rudian *was* a sinister, ruthless, ice-blooded crime lord. There was no room in the performance for anything less. The warden sized him up for the span of a heartbeat, then another, and another. Octavio walked past Rudian and the others and keyed his command access into the beeping pedestal console. The controls chimed to acknowledge the receipt of the correct codes. He glanced over to Mocsnarb.

"Enough to buy planets," he said.

"Whole star systems," the vice president replied.

A glowing crimson window appeared on the surface of the spherical room. It floated down to eye level with the platform. Inside the empty room was a humanoid, a woman. Unlike the other prisoners, she did not move, only stood like a statue.

"What is this?" Chain asked. Rudian heard the anger and concern in his voice, but only because he was highly skilled in doing such. It was fortunate the warden was not as astute at reading people.

"Full-stasis containment," Octavio said. "It was the only way they could catch her."

"Who's 'they'?" Pana asked.

"The Sultah of Uranni. They laid a trap for her after she stole the royal jewels twelve comps ago. They paid quite well for us to keep her frozen."

"How were you planning to get that by Amnesty Universal?" Rudian asked.

Octavio shrugged.

"All prisoners are subject to the sovereign laws of the government that tried them and convicted them. Stasis imprisonment in perpetuity is one of the Uranni's more merciful punishments."

"So, she's been in there since she was arrested?" Pana asked. "How could they possibly try her like this?"

"Quickly." The warden glanced down at the data that fluttered across the window before him. "She's been in there four comps, eight xtents."

"That's inhumane," Pana said. Rudian winced. She had forgotten her character; the hardened underworld enforcer was sounding a lot like a naive young knight.

"Do you understand what Lera Trade *is*? She's no thief, no mere criminal. She is an entropic savant. She has an intuitive sense of the flaw in things—people, constructs, relationships, machines, computers, locks, plans, tactics, societies, governments . . . anything! She can infiltrate them, understand them, subvert them, and break them. She's been sowing chaos and anarchy in her path since she was able to crawl—her brother, as well."

"I heard he was dead," Rudian said.

"Doubtful. So, do you wish to have a fundraiser for her legal defense, or shall we wake her up and get that code."

"Please proceed, Warden," Rudian said.

"Guards," Octavio said to the war-constructs that had followed him in. "I will be awakening the prisoner. If you sense the slightest indication of violent intent—increased pulse, pupil reaction, anything —you are to use maximum non-lethal force to subdue her. You do not require any further authorization."

"Understood, Warden," the constructs all said as one.

Octavio tapped a few codes into the console and waved his hand over a scanner. There was a long tone to verify the command. "Confirm and execute," the warden said to the machine. The red field that suffused the cell faded away, leaving the glittering golden force field in place at the front of the cage.

Lera Trade was of average height with an athletic build, like a runner. She was dressed in a dark-blue bandage tunic and gray culottes. She had striking, almost-noble features, but she obviously worked very hard to not carry an aristocratic bearing. Her eyes were wide and brown, and one could immediately see the frightening, almost predatory intelligence that gleamed in them.

Lera's confusion at her situation lasted less than a second. Then, she sagged and fell to the floor, like a puppet with her strings cut. Rudian stepped forward, as did Chain. The constructs leveled countless barrels at the slumped form, even through the force field.

"Lera Trade," Rudian said. "My name is unimportant." Her head popped up at the sound of his voice. She kept the smile off her face and eyes, but both she and Rudian knew who each other was, and they both knew that they knew. "I speak for the Samtok."

"Figures," she said, trying out her voice after four completions of silence. "They always sounded pretty pompous. Don't tell me; this is about the Sarreene job, right? I figured you boys would turn up sooner or later for your cut."

Rudian remained composed, but inside he was dancing. *You wonderful, wicked, brilliant woman! As sharp as ever!*

"Very astute," Rudian said.

"Yeah, that was why I let myself get caught. How long was I under?"

"Four completions. A little over that, actually."

Rudian saw the spark of shock and sadness pass through Lera; then it was buried deep.

"Well the compounded interest on the principle should cushion the sting of that. No greater power in the universe. Get me out of here, and I'll pay my tribute, like a good little master criminal."

"Code to the accounts first. Then you go free."

"Riiight. Because all of you look like such respectable, trustworthy folk."

"You don't have a choice. You're in Balisk, at the edge of a black hole. The only thing keeping you from being swallowed up by entropy right now is some good old Tribanni spatial know-how." Lera took in the words, read the subtext, and then began to plug it into the plan that had been burning in her brain since the stasis field had snapped off. "There's no escape, unless we allow it. Isn't that correct, Warden?"

"Cooperate with them, Trade," Octavio said. "You do that, and I'll leave the stasis field off. Knowing you, you'll be loose and out of here in less than a cycle. Be a hard-ass, and the red lights go back on, and you sleep until I decide to let you wake up again. How many people, how much of the world you know do you really want to have slip away from you?"

"That's a convincing argument, Warden. You overcame my objections. You missed your calling in sales." She looked to Rudian, "So, I lose the whole score for not getting permission, is that it?"

"Exactly. But you stay alive, and you get your freedom back."

"The codes," Chain said, "We have part of them." He repeated the formulas exactly as Ambassador Neste had given them to him. He saw the recognition flicker in Lera's eyes. "Now, the rest of them."

Lera began to speak. She had altered her tonal inflection and her pitch to exactly match those of Warden Octavio. The numbers, letters, and phrases she spoke went on for a moment. Then she said, "You got what you wanted. I hope the lot of you choke on it. It's getting so an honest thief can't make a decent living around this universe."

"Thank you," Rudian said. "Now, if you'll excuse us, we need to get our representatives to your shadow bank and transfer that money as soon as possible." The preacher nodded to Mocsnarb and Octavio. "Gentlemen, after you."

Octavio looked at his dead men and Lera. "Commander," he called over his shoulder, as the party made their way back toward the flash booths, "attend to the dead and injured, and make sure you turn the stasis field back . . ." A howling chorus of alarms went off. Red emergency lights flared to life everywhere. "By the Mother, no! Not now!"

"What is it?" Rudian asked the clearly terrified Octavio.

"A catastrophic failure in one or more of the spatial anchors!" the warden nearly screamed as he began to run toward the booths, taking Mocsnarb by the cuff. "We have to evacuate before the whole damn planet's devoured by the singularity. Commander! You and your unit with us. Make sure we get to the executive garage safely!"

"Yes, Warden," the commander replied. Louder klaxons were blaring now. A calm, programmed voice urged all personnel to abandon the station at once.

"Hey, hey! Get me out of here!" Lera shouted to the departing warden, some panic in her voice. Octavio ignored her.

"Get Mocsnarb to safety," Rudian said. "Secure the money! We'll find you."

"Right . . . right!" Octavio said as he, the counterfeit vice president, and the crew of war constructs disappeared into the flash booths and were gone. All the stress and tension slipped from Rudian, and he looked over to Lera, grinning in her cell. She was examining the force field.

"Bravo," Rudian said. "Always a pleasure to work with an artiste."

"Chain put you up to this, of course."

"He is a brute," Rudian nodded. "Uses a plaser when a scalpel will do."

"I'm standing right here," Chain said. "Lera, this is Ratari Pana Goss. Pana, Lera Trade."

"Pleasure," Lera said. Pana nodded a bit curtly. Lera chuckled and ran a finger along the force field. The glittering intensified wherever she placed her finger. "Ah, you're not a P-41," she said to the force field. "It's newer, a P-43? Two iterations, perhaps? Yes, but they still didn't work that little kink out of it, did they? Lady Pana, would you be so kind as to apply about a 1.5-g field in an eighth-of-an-inch cross section . . ."

Lera's finger hovered for a moment, moving ever so slightly. She placed her finger on a spot, finally, to the left of the field. The spot sparked and flashed brightly.

". . . here, and hold it for a moment, please."

Pana looked a little incredulous, glanced at Chain, and then gestured toward the force field. Lera slapped the spot hard with her palm, and the whole field sputtered and collapsed.

She backed up and made a running jump to clear the distance between the opening of her cell and the catwalk platform. Rudian laughed as she ran to him and hugged him. "You dodgy old coot! It's good to see you."

"You too. Let's get you away from this dreadful place. Too bad it's not actually falling into the black hole. Good riddance, I say."

They all headed for the flash booths.

"That was a nice bit of work, there, giving me the info on what you needed by letting me know I was in Balisk. All their command systems are tri- or quad-neutrino encrypted. It'd take me awhile to crack them, but the notification systems are super-low priority. I slipped right in and gave them a bit of a scare."

"They'll be halfway to the Black Widow Pulsar before Octavio realizes he's been duped," Rudian said.

Lera turned to Chain. "And what exactly are you dragging me into this time?"

"The usual," Chain said as the doors to the flash booths opened. "I need the impossible."

"Well," she said, running a finger along the lapel of Chain's corporate suit, "If someone was able to get you out of those smelly leathers, then nothing's impossible."

"Ouch," Chain said as the doors slid shut.

# 24

The People's Arena on Durco seated two hundred fifty thousand beings. It was packed to capacity, and everyone waited for the show to begin.

Ray and Neste were literally in the sky boxes—a series of floating private boxes that flew far above the sea of beings below. A local pilot in a traditional Durcoian steward uniform—a long, double-breasted turquoise coat and an Iridium mask—flew the box from a recessed cockpit on the roof. The box had an interior lounge with comfy couches, monitors for watching the concert, a fully stocked and manned bar, and long buffet tables piled with food. One wall of the lounge was transparent with an open doorway that led outside to a balcony that ran the length of the box.

On the balcony were more couches and chairs to enjoy the show and another bar in case it was too far to walk inside for a refill. Besides the six teal-uniformed locals who acted as catering staff, Skye had invited about a dozen guests for the box, as well as Ray and Neste, who stood on the balcony. Their state-sponsored shadow, Trannixx, reclined on one of the chairs nearby, sipping a drink and trying to act like he wasn't watching their every move.

"Man, this is different from any show I've ever been to," Ray said to the diplomat. "They were usually in some sketchy club with a few dozen people. You got a stamp on the back of your hand, and the drinks were all in red Solo cups."

Ray felt the shiver of the tiny thread line slipping into his ear.

"Durco was a paradise, once," Neste's voice said in his ear. "The surface is glorious. The suns have fire-fall arcs constantly flowing between them. The beaches are pristine and peaceful. Over ninety-nine percent of Durco is water. Many more tourists than this used to come before the current regime took control. Now, the surface is only for the elite and those who can afford it.

"The majority of native Durcoians now live in hunger, darkness, poverty, and fear. The reason the president set up this event tonight, is broadcasting it all over the world, is letting the proles be here and giving them the power ration to view it, is because there is great unrest here. He's throwing the people a few crusts in hope of calming them down a bit. His last violent crackdown against dissent cost him the sanctions Durco is currently under. He murdered more than three hundred thousand of his own people in this very city. Cut off the air in some districts, flooded others."

"Why don't they do something?" Ray asked softly, almost whispering, "They've got the numbers."

"The oppressed almost always do. But the representative government is in the pocket of the president and his backers. No weapons, no public assembly, no unmonitored access to communications, no real free media. People who speak up publicly . . . just go missing. Being here would make my skin crawl . . . if I had skin."

"And this is the guy Skye insisted he had to play a gig for tonight." Ray sighed. "I don't get it. He seems legit. His lyrics seem honest as hell, but he comes off really 'Whatever, man.'"

"It makes little sense to me as well. He and his band have a reputation for supporting the cause of universal sentient rights. He is one of the wealthiest beings in the Known Galaxies, and he contributes significant amounts of his income to charitable agencies, or so the stories go."

"Maybe he needs the tax break," Ray said as the lights began to dim. The crowd roared as one. An announcer's cheesy stadium voice filled the very air, which was seeded with countless nano-speakers. "Good evening Durrrrr-co!" The crowd gave another outburst at the mention of their name. "Welcome to all of our esteemed guests and all of you watching tonight through Republic Channel 4 . . ."

Ray noticed many of the sky boxes sliding into a semicircle formation, at least twenty stories above the crowd on the floor, ensuring the guests all had an optimal viewing position. Their box drifted up very close to another one that had a cadre of armed troopers on the balcony. Among the troops was the president, looking as he did on the giant dome projection. He was sitting in an ornate, almost throne-like chair. He smiled his supernova smile to Ray and waved jovially.

The announcer continued as the stage darkened, his powerful voice everywhere. "Your esteemed beloved father, President-for-Life Boren Naz, and the Department of Cultural Hygiene are proud to bring you . . . for one night and one night only . . . the . . . greatest . . . band in the Known Galaxies . . . Skyeeeee Salvo and the World-Breakers!"

The audience went mad, screaming in excitement as the lights flared to life on the stage and the World-Breakers began to play. They were all humanoid, but there the similarities stopped. They were obviously from very different parts of the universe.

Two of the band members were on a hovering platform near the back of the stage. An array of floating discs that looked like drumheads of different sizes and shapes encircled them, and they danced in place, turning to use different surfaces as they did. They used their bare hands to drum a multi-layered tattoo between them that drove the relentless beat forward and carried it out across the stadium.

Two other band members—one on either side of the stage—played by holding spheres the size of basketballs between their hands. They pushed and slid their fingers and palms across the surfaces to make sounds that seemed to Ray to be like a variety of string instruments.

The final member of the World-Breakers looked like he was playing a large yellow octopus, cradling it like bagpipes. Several of the creature's tentacles were attached to the player, one to the side of his head, another actually in his mouth and partly buried down his throat. The instrument made a wide range of sounds, like wind instruments. It also sang backup from a chorus of mouths scattered over the "bagpipe's" body. Ray was amazed and a little freaked out by this, even more so when Neste pointed out that the "instrument" was also a member of the band.

The music thrummed and swirled around the audience. Hands clapped and voices were raised in howls of pure joy. A single figure still stood in darkness near the edge of the stage, brilliant planes of light appeared around him. It was Skye, his tattoos drawing a bird-like mask of sun-fire-dawn over his face that made Ray think of Egyptian gods. Parallel lines of silver grew outward from his back, forming holographic wings of cool lunar radiance. The shadow slapped his hands together and drew them back horizontally. Glowing cords of energy spread out as Skye's hands moved further apart. The strands remained in space before him; they moved as he moved. He began to play them, making chords, strumming them furiously the way you might a guitar's strings, and their sweet sound added to the alchemy of the band's music.

"Hello, Durco," Skye's voice rumbled across the stadium. "Tonight, everything changes. 1-2-3-4!"

The music flared like a nova at the same time the lights did, spot-lighting Skye. His tattoos shifted and swam across him like schools of glittering neon fish as he stared directly into two-hundred-fifty thousand sets of eyes and began to sing to each being with everything in him. The opening number was called "Sunfall," and it was apparently a classic. Ray heard hundreds of thousands of voices singing out below him, around him. Skye danced and strutted his way across the stage, each lyric, each word sweet, dripping with raw emotion. Ray found himself head-banging, and his hands were slapping in time to the bass and the drums. Even if the guy was a fake, he sure as hell knew how to wail.

The first song wrapped, and the crowd swelled and roared. Skye stood at the fore and took the full force of the crowd like a crashing wave. "How is everyone feeling tonight?" The crowd responded to the litany, and Skye grinned and nodded. "Yeah, good, good! Sounds like you folks don't get to yell too much around here, huh? Feels good, don't it?" There was laughter and, beneath it, an undercurrent of nervousness.

"It's okay," Skye said walking back among his smiling bandmates. "Nobody's going to arrest you for having a good time . . . at least not tonight." More cheering, more laughter; it grew stronger, more certain. Skye made his way back up to the front. "Here's one off our sixth pill; I think you know the words. It's called *Break!*"

The band pushed back against the energetic crowd, sending out a wall of sound. Skye spun it, shoved it in their faces with his voice—an angry, mocking cry this time, a demand— almost as if he were daring the crowd to follow him into the music. The audience took the bait.

*I don't want to live between monsters,*
*I don't want to lie to play it safe,*
*Take you out past the barbed wire, baby,*
*Take you out, gotta keep the faith!*

The bagpipe octopus's mouths began to drone the chorus in several different voices and ranges: *Nobody owns nobody owns nobody owns nobody owns . . .*

It was hypnotic, and it reminded Ray of some of the old punk that he loved. He glanced over to the other box. They were close enough for him to see that President Naz was fidgeting and looking a lot less pleased with himself. The crowd was getting into it, though, even if the president wasn't, surging like a tide below them. Everyone in the seats was up, stomping, thrashing. It was impossible not to.

*Keep your head down, baby, keep your meaning tight,*
*Don't meet their eyes now, lover, 'less you want a fight,*
*Secret hunting agents, secret killing men,*
*Put your hands up, baby, throw them down again!*

"I will say this," Neste said through the thread. "In his way, he's as skillful at manipulating a crowd as Rudian." Ray disagreed. This wasn't manipulating as much as it was an exorcism—coaxing the audience's feelings to the surface. Skye was a master of it, almost a magician.

*Nobody owns nobody owns nobody owns nobody owns* . . . The audience was singing along, chanting the chorus. The whole stadium shuddered at the sound.

The crowd was moving now as a single, frenetic force, surging in time to the music, to Skye's words. Ray glanced over to see their handler, Trannixx, sitting up in his lounge chair now, looking concerned and seemingly staring off into space. He was probably on his comm. He looked over to the president again. His lips were moving, and Ray was pretty sure there was a high-level conference call going on right now.

Below, Ray spotted waves of visored military troops like the ones that had shaken them down when they arrived. The troopers were gathering at the periphery of the crowd on the floor. More were moving up the stairs to disperse themselves among the aisles of seats. Hovering triangular constructs, about the size of refrigerators, drifted down from the shadowy rafters. Barrels, communication dishes, and antennae slid into view from a few dozen of the unmanned crafts. They scattered about the sky throughout the stadium. There was nothing overt yet, just a reminder to the people about who was in charge.

"Uh, Neste?"

"Yes, I sensed them too."

*Time's a curtain, baby, dropping flight,*
*Time to break free baby, time to break tonight!*

The chorus grew in speed, in intensity, whipping the crowd into a frenzy. Then, it was over. Silence, then thunderous applause. The band waited a heartbeat and then fell into the next song. It was also powerful, but it was safer, lyrically. Skye had brought them to the edge and then pulled them back. Ray felt the authorities' apprehension begin to recede, just a little.

Skye and the band kept repeating the process for the next few hours. They'd play songs Ray was sure were on Secretary Trough's banned list. Then, when the crowd was ready to go and the republic security personnel were ready to do something about it, they'd drop back to good, but politically-neutral, songs and things would get less tense.

Through it all, Skye showed them a way to escape the ID checks, the surveillance, the guns, with song, music, and dance—a freedom no tyrant could ever touch, ever steal. On his throne in the sky, the president hunched, and crossed his arms like a petulant child. His lips were pursed, and there was anger and distrust in his eyes. He was afraid, Ray realized. With all his troops, truncheons, guns, cameras, and secret police, he was still afraid of what this music could do to his empire.

The evening was coming to a close. The audience was raw. Most of the quarter-million beings had been dancing, writhing, shouting, and applauding for hours now, pushed closer and closer to the brink of physical and emotional catharsis by Skye and his band. Most everyone was damp with sweat, their muscles warm and loose. The powers that be were equally on edge, ready for this debacle to be over so they could turn off the cameras and herd the people out and back into their neighborhood pens.

"Well, Durco," Skye said to the shrieking, breathing organism that was now the audience, "looks like it's about time to wrap this up." There was an audible single voice of "No," from the crowd, followed by chants of "More, more, more!"

Skye smiled and looked back at his mates. They were grinning too, and a few laughed. Skye nodded his head. His lunar wings reappeared, fanning out from his back, as he and the other band members all began to rise on gravitic platforms similar to the drummers' risers. The whole band ascended higher and higher, while a lone, strong guitar riff began to thrum and repeat. It sounded familiar to Ray, but he couldn't place it.

"Oh, we are not going to stop playing, oh no!" Skye said to the crowd now stories below him. They roared and whistled in approval. Hands were clapping along with the contagious riff. "When I said it was time to wrap this up, what I meant was it was time to get you—*all* of you—free!"

Then, a couple of things happened at once. Ray's comm and plaser augments both came back online with full capabilities. At the same time, he saw a lot of agitated activity over at the executive box next door. The troops were in an uproar, almost a panic.

"All of you, Durco, all of you who have been shit on—have lived with a boot on your throat—have feared the secret police boogeymen would take your children in the darkness your whole lives. All of you just got full, unmonitored, unedited, uncensored comm access. All of you who have had a gun stuck in your face, who felt powerless while you watched people being put up against a wall and shot for stealing food . . . well, you have guns now too—you have power in the tips of your fingers!"

The music picked up, with more instruments now, building. Ray saw the helmeted troopers, tens of thousands of them on the arena floor, thrashing about in pain and collapsing. The ones in the president's box struggled to pull their helmets off, but it was too late. They fell too.

"And the ones who have kept you in fear, kept you from living, from singing, from dancing, kept you from freedom, they are blind now; they are disarmed!"

The crowd was roaring, surging. Random blasts of plaser fire were being shot out of citizens' hands into the air, creating plasma-cloud fireworks. Citizens blasted the pyramidal weapon-drones, raining down fire and sparking debris.

Ray saw a commotion inside their own box. The service personnel had plasers and were ordering many of the guests onto the floor. One or two resisted and were electro-stunned by the ionized laser beams firing from their hands.

Trannixx was up, out of his chair, and trying to reach anyone on his now-dead comm. He was drawing his pistol, since his weapons augment was also apparently offline. He was aiming at a young olive-skinned Durcoian woman, stepping out, her hand glowing. The republic agent had the drop on the rebel. Ray raised his arm, and his hand began to glow too. "Drop it!" he called out to Trannixx, who spun to shoot him. Ray fired without thought, and Trannixx crashed back as a ball of plasma tore apart his chest.

"Oh shit." Ray gasped.

"Thanks, Ranger!" the girl said. "We're trying to stun as many as we can and take them alive to stand trial. He didn't give you much choice, though."

"Are you all right, Ray?"

It was Neste. He had withdrawn the thread from Ray's ear. Ray blinked. His heart was thudding in time to the drums; he was sweating and trembling. He looked at his still-glowing hand, shaking, and ordered it to still. It did.

"Yeah. I'm . . . good."

"Right now, every citizen is armed and able to reach out to others, to the revolutionaries who have been planning for this day for over a year," Skye was saying as the music built. "The revolution controls the communication networks now, including the ones used by the military and the secret police. The revolution now controls the systems normally used to drown you, to suffocate you, to oppress you with fear. About a third of the military has joined the revolution!

"Now listen to me, Durco. Tonight, arrest the criminals who have done this to you. They think you can't be trusted to govern yourselves, to act civilized, not like vengeful animals. You have all the power now, and all the responsibility that goes with it. Don't be like them, don't prove them right. Show them justice, not vengeance. Take away their freedom, not their lives. Rise up and fight! Take your world back!"

The stadium was in chaos. The massive windows that had been showing the concert were now showing scenes of mass uprisings everywhere, across the planet. Others showed revolutionary leaders talking to the population. Plainclothes security agents and unhelmeted troopers were rushing in to confront the crowd, and they were meeting withering plaser fire—mostly stunning but some explosions of plasma here and there. Windmilling security agents and flailing troopers plummeted, thrown from other sky boxes, crashing among the turbulent rivers of people on the stadium floor.

The band was still playing. Skye pointed up to the president's box, only a few stories above him. "And now we close with a little music from a place a long way away from here. Music to start a revolution to. Mr. President, this one's for you!" The drums dropped in, and Ray realized what he was listening to. It was the Clash's "London Calling."

"Mr. Ambassador, Ranger, you better get inside," the young rebel said. "Skye asked us to make sure you two were kept safe just before he went on."

"It doesn't look like anybody's too safe around here right now," Neste said as he moved toward the interior with the rebel. He looked back to see Ray sprinting to the edge of the balcony. "Ray! What are you doing?"

Ray sprang up to the rail closest to the executive box and without a thought, or a look down, jumped.

There was a dizzy second of uncertainty, washed away in adrenaline, and then he was on President Naz's balcony. The troopers were still down and unmoving, lost in the feedback haze of their own helmet comms being sabotaged. Ray scooped up one of the troopers' rifles and headed for Naz himself. The president was screaming something about "Get him on the damn comm, now!" His eyes widened as Ray was suddenly upon him, jamming a rifle barrel in his face. Ray grabbed the president and stepped behind him as the two surviving security agents, bloody and wounded, rushed out of the interior lounge and leveled their own back-up pistols at Ray.

"You're under arrest, asshole," Ray said.

"Who the fuck is this?" Naz snarled, then pulled back his anger as he felt the rifle barrel tucked against his neck and jaw.

"I'm a Ranger. You're a scumbag, and I'm arresting you in the name of the people of Durco."

"Shoot this prick!" the President said out of one side of his mouth.

"Uh, sir, we can't be certain we wouldn't hit you in the process."

"What the hell do I pay you bait-brains for?" He glanced to Ray. "Shoot away alien scum. I'm just a decoy, a clone double of the real Naz."

"Okay. Here comes a little off the top."

"Wait! It's me, it's me. We couldn't afford the damn clones after we built the presidential night club."

Skye's hovering platform reached the level of the executive box, just as he finished "London Calling." His tattoos were blazing with the light of a man-sized sun; his fists were wreathed in energy. "Good night, Durco. You've been amazing! Good luck!" He looked at Naz. "Boren Naz, I place you under arrest in the name of . . ."

"I already did that," Ray said.

"He already did that," Naz and the injured agents said at the same time Ray did.

"Oh," Skye said. "Oh well, that's . . . that's great." His tattoos diminished back to normal radiance. "Did he surrender?"

Ray glanced around the rifle barrel and gave the dictator a questioning look.

"Sure." Naz sighed. "What the hell? Fucking musicians."


It was dawn in the capital city when Ray, Neste, and Skye prepared to leave Durco. The automated light cycle lightened the artificial mini-suns within the various domes and bubbles of the city. The announcement of Naz's capture had raced around the world overnight and had taken a lot of the fight out of the loyalists. The next few weeks would be stressful and uncertain, but it looked as though the revolution had succeeded.

The World-Breakers were leaving in their tour bus—the "bus" being a heavily armored, two-story war machine and luxury hotel on twenty puncture-resistant wheels. A dozen escort vehicles accompanied the mobile fortress, and fans, groupies, and roadies were all saying their goodbyes and loading up to head on to the next gig. Skye embraced his bandmates and their families and waved goodbye to them as the massive bus groaned and hissed. It pulled out of the stadium parking lot, headed for the highway tubes and the Queen's Road.

"So," Ray said as he walked up to Skye, "is this some kind of weird hobby for you, starting revolutions?"

Skye chuckled. "The idle rich are difficult to keep amused. We've been at this for a while. We only target people like Naz, and we just provide the means. It's up to the people to free themselves."

"I take back a lot of the things I was thinking about you."

"Don't. Most of them are probably spot on." They walked toward the Galaxie. A group of the rebel leaders was speaking with Neste as they approached.

"As soon as the present crisis with the Yateveo has been resolved," Neste was saying, "I will have the Shield Pact diplomatic corps contact your people about recognizing your new government, opening diplomatic relations, and lifting those sanctions."

"Thank you, Ambassador," said a Durcoian woman named Irown, who was the provisional leader of the revolutionary government. Irown turned to Skye and Ray. "How does it feel to be the first hero of the revolution, Ranger Cosa?"

Ray saw a dark cloud drift momentarily across Skye's face, and he grinned. "Pretty chill, actually."

"That will be a great quote for the history books," Skye said under his breath.

Irown embraced the musician. "Thank you, Skye. Without your help, we could never have pulled this off."

"You did this yourselves. You risked everything. I'm glad I could help in some small way." His face grew stern. "Don't forget the people who believed in you, who fought and died last night for you." He looked from face to face of the planet's new leaders. "If you do forget them, then I'll be back for all of you." The leaders nodded, solemnly. Skye shook their hands and embraced them, then continued toward the Galaxie. Ray and Neste followed.

"So, where are we meeting Chain and the others?" the musician asked.

"A place called Onao," Ray said.

"Never heard of it. Doubt they have room service."

"Ranger Cosa?" A young man with a trooper assault rifle slung over his shoulder raced to catch up to them. Ray turned to meet him. "Here." The rebel handed Evan's forty-five pistol to Ray. "I'm afraid we couldn't recover your other stolen property, but we found this, and I wanted to make sure you got it back!"

Ray took the old pistol and tucked it away.

"This is the only thing I really cared about them taking. Thank you."

The young man smiled and looked at Ray and Skye.

"I've never seen a Ranger before. They told us growing up you weren't real, only a fairy tale, but a lot of us never believed that. Maybe someday I can be a Ranger."

Skye started to say something but stopped himself. "You can be anything you want to be. Don't let anyone tell you different. May Shylah ride with you."

The young rebel smiled and ran off.

"I knew you were an old softie." Ray chuckled. He paused to look at the Galaxie and remembered the first time he had seen it in Bingo's parking lot. It seemed like a hundred lifetimes ago, but it had only been about a week. He thought about Juanita and Lu and hoped they were okay.

Skye looked at the car too, and whistled. "Any chance I could drive this sexy beast for a bit, hero of the revolution?"

"Space you?" Ray grinned. "Am . . . am I getting that right? Space you?"

Skye laughed and nodded. "Space you," the singer confirmed, slapping Ray on the back. "We'll make a citizen of the universe out of you before you know it, Earth boy."

Skye wanted to listen to some Earth music. Ray found him some Dead Kennedys with Cassandra's help. He seemed to approve of "Police Truck." They were in the highway tubes in minutes and then onto the Queen's Road, the light of galaxies guiding their way to rendezvous with the others.

---

## 25

Orrenhawl was a frozen, abandoned world. That made it the perfect place for one of the Lords of Glass to hide from Death's Muse.

Landran had once been very wealthy. He had gotten into the Glass business as a young man, took some great risks, and made and lost many fortunes before he was thirty. Fortunately, over the course of his eighty-comp career, he followed the proper progression of getting smarter as he got older and managed to hide money away, invest it, and put it into legitimate enterprises. By the time he reached the age of one hundred, he was completely out of the Glass business and set for several lifetimes.

"Glass" was the slang used for the fist-sized clumps of crystallized proteins that had been discovered embedded in the skulls of animals on a world named Isokan, in the Rusak Galaxy. They produced an amazing variety of telepathic hallucinations in virtually all species, tapping into the fundamental deep structures in their consciousnesses. The discovery and importation of Glass in the last few centuries had changed everything in intergalactic society.

Many intergalactic religions used Glass as part of their sacrament for communing with whatever powers they worshipped or with the universe itself. The crystals were also capable, when used with other drugs or disciplines, of wildly boosting the strength and range of a psychic's powers, especially telepaths. Glass's legality varied from region to region of the Known Galaxies. In most places, its use was highly regulated by the government, to ensure its abuse didn't lead to telepathic addiction and a host of other health and social problems.

Glass was rare, since the poachers and dealers had hunted the animals who produced the crystals into extinction over a hundred completions ago. It was estimated that no more than a billion intact crystals existed across the whole of the universe. Finding Glass and obtaining it was dangerous and, usually, highly illegal work, but a single score could make you wealthy enough to buy and sell whole regions of galaxies.

The scarcity of Glass had led the underworld to innovation. Landran was one of a group of investors who backed a successful undertaking to "clone" the protein chains within the original crystals. The result damaged the original crystal but produced a multitude of new crystals that worked almost as well as Glass but burned out after prolonged use. The new, cheaper manufactured product known by the nickname "Krys" flooded the Known Galaxies and created epidemics of addicted beings, lost in mazes of alien thoughts and dreams.

Krys made Landran and his associates even more wealthy than they already were. Now a legitimate businessman on the prosperous core world of Sukalia, Landran knew his family was secure. He had provided for endless generations of his children and their heirs with the limitless wealth he had obtained by pushing drugs and destroying lives. He slept well at night. The Glass he had in his personal collection helped him with that.

Then, one night, more than twenty comps ago, he had received a message from one of his former business associates, a Lagriean named Arlox, that something was very wrong.

"I think she's found me, my family," Arlox said in his frantic comm recording. "If she comes, you must beware, my old friend. She comes for us all."

Landran didn't need to ask who "she" was.

He dispatched his best agents to the private world his old partner owned. They reported back that Arlox was dead. His seven mates, their children and their grandchildren, everyone who bore his blood, were dead; all his servants, their families, his private army, his attorneys, his retainers were dead. All were murdered in the most brutal and hideous ways imaginable. Arlox's properties had all been burned to smoldering craters by plasma bombs. His funds had been stolen away from his secured shadow-bank accounts.

Landran had tried to discount it as revenge from someone else in the Glass trade, for some old slight. Such things did happen from time to time in the business. The justifications didn't take, and he began to not sleep so well. He hired more security, sent out feelers for any information about her current whereabouts and latest victims. As usual, there was no solid intelligence, only rumors and myths.

Anyone who had anything to do with Glass or Krys had done the math at one point or another. How could they help but do it? There were countless trillions of beings spread across near-infinite space who trafficked in, profited from, and used Glass and Krys, from thieves and murderers to priests and government spies. The odds that she would find her way to Landran and inflict her terrifying attention upon him and his loved ones were infinitesimal. Still, there were so many dead on so many worlds, so many victims.

Landran decided to not take any chances. He moved his family to a private compound swarming with guards and combat constructs on a distant world he didn't even own. He took off in the opposite direction toward a little-visited galactic cluster made of mostly still-white-hot stars. He took an army with him. Another army guarded his wife and five children.

None of it mattered. His family and all their protectors were butchered. The anger welled in him; he did what so many before him had done. He put out a contract on her head, enough money to attract the universe's greatest killers. Then came the comps of running, of hiding, of alcohol, and drugs to try to sleep, to not think of his children hacked and hewn, to not think what she would do to him.

Landran no longer worried about spending money; he spent treasuries of it on traps to lure her in and make her pay for his family. She would ignore them and then strike at his servants, his attorneys, those who represented him in the endeavors. Soon, no one wanted to work for him or even be in the same room.

He spent even more money, he had to, to send out investigators to scour the commospheres of all the core worlds of the Known Galaxies trying to find her, to get a solid scrap of information about the most dangerous and prolific serial killer in the history of the universe. All that came back was news that more of his old associates were dead along with anyone connected to them. The only solid piece of intelligence any governmental, criminal, or law enforcement organization had on her was the piece she, herself, had volunteered to them, left at her first crime scene.

Her name was Ajeet.

Landran had his appearance and his genetics altered to disguise himself. It cost him even more of his dwindling fortune. He even considered a telepathic body jump to throw her off the trail, but there was no way he could afford it. He'd insisted on hanging on to his collection of Glass, hopelessly addicted to it by now, even though parting with a few of the crystals would have made him a fantastically wealthy man again.

He thought that the alterations had succeeded in hiding him for a time. He settled into his new face, his new life, on a quiet little world named Mehiri, with beautiful skies and sunsets, warm winds, and a global network of shallow tidal pools. After so many comps of running and hiding, he began to put down roots once again. He fished, he made friends, he grew tan, and his hands roughened from tying nets and pulling them in from the pools. But soon the feeling of being stalked, of being watched, returned, followed by the dreams of her coming closer each night.

Eventually, he met a woman who reminded him of his beautiful wife, lost to him more than twenty comps ago. They married. He never told her who he had been before he came to Mehiri. The only time he yelled at her was when she discovered his box of Glass and almost touched one of the crystals. In time, they had a child, and Landran insisted they give the baby his late little girl's name. He never told his wife why he picked that name, but she agreed out of love for him.

A few comps passed. One night, Landran didn't come straight home from work. One of his fellow fishermen had just opened a new batch of thistle wine, and he and his friends sat and passed the jug back and forth, watching the golden sun set across the waters. He arrived home after dark and discovered his house consumed in flames. He found his wife and baby girl cut to pieces on the front lawn, among the flowers of the garden they had planted. They were laid out in the shape of Landran's old merchant mark, the one he had used the whole time he had dealt in Glass. He found his box of Glass sitting at the base of the symbol made from his loved ones. Inside the box, his crystals were gone. They were replaced with his wife's and child's hearts.

Landran searched frantically for some place, any place, he could hide, could live out his days in peace. That was when he heard about an old abandoned lodge, on a forgotten planet, in a mostly empty galaxy. He killed the being who told him about Orrenhawl, after he had wrung out every scrap of information about the ice world. He then tracked down and killed the being who had told the-now-late being about the world. He hoped that that was far enough back to keep Ajeet from picking up his trail.

Landran arrived on Orrenhawl and found that the once-majestic lodge had fallen into disrepair, but it would do for his purposes. The buildings and grounds stretched over two hundred acres of land near the ramp to the Queen's Road, the single way onto and off the planet.

He mined the road off the ramp with surplus fusion mines he had bought cheap off an arms dealer. He settled into the dark, hulking building, activating a few small photon furnaces to give him power. After a time, he took to hunting to supplement his food. He never slept more than an hour at a time, and he never recovered from the loss of his Glass.

In the deep of winter on Orrenhawl, in his one-hundred-thirty-second comp of life, Landran awoke and saw her standing before him, her silhouette lit by the photon furnace's dim light. Her ears were high and pointed, and she stood on hocked, back-facing legs with cloven hooves. She had no eyes, no mouth on her vertically elongated head. In her hands, which resembled segmented hooves, she held a yard-long scepter of dull and scored silver.

"Please," Landran whispered. "You've hounded me most of my life, taken everything else away from me and murdered everyone who mattered to me. Isn't that enough torture? Isn't that enough for whatever you think I did?"

*No,* Ajeet said without a mouth. The photon spear in her hand ignited with a wicked hiss.

The being known as Landran screamed. The totality of what he was—his every memory, his every thought, the very essence of his awareness, his consciousness—was torn out of him and devoured. Then she went to work on his still-screaming flesh.

## 26

A re we there, yet?" Rudian asked for the hundredth time.

"Do not make me pull this truck over," Chain said. He, Lera, Pana, and Rudian were in the tow truck headed for the rendezvous on Onao with Ray, Neste and, he hoped, Skye.

"My dear Chain, it is utterly barbaric to keep us sealed up in this rolling grease-trap with no stops for sustenance or the relief of biological requirements. I thought I taught you better, my boy. Besides"—Rudian glanced over to Lera, who was sitting beside him in the back seat—"she keeps scooching over!"

"You're really good at pretending to be other people, Rudi," Lera said with a yawn. "Could you try to pretend to be someone who has a personality?"

Chain chuckled at that.

Pana shook her head with a smile. "Always a pleasure to work with professionals."

Chain reached past her and flipped open the glove box. Papers, wadded up toll receipts, and baggies of questionable substances shifted forward as the door flipped open. Chain retrieved one of the last of his meat-stick snacks that Lu had given him back on Earth. He handed it to the preacher.

"There's your sustenance. As for relieving yourself, roll down a window and pray the winds are kind to you."

"Magnificent," Rudian grumbled as he pealed the plastic sheath off the meat stick. "We could have taken my bus, a much more pleasant ride."

Lera sniffed the air and made a face at the meat snack.

"That thing is disgusting . . . give me some."

"Get your own!" Rudian looked up at Chain, pleadingly. "It's mine. You gave it to me, right?" He glanced back. The stick was now in Lera's hand, and she was munching on it.

"Just as I suspected." She took another bite. "Repulsive. It has more preservatives in it than a Nasrurian mummy."

"Madame! Have you no shame . . . oh never mind, you don't! Chaaaaain!"

"Share, or I'll shoot you both." The Ranger sighed and glanced over to Pana. "Then I'd have to get my back seat detailed . . . the struggle is real."

"You think Ray and the ambassador are okay?" Pana asked Chain while Lera and Rudian squabbled in the back. "I should have gone with them. That was my mission."

"I trust Ray, and you do too, or you would have gone with them. We needed you with us, Pana."

"A prison escape is not exactly what I ever expected to be doing on my first assignment away from Norama. Still . . . it was . . . exciting."

Chain grinned. "We'll make a Ranger out of you yet, Ratari."

"Shylah forbid." She chuckled. "We've been gone four cycles. I pray the Yateveo haven't made their move."

"Me too," Chain said. "The Yateveo are pretty conservative. They won't go until they think they have enough troops to be unbeatable. They want overpowering numbers, and given their biology, that will take a while. We need Lera and Ajeet to get us in, to break through and give us time to do what we have to. We needed Rudian and Skye to get to them."

"So you say. You *are* talking about Ajeet? *The* Ajeet. The serial killer."

"I am."

"Why in the Mother's name do we need an unstable killer, and how exactly do you intend to find her when the whole universe has been unable to do so?"

"Skye and Ajeet have a . . . special connection," Chain said. "I don't entirely understand it myself. He's a projection empath, able to use music or even his voice to affect other beings' emotions. He's never used it to manipulate people. I think the feedback of that would hurt him pretty bad, but he can sense feelings buried inside people and help them pull those up to the surface. He would have made a hell of a therapist, if he weren't so busy getting rich. 'Jeet's a powerful telepath from a race of telepaths. When she and Skye worked together before, they connected on some very deep levels. They're . . . they're as close as any two beings can be. If anyone can find her, it's Skye."

"You said her people are telepaths," Pana said. "Where is she from?"

"Isokan."

"The world Glass came from?" Chain nodded. "But Isokan has no sentient life on it."

"Not anymore," Chain said.

Onao was a nexus of roadways. Located in the Kona Galaxy, the planet was a crossroads for travelers on the Queen's Road coming from seventeen different galaxies. Large sections of Onao were dedicated to travelers, their vehicles, and their money. The place reminded Ray a little of the Bingo Truck Stop, but only a little.

As Ray, Neste, and Skye wandered the lot, heading toward one of the hundreds of restaurants, gift shops, motels, and malls that dotted this particular exit of Onao, he saw alien families in RV-like vehicles with tank treads. A pack of seven-foot-tall, six-armed, horned, flax-skinned beings was riding two- and three-wheeled motorbikes. All the bikers had the same tattoo symbol on their bare chests or backs. Ray gave them plenty of space. They looked badass.

Ray was happy to find Chain's old tow truck waiting in front of the restaurant Chain had suggested as a rendezvous point. The place was called Olgav's Feedery, and had a holographic, tapir-like alien cartoon character dancing around the sign under the door. They went inside. The place was packed with families, truckers, and the pear-colored local humanoids. Music was playing from the small control consoles at each booth and table. Ray spotted Chain and the others at a long table in the corner of the main dining room. Chain waved and gestured them over.

Besides Chain, Pana, and Rudian, they had been joined by a slight humanoid woman with metallic hair and champagne-colored skin. Old friends greeted one another, and new acquaintances were introduced. Skye gave Chain a curt nod, and Chain returned it, but they did not embrace or even shake hands.

Ray was introduced to Lera, who looked him up and down like he was on the menu. Chain stepped in before she could make a move. "He's green, and you should be ashamed of yourself."

"In my defense, I am just out of prison." She gave Ray a beaming smile. "Pleasure to meet you, darling boy."

They ordered enough food to feed an army, and it occurred to Ray as the second wave of plates and platters arrived that that was exactly what they were. The beings sitting around this table were going to invade a heavily armed planet and take on a monstrous army that vastly outnumbered them. It was sobering, and then frightening, to realize he was part of this, until he saw how completely at ease the other Rangers seemed.

"So, the caper is the ambassador's home world," Lera said in between massive bites of food. She and Rudian seemed to be in a competition to see who could put more away faster. Chain nodded as he, too, wolfed down copious amounts of the spread in front of them. "Triban would be a tough nut to crack even without an occupying army of blood-drinking nihilists," Lera said. "Your Excellency, you do have the security codes we'll need?"

"I do." He had several small tendrils in a bowl of some kind of slate-gray liquid. "There is, of course, the possibility that they have changed them."

"No worries." Lera drained a tall glass of a frothy, fermented drink before she replied. "If I have a notion of how the encryption system is set up, I can break it. You ready to phase the world out of this continuum?"

Neste paused, and Ray felt his hesitation. So did most of the beings at the table who stayed alive by reading motives.

"Yes, of course."

"You sure about that, Ambassador?" Chain said.

"You seem a bit . . . uncertain," Rudian added.

"I'm not looking forward to the prospect. The calculations are taking up more of my processing capabilities than I've ever had to employ before, so please forgive me. The calculations will be ready when we reach Triban, I assure you."

"Good," Lera said. "I've run the numbers, and with the estimated forces we've got against what they are cooking up, the best we can hope for is a brief holding action once we're in. If you can't phase the planet away, we're going to be slaughtered."

The table grew silent as Lera went back to really enjoying her drink. Chain narrowed his eyes at Lera and shook his head. He looked back to Neste. "I understand how difficult a choice this must be for you, Neste, but we do need you to stop the Yateveo."

"I will be ready to do what I must."

Ray felt for the ambassador. Deep down inside of him he was a father terrified for his child. All this pressure to destroy his home, so many of his people. He wondered why Neste hadn't mentioned his kid to anyone else.

Chain glanced across the table from face to face. "Okay, our next move. Skye and I go fetch our last teammate. I need the rest of you to head back to Ray's home world, Earth, with him. We'll meet you at the rendezvous point that Ray's friends back on Earth have set up. It's a world called Trull A-17."

"What?" Ray said. "What rendezvous? What are you talking about?"

"Is Earth where the . . . thing we need is?" Lera asked. Chain nodded.

"What thing we need?" Ray looked at Chain accusingly. "What are you doing to my planet, man?"

"Relax. I need you to catch up with 'Keem and Mateo and see if they did what I sent them to do, and then follow them to the meet-up point."

"You . . . you asked them to do something?" Ray was feeling a little dizzy. "When the hell were you going to tell me?"

"I just did," Chain said calmly. He looked at the others. "I'll pick up the tab."

"You most certainly will," Rudian said, dabbing his lips with a napkin. "You are the one, after all, with a covert operations spending account."

"Could you say 'covert operations' a bit louder, Rudi?" Chain said.

As everyone got to their feet, Chain confided in Ray. "Everything's okay. I asked Mateo and 'Keem to help me with something I knew we wouldn't have time to do ourselves. Nothing dangerous. It's going to be great; you'll see." He walked away, and Skye slid up.

"'It's going to be great.' That is *exactly* what he's said to me every single time he's screwed me," he said to Ray and then walked toward the door.

Lera and Rudian brushed by the concerned Ray, nodding in agreement with each other.

"Oh, yes," Rudian said, "royally screwed."

"Every time," Lera added. They walked on.

"'It's going to be great,'" Rudian said to Lera.

"It *is*!" Lera replied. "Great!"

Ray rubbed his face and tried to console himself with the thought that at least he was headed home, no matter what was waiting for him there.

"Great," he said to no one.

# 27

Chain's tow truck sped along the Queen's Road, headed away from Onao and the others. Skye sat in the passenger's seat, quiet, almost brooding. His tattoos were shut down for the moment.

"What's your take?" Chain asked the musician. "Where is she?"

Skye said nothing. He leaned an arm out the window; the cool breeze of the road tugged at his jacket sleeve.

"All right, let's get this out of the way," Chain said. "You still blame me for how things ended up last time. I'm okay with that."

Skye glared over at him and shook his head in obvious disgust. "I'm sure you are." The singer fished out a small device from his jacket. It resembled a set of brass knuckles but with a slender metallic tube attached to it at a forty-five degree angle, facing toward Skye's lips, and a squat cylinder mounted under the handset. Skye keyed the pipe on with a push of his thumb and took a long drag on it, exhaling rust-colored smoke.

"One of the biggest problems I've always had with you, Chain, is that I don't know if I can trust you. I have no idea who you really are. I can't get any kind of read on you at all. You are an emotional dead zone. After everything last time, I thought maybe you were some kind of psychopath, with an emotional landscape only for yourself, but that isn't the case, is it?"

Chain said nothing, just kept driving.

"I've seen you care, and no psychopath is that capable of pretending. You have emotions and feelings—strong feelings, I'd wager—but you shield them from me, from everyone, all the time. And that makes me distrust you more than if you were insane."

"Where I grew up," Chain finally said after a long time of silence, "you learned to block your feelings, your thoughts. You had to. They were a weakness, a weapon that could be used against you by the others. I don't apologize for it, but I do acknowledge it would be disturbing to someone with your talents. Trust me, I feel. There are times I try very hard not to, but I can't. I know you blame me for what happened to Meadow and the others. I do too, but it doesn't change the fact that if I had to give them those orders again, had to send them back in, I would."

"I . . . I know. It was the only way. But, damn it, she *loved* you; she respected and trusted you so much. They all did . . . *we* all did."

"I know. I know."

"This greenie, Ray, he's got the look too. You tell him to go piss on a supernova, he'll ask you 'how long a stream.' I couldn't keep meeting people, liking them, loving some of them, and then watching them march into the grinder for you, for the fucking invisible Queen and her void-damned children."

Chain chuckled.

"What?" Skye asked, taking another hit on his pipe.

"Just a very, very apt description."

"*Highwaymen, you do the driving, Highwaymen, you do the dying,*" Skye sang.

"I always liked that one," Chain said.

"Charted pretty good in the outer systems, not as good in the cores." He put the pipe away and summoned his hovering energy strings from between his fingers. He strummed softly as they drove on. "People never get tired of the myth. Not so much on the reality." The musician played, and Chain drove.

"I . . . haven't been with anyone since Meadow," Chain said, after a time. "Not so sure I ever can be again. I know you can't feel that . . . but I can."

They stopped on the shoulder of the Queen's Road that overlooked the Barthram Expanse, a 200-thousand-parsec nebula of phlox and sapphire punctuated with the sharp lighthouse flashes of a thousand variable stars. They left the truck idling and stood at the rail. If you stepped over that barrier, you'd find yourself floating in the depths of space, the Road seemingly gone.

"You can still sense Ajeet, can't you?" Chain asked quietly, as if he were in a temple. Skye nodded, not taking his eyes off the awe-inspiring beauty laid out before them.

"I had to close myself off from her. I hated doing it, but it was . . . too much. She's killing children, Chain, innocent people caught up with the ones she blames. I had to shut her out."

"Could you try to sense her, to find her?" Skye looked over to him. "Please."

Skye sighed and looked back to the living masterpiece drifting before his eyes.

"How can there be something like this in a universe full of such . . . ugliness?"

"Balance? I don't know. I know Ajeet is . . . sick, but sometimes she's done extraordinary good, saved lives instead of taken them."

"Under your guidance, of course," Skye said. "You see her as a weapon. I see glimpses of how she was before her life was amputated and she lost her mind, lost her way."

"I need the weapon. I need you to take care of your friend."

Skye closed his eyes and concentrated on his breathing. After a few moments, he winced and almost doubled over as if he had been stabbed or punched. Chain took him by the shoulders and held him up.

"You okay?"

Skye nodded and righted himself.

"It feels . . . it feels like . . . I smell sickly sweet flowers, decaying, choking . . . the crunch of ice under her hooves. Blood in the snow. All the voices in her, singing, laughing, crying, screaming . . . all her charges now, her children. The sadness . . . like the bow drawn back on a lone violin, vibrating, quavering in the darkness. Staring over the event horizon into the place where the very idea of light dies. She . . . she just killed someone . . . not long ago. I felt her. She doesn't get pleasure from the kills, she never has, just the hunt. There is a peace, a terrible peace, that comes to her when she . . . inflicts the pain, at the end, when she finishes them."

Skye was pale, and he was sweating even in the chill of the Queen's Road. Chain started to say something, and the singer stopped him.

"I know. I know where she's going, where she always goes after a kill. She's going home."

Isokan was a world of impossibly tall mountain ranges that extended beyond the planet's atmosphere and into the fringes of space. The planet was stark in its rocky, frozen beauty. Completely covered in snow most of the year, there were only two life forms that had developed and endured on the planet.

Only one thrived now.

Ajeet had arrived home only a few days ago from the conclusion of her hunt on Orrenhawl. She traveled the Queen's Road in a powered suit that augmented the strength of her four legs and would take over for her when her legs tired. She hated the suit and its technology; she despised the Queen's Road. If it had never been created, then other species would never have made their way to her home.

The first off-worlders couldn't communicate with her people, thought them mere animals and treated them accordingly. Eventually, though, telepaths came to Isokan. They told those from other worlds that Ajeet's people were intelligent. But no one listened, not when there was so much money to be made. The hunters and the poachers had discovered her people's souls and begun to steal them, abuse them, turn them into Glass—all to become "rich," a concept Ajeet's people never fully grasped. They had all they needed to live, to thrive, to be happy. Why strive for more than that when it would never satisfy you?

The reason Ajeet wore a Ranger's signet on one of her forelegs, like an arm cuff, was because of one such telepath who died saving some of her family . . . at least temporarily. She knew that not all those who lived on the endless worlds beyond her own were evil and selfish. She just no longer cared.

Her people had never fought one another, never warred or needed police. Once every few centuries, a sick individual might arise among her people who abused their ability to draw sustenance from the psychic lichen and would drain others of their kind into mind-soul death. Such diseased, pathetic creatures were put down for the good of all, including themselves, and their souls were not allowed to be added to the Great Story.

It came as an utter shock and horror to Ajeet's kind that there were whole species, whole worlds and galaxies of beings who harmed one another, who murdered. Their descent onto her world was a nightmare of which they had no comprehension. How could the whole universe be so ill, so afflicted, save for her tiny, lonely world?

It took centuries to slaughter all of her kind, to cut their souls from their flesh, to plunder and empty the tens of thousands of caves beneath the living rock that held the souls of all of her kind that had gone before. She could not say why she had ended up being the last. She wished with all her power she were not.

In the empty catacombs that had held the essence of her kind, she wept as her kind did. She had no eyes, so her soul wept, stretching itself across the silent psychosphere of her world. In times before the hunters came, her cries would have been met with the comfort and love of all the souls of her kind, joined together to share the joy and the sadness. Now, Ajeet of Isokan cried alone.

In time, she went mad, with no voice but her own to keep her company, to soothe and teach and minister to her. She knew she was ill. She no longer cared. She would sense the arrival of more hunters on her world, and she began to hunt them. She took one of their tools

—the photon spear they used to cut the souls out of her people—and she began to use it on them. She did the unforgivable and tore apart their essences, their souls, and fed upon them. Over time, she came to drink their fear of her and found it sweet.

Finally, they stopped coming to her dead world. So, in time, she went to theirs.

Ajeet carefully placed the late Landran's Glass collection onto the rocky shelves of one of the caves of the Great Story, one crystal at a time. She heard the frightened, fragmented voices of the stones, so long abused and damaged by alien minds. She tried to soothe them by singing them a very old song the mothers would sing to their newborns. The other souls that resided on the shelves joined her voice to welcome the newcomers and reassure them they were safe and home. *He cannot hurt you anymore,* she said to the souls she had recovered a few years back when she had killed Landran's second family. It would take time, but the souls would recover themselves as much as they could. She placed the artificial souls of the off-world beings called "Krys" that she had recovered on her way home on the shelves as well. They were warped and stunted echoes of the true souls of her people that had been used to make them, but they, too, deserved peace.

As she said goodbye to the souls in this cache, she reinforced the mind-shields that hid this cave from the sight of all but her. If a telepath were strong enough to pierce her deception, they would die a most excruciating death at the hands of the mind traps she had prepared and reinforced before they ever laid hands on a single soul.

Back on the surface, she sensed their arrival, felt Skye's soul once again open to her. She would be lying to herself if she didn't admit a thrill of happiness at feeling him again, but her excitement was diminished, because he was not alone.

. . .

"I've never been to Isokan before," Chain said, his breath a mask of mist in the cold gathering twilight. They had parked the truck near the edge of the ramp onto Ajeet's home world and gotten out to look around. "It's beautiful."

"If the Shield Pact, or any of the major governments, had tried to do more than just pay lip service to stopping the flow of Glass, they could have saved this world and her people," Skye said.

"Big business, big money," Chain said. "You'll always find politicians sniffing around. Too bad 'Jeet's people didn't have a lobby." He paused for moment. "Is she here?"

"Yes. She sensed us arriving."

*Hello, Skein, Chain.* Ajeet's thoughts were strong and clear. She was either transmitting them from a distance or telepathically blinding them both to her presence near them.

"'Jeet," Chain said. "Long time. How are you?"

*In pain. You are still a thought-shadow to me, Chain. I see nothing but what you allow me to perceive. I'm not used to being blocked so casually. It used to trouble me and Skein very much, didn't it, Skein? I still don't like it . . . or you.* She regarded the musician. *How are you? Still singing inside and out, I sense?* Skye smiled at the remark. *You have opened yourself back up to me. Was that so you and Chain could find me?*

*Yes,* Skye thought. *In part. In part, I've wanted to for a long time, but what you do . . . it hurts me, 'Jeet.*

*I understand.*

"We need your help, Ajeet" Chain said. "The Yateveo have returned, and they have taken over a world and are holding billions of beings hostage. They intend to swarm out and take over more worlds. It's the start of another war."

*It amazes me you people can keep track of all of them. You hold them so often. Why should any of this mean anything to me?*

Chain looked to Skye and then looked around, trying to figure out which direction he should address. "You've helped us before . . ."

*You mean I killed for you before,* she corrected him. *The circumstances upon which we met necessitated we stand together or all fall. After that, I merely tolerated you and the others because it allowed me to remain in Skein's company.*

"Killing is precisely why I need you," Chain said. "They have names for you on every world you've visited in your 'work.' 'The Void-Bringer,' 'Pain Sculptress,' 'the Night's Knife.' I think the most apt one is 'Death's Muse.' You have a gift for murder, a taste for it, and that makes you valuable to me. You don't have to like me, and I don't have to like you. In point of fact, I think you're insane, but I do understand why you went mad, why you do what you do."

A montage of terrified screams, cries of utter pain, and hissing, choking death, ripped through Chain's and Skye's minds. It was what passed for laughter from Ajeet. *You know nothing, less than nothing,* she said. *You never will.*

She was between them now, visible. Her fur was black with patches of silver. Skye was pretty sure there was more silver now than the last time he had seen her. Her head was elongated and vertical like a horse's, with large flaring nostrils. Her ears were up high on her head and pointed and cupped like a goat's. She had no mouth, no eyes.

A raised lump of flesh rested slightly up and center of her "face." This was her soul. The crystal was embedded in her skull and under her flesh. She was on all four of her powerful backward-bent legs. Each of her hooves was cloven. A beautiful mane of wild black-and-silver hair ran from between her ears and down her long, muscular neck. She wore no clothing and carried only a yard-long metallic staff —the photon spear she had long ago claimed from a hunter. The staff had a strap that was slung over her neck, and it rested on her back.

"Think what you will," Chain said. "You are the best killer in the universe, and I need you. You'll either help us, or you won't."

She turned her sightless face toward Skye. *Why should I help him, Skein?*

Skye looked at the ice and snow at his feet and then looked at Ajeet. He wanted to reach out and touch her but he knew now was not the time for that.

"If the Yateveo succeed, they will spread across the civilized regions of the Known Galaxies quickly. The death and chaos they inflict will make it much harder for you to hunt down the others you want to kill. In fact, they will most likely kill many of those you seek, denying you your hunt. It's in your long-term interest to help us."

*Why are you helping him?* she thought to Skye. *You distrust him as much as I do. Are you here to save lives? To stop an ancient evil?*

*Yes,* Skye thought to her. *That's part of it. I'm sick of war and death, but not so sick I could sleep knowing I didn't try to help. The main reason I came when Chain asked, though, was to see you. To make sure you were all right.*

Ajeet stood on her hind legs. She towered over the other two Rangers. Her fore-hooves split apart into rudimentary "fingers," and she let the photon spear drop into her hands. She looked down at Skye. *I've missed you too, Skein, very much.* She reached out to an open channel of telepathic transmission so Chain could hear her as well. *I'll go with you, Chain—shadow man—and I will kill. Not for you, but because Skein feels strongly about this latest fool's crusade of yours. I can feel it. I do it for him. Is that clear?*

"Perfectly," Chain said with a nod. "We'd best be on our way. We don't have much time."

*You never seem to,* said Death's Muse.

# PART III

# RANGER

# 28

Port Arthur hadn't changed a bit. If anything, it seemed smaller to Ray, coming off the exit from the Queen's Road. It was night, and it was the middle of a summer thunderstorm. Lightning cut the sky, and thunder cracked it. His passengers struggled to see past the darkness and the rain.

"You don't control your weather here?" Pana asked.

"More like it controls us," Ray said. "We had a really terrible storm here about two years ago. It wrecked the place pretty bad. We've been rebuilding as best we can. Folks around here don't like rain, but we're tough, and we don't scare easy."

"Clearly," Neste said. "Ray, I think it's best if you find me a place to work where my physicality won't disturb your neighbors."

"I'm taking you all to my house. Then I'm going looking for Mateo and 'Keem to see what Chain has gotten them into."

"May I come with you?" Pana asked.

"Sure. We'll find you something a little less conspicuous to wear."

Ray was able to sneak everyone into the house under the cover of the storm. Everyone got soaked making it inside except Neste, who seemed to remain dry even though he almost looked like flowing water. "Well, here's *mi hogar*. Sorry the place is kind of a wreck, but please make yourself at home."

Rudian looked around. "My dear boy, I had no idea you lived on such a . . . rustic world. There's no commosphere, no makers . . . how do you people . . . live?"

"Rudi means no offense," Lera said with a chuckle. "He hasn't had to rough it in a long time. Thank you for welcoming us into your home."

"We have cable." Ray nodded to the TV in the living room. "I just paid the bill, so it should be good. And we have Wi-Fi. It's not the same as a commosphere, but your comms should be able to pick it up. I'm guessing it's a little like AM when you're used to stereo."

"I have no idea what you just said"—Rudian patted Ray on the shoulder—"but thank you, dear boy."

Ray assigned sleeping quarters. He gave Rudian his brother's old room; Pana, his; and Lera, his parents' room. He'd sleep on the couch. He directed Pana to Juanita's closet, and then he grabbed a shower, a shave, and some clean, dry clothes while she searched.

Feeling a million times better, he grabbed one of his old Memorial High School baseball caps to keep the rain off his head and sat on the edge of his bed, tying his Chucks.

"Is this acceptable?" Pana was dressed in Juanita's old Texas A&M hooded sweatshirt with a T-shirt underneath, a pair of old, well-worn jeans, and some running shoes. Her short wet hair was swept back from her face.

Ray smiled. "Yeah, you look great. Most folks will figure the ward you're wearing on your forehead is just some kind of body jewelry."

"If you don't mind my asking"—she stepped into his room—"who are these people?" She held a dusty, framed photo that Juanita kept on her dresser. It was from about five years back. She sat on the bed next to him. "Is this your family?"

"Yeah. This was one of the last pictures we got of everyone together. It was at Christmas. My friend Lu took it. That's Juanita, my mom."

"She's beautiful."

"Yeah, she sure is. My dad said thinking of her is what got him through all the fighting. Like I told you, he was in the military. He fought in a war called Desert Storm, back before my brother and I were born."

"That's him?" She pointed to Dad in the picture. He was frail, almost skeletal at that point, with a blanket wrapped around him. About a month after the picture was taken, he was back in the hospital for the last time.

Ray nodded. "That's my pop."

"I can tell he's a warrior. The look in his eyes." That made Ray smile. "My grandfather had that same look. He fought in the war against the Fireborn long ago. Even when his body was failing him, when he was fighting his last battle, he never lost that look."

"Yep, the baddest of the badasses. That was Pop, right up till the end."

Pana pointed to Ben and Jess. "Your brother and sister?"

"Brother, yeah. But this is Jess. She was my girlfriend. They're both gone."

Pana glanced over to Ray, but only for a second.

"I'm sorry."

"Yeah, me too."

"Your brother looks a lot like you and your father."

"Thanks. Yeah, Ben kind of took over after Pop died. Juanita . . . Mom, she kind of lost it. She really loved Pop. She . . . couldn't handle losing him, so Ben picked up the pieces. He dropped out of college, worked a few jobs, and raced for extra money on the weekends. He loved the racing. He had ice water instead of blood, could take a hairpin at a hundred, and laugh while he was doing it. He wasn't reckless; he was just . . . sure. I miss him a lot."

"And now you do the same," Pana said. "You take care of your mother, of your family."

Ray shrugged. "I try. Not much left to take care of. I'm not as strong as my dad or Ben. Someone had to do it, and I'm all that's left." He handed the picture back to Pana. "The funny part is all this crazy shit—intergalactic highways, laser guns, aliens, and vampire trees—it seems more real to me than the last few years. I feel like I'm sleep-walking through my life, like there's a hole in me, and all the color is just gushing out." He looked at Jess in the picture, laughing, alive, their arms tangled around one another. "Just put one foot in front of the other, I guess."

He closed his eyes, and there was Jess, limp on the floor in her room. The white-hot dagger of pain stabbed him again, as if no time had passed from then to now. *Pain lets us time travel,* Ray thought. It was sharper than memory.

"A person who feels no reason to live," Pana said, "will find a way to stop living."

"Yeah, you're right." Ray stood. "They will. They do. Come on, let's go find Mateo and 'Keem."

"Ray"—Pana set the picture on his night table—"the dead can give us reason to go on, as much as they can take it away. Your family has many warriors within it. You honor them by going on."

She brushed past him as she headed downstairs. Ray looked back at the picture and then followed her down.


"They left?" Ray asked Rudian, who was on the couch and had already mastered the art of channel surfing.

Rudian nodded, pausing his search on a local access channel that was showing some televangelist preaching. He had hair much like Conway Twitty's. "Nice hair. Yes. Lera said she had something to take care of, and she needed the ambassador's help. You happen to have one of these bibles he's going on about here?"

Ray growled and dug his grandmother's bible up from under a pile of long-expired fast food coupons and other Jurassic junk mail that had never made it to the trash can. He handed it to Rudian. "Did they happen to say where they were going, or how they were getting there?"

"Uh . . . no," Rudian replied and went back to his exploration of Earth's pop culture.

"Come on," Pana said, pulling up the hood on the sweatshirt. "I'm certain they will be fine."

"We don't have a lot of . . . talking metal fountains around here," Ray added.

"Tribanni can alter their forms relative to their mass," she said. "Neste may look like a metal humanoid now."

"Oh, that's much better," Ray said, walking out the door. "I'm silly to worry. Hey, have them comm me if they come back."

Rudian grunted and gave a dismissive wave.

Pana closed the door behind her, and a second later, Rudian called out, "Bring back . . . Doritos . . . is it? And some of this 'KFC' they keep talking about as well."


Ray called Lu first, as they drove down the rain-slicked, black-mirror streets of Houston Avenue.

"Hey, man, it's Ray."

"Are you back?" Lu asked. "Did you guys pull it off?"

"Yes, but just for a little while, and no, not yet. How's Juanita?"

"She's . . . she's okay. Doing a lot better."

"Lu, you don't sound so sure."

"Yeah, well, she is okay. She's detoxing, and she's getting therapy. She . . . just misses you a lot, Ray. She thinks you've dipped out on her."

Ray felt a knot in his stomach.

"She's not buying the working-out-of-town thing?"

"I think she is, but she's mentioned how you're not coming to see her and how you must be getting at least a few days off. She's just sad, man."

"Okay." Ray sighed, and Pana gave him a concerned look. "One way or another, this thing is almost finished. I'll make it up to her."

"The doc told me he's been trying to call you to discuss family therapy. She'll be ready to head home in about three weeks. He says you need to be part of her recovery . . . or you need to leave her alone. I'm sorry, Ray. I can't tell him you're off fighting space monsters."

"It's okay," Ray said softly, his voice almost lost in the rain. "Tell her, and the doc, I'll be back soon."

"Sure." Lu paused for a moment. "Where are you?"

"Driving down Houston. I'm trying to find Mateo and 'Keem. I've tried calling both of them but no answer. You seen either of them?"

"Not since you guys left a week ago. But Ciudad Aztecas were all over the news for the big firefight over at the Gould-Wright ship-works, when you guys were fighting the evil space-shrubs. A lot of them are in jail because of that. Oh, I heard a really weird rumor from Shelly's brother's girlfriend, Ashanti, the other day down at the Chug-n-Lug."

"What?"

"There's like *X-Files* guys—government agents—crawling all over Gould-Wright."

"You're kidding me."

"No, no. There was something on the news last night about CDC guys from Atlanta being here, supposedly chasing down cases of mumps or something, but I've seen a lot of Men in Black wandering around and more army guys than usual, too."

Ray recalled 'Keem's story about running into aliens in Afghanistan and how the military covered the whole incident up. Maybe there were people on Earth who knew more about aliens than the majority of the population. He worried about Neste and Lera wandering the streets, getting caught, and ending up in some secret government lab.

"Hey, I can call Jorge who used to work with us. His brother-in-law is a Ciudad Azteca. I bet he'd know how to get a hold of Mateo. Want me to call him?"

"Yeah," Ray said. "Thanks."

"Where are you? We can meet up."

"How about Bingo's?"

"See you in ten," Lu said.

"Your friend?" Pana asked.

Ray nodded. "Lu. He's the best."

. . .

Lu met them in the parking lot of Bingo's. They gathered under the large awnings that shielded the people using the rows of gas pumps from the rain. Lu stumbled a bit with his words when Ray introduced him to Pana. She smiled at his unintentional awkwardness. "A knight?" Lu asked, shaking his head, "A . . . *space* knight? Like out of *Star Wars* or something?"

"I don't know what *Star Wars* is. I'm sorry." She shook his hand. She was a little put off by the intimacy of the greeting after a lifetime of bowing the proper amount in relation to your social rank. She got the gist of it, though; both people shaking were equals. For all its backwardness, she liked this about Ray's world.

Lu looked to Ray disapprovingly.

"What? We've been on Earth, maybe, four hours," Ray said.

"No excuse." Lu nodded to Pana. "I'll make sure you are introduced to one of Earth's greatest cultural milestones."

"Sorry to interrupt you there, player, but did you find Mateo?"

"Yeet. His guy is going to reach out to him and let him know you're back in town, and I told him to call you or meet us here." Lu looked at Pana, "Lady Pana . . ."

"Oh, no, I'm not a lady." She laughed. "Just 'Pana' will be fine."

"Would you do me the honor of buying you your first Earth corn dog?"

"Uh . . . I'd be . . . honored?" She glanced to Ray. Ray nodded with a smile and followed them inside the store.


About an hour later, Mateo's Nova appeared out of the rain and glided to a stop near the windows where Ray, Pana, and Lu were sitting. The *mara* leader climbed out, dressed in a half-buttoned red-and-black cowboy shirt and baggy jeans. They rushed out to meet him.

"Good to see you still alive, Ramon." Mateo and Ray bumped fists. "Who's Cinderella?"

"Pana, Mateo. Pana's from out of town. Chain wanted me to check on you and 'Keem. He said you guys were taking care of something for him?"

"Yeah." Mateo nodded. "Let's go back inside."

They took over a few of the tables by the windows. Pana actually had a second corn dog on Lu. Ray and Mateo both had Jarritos sodas. The rain was almost falling sideways outside, and the lightning made the night into day.

"I heard your crew had some trouble with the cops," Ray said.

Mateo nodded. "Been going to a lot of funerals, lately. It's hard to explain to wives, old ladies, and little kids that the person they loved got whacked fighting to save the world from evil trees from fucking outer space. Everyone thinks it was some kind of internal thing. So, I look like *el cabrón*."

Ray didn't know exactly what to say. He remembered how bravely Mateo's people had fought to save their loved ones. It seemed so unfair that no one would ever know.

"It's all right. It needed doing, right?" Mateo said.

"What did Chain ask you?"

"He came to me and 'Keem the night before you two bounced. He told us to go hunting for Rangers—guys with rings like you and him wear. He said we'd need backup, in case the government guys you were going to ask for help turned out to be chicken-shit. He gave us the name of a couple of places . . . planets, I guess, where Rangers hang. He sent me one way on that highway—the Queen's Road, or whatever—and 'Keem, the other way. Let me tell you, man, that was one crazy-ass road trip."

"I'm familiar." Ray looked down at Mateo's hands. "How'd you travel? You don't have a signet."

Mateo slipped what looked like a coin out of his pocket. "He gave each of us one of these."

The coin was a little larger than a quarter. It was made of black metal, like the signets, and it had a symbol engraved into both sides: a hendecagon, an eleven-sided geometric shape. Inside that was a decagon, a ten-sided shape; inside that was a nonagon, a nine-sided shape, and so on, diminishing down to a single point at the center of the disc. It struck Ray the symbol on the coin was the same as the faded bumper sticker on the Galaxie. Mateo handed the coin to him. It was icy to the touch.

"What is it?" Ray looked more closely at the coin, felt its weight, its coldness, in his hand.

"It's called a guidestone," Pana said. "It allows its user to find and travel the Queen's Road, going anywhere you can visualize or name. It works a lot like a Ranger's signet." She looked to Ray, "Chain never discussed any of this with you?"

"Vaguely, once. Seems there's a lot of details he didn't bother to clue me in on. I guess I really hadn't wondered how all those other people were moving along the road. We've been kind of busy."

"The guidestones and their lesser version, called tokens, have existed as long as the Queen's Road has," the knight said. "The Royal family gifted them to beings and seeded them across creation long, long ago, eons before the Rangers were created. They say Rangers have the ability to create new guidestones and tokens as they wish. It was part of how they helped raise and mobilize forces for the Shield Pact back during the Lytch War. Those 'coins' are the lifeblood of intergalactic civilization, one of the most valuable commodities in the universe."

"Cool," Mateo said. "All I know is Chain just kind of did this magic trick thing. He put one hand over the hand with the ring and, ta-da! When he moved the hand away, he was holding one of these guidestone things between his fingers. He told me to focus on the names of the places he gave me and then focus on home when I was ready to come back. He gave me and your boy 'Keem a shot of something to let us be able to understand most of these guys we ran into."

"Probably a translation augment," Pana said.

"So, what happened?" Ray asked.

"We told them about the Yateveo and fighting them on Earth. Dropped Chain's name. Those guys party *hard*. I mean, I hang with some serious motherfuckers, and these Rangers make them look like fucking Jehovah's Witnesses. Between me and Pawn Shop Commando, we gathered up close to fifty Rangers, all set to meet us at the rendezvous point Chain gave."

"Let me guess," Ray said. "Trull A-17."

"Yeah." Mateo checked his phone's clock. "Supposed to be there by tomorrow night. Me and 'Keem and my crew are heading out early tomorrow to get there. My old lady's pretty pissed with you right now, Ramon. I'm supposed to be with her."

"After everything that happened before, you still have people willing to go?"

Mateo nodded. Ray could see the pride in his eyes.

"Ciudad Azteca," he said, like that was explanation enough. "We're descendants of warriors. We owe those leafy motherfuckers some payback for our brothers in the ground."

"So, I take it you are a member of one of Earth's militant orders, a knight, yes?" Pana said.

Mateo laughed. "Yeah, I like that, an eagle knight. I'll make sure we leave our tags out there in the final frontier to let everyone know who cooked the walking broccoli." He glanced over to Ray. "We good? I want as much time with my wife and kids as possible before we ride."

"Yeah," Ray said, "we're good. See you tomorrow on Trull."

Mateo gave Pana a mock salute, gave Lu a dismissive wave, and strutted out the door, lighting a cigarillo as he climbed back into his Nova. The car snarled and pulled out, lost almost immediately in the dark curtain of rain.

"He's . . . he's not really a knight," Lu said to Pana, munching on his corn dog.


As they were leaving Bingo's and heading home, Lu and Ray gave each other a quick hug. "I'm tired of this goodbye shit," Lu said. "I should be going with you guys."

"Take care of Juanita. If I don't make it back, I need you to try to explain all this crazy shit to her."

"Make sure you make it back. You got people here on Earth that need you alive, not dead and a hero."

Ray fought against the hole inside him that ate all the light, all his future.

"I'll do my best." A thought struck him, shooting up out of the gnawing sadness. "Here, let me try something." He placed his right hand over his left and touched the ring. It was cold, like it had been sitting out on a winter's night. He felt it, felt the tiny raised gemstones. Each of them was warm under his touch. Ray closed his eyes and concentrated, tightening his grip on the ring with his fingers.

For the briefest of moments, he had a sensation that felt a lot like walking past an open door and glancing inside, seeing someone there as you pass. There was a presence associated with the warmth of one of the stones, an awareness turning toward him. Whoever it was, he could sense they were startled by the contact. *"What the void?"* the presence seemed to say in his mind. *"How did you . . . ?"* and then it was gone, like a door slammed in his face. Ray smelled the scent of lavender, as if it had wafted through the doorway as it closed. The scent remained with him for a few seconds. A name was associated with the scent, now, in his mind—Krace.

"You okay?" Lu asked.

Ray opened his eyes. "Yeah, yeah, just got a weird . . . thing happening. Give me a sec."

"You need a space-exorcist or something?"

"Just shut up and give me a minute."

"Okay, okay!"

Ray closed his eyes again. He pushed away the thought of the mind he had brushed against when he touched the stone and focused on the sensations of the coin, of the guidestone. The shape of it, the weight, the chill, like the vacuum of space. He began to imagine it under his fingertips, feeling it between his fingers. His whole hand felt cold now, freezing, burning. He kept going, kept willing the cold into shape, a form. He pressed the symbol he had seen on the coin into the cold with sheer will. He felt the cold ease, the burning stop, and he opened his eyes. He pulled his hand away from the ring. A black coin rested on it. He could feel it and he plucked it up with his right thumb and forefinger. It was a guidestone, exactly like Mateo had.

Ray handed it to Lu.

"You're kidding me," Lu said, holding up the coin.

"Now, if I don't come back, I want you to wait a while, a few months, and then you come look for me. If you can't find me, I'm probably dead, but at least you can prove my story to Juanita, and she'll know I didn't just run away and leave her."

Lu clutched the guidestone and winced a little at the cold. "You got it. I'll take good care of Juanita and this."

"I know you will. You're the most reliable person I know."

Ray climbed into the Galaxie and watched as Lu sped off in his car.

"That was a very great honor you gave Lu," Pana said, having watched the exchange.

"It was as much for me as it was for him. I don't want Lu heading out there, especially after some of the stuff I've seen. I have to come back to keep that from happening." He glanced over to Pana. "I guess I found a reason, huh?"

# 29

Dawn was close, a feeling of something gathering in the darkness. The rain was tapering off. Khan Hakeem stood at his partially open patio door, smoked a cigarette, and tried not to think of his sleeping wife and children. He tried not to think of anything, to just be. That was one of the secrets to surviving in war.

He wished he had some of the Player cigarettes his father had smoked his whole life. He and his brothers had picked up the habit from their father, of course, and chose the same brands, except for his older brother, Jal, who insisted on smoking American Marlboros, just to be different. Once the war began and 'Keem and his brothers and father had been in the field, they smoked whatever brand they could find. However, when he thought of his father, he smelled John Player cigarettes.

He would smoke one more, and then it would be time to go. His gear was packed, his truck gassed up and ready. He remembered the morning his father and he and his brothers had headed out to work with the Americans for the last time. His mother had made breakfast and strong, hot tea, and he had never forgotten the look that passed between his parents, as they parted for what turned out to be the last time. 'Keem felt his insides ache at the thought of never seeing his beloved Sharjeela again, or their babies, or his son, off at war himself.

The lieutenant who made it out of the cave with him after battling the alien monsters always said that soldiering was better suited to the young than the old. *Once you get to a place in life when you think before you charge, when you hesitate because you got so much to lose, you're halfway to dead, my friend.* 'Keem was feeling that now, especially after what he had seen and fought here in Port Arthur. *Don't think about it.*

He had been surprised when he saw the lieutenant walk through the doors of City Pawn, just a few days ago.

"I'm looking for some army-surplus rations," Sam Barrows had said, with a wide grin. Barrows wore a suit and tie now, and his gaunt face had widened a little. He still wore his graying brown hair short, close to military style. "Some MREs, if you got 'em. I'm prepping for the zombie apocalypse."

"You mean Meals Rejected by Everyone? I do not sell that garbage in my store, sir."

They had embraced, warmly.

"How are you, Hakeem?" Barrows asked. "How's Shar, the kids?"

"Very well. Blessed. Look at you! I see you gave up your uniform when you no longer could fit in it!"

They both laughed.

"Yeah, yeah, yeah, I put on a few pounds. Civilian life does that to most of us. You still living on cigarettes and tea?"

"Better than MREs," 'Keem replied. "What are you doing here?"

"That is a long story. Buy you dinner tonight?"

"Of course."

They met up at a seafood place over in Houston, had a few drinks and some excellent food and caught up.

"After what happened over there," Barrows said, "I got sent stateside."

"I remember. Thank you again for all you did to get my family and me over here to the States."

"You earned it. I only wish your dad and your brothers could have made it over with you." Sam raised his beer. "To Shahpur, Qammar, Farjaad, and Jal." 'Keem raised his own glass. "To them."

They clinked glasses and took a drink. Then, Barrows got around to why he was in Port Arthur.

"Since 2010, I've worked for an . . . organization that gathers intel for the US Government and provides analysis on things like we ran into." 'Keem chuckled. "Are you now a Man in Black?"

Barrows rolled his eyes. "Very funny, I never hear that. You should write that one down. I'm looking into something local here that happened last week. You hear anything about some . . . weirdness?"

"I own a pawn shop." 'Keem took another sip of his beer. "Weirdness walks through my door on a daily basis." He leaned in toward Barrows and lowered his voice. "Can you tell me anything more?"

"I wish I could. It's all sealed up tight. Unless you're looking to get out of the pawn and loan business and go to work for me?"

"I wish I could help you, but my action-adventure movie days are over."

"I'm more than a little envious of that. It's great to see you, Hakeem, no matter the reason."


"Baba?" 'Keem turned to see his youngest son, six-year-old Mateen, standing there in his *Sesame Street* pajamas. "Why are you not sleeping? Are you going to the store so early?" 'Keem smiled at his boy, who wandered over to him, still half-asleep and rubbing his eyes.

"Why are *you* not asleep?" 'Keem asked as he picked Mateen up. The boy giggled, and 'Keem held him close.

"I have to go out of town for business. I'll only be gone a few days."

"But you just got back from a trip. Can I go too?"

"Not this time, but when you are older, yes."

"What is this?"

It was Sharjeela. She was wearing one of 'Keem's shirts that fell to her knees. Her black hair was a tousled mess, but she looked perfect to Hakeem.

"Mattie, what are you doing up? Back to bed, young man. Don't trouble your father."

"He's no trouble," 'Keem said with a smile. He kissed Mateen, hugged him tight, and then set him back down. "Your mother's right. Off to bed with you. If you are good, maybe I will bring you and your sister back another present."

On one of the worlds Chain had sent him off to, 'Keem had found a big fuzzy stuffed toy that looked like a blue fur-covered marsh-mallow with straw-thin arms and short, squat legs. Its wide, goofy face was built into its vaguely cylindrical body. The merchant had told him it was a representation of Wombly that had a limited artificial intelligence inside it, so it could walk, talk, bounce, and play with children. Hakeem had managed to come to an arrangement with the merchant and brought it home to the kids. It was comforting to know that haggling was a thing out in the stars.

Mattie grinned and play-raced to his room, shuffling his footie-covered feet on the floor. "Goodbye, Baba! I love you!" A second later, they heard him jump into his bed with a whoosh of air. Hakeem and Sharjeela laughed.

"Please . . . no more alien robot toys," she said. "That thing keeps on trying to help me cook."

"Maybe a pet this time." 'Keem pulled her to him, felt her warmth.

"Oh, no. No, no, no." She shook her head in mock indignation. "It might eat the robot, and then we'd all be in trouble." They chuckled, and the laughter faded. They looked at each other, held each other's gaze, finally, they kissed for a long time.

"You know how proud of you I am. I wish you were not going again. I thought when we came here, we'd never have to deal with guns and wars, and parting, anymore."

"Me too. I didn't expect any of this, but they need me . . ."

"These Rangers."

He nodded. "Yes."

"Are you sure you can trust them to have your back, to keep you safe?"

"The ones I have met are . . . rough souls. People who fight wars usually are, but they fight for a cause they believe in. They fight to keep us all safe, and we never even knew they were out there."

"The monsters"—she glanced back to make sure Mattie was off to his room—"if you don't stop them, they will come back to Earth?"

"Maybe never in our lifetimes, our children's lifetimes. But they will be slaughtering other people's children. I cannot sit by and know I did not do what I could to stop such an evil. We've both lived through what can grow when men do nothing in the face of evil."

Sharjeela was silent. She nodded and then kissed him again.

"Hurry back. We'll be waiting."

"I will."

"And no pets," she said, mustering a smile.

"You stole *what?*" Ray said.

He and Pana had returned home to find that the wayward Ranger and the ambassador had returned.

"The Yateveo's transport," Lera said. "We need it."

"Did you bring me any Doritos?" Rudian asked from the kitchen. Ray returned to find the living room and dining room spotless and organized. Now the preacher was battling the kitchen mess.

"The big, black, shiny pill-shaped thing that I grounded at Gould-Wright? The one probably guarded by a bunch of military black-ops guys?"

"KFC, then?" Rudian tried again. "A greasy bucket of Earth's finest cuisine?"

Lera looked to Neste. "Yes," they said in unison to Ray.

"This is what a stroke feels like," Ray said to Pana.

"No worries," Lera said. "The guards didn't see a thing. Chain told me you and he had removed the thing's core, so I needed Neste here to help me unstick the thing in space-time and get it moving again."

"Where is it?" Ray asked.

"Parked it out front." Lera laughed when she saw Ray's expression. "Calm down, Earth boy. You really need some serious stress relief, if you know what I'm saying."

"We folded it into hyperspace," Neste said. "For all mundane purposes, it doesn't exist in real space. No one can see it or interact with it, until we unfold it."

"It's part of the plan," Lera said. "The Yateveo expect their people back, and they expect them back in that transport."

"A Trojan horse," Ray said.

"Is that what you guys call it here?" Lera said.

"Why didn't you tell me you were going to get it?" Ray asked, a bit more anger creeping into his voice.

"Because, greenie, you don't run me. No one does," Lera said, some of the amusement slipping from her voice. "If we had all gone clumping about over there, we would have alerted the guards, and you obviously don't want that, do you?" Ray remained silent. "I took exactly who I needed to get the job done properly. That's how I work. It's very sweet you think you have to 'take care of everything,' but I do not need your care. I think you will find that with most of us, we're very good at working alone. That's what Rangers do."

"I really think the takeaway from all of this is that none of you brought me any food," Rudian said, returning to the entry hall in one of Juanita's aprons and wearing rubber gloves.

"I know you're super competent"—Ray nodded to Lera and Neste —"all of you. I'm just used to, y'know, looking out for people who need that, even though I kind of suck at it. Hard habit to break, but I'll try." He headed for the stairs. "We've got an early morning, if we're going to make the rendezvous with the other Rangers. I'll grab a pillow and blanket so I can crash down here. If you need bedding or towels, they're in the closet across from the bathroom."

After he departed, Rudian looked at Lera. "Way to kick the puppy, you evil bitch."

"What's a puppy?" Lera asked.

"Some cute little innocent thing they have around here. I think it's what they make KFC out of." Lera shrugged and walked off. Rudian went back to cleaning the kitchen.

"Your Excellency," Pana said to Neste, "will you need a place to rest?"

"No, thank you, Ratari. Just a quiet spot to continue my calculations."

"Goodnight then," she said with a bow.

Neste struggled to tell the knight, but failed. He would have to tell his new friends soon. Time was burning away. They deserved to know the truth, his truth, before they risked their lives. The ambassador turned inward and proceeded with his work, pushing his internal battle as far away from him as his minds would allow.

# 30

F lag General Xeris Fulry hadn't commanded a unit in the field since the final year of the third war with the Leth. That had been seventy-seven comps ago. He was a competent commander, not the most imaginative fellow, but he looked out for his troops and never shirked his responsibility or passed blame on to someone who didn't deserve it. The Mother knew he wasn't commanding this action against the Tribanni home world for glory or to get a new combat ribbon added to the collection he wore on his dress uniform. He was middle aged, and some younger officers suspected this had something to do with recapturing past glories. It didn't.

The reason he was out here, sitting in a two-story command transport on the Queen's Road, was because he had read enough military history to know what the Yateveo had done to countless millions of worlds. He was thinking of his daughter, his grandchildren. He wanted to be absolutely sure the Yateveo never broke out from Triban, never threatened another world in the Shield Pact or beyond.

Though he disagreed with the mystical myth of the Nemesis forces somehow appearing and disappearing during the Lytch War—the same myth that Ranger, Chain, had brought up during the initial briefing—Fulry wanted to leave nothing to chance. He had established rearguard forces some distance away from all the ramps that led to and departed from Triban. Nothing was going to get past them.

The orders from the High Marshal himself were to hold, to contain, anyone from leaving Triban and wait for Chain and his Rangers to infiltrate and destroy the planet before the Yateveo could break out. His forces—a good quarter of the Norama home guard— had been here for days. They were getting bored. Media had begun to show up, asking all kinds of questions: was it a hostage situation? If so, with whom? Was it an epidemic? A revolution? Had the hardline Tribanni transcendentals finally made a grab for power? The orders from High Marshal Thierry were to say nothing, keep the media back, and make sure none of his commanders or enlisted troops leaked anything. That was like trying to catch nanites with a fishing net.

Word that part of the infamous Nemesis coalition was still alive, still active, and preparing to start the cycle of madness and death all over again—the Known Galaxies didn't need that right now. The Shield Pact didn't need it. There were already fractures in the alliances that grew daily. The old bonds of camaraderie that had pulled them together against a seemingly unstoppable enemy loosened, the fires that had forged those bonds had grown cold.

No, it needed to be stopped here and now—quickly, decisively, and quietly.

"General?" One of his aides pulled him out of his thoughts. "A courier from the fast-attack rearguard just arrived. He reported that the eighty-second encountered a Tribanni transport speeding away on the Queen's Road toward the Black Flame Regions. They are pursuing it and attempting to disable or destroy it with non-radiant weapons."

"How in the void did the Yateveo get around us?" Fulry slammed his fist down on the monitor console, then stood and grabbed his field cap. "Order units from the one-oh-third to assist in the pursuit, and put all units on full alert. Evacuate the civilians now! It's starting." The general looked around the command-and-control center. "Notify Norama. Where in Shylah's name are those damn Rangers?"

. . .

Trull A-17 had been a garden world once. The natives were small, inoffensive humanoids who had developed a culture on a bedrock of hedonism. Because of their proximity to so many main routes on the Queen's Road, and their hospitality, their world became a destination for travelers from across the Known Galaxies, famous for their food, their music, their dance, and for their moral adventurism.

When the Agar Militia had passed through the region, the Trull had refused to provide them with a tribute of raw materials for their ongoing cosmic campaign of domination. It was against their pacifistic beliefs. The Agar dropped an asteroid on their planet from orbit for their refusal. Most of the Trull died as their world did. The survivors were taken into captivity and sold into slavery across the universe. The phrase "a Trull's errand" had come to be known universally to mean "an unwise venture."

That made Trull—now a cracked shell of a world—the perfect place for the Rangers' rendezvous.

Ray, driving the Galaxie, and Lera, driving the Tribanni transport, arrived off the exit to the abandoned planet. They were greeted in the crumbling ruins of a Trull city by a caravan of vehicles, including Mateo's Chevy and 'Keem's pickup. They made their way through the throngs of beings milling around the bizarre array of transports.

Ray spotted a series of hovering disc platforms connected by loose, rope-like silver cables. Some of the platforms had a mounted seat, a windscreen, and a control panel; others had cargo lashed down on them. There was a craft idling on jets of flame. It had three rear-facing engines, like the tines on a pitchfork, and a sunken cockpit with a full back seat. Two massive cannon-like weapons were forward mounted on it, and a third was rear-mounted. Another craft looked like a sled, pulled by a pack of snarling, frothing dire-wolf-looking things with bright red fur, sharp metallic antlers, and eyes like television screens.

Eventually they spotted Chain's tow truck and parked nearby.

"This is like the weirdest car show I've ever seen," Ray said, admiring a hundred-yard-long horizontal obelisk with more than fifty wheels that looked like it was made of blue marble that glowed and pulsated with a milky inner light. The beings either standing near their vehicles with obvious pride, or wandering the rows checking out the assembly, were as varied and strange as their conveyances. Many were humanoid, but not all. Ray did spot that all of them wore Ranger signets. They wore them as rings, arm cuffs, bracelets, collars, belts, thigh cuffs, earrings, bellybutton rings, septum piercings, or headbands.

Ray, Rudian, and Pana met up with Lera and Neste, and soon they found Chain and Skye.

"Where is she?" Lera asked.

*Here,* a voice whispered in everyone's minds. *I perceive no value in being seen.*

"Ah, Ajeet, dear," Lera said. "It's nice to see you're as sociable as ever."

"'Keem and Mateo outdid themselves," Chain said. "We can use the help."

They found the two Earth men near the center of the gathering, greeting the arriving Rangers. 'Keem and Mateo were both armed with the abolisher rifles and pistols that 'Keem had recovered so long ago. 'Keem also had his army-surplus flame thrower. There was music coming from a multitude of car speakers, laughter, and a babbling river of voices.

"Hey!" Rudian said, narrowing his eyes at one of the gathered. "That bastard owes me money! Excuse me."

Introductions were made all around, and Chain found himself swamped by fellow Rangers greeting him.

"The man's got juice," Mateo said to Ray as they watched Chain work the crowd. "I didn't run into a single Ranger who didn't know Chain personally, and all of them wanted to fight for him. Guy's been around forever. Apparently, he fought back in that Lytch War thing, five hundred years ago."

"Can you imagine being that old?" Ray said.

"Shit, can you imagine living through five hundred years of all this?"

"I'm surprised this many came," Chain said to 'Keem as he worked his way clear of the crowd.

"We mentioned you and the Yateveo. That was all it took."

Chain climbed a crumbling staircase that led to nothing but gave him a little elevation over the gathering. He whistled loudly and everyone and everything fell quiet.

"I appreciate you all coming."

"You'll get the bill, Chain!" a voice came up from the crowd, followed by peals of laughter.

Chain laughed too.

"If we make it out, Grath, old son, I'll pay you the same as last time —all you can drink."

Laughter and cheers went up from the assembled. Chain gave them a second, then he went on.

"We're hitting the Tribanni home world. Some of the Yateveo survived the war somehow, and they've taken over Triban. They're building up their strength, and then they intend to make a run for about a hundred core worlds. They get embedded, it will be harder than digging out Herberian sand fleas. So, we're going to stop them now. By Shylah's blood, we're going to wipe out every last one of those death-loving, void-shitting bastards before they can do any more harm!"

The Rangers bellowed again. Guns and beams were fired into the air, wildly. Chain let them get good and fired up before he continued.

"You all know Lera Trade." There were roars of approval, a few wolf whistles, and some scattered shouts of Lera's name. "You all know what she's done, what she's capable of doing. Lera's got the plan. Check in with her, and with me, to get your assignments. We don't have much time, so make your preparations, make your peace with whatever's waiting for you when you die, and get ready to roll!"

The Rangers chanted Chain's name as he descended the stairs and the gathering turned into a party with a purpose.

The plan was made up of parts that built one on top of another.

The crux of it would hang off Lera and Neste. Ray and Pana would go with them to act as security and to draw off any fire. Rudian would make his way to the Shield Pact forces and coordinate with them. 'Keem would lead one of the feinting tips of the assault, commanding a group of the Rangers going in. Mateo, his gang members, and the remaining Rangers would act as a second layer of rearguard to make sure none of the Yateveo broke through.

The most insane and dangerous part of Lera's symphony of chaos was to be handled by Ajeet and Skye. *He should not accompany me,* the serial killer protested. *It is too dangerous.*

"I'm coming along," Skye said, "because you'll need me for the second part of the plan. I've done crazier things on stage. It'll be good."

*You think I will go out of control without you there, slaughter the wrong people.*

*Maybe,* Skye thought back. *That much death around you, projected into your mind, you could. Also, you need someone to watch your back. You're not indestructible, remember?*

Skye felt Ajeet's surprise at his concern for her safety, like someone recalling something long forgotten. He felt a thrill of appreciation, like a ray of sunshine piercing a bank of storm clouds.

*Very well, but you will slow me down.*

Skye smiled, and let her feel it. *I'll try to keep up.*

As final adjustments were being made to the particulars, a Ranger on a four-wheeled ATV-like vehicle hauled ass down the ramp from the Queen's Road and rushed to reach Chain's side. After a terse conversation, Chain ascended the stairs again and called out to the assembled force.

"All right, I just got word a Yateveo transport somehow got past the Shield Pact's army. They're in the wind. We don't have any more time; they're mobilizing. You all know what's expected of you. You all know who suffers if we fail. We are the last line, as we have always been, as we'll always be. May the Mother ride with you, may Shylah guide your aim, and may I see all of you on the other side of this. Now, highwaymen, let's ride!"

Engines thrummed to life; the music of a hundred worlds blared and shook the air. Goodbyes and good lucks were quickly passed. Jugs and flasks, pipes and pills, were exchanged with hugs, kisses, handshakes, and stoic nods. Prayers were chanted, or sung, or whispered. Weapons were powered up, chambered, checked, and stowed.

Chain nodded to Ray, both in their cars, ready to launch. "Graduation day, Ray," Chain said over the snarl of motors, barely contained. "Keep yourself alive. Do your job. I'm counting on you."

Ray nodded. "Beat you there."

The Galaxie spun out in a hiss of dirt and loose rock. Chain laughed and followed. The Ranger army rushed forward, speeding up the ramp, rocketing across infinite worlds, leaving in their wake only a swirl of dust and diesel among the ruins of the dead.

# 31

**K**reesh of the Yateveo observed the multitude of his battle leaders from the large depot complex that housed thousands of the black mirrored Tribanni capsule transports. Tens of thousands of Yateveo troops marched through the walls of the transports. Each carried a Tribanni weapon—a spatial corrugator, better known as a "rip gun"—with their lower arms. A quarter-million of the humanoid Tribanni had been converted into proper tools of the invasion; they marched into the transports as well. All were armed and now more than happy to fight and die for their new masters.

It was an old battle tactic of Kreesh's people to turn the population into weapons. The meat-animals had little compunction about killing the Yateveo, but they hesitated to turn their weapons on their own, especially children. It was yet another weakness of the food animals, another example of why they did not deserve to exist.

The Yateveo had been forced to be very careful about how many of the hostages they converted and when, lest the Tribanni discover too soon and rise in angry, desperate rebellion. If Kreesh had his way, this would be the fate of every food animal on the planet, but the Yateveo were not yet ready, not yet strong enough, to be so bold. But their defeat, so long ago, had taught them well. They would not make the same mistakes again.

If the Shield Pact had moved against them sooner, the Yateveo would have been defeated, destroyed to the last, but their allies hidden across the Shield Pact had done their jobs very well, and the mighty sword the Pact worlds held was now in trembling, hesitant hands. Now, more than a million Yateveo marched to war, to conquest. They were all young, their skin still smooth and soft from their infancy in the blood fields, but they were ready to fight, and with the converted Tribanni as cannon fodder, the soft, decadent worlds they had chosen as their initial targets would fall.

Kreesh addressed his most senior aide. "Once the transports are loaded, begin departure. The Pilgrim has said he will get them all past the Shield Pact forces, as he did our scout craft. Have all the defenses at all the entrances from the Queen's Road on high alert. Once the crafts depart, the food animals may become desperate enough to grasp their courage and dare to assault us. We will hold this world. It still has many secrets we must rip from it."

"Yes, Eldest." The aide began to depart. Then, it paused and turned. "Eldest, our scouts at the fringes of the Queen's Road report the Shield Pact is firing on a Yateveo transport breaking through their lines and headed toward us. It may be Elder Hooruuul and his hunt party you sent to silence that Ranger."

"Perhaps, but it could be a trap. Confirm the dimensional encryption code for the transport if it makes it to the ramp. If it's Hooruuul's ship, then deactivate the mines and let them through. Otherwise, let them hit the gravitic singularity mines."

"Yes, Eldest."

Kreesh started to depart as the fleet of transports lifted off the ground and began to drift away.

"I will be speaking more with the Tribanni scientist. Keep me informed."

. . .

The Tribanni transport Lera had stolen off Earth was wreathed in clouds of anti-tank flak as it zigzagged through the lethal corridor of Shield Pact artillery. At the controls, Lera laughed as she banked close enough to bang the paint off a Pact combat prowler.

"Sorry, officer," she giggled, jamming the accelerator ever closer to the red.


In the command-and-control center, General Fulry was directing his men as the window in front of him showed an animation of the veering, erratic course of the speeding transport through the Pact defenses. The pilot seemed to know exactly which way to turn and shift to avoid the closing net of troop and vehicle fire directed at her.

"Remember, General," Rudian said, stepping to his side, "it has to look authentic. Your men need to put up a good fight for show, but we're all on the same side here."

"Anyone mention that to her?" Fulry shook his head at another near-collision.


Lera swerved the transport toward a barricade and slowed just enough to give the troops time to scatter before she pulverized it, hitting it in the exact spot at the exact speed to send it flying skyward as debris. Alarm gongs and tones were a background to her soft humming and outbursts of laughter as she came ever closer to the exit ramp to the Tribanni home world. She checked her internal comm clock.

Right on time.


The Ranger assault force roared forward—part of it well behind Lera's craft, and the rest following Chain and Ray—heading toward another ramp down onto Triban. As they neared the ramp, Ray looked over the edge of the Queen's Road, past the shoulder and the barrier. The shimmering black-mirrored orb that was the Tribanni home world came into view. The distant sun reflected off the feature-less planetary sphere. It would have been beautiful any other time.

In his rearview mirror, just before he pulled ahead of Chain's truck —which was hauling a large dull-metallic orb by its tow sling—Ray saw one of the larger Ranger transports fire a silver projectile, the size of a car, off the back of its massive rig. The capsule cleared the barrier of the Road's hyperspace interface and fell back into real-space and real-time, hurtling toward Triban from low orbit. He checked his comm; the launch had taken place right when Lera had said it needed to.

"Good luck you two," he muttered, thinking of Skye and Ajeet.

"They'll be fine," Pana said. "I hope the same can be said about us."

"Cassandra, full combat countermeasures . . . and give me some-thing out of the racing folder," Ray said. The car was filled with Lil Wayne's "Uproar." This was just another run, Ben beside him, racing for bill money.

"We got this," he said, jamming the gas as the Galaxie screamed into the turn and down into hell.


The reentry capsule plummeting downward to the surface of Triban was glowing white hot now, its silver shell charring and blackening as it tumbled downward. Inside, Ajeet crouched still, her head down— perhaps in meditation, perhaps she was napping. She wore a drop pack on her back slung next to her weapon. Skye, dressed in a low-orbit evac suit, clutched the handles on the sides of his acceleration couch and tried not to think about the gravity compensators failing and turning them both into jelly.

"You . . . you don't need a suit?"

*My people are used to very thin atmospheres. I will find a soft place to land. Are you regretting coming with me?*

The sphere shook as it hit turbulence, and Skye white knuckled it for a second.

"No," he said, then, "yeah, a little. This part anyway."

*I will give the thief her due, they won't be expecting this.*

"You're right. There aren't too many species stupid enough to undertake old-school real-space travel with the Queen's Road around."

There was a loud cracking sound and then a groan.

*I can feel your anxiety.*

"Sorry, I can shut myself off until we—"

*No. I'd rather have your fear than feel nothing.*

*I'm sorry I cut you out,* Skye thought, noticing the indicator light on the capsule's display had shifted from red to yellow. *It . . . I. . . I wasn't a good friend to you.*

*One such as I cannot be too critical of friends,* she said. *Friend,* she corrected.

*I truly missed you, Ajeet.* Skye tangled himself in her thoughts, her emotions, like an embrace. *Sometimes at night, I thought of opening back up, of taking a peek, and seeing if you were okay. I'm sorry I didn't.*

*What I am . . . what I do,* she said, *is . . . difficult. I understood. I was never angry.*

*But I did hurt you,* he thought. The programs in his suit were telling him to stand by for capsule disengagement. The whole thing was shaking violently now, the cracking sound was terrible and deafening.

*Yours has always been my sweetest of pains. You're worth it.*

The green light flashed on as the capsule exploded around them. The undeniable forces of the universe tore them apart from one another. The two tiny figures and the glowing rain of sensor-jamming debris fell through the mirrored surface of the planet's upper atmosphere, swallowed by the darkness.


'Keem's and his men's transports came down off the ramp appearing on Triban and into a withering rain of crossfire from the Yateveo warriors' rip guns. The first four vehicles down hit the gravitic singularity minefield and began to crumple and collapse into something the size of beer cans. These cars were all remote controlled from the occupied transports at a distance.

The driverless cars folded under the relentless edicts of gravity.

That was when the plasma bombs inside them went off, filling the immediate area with seething, annihilating plasma. A few of the bolder Yateveo died, enveloped in the furnace of the instant artificial suns. Others were burned and forced to fall back from their entrenched positions.

The second wave of vehicles came off the ramp and fanned off into two columns. Rangers poured out of the vehicles, firing and advancing forward, as the third and final wave blocked the ramp and disembarked to support their fellows. Rangers fell as the Yateveo defenders tried to regroup and retake a few of their abandoned defense points. 'Keem and his people made sure they didn't have the time, leap-frogging columns forward and tossing incendiary grenades as they went.

'Keem heard the man to his right scream and fall as he was hit by the spatial shredding force of a rip gun blast. He gave a count of five, as he had told his men to do, then knelt and directed the stream of his flame thrower in the direction the heaviest fire was coming from. He saw one of the Yateveo stagger out from behind cover, coated in devouring fire. It made a sound like the whistle of a teakettle full of boiling water.

"Left flank, advance! Right cover!" 'Keem shouted as he also transmitted it over his comm.

His men moved forward.

Per the plan, the rear guard of 'Keem's forces sent a driver back up the ramp to give a signal to the Shield Pact. A green flare soared skyward and a cheer went up from the Pact forces.

"There's your signal, General," Rudian said. "The Earther's done it. They've broken through."

"They won't be able to hold that ramp very long." Fulry looked to one of the C-and-C dispatchers. "Have the one-eighty-second advance on that ramp and support the Rangers. Tell Commander Issa I expect her to hold that position!"

"Yes sir," the technician said, rapidly transmitting the orders.

"Sir, shouldn't we contact Norama for confirmation?" the general's aide asked.

"I'm not waiting around half a day to hear back from a bunch of politicians when we have people fighting and dying to give us an opening right now."

"Yes, sir."


Chain's force split from Lera's on the Queen's Road. Ray followed Lera down while Chain and the remaining Rangers shot past the Shield Pact defenders at the next exit, and took the last ramp to Triban. Lera's plan was a four-pronged attack centered at different access ramps to Triban, most of them acting as misdirection and to draw off enemy forces, concentrating them so Ajeet could more easily dispatch them. Lera Trade's ego would be insufferable, Chain thought, if she wasn't every bit as good as she thought she was.

The minefield was coming up fast as Chain's assault group spiraled down their ramp.

"Stand by," Chain called into his comm. "Everyone holds near the top until we see what this thing does. Give me a little room."

As the base of the ramp approached, Chain jerked the truck into a wild, hard spinning turn. The large spherical device he was hauling in the sling was something Lera and Neste had been cooking up in theory for a while now; no one had ever tried to build one on such a small scale. It took a handful of crazy-ass Ranger engineers to make the thing a reality. Chain brought the truck to a full stop at the end of its 180-degree turn as he flipped the release and hurled the anti-black hole bomb out of the tow truck's sling straight into the center of the minefield.

As the osmium-cased bomb set off the first few gravitic singularity mines, its own spatial adjustment field—constructed by Neste—kicked in, making the orb momentarily super-massive. Tribanni engines within the bomb sent out powerful kinetic velocity charges, radically and rapidly increasing the angular momentum of the exploding mines' event horizons, ripping them apart and collapsing the baby black holes in a massive discharge of radiant energy.

The bomb survived the few seconds it needed to in order to blow a clear path straight through the minefield. Chain brought the tow truck around and raced through the gap, ramming the main Yateveo barricade as the creatures tried to comprehend what had just happened.

Chain saw the radiation gauges on his comm jump wildly then diminish.

"It's hot going through, but nothing you can't handle," he called out to the Rangers following him across.

A Yateveo was picking itself up from behind the smashed barrier. Chain fired a plaser blast from the rifle in his front seat through his open driver's side window, blowing a hole in the creature's trunk before it could open fire on him.

"Send the word back up the ramp, to Rudian, to the general. We're in."

Lera's transport hurtled down another ramp. She didn't brake for the minefield. Either the Yateveo had deactivated it, thinking she was their compatriot returning from Earth, or they hadn't taken the bait and her Tribanni craft would create a massive multi-spatial explosion, annihilating everything for miles in all directions. She knew, *knew*, they had to shut it off.

"Hold your fire," the Yateveo commander ordered. "Try to raise the hunt party inside."

Lera crossed the field and laughed, pleased with herself.

Ray's Galaxie hit the bottom of the ramp and didn't slow for the mines either.

"Alert! Minefield reactivated! Closing," Casandra said.

"Guess they figured out it wasn't their guys driving the transport," Ray shouted to Pana over the weapons fire. "All you!"

The knight closed her eyes and reached out with her ward, feeling the lines of force being summoned to devour them. The mines began to rupture when the car crossed their proximity field and created tiny gravitic singularities. Pana held the mini-black holes closed, smothering them as they each imploded. Sweat ran down her face as she willed all the gravitic forces at bay until the Galaxie was clear, and the minefield had been rendered inert.

Ray jumped from the car and fired plaser blasts from both fists, wounding two of the Yateveo warriors. He ducked as a spray of venomous spines clattered against the car's roof. Lera rose up out of the Tribanni transport with Neste by her side. She fired on the two Yateveo that were pinning Ray down. Blacklight lasers—powered by anti-matter and hissing like serpents—fired from her hands and cut the wounded monsters in two.

A squad of Rangers rushed out from the side of the transport and began to fire and advance on the Yateveo who returned fire with more wooden spines. A couple of the Rangers groaned as they were hit, but returned fire as they died.

Another cluster of Yateveo defenders fired their rip guns, trying to avoid the hull of the transport, crushing and tangling the rubble and debris the Rangers used as cover as they continued to advance. Two of the Rangers had plasma guns and fired ugly streams of super-heated energy that melted through defensive barriers and the Yateveo behind them. Ray cut left, covered by the Rangers' plasma blasts. Lera's blacklight beams tore through another Yateveo. A rain of poison spines bounced harmlessly off Neste. Lera quickly ducked behind him, then bisected the ambassador's attacker with a slashing gesture of her arm and another blacklight beam. A surviving Yateveo advanced and pivoted to get a clear shot on her, but she had already moved, as if she knew where it was shooting even before it did. A thread-like barbed line shot from Neste's body and embedded itself in the Yateveo. The Tribanni ambassador sent a power beam down the line and into the monster's interior, burning it internally and in seconds reducing its insides to ash. The smoking, chitinous corpse collapsed and Neste withdrew the line.

Ray's flanking maneuver had worked, and he popped up, bypassing the Yateveos' cover. He had a discarded rip gun in his hands and he fired rapidly on both remaining warriors. Even though he knew they were monsters, Ray felt sick to his soul as he watched the Tribanni weapon crush and fold them, as if the space around them could no longer contain them.

A squad of the Yateveo had regrouped to the right and advanced, firing a barrage of spines and rip gun blasts at the Rangers. The poisonous stakes hit the ground and smashed into splinters from their highest arc. For a second Ray wondered what had saved the troops. Then, he saw Pana dropping down among the enemy. The Yateveo towered over the knight, but she used their size and bulk against them. Summoning a "blade" of a hundred g's along the edge of her palm, she chopped at the base of the monsters' trunks, ripping them open and flattening them under unendurable mass. They slashed at her with barbed, branch-like tentacles. She spun and jumped, virtually weightless, narrowly missing the tendrils and getting them entangled with other Yateveo. As the creatures struggled to get free, Pana smashed them, broke them, and left the cadre of warriors a bloody, oily pulp on the ground. Another battle group fell back, retreating at the sight of their defeat by the small, lone humanoid.

The battlefield was eerily silent for a moment. Pana struggled to stand. Ray rushed to her side.

"You okay? That was amazing!"

The knight gave him a shaky but dismissive wave. "I'm fine."

Lera hopped down from the transport. "More than fine, I'd say."

"I feel like someone poured lead into my skull, and it drained down into the rest of me. I've never tried to hold back that much gravity before, even at combat graduation."

"I told you that would work. Everyone else good?" Lera asked.

Ray nodded.

"I'm fine," Neste said, a weariness in his voice.

"We're right on schedule," Lera said. "Everyone should be in by now. The Yateveo should be in utter chaos, trying to figure out which feint isn't a feint, but the tip of the spear. The way should be clear for us to hit our objective."

Ray turned to the surviving Rangers. Some stood watch while others tended to the dead and dying. He saw Rangers taking the signets off the dead. One of the Rangers—a big orange humanoid named Targus—approached Ray.

"Get going to your objective. We'll hold here. They'll be back soon, so we'll find some places to hole up. Chain's guys should be working their way toward us too, so keep monitoring your comms."

Ray nodded. Targus jerked his thumb back toward the ramp to the Queen's Road, "We'll send a runner back up to get the Shield Pact guys off their asses and down here to reinforce us. Shylah protect you, Ray. I hope the plan works and quick."

"Me too," Ray said.

Ray, Lera, Pana, and Neste advanced through the flames, giant bodies, and debris. Ray told Cassandra to put the Galaxie into defensive mode and wait. Pana steadied herself and picked up a rip gun from the ground as they carefully proceeded deeper into the city.

As they marched toward their destination, moving cautiously, alert for ambush or sniper, none of them, not even Lera, seemed to notice the being known as the Pilgrim of Chaos watching them from an elevated terrace. The humanoid garbed in black and jade smiled in approval. They were quite good, these Rangers, and they used the principles of entropy against the Yateveo. He liked that. Old eyes in a young body watched the direction the party was headed. The Pilgrim nodded as if it all suddenly made sense to him. He vanished from view like the hope in a broken promise.

## 32

The Yateveo invasion forces were on the move. The transports headed up the multitude of ramps out of Triban and onto the Queen's Road. As promised by the Pilgrim of Chaos, they found the roadways clear, the Shield Pact forces behind them somehow. It was impossible. The ramps' entrances had been swarming with Shield Pact troops and armored vehicles. It was as if the Pilgrim had simply moved the Yateveo farther down the Road without having to cross the intervening space. The Pilgrim was still as powerful and mysterious as he had been when he first approached the Nemesis eons ago.

They accelerated, speeding toward their targeted worlds and their glorious destiny of death. Within moments they found themselves facing down a second blockade along each roadway out. This time it was the Queen's Rangers.

Mateo's force saw the black-mirrored ships on the horizon of the road. He raised a hand out the driver's window of his Nova, and revved his engine loudly, like a battle cry. His fellow Aztecas and Rangers responded. He knew once they started moving on the Queen's Road, he'd lose comm contact with the other cars.

"Okay, we do this exactly the way we talked about it, okay? No fucking around and no doing anything stupid. Let's weed-whack these assholes!"

He hit the play button on his car's stereo. If he was going out, he was going to be carried out on music. Baldacci and Misfit Soto's "Death Wish" shook the car's windows with its bass. Mateo dropped his arm and the defenders raced forward toward the Yateveo fleet.

Skye's suit reported to him that they were low enough now in the atmosphere that he no longer needed oxygen from the life support system. He sent a mental command to the suit and it peeled off him and fell away. He welcomed the whistling, cool Tribanni atmosphere on his skin. He still had the lift pack on and the controls to trigger it. Glancing downward, he saw a dark mote that was Ajeet, aiming herself toward the sprawling city complex, laid out below them like a massive motherboard.

*The Yateveo's minds are very . . . diffuse,* Ajeet projected to him. *I've spotted a large group of them moving toward one of the Ranger emplacements.*

The dark speck grew smaller as she straightened her body and accelerated downward. Skye laughed and did the same.

"Eldest," Kreesh's aide said, "forgive the intrusion."

"What?" Kreesh was irritated that his meditation upon the Stillness had been interrupted.

"Enemy forces have taken three of the passages from the Queen's Road to here. They are on Triban, now, Eldest."

"The Pact worlds actually grew the spores to come at us?"

"No, Eldest, it's the Rangers."

"The Rangers? Decay their miserable hearts! How?"

"Unsure. They are a small force, but they used some very . . . unconventional tactics to land, and they are outnumbered by our forces five hundred to one. We are holding them at present and it appears the Shield Pact is moving to support them."

"Send in our reserves. Wipe them out before they can be reinforced."

"That's the other urgent news, Eldest." The aide moved back a little. "Some unknown force is . . . wiping out our reserves before they can be deployed. We believe a quarter of them to be dead already."

"What? You're talking about twenty-five thousand Yateveo warriors. There's no way the Rangers or the Pact snuck an army past us."

"Yes, Eldest, yet they die. They plead for support."

"Yateveo *pleading?*" Kreesh said in disbelief. Anger stirred his ichor; his upper tendrils whirred like a rattlesnake. "Split our remaining forces—all one-hundred thousand Yateveo. Half to reinforce our . . . reinforcements and obliterate whatever unit is taking them out, the other half to retake the choke points."

"Eldest, that will leave much of the infrastructure and the population unguarded."

"I know that!" Kreesh said, the rage stabbing him again. He inadvertently aimed the rip gun at his trembling aide. "Send out a general commosphere transmission: any Tribanni who attempts to leave their home for any reason will be killed on sight. Leave a token force to guard the organic Tribanni hostages. Tell them to begin full conversion of all the Tribanni children now! We need the troops."

"Yes, Eldest." The aide rushed away, taking one of the guards with him.

Skye was still airborne. He had used his lift pack to slow his descent and then drift down once they reached terminal velocity. He had it in hover mode now and was several hundred feet up watching Ajeet slaughter a Yateveo army.

The enemy forces had been moving toward one of the places the Rangers had established a beachhead. Ajeet had reduced power to her lift pack enough so that the drop wouldn't kill her. About eighty feet from the ground, she killed the pack completely and landed in the middle of the Yateveo, igniting her photon spear.

Watching Ajeet work was mesmerizing, and horrifying. The closest comparison that Skye could think of was watching natural destruction on a cosmic scale—suns going nova, galaxies colliding, a black hole devouring countless worlds.

Every movement was precise and led to a death—nothing wasted, no hesitation, no fear. The photon spear's blade was designed to cut effortlessly through anything except crystal, which diffused the blade into harmless light. The poachers back on her home world used the spears to cut away bone and flesh to get to the soul crystals embedded in the Isokanians' skulls. She kept it as a reminder of what her prey had done to her people and because it was an extremely effective weapon.

She was on her hind legs now, a flutter of motion, only seen long enough to end a life, then gone before the giant tree-creatures even fell. They were whipping at her with their greater barbed tendrils, launching volleys of poisonous spines, and curdling the very air with blast after blast from the Tribanni rip guns. Nothing. It was like attacking a spirit, a ghost. The warriors died and died and died and died.

Ajeet was the most formidable combat telepath Skye had ever met. Not only could she track her targets with her mind, she gained an innate awareness of their most vulnerable points. She could disrupt an enemy's thought process enough for them not to see her, to miss her when they had a clear shot, and for her to know exactly which way they were going to move, what they were going to do, just before they did.

A column of Yateveo was advancing on her, spraying her with rip gun fire, as she appeared and disappeared. The force was starting to unfold, trying to englobe her. Skye brought his holographic tattoos on line, bringing their generation grid—knitted just beneath his flesh—up to four hundred percent standard power. He was a man-sized sun burning in Triban's patchwork sky. He gestured toward the startled Yateveo and holographic laser bolts tore through them, incinerated them before they had a chance to raise their weapons and fire on him. Hot ash that had been the enemy swirled around Ajeet.

*They were shooting their own,* Ajeet said. *You deprived me of a combat asset to show off and look pretty.*

*They were trying to flank you,* Skye thought back. A shower of Yateveo spines soared upward at him. They drifted down as dust. His generation grid was reading at three-hundred-twenty-seven percent now but holding steady, well above the red line.

*They would have failed.* Ajeet killed two more Yateveo and moved slightly to one side to let a third shoot and kill his comrade. *I have this well in hand, thank you.*

*I knew there'd be a thank-you in there somewhere.* Skye engulfed his would-be snipers into burning, collapsing pyres with a barrage of laser fire. He was at three-hundred percent now. His skin was tight and sore, but he hardly felt it through the adrenaline haze. *I'm really glad you got this, too, because there's about half a platoon coming your way.*

*What took them so long? I was running out of targets.*

Mateo's fleet of cars collided with the oncoming Yateveo invasion force. He swerved his Chevy at the last possible second to avoid the big, featureless capsule barreling down. He knew from the fight back on Earth these transports packed more punch than an 18-wheeler, and he and his people would lose a game of chicken with them. The music throbbed in his ears, as he tossed the first of the C-4 IEDs that 'Keem had made, under the gravitic suspension of the transport that he had just avoided. Rangers and Aztecas following him in were tossing similar bombs and grenades. They couldn't stop them with abolishers—the guns 'Keem had recovered from the cave in Afghanistan—because yada-yada physics or some shit, but no one said they couldn't fuck up these alien hoopties' "tires."

He watched in his rearview mirror as his bomb went off under the Yateveo vehicle and saw the transport buck and swerve, smacking into another member of the Yateveo convoy. A Ranger on a fast-moving motorcycle slid between the colliding vehicles and dropped a grenade behind him, just clearing the two transports before they traded paint. Another explosion and one of the transports crashed over the side barrier of the Queen's Road and tumbled into deep space, lost forever.

More Yateveo ships flipped into the air from blasts and then rolled and tumbled, crushing some of their own transports but also crashing into Ranger and Azteca cars, totaling them and killing the passengers. Mateo tried to not think about more of his people dying, or about how the other intercept groups had done. He needed to keep his mind on the job. He saw Spyder, a hero of the fight in Port Arthur, zoom by on his Honda rice burner. He was weaving around the tail end of the invasion force and heading straight for the Shield Pact guys to get them out here to help pin the Yateveo down.

They had managed to take out maybe a third of the Yateveo craft. The others roared on, further down the road. Mateo and the survivors of the pass brought their cars around and went after the fleeing transports.

The Yateveo ships accelerated as some of the pursuing Rangers fired rockets, missiles, and conventional beam weapons at them. That was when the Yateveo ran into the debris field Mateo had arranged for them—enormous piles of rubble, twisted steel girders, and other scrap gathered up on Trull A-17 and carted off by Rangers with large capacity cargo vehicles. It was a literal mountain range of debris blocking the Queen's Road. The Yateveo transports tried to stop or increase the height on their gravitic suspension fields, but there was too little distance, too little time, and too much junk.

The transports smashed into the barrier and then into each other, some climbing up the backs of already crashed ships, before tumbling back down to hit the ground and roll into more oncoming vessels. Mateo and the other drivers pulled to a stop and watched the pile-up. By the time the Shield Pact forces arrived with Spyder, there were dead Yateveo everywhere, thanks to Ranger snipers and rocket launchers picking them off as they attempted to exit the transports and establish a defensive line.

"What's the word?" Mateo asked Spyder. "Anything about anybody?"

"They made it down. Fighting's thick. That's all I got, man. Sorry."

Mateo lit a cigarillo and admired the view off the Queen's Road. He'd come a hell of a long way from selling weed and pills off Ninth and Dequeen Boulevard in Port Arthur. He thought about his baby boy back home and he knew, he *knew* he wanted better for his son. One of the Rangers, a crocodile-looking motherfucker named Jobblis, walked up to him.

"You did real good Earthman. But you forgot something." Mateo turned and looked at the alien. Jobblis opened his hand. A Ranger signet rested in his palm. "Yorgobb bought it back when we strafed them. He dropped this. I know he'd want you to hang on to it for him."

Mateo picked up the ring.

"You put this on it stays on, right?"

"'Til death parts you, yeah," Jobblis said. "Think it over, but you earned it today."

Mateo looked at the signet for a long time, at the border between the road and the deadly beauty of space. He slipped the ring into his pocket and turned from the pretty view to go check on his people, all his people.

## 33

R ay, Lera, Pana, and Neste made their way deeper into the corridors of their target—an environmental monitoring station. The structure was a little over a mile out from and below where the vicious fight between the Rangers holding the ramp and the Yateveo eager to reclaim it was going on.

The station was one of thousands across the planet, and it regulated aspects of daily Tribanni life such as the weather, temperature, and overall environment. The stations, Neste had explained to Lera and the others, also housed monitoring and emergency interface controls for the spatial anchors that reinforced the planet's dimensional existence. The anchors were needed because of the complex web of spatial overlays that made Triban an amalgam of millions of different worlds from across the gulfs of time and space.

As Lera had planned, Ajeet's onslaught had drawn the Yateveo guards off the relatively insignificant structure, and they had entered easily, bypassing detectors, alarms, and locks with little delay. Ray and Pana were here to stand watch and let Neste do what he needed to do: cut Triban loose of its anchors and let it slip off into another dimension, taking the Yateveo with it.

The central control was an elevated office overlooking a vast floor of blocks of machinery. It was designed, in Tribanni fashion, to look more like art than cold science. The sabotage party cleared the machines and ascended the ramp that led to the glass-enclosed office. Pana had point, Lera and Neste followed, and Ray brought up the rear, waiting for an ambush, a guard, anything.

Ray was still knotted inside from all the shooting and killing. He knew there wasn't a choice here. The Yateveo couldn't be reasoned with. They viewed people as food and slaves, that was it. It was the act that affected him, watching the repercussions of firing. Those images burned into his brain. He didn't know if he was cut out for a lifetime of this; he wasn't Chain, or Mateo, or 'Keem, or Pana. They were warriors, he was . . . just a guy. He shook off the mental fog of distraction and focused. Across this planet, people were fighting and dying to get them here. They deserved him to be fully present right now.

They had reached the doors to the control room. There was a catwalk of sorts that ran outside and around the room. They stood on that while Lera examined the door. Like the other Tribanni doors in the complex, there were no buttons to push or panels to enter a code into. You couldn't break it down, because it was anchored in space. It only opened for the proper code.

"Neste," Lera said.

The Tribanni ambassador scanned the lock and transmitted his access key. There were very few locked doors on Triban, the Tribanni were a peaceful and thoughtful species, but access to these controls had to be limited. His position in the Encompassment and his academic reputation gave him access to most places. *A peaceful and thoughtful species.* He was about to undertake an action of horrible consequences. He had initially agreed to the proposal to get to go along, to help his daughter if she was still alive, to help his people. Now he was a few steps, a few moments, away from the unthinkable.

The door faded away with approval of the code, and the team entered the control room.

"Attention all Tribanni citizens, and civilian hostages." It was

Chain's voice coming over every comm unit. "This is Her Majesty's Rangers. We have liberated the commosphere from your captors."

"Ah," Lera said, "a few minutes late, but close enough for government work, Chain. Very good."

Chain's transmission continued.

"Forces of the Queen's Rangers and elements of the Shield Pact's military are presently securing your world from the criminals who have taken it. Please remain calm and in your homes. We will be giving you additional information as it is relayed to us. Be strong and be brave as you have been throughout this situation. We are coming for you and your children. Rangers out."

Neste located a hovering row of geometric shapes. "This console, Lera."

She nodded. "You have any trouble accessing it for what you need to do?"

"No . . . none whatsoever."

"Very well. I've calculated the optimum time 'til phase-out to give the assault forces, any hostages Chain and 'Keem's people can free in the allotted time frame, and, of course, us, sufficient time for retreat."

"Ray and I will be outside standing watch," Pana said. "We'll give you as much time as we can."

"Wait," Neste said as the Knight and Ranger headed for the door. "I'm sorry . . . I'm sorry I brought you all here . . . that I didn't say any of this sooner. I can't go through with this."

Ray, Lera, and Pana exchanged looks.

"Excellency," Lera said, "I know you are feeling conflicted, but there's no other way. Why did you say you could do this, and come all this way?"

"I was buying time. I knew you'd only bring me along if I could offer a solution. I needed to get home, I needed to be with my family."

"I've run the permutations," Lera said. "You have too. If we don't do this, and very soon, the Rangers will be overrun and mostly slaughtered. The Shield Pact will not fully commit to this battle and will pull back what support they are giving us now, if this isn't resolved decisively and quickly. The Yateveo will be victorious. Given a little more time and access to your technology, they will convert your atmosphere. Your people will all suffer and die, then billions more will as well."

"If I do this, if I tear Triban out of space-time, it kills all the Tribanni here, and it will kill all the non-organic Tribanni anywhere else in the universe."

"What are you talking about?" Lera seemed genuinely surprised.

"My people, once they transition to this form, draw primary energy as individuals from spatial interface broadcast power. It's a fixed connection. All that apparatus is here, on the home world. Destroy the home world, you kill more than 99.9 percent of the Tribanni people. It's genocide, Lera. Could you do that to your own? Even for the most noble of reasons?"

Lera paced like a captured tiger. It was the first time Ray had not seen her looking smug and self-assured. She opened her mouth to speak several times but didn't. She shrieked in frustration and drove her fist into one of the immutable statue consoles.

"Void damn it!"

"I'm sorry. I figured we'd find another way, find an opportunity here."

"Sorry?" Lera snapped. "Do you know how many people are dead already in this little outing? Do you have any idea? I knew you were on the edge, but I figured on your cool Tribanni aplomb, your rational mind, seeing that there simply wasn't another way; I calculated it would win out over any gross, oversimplifying emotional concerns—"

"Lera," Ray said.

"In roughly twenty-six minutes, our safety margin ends." She started pacing again. "That's when the Yateveo get wind of all our little misdirection and parlor tricks and they start aiming their guns in the right places. Things stop being easy then, and the slaughter begins in earnest—"

"Lera!" Ray said, getting angry, "Stop it!"

"Oh, the tactical genius who lives one step up from a cave has spoken."

Lera spun and got in Ray's face. It hadn't occurred to Ray before this moment how high-strung Lera Trade truly was. This was the price of her brilliance. She was like a precision instrument; too much deviation threw her off, way off.

"I had this planned out perfectly, *perfectly*! Every detail, every variable accounted for. Do you understand? How could you?"

"Lera, it's his little girl," Ray said. "His daughter. Neste's daughter is a hostage. You're asking him to kill her."

Lera blinked and stopped as if she had been struck. She stepped back. Paced slowly now, her head down.

"Nobody told me," she said. "I . . . didn't pick that up. I *should* have picked that up. Rudian . . . Rudian is better with reading, with getting people details . . . than I am." She turned back to them, calm again but the mania wasn't in her eyes. She looked defeated. "I work better with people in the abstract. I don't . . . do . . . real people very well. 'Nobody told me.' What a stupid excuse."

"Should we get on the comm to Chain, tell him we need to abort the mission?" Pana asked.

"Wait!" Ray said. "Come on! We're right here! We got freaking universal geniuses in the room. Lera, Neste—there has got to be a way we can do this!"

"No," Lera said. "Given the elements we have to work with, it's the only option."

Ray turned to Neste. "What if we just *partially* phase out the planet? Just enough to shake the Yateveo loose?"

"The Yateveo are still organic, just like our children. We filter them out, we filter all organics out. I'd need Yateveo DNA to differentiate, and the calculations would be immeasurable, even more than I've been running the last week. Besides, the whole hypothesis is moot. Once we disengage the spatial anchors and the planet slips away, there's no 'brake,' no apparatus in place to hold it partly out of phase long enough for the plan to work."

Lera had been looking through the glass windows of the office, her reflection a ghostly shadow on the surface. She was nodding slightly. Ray thought her lips were moving, silently. Her finger moved over the glass as if she were working out an equation and needed some visualization to move through it.

"You *have* Yateveo genetic material," Pana said. "You fried that soldier back at the beachhead. You should still have a little on your thread, I'd imagine."

Neste was silent for a moment. "I do. However, as I said there is still the matter of the calculations and . . ."

". . . The anchors!" Lera spun. "Yes! The anchors. You cut them, and the planet falls away"—she made a little 'bye-bye' wave with her hand —"*all* away. But what if you had trillions of hardline connections here in the home space-time to tether the planet, just long enough to shake the Yateveo loose like leaves on a windscreen?"

"The spatial interface we use for broadcast power. Yes! Yes, that might work—not for long, but long enough. But the calculations! Even if I use my maximum mirroring processing power it would still take . . . days at least."

Lera gestured to one of the access panel art pieces. "You have access to the central processors right here. You can increase your calculation time through that considerably, Neste!"

"I could, but . . ."

"But nothing! I'm a genius."

A tone sounded through the comms. It was Chain again. He sounded tense.

"Attention all Tribanni citizens. The Yateveo are currently undertaking conversion of the hostages. This is a death sentence for them. Any Tribanni able to fight for your world, for your children, now is the time. Our forces are coming, but we are facing stiff resistance. We need your help; they need your help. Arm yourself and attack any Yateveo on sight. Show no mercy, for they have none. Good luck!"

"We're out of time." Slender tendrils slid from Neste's frothing, tumbling form and connected to the central console. "I'll get underway."

"Remarkable." The man's voice came from the doorway. "You people are absolutely remarkable." He was humanoid, dressed in black, with an open doublet festooned with a black-and-jade diamond pattern. He slipped back the hood on his tunic revealing a tangle of curly ink-black hair and merciless eyes of green malachite. "I'm afraid I can't allow you to proceed, of course," the Pilgrim of Chaos said, "but I wanted you to know how impressed I truly am."

# 34

"B ang," the Pilgrim said, raising his hand. A sizzling particle beam flew straight toward Neste.

"No!" Pana shouted and launched herself, taking the blast square in her chest. She tumbled, crashed through one of the windows, and lay still on the catwalk outside the office. Before she had fallen, Lera and Ray were firing on the man in black and green, but he was gone before their beams could find him.

"Keep going, Neste. We got this," Ray said as he and Lera headed out the door, sweeping for the Pilgrim as they advanced cautiously. Ray moved to Pana and knelt by her side. The knight was unconscious, maybe dead.

He stood and then dived for cover as a blast from the Pilgrim arced toward him. Ray scrambled on his elbows and knees to get into a position to return fire. But the Pilgrim was gone. A strong hand grabbed him by the back of the neck and hurled him off the catwalk, crashing into the banks of machinery-art below. Pain stabbed Ray, but he brought his arm up quickly and fired on the Pilgrim with a plaser bolt. He lost sight of the man in black and green in the expanding cloud of super-heated gas.

He groaned and struggled to get up. His back ached, and a sharp pain lanced his side. A dark shape arced through the air and landed in front of him. It was the Pilgrim; his face was smudged with soot and red from minor burns.

"Close." He backhanded Ray. The Ranger saw lights strobe behind his eyes as his brain was sloshed around inside his skull from the impact. Everything was dark for a moment, then he was again on his ass, crumpled up against one of the immutable blocks of machinery. His face was numb and when he touched it, his fingers came back wet with blood.

"I could have killed you a few times already," the Pilgrim said, kneeling on his haunches. "But you are a paradox, Ranger, and I enjoy those."

"Lucky me," Ray tried to say through puffy, swollen lips and loose teeth.

"I am, among other things, a scientist. I pride myself on my powers of primate observation. For example—excuse me."

The Pilgrim rolled suddenly, a hissing black-light beam cutting the machine he had been near into two sizzling, inert pieces. He came up firing twin particle beams at Lera on the roof of the office, one from each hand. The beams missed her as she launched herself off the roof, and instead blew a car-sized hole in the ceiling of the vast underground complex in a display of brilliant blue-white light. He stood and glanced back at Ray, who was struggling to his feet, raising his arm.

"Where was I?"

The Pilgrim shot Ray with a particle beam bolt through his shoulder. Ray moaned in pain. The bolt knocked him back down and burned a hole through the machine behind him.

"Oh, yes. A paradox. That was four times now I could have just ended your life, by the way, if you want to keep count."

Ray was fighting to stay awake; the pain in his arm was cold. He thought he might be going into shock. He remembered Lu telling him once that really bad burns felt cold because the nerves were being obliterated. He tried to focus on what the bastard was saying, standing over him.

"As I said. I am a very, very observant person, and I take you for someone who is ready to die. I've seen it at least a half dozen times since you arrived here on Triban. Your body language, the reckless way you fight. It's clear you're new to the whole fighting thing, but it's more than that. Your fight is inside you. You long to stop hurting, to stop having to trudge on and wade through the sewer of existence. Every, single, moment is a battle for you, Ranger."

"Fuck you," Ray mumbled. He was going to raise his other hand to fire, but the Pilgrim shot him again, this time low in the guts. He thought he was going to vomit. Another black-light blast from Lera created an explosion that blinded him for an instant. His eyes flickered to see the Pilgrim crouched behind the smoking remains of another machine. Ray noticed the Pilgrim's upper chest was burned and smoking. Lera had managed to get a hit.

"Any more stunts like that and I will just kill him," the Pilgrim called out to Lera. He glanced over to Ray. "Ah, good. I set that on low power. Just enough to keep you from doing something stupid, but not enough to shut you down. Oh, no. I really want to know the answer. Why does a person living in constant pain, in constant sadness, a person I'm quite certain has contemplated diving into the abyss himself, fight so hard for life, to live? You seem terribly conflicted."

The pain in Ray was beyond his vocabulary to describe. It chewed at the edges of his consciousness, made it hard to think, to concentrate.

"Let's look at the facts, shall we?" the Pilgrim continued, seemingly oblivious to his wound, to the destruction around him. "Life is a program—be born, eat, excrete, procreate, die. Lower life forms have the merciful absence of the delusion we higher forms cling to like a drowning man to a life preserver. The illusion of meaning, of purpose."

The machines filling the room began to whir and hum, a chorus of activity.

"Ah, your Tribanni friend is making some progress. Pardon me, I need to address that."

He stood and fired a massive particle beam from both fists straight at the control room.

"Don't!" Ray shouted and struggled to focus and fire his plaser. Lera Trade launched through the air from the dark rafters of the ceiling.

"Damn it!" were the last words she shouted as the blast enveloped her, taking the brunt of it and saving the control center and Neste. Her smoking form landed with a thud near Ray and the Pilgrim. It remained still.

"You see!" The Pilgrim spun, his fists still smoking. "That, right there! Why? I observed her too, a magnificent creature. A perfect survivor. Why override her biological program and do that? It makes no sense to me. Every cell in that woman wanted to live, at any cost, and you, you want to die so badly you practically scream it. Even your friend in there, the Tribanni, even if he were to live long enough to complete your little plan, his memory core, his essence, would be fractured and ruined in the process. He'll die either way. Tell me why, Ranger, explain that to me."

Ray slid his good hand into his jacket to hold his guts in. It was like his thoughts, his perceptions, were covered in cotton gauze.

The Pilgrim shook his head. "Are you all just so enamored, so wrapped up in the idea that life is precious or rare, or deserving of preservation? Because it's not. This whole universe is geared toward death, toward ending. That's why the only reason I can imagine for fighting against the cosmic force I back in this war is delusion, madness."

Ray was with his dad. He was small, very young. Ben was there too. Ray was crying, he couldn't remember all of it, he was so young. His dad was telling him something, something Ben repeated. Something Juanita . . . Mom, had told him too. A truth, even if it was a hard truth to keep in front of you all the time.

"You've lost people," the Pilgrim said with real sympathy in his voice. "You've seen past the delusion; you know the truth. Tell me, Ranger, do you want me to kill you before I finish off the Tribanni, or after? Or would you rather face the uncaring cosmos on your own terms? I'll allow you to kill yourself, if you wish."

He thought of Jess and he remembered something he had learned standing beside her corpse on the gurney after she had managed to finally end her own life, remembered how hard he had tried to reach her, to save her. He saw the look on Mom's face when she stepped out of Pop's room and whispered, "He's gone." Ben on the mortuary table, Mom weeping on his shoulder and Ray feeling sick and numb and wanting it all to go away. Physical pain had limits, had boundaries, no matter how extreme. Emotional pain did not.

Ray slipped the microwave knife out of his jacket pocket. He looked at the Pilgrim, looked past him. The man in black and green's eyes grew a little brighter as he saw the Ranger bring the blade out.

"So say it, tell me," the Pilgrim said. "Tell me you want it to end."

"Pass." Ray hurled the knife away.

"What is wrong with you, Ranger? Why? Why would you possibly want to go on?"

"Because . . . I want to watch her kick your ass."

Lera Trade—burned, bloody, but very much alive—scooped up the microwave blade, snapped it on, and burned through the Pilgrim's nerve cluster in his right bicep. She followed it up with a spinning roundhouse to the side of his skull. The Pilgrim crashed into a bank of humming machines and turned to fire on her with his left hand. Her blade stabbed through his hand at the moment of discharge and his lower left arm and hand were blown apart by his weapon's malfunction. The blast hurt Lera too, and she skidded along the floor, managing to slap the ground to slow her momentum and come up in a crouch, blade still in hand. Her hair was burnt, her face and upper chest badly burned, but she was grinning.

The Pilgrim regarded his lost arm, hocked up some blood and spit it on the floor.

"You remind me of my mother."

"Really?" Lera said, slowly circling him. "Did she breast feed?"

"No," he scoffed.

"Well that explains a lot."

Lera came in hard and fast, the shimmering microwave blade humming. She slashed, but the Pilgrim banked and avoided the cut.

"I've never had anyone, other than my brothers and sisters, ever sneak up on me before. You're very quiet."

"Thanks. I watched how you moved and reacted when you were up on that terrace watching us, thinking no one saw you. It showed me enough to be able to creep up on you, at least while you were in mid-gloat."

She kept coming in and narrowly missing him. He waited until she was in tight and launched out a vicious snap kick. Lera dodged it. He advanced with a roundhouse kick that caught her in the side. She grunted and staggered back.

"You and I are very much alike," the Pilgrim said, kicking and advancing. "We both court Chaos, know it by its true face. It's been a loyal mistress to us both."

He launched a bone-crunching punch with his injured right arm. It knocked Lera back, almost off her feet, but she recovered. He pressed the advantage.

"I heal quick," he said.

"I'm impressed." She ducked and then slashed back with the blade. She was retreating toward the ramp at the base of the control center. "I've only known one other person who ever laid a finger on me in a straight fight."

"I'm honored to be in such exclusive company. Tell me, how did you survive that blast? It should have reduced you to cooked meat."

"Oh, that." A smile played at the edges of her bloodied and burnt face. "She deflected most of the blast for me."

The Pilgrim's eyes flicked up toward the catwalk outside the control center. Pana, barely on her feet, was slumped against the corner of the building.

"Bang," Pana said.

She gestured down at the Pilgrim and his feet froze, too heavy to move. Lera drove the microwave knife deep into his chest and ripped it upward.

As they stood, in an embrace of sorts, Lera whispered in his ear.

"Silly boy. Just when you think Chaos is your mistress, that's when she slips the blade in."

The Pilgrim half laughed, half coughed. Blood spilled from his lips and he collapsed at Lera's feet.

Ray wanted to clap, to cheer, but he was having trouble staying awake. He felt a strange sensation like acceleration but without moving. The whole chamber, the whole planet, became pale and washed out around him, like it was made of rain trailing down a glass window. Lera was shouting something but he couldn't hear her over Jess, over Pop, over Ben. He felt like he was forgetting something important as the void swallowed him and his heart became still.

They were overrun. Skye had already fallen, his holographic weapons array exhausted. Ajeet sensed he was dying. She fought her way through the walls of barbed thorns and the waves of poisoned spines, killing anything that got in her way to reach him. *Priest, healer . . . Rudian! Attend!*

She knew he couldn't hear her in the infinite corridor of the Queen's Road. She stood guard over Skye's unmoving form and kept fighting. She was injured, badly, but it didn't matter now that the only vital part of her had already been slain. *Come,* she called to the swarming Yateveo, *you want the end of all things, I am the end of all things!*

'Keem and his men were being pounded by Yateveo fire. Even with the help of the Shield Pact troops, they had been pushed back, with nowhere left to retreat. The dead were everywhere. 'Keem said a goodbye to his family and ordered his men to keep firing.

Chain's men were all dead. They had fought like demons, but there were too many of the monsters. He was holding the commosphere control center alone now. The Yateveo were spilling in, rip guns crushing the very space around him. He stood and called to his gauntlet. The chain whirred in his hand. Rifle in one hand, chain in the other, he bellowed out the ancient battle cry of his family, and charged the lumbering, thrashing forces of death.

Neste's final calculation slipped into place, like a key in a lock. His minds, his infinite roaring river of thought, crashed against the rocks of the finite. He felt his intellect splinter, crack like ice on a frozen pond. A million thoughts, a million mirrors, spilled out before his awareness. Triban was free, no longer anchored in time and space. The world was slipping into an infinite number of other realms, all at once. Neste stretched his perception, his focus across as many dimensions as he could before his very essence began to fracture and diffuse. He engaged the hastily calculated genetic filter and fed it the Yateveo. The world and everyone in it became a thing of smoke. Except the monsters; they began to slip, to fall.

The Yateveo everywhere on Triban were ripped away, sucked through the fading planet like meteors in inverse.

Kreesh, eldest of the Yateveo, felt himself sinking through the floor of the command center where he was directing the extermination of the Rangers and their allies. *This cannot be. We are the destined, we serve the Stillness, we cannot end like this!* The Pilgrim of Chaos, bloodied and maimed, appeared from thin air. He touched the Yateveo leader's trunk, almost falling against it.

"Not done yet," the Pilgrim whispered, blood dripping from his lips. The world became as mist and the Pilgrim and Kreesh were gone. The other Yateveo, abandoned by their champion and their eldest, howled in anger and fear. They fell into the cold, empty crevasses between all things.

*One last task.* Neste held the thought together by will alone. He tested the connections, the intangible, invisible beams of broadcast power that kept all the non-organic Tribanni off the home world alive and powered. He reinforced the connection, gave it substance, and then he called out to all of his kind, everywhere: "*Stand, hold. Be strong, for the children, for all of us. Do. Not. Let. Go.*"

He felt the Tribanni becoming the anchor for their world. He could feel some of them succumbing to the strain, but that made the other hold fast even stronger. The determination, the drive of the Tribanni to save their planet, to save their own was like a song in Neste's crumbling mind. He sang it too, sang it to his daughter, to his son. Neste's last thought before tumbling into the darkness was of them.

It was a good last thought.


The battlefields grew silent. Triban returned to color, to substance.

It was over.

## 35

Ray woke up a few times, but always the darkness reclaimed him. He heard a voice whisper in the crowded, claustrophobic black. It told him something he knew was true, but he refused to listen to it. He needed to get home.

Ray opened his eyes. He was in a bed. He felt warm and clean. He wasn't in pain anymore. Chain was sitting near him.

"You snore." The Ranger laughed. "How are you?"

"I feel . . . fine," Ray said. "What happened, where are we?"

"Norama. Long story short, we won. The ambassador phased the Yateveo off the planet and was able to pull it back." Something awkward and painful hung in his voice.

"He's dead."

Chain nodded. "They tried to retrieve the core of him, but it got cracked and burned pretty bad running all that power through him to direct the phasing."

"Can't they . . . make a new him? Use his DNA or a backup copy or something?"

"The Tribanni have their own way of doing things. A lot of it depends on the ambassador's last wishes."

"Okay, well how's Pana? Lera? How bad was I hit?"

"You, uh . . . you died a few times." Ray let the words sink in. "Pana too. Fortunately, Rudian was able to stabilize you both and we evacuated you back here as quick as we could. She's on the mend. Only thing that saved her was she managed to use a gravitational lens to redirect a lot of that first particle beam she got hit with."

"Yeah, who was that guy?" Ray sat up in bed. "The guy in green and black. I think he works for the Nemesis, or the other way around."

"We're unsure," Chain said, and Ray knew it was a half truth. He decided not to push it on his first day of being alive again, and all. "There was no body. He either fell through with the Yateveo, or he crawled off somehow."

"Swell. Besides Neste, we lose anyone else?" Ray was afraid to ask but it was better to know now than feel the gut punch later.

"Lot of people dead. The damn Yateveo were converting people when Neste tossed them out. They had already converted a bunch for the invasion forces too. More hostages alive than dead, so that's something.

"There were a lot of Ranger casualties, some Shield Pact troops too. It's a mess, but it would have been worse if we hadn't gone in. We stopped all their transports except that first one, and the Shield Pact and a bunch of the Rangers are tracking it. We'll find them.

"'Keem and Mateo are okay. They waited around for you for a few days and then took off for Earth once they knew you were going to recover. They both got offered signets. 'Keem turned them down, but Mateo's mulling it over."

Ray glanced down at his hand. The signet was gone. "What the hell!"

"Relax, it's right here." Chain held the ring up and placed it on the tray table in front of Ray. "I took it off when you were clinically dead. I figured your stubborn ass would pull through and I wanted to make sure you got a choice this time. You earned that."

"What do you mean?" Ray picked up the signet.

"Evan was dying. He didn't have time to give you a lot of options. He figured you for a good man, and he was right, but after all this, I figured I'd let you decide for yourself if you want that ring on your finger for the rest of your life or not."

Ray looked at the black metal band, cool to the touch, the glittering gemstones.

"Who's Krace?"

Chain froze. "Where did you hear that name?"

"Who is she?"

"She's the Queen's daughter, one of the royal family, a princess. Why?"

Ray took the signet, held it tight in his hand.

"How long have I been out?"

"About four days." Chain recognized the technique of switching subjects. He didn't like it, and that made Ray feel a little better about doing it.

"Okay, good. Lu's not riding to my rescue and Mom's not out of rehab yet."

"*Mom,*" Chain said. "Not Juanita."

"Who's still hanging around?"

"Don't use that 'change the subject' bit too much," Chain said, "that's my thing. Lera's in the wind. She's got too many prices on her head to stay put long. She kissed you while you were out, by the way. Said you were a 'clever boy.'" He placed the microwave knife on the tray. "And thanks for letting her borrow this."

"Skye okay? Crazy horse lady?"

"Yeah. He's here. He's touch and go but getting treated. Ajeet vanished. No idea where she's gone off to. What she did down there was . . . impossible. She and Skye pretty much kept all of us alive until Neste had time to phase the planet."

"Rudian?"

"Milking the hero routine for all he, and the Shield Pact, are worth, of course. Been all over the media. He's hoping the spotlight will keep the Fellowship of the Whispered Word off his ass for a spell. He's even been big enough to give some of you all credit for saving the day too. There's going to be an award ceremony in a few cycles if you'd—"

"I got to get home," Ray said.

"Of course. I'll get you a guidestone, so you can make your way back. I'll get them to give you a translator ject too, so you can say your goodbyes."

Pana was in and out of consciousness. She gave Ray a drugged smile when she became aware of him beside her bed.

"Never underestimate us lowborn," Ray said. "We're sneaky fuckers."

She laughed and winced a little. "That we are."

"You're going to get a medal, a big ceremony. So, heal up quick. You don't want to sleep through that."

"You're leaving?"

"I got to. My mom . . . is a mess, but she's my mom. I got obligations." Pana nodded. They held each other's gaze for a little too long.

"It was good riding with you, Ranger," she said.

"It was an honor to fight by your side, Ratari." Ray took her hand. She squeezed his and then drifted back off to sleep.

Ray found Neste in another wing of the medical facility. He was an organic embryo floating on a monitor window. Two humanoids, an older man in his forties and a young girl in her mid-teens, were watching the monitor and holding hands. They favored each other strongly.

"Hi. Sorry to interrupt. My name is Ray Cosa. I'm guessing you're Tion," he said to the man, "and you've got to be Veme. I was a friend of your dad's."

"Pleasure," Tion said shaking Ray's hand. Veme smiled and nodded. She looked thin and haggard from her hostage experience.

"Thank you for saving us," Veme said.

"It was your dad who saved everyone." Ray glanced over at the monitor. "So what happens to Neste now?"

"He starts over, grows up, all over again," Tion said. "Those were his wishes. Some non-organic Tribanni opt for a stored backup but that leaves gaps in memory from the time of the last download. I was really surprised he chose this way, after all the grief he had given me about not making the transition myself." Tion smiled. "Always full of surprises, our old man."

"There's something really nice about that, about starting over," Ray said. "Who will look after him?"

"We will," Veme said, "once he's born, the same way he looked after us."

Ray smiled and nodded. He turned back from the monitor, to Neste's children.

"When he's older, could you please give him a message, in case I'm not around to do it myself?"

"Of course, Master Ranger," Tion said.

"Tell him, I knew he'd save her," looking at Veme, her eyes welling up with tears, "and that I said thank you, for being a good friend. It was nice to meet you both."

Ray headed toward the door, then paused. He looked back at the screen and turned around.

"If you guys don't mind, can I tell you a little about my time with your dad? I know it wasn't much, but he was so proud of you and he talked about you both to me. I think you would like to hear it. Maybe you could tell me a little about growing up with him, too."

Neste's children looked to one another and then back to Ray.

"Please," Veme said.


Skye was unconscious when Ray came to his room. Night had fallen. Machines churned his blood and breathed for him. His room was full of flowers—some real, some animated, and others holographic. Ray stood by the bed and searched for a sign of life, of motion, but the musician was still and pale. Chain said he had taken quite a few hits from the Yateveo spines that killed Evan and scratches from envenomed barbs too. There was no known antidote for the toxin. Chain said the doctors flushed Skye's blood, and replaced it with cloned blood. They had used neurological blockers to try to fight back the damage to his nervous system, and there was talk of building him a new one altogether.

Ray felt a strange presence, a chill at his back, but he saw nothing.

*I sense the concern in your mind,* Ajeet thought to him. *He is strong. His soul is strong. Do not despair. I will tell him you visited when he awakens.*

"Thank you," Ray said, but the presence was gone. Only shadows and flowers remained.

Chain was waiting with the Galaxie outside the medical center. He flipped a guidestone to Ray, who caught the coin in mid-air.

"Where you headed now?" Ray asked. "Back to gambling in rat-hole truck stops?"

"As tempting as that sounds, I'm going to be working with the general and the High Marshal for a while. I want to know how the Yateveo showed back up and make sure none of the other Nemesis are creeping about again. That would be very bad, for everyone. How about you?"

"Help my mom, pay Lu for all the shifts he covered for me. Get the Galaxie detailed. Maybe see about going back to school. I don't know."

"Sounds like you found some reasons," Chain said.

"A few." Ray held out his hand. "Thank you, for everything. You changed my life."

Chain shook his hand. "You did that, Ray. Your family would be real proud." As Ray climbed into the car, Chain added, "See you around the cosmos. You can ride with me any time, Ranger."

"In *that* P-O-S truck?" Ray scoffed.

Chain broke out laughing.

Ray started the Galaxie, and pulled away into the evening traffic toward the ramp to the Queen's Road, the first step in his long journey home.

. . .

Juanita walked on her own out of rehab. Ray had to admit she seemed like her old self. She looked ten years younger and her eyes had life in them again. She smiled at Ray and laughed when he opened the passenger door to the Galaxie.

"That new ride you've been telling me about. How fancy!" She slid into the car. Ray closed her door and then put her bags in the trunk. He went around, started the car up, and they pulled away.

"How're you feeling?" he asked.

"The same way I felt the last hundred times you asked me," she said with a smile. "I'm not going to break or melt in the rain, Ramon."

"Just checking."

He had made it home and spent the following week and a half before her discharge in sessions with Juanita and privately with her counselor, getting her ready to come home, and getting himself ready too.

"She's going to need consistency, support, but not smothering," the therapist said. "She has to be the most invested person in her recovery. And you, you need to get yourself to some Al-Anon meetings too, Ray. It's understandable you have anger issues, but if you want to be a part of her recovery you have to process them. You need to love her and stand by her through the good and bad, but you have to do that in a healthy way for both of you."

It had been rough at first. She felt like he had abandoned her, given up on her. Ray worked hard to dispel that. "I had a really hard job I had to do," he explained in one of their first visits. "I'm sorry I made you feel that way, but the job's done, and I'm home."

"I wouldn't blame you if you did walk away," she said, her voice tight in her throat.

Ray leaned forward on the couch in the visiting room. "Look, I'm not going to lie, we've hurt each other. I ran into this guy last week . . . at work. He kept trying to convince me there was no point to any of it. That life's all pain and why even try, why even bother?"

"That's how I felt after we lost your dad," she said. "I was so selfish, so caught up in my own fear and hurt. I . . . I abandoned you boys."

"You just got lost. It's easy to do. So, this guy was banging on me hard, when I remembered what you and Pop both used to say when we were little, when we'd mess up, when we'd give up. You remember?"

Juanita sifted through her memories, like walking a minefield. She paused and looked to Ray.

"Anything worth anything ain't easy," she said. "Your dad said that all the time when we dated, when we first got married. It's true."

"That kept me going. Kept Ben going too. More times than I can tell you. We used to remind each other of it when things got bad." He looked over to his mom. "I'm going to remind you of it, too. A lot."

She smiled the way she used to, a long time ago. The thing in the wasteland of the darkness whispered to Ray that her chances for relapse were high, that this moment, this victory was fleeting. *This whole universe is geared toward death, toward ending.*

"Who's the new girl?" Juanita asked. Ray looked confused. She nodded to the Ranger's signet hanging on a chain around his neck.

"It's a . . . complicated relationship. Hey, you want to go grab Lu and get ice cream? To celebrate?"

Her laughter chased the dark whispering thing away.

"Sounds wonderful, *mi cielito.*"

Ray wasn't blind. He saw all the signs of death and decay crowded around him. Closed shops, destroyed homes, ruined lives, people shuffling like zombies down empty streets. He glanced over to his mom. Thought of all the people who'd lost everything, who had every reason to roll over and die, who had instead stood and rebuilt. He thought about the war between hope and despair, life and death, that was beginning out there among the endless wonders and terrors of the universe, along the Queen's Road.

Perhaps you counted your victories a day, a moment, at a time. A step at a time. Even if the void was inevitable, the journey to it was yours; you owned it.

The Galaxie thrummed along. The wind was warm and sweet through the open windows. Sunlight flashed and reflected off the water. Ray ignored the cold of the signet's metal against his chest and tried to focus on the sun and the wind kissing his face.

**THE END**

# ACKNOWLEDGMENTS

I'd like to thank Steve Feldberg of Audible Originals for his hard work, belief, and support in making *the Queen's Road* into an audiobook reality.

Thank you to Lucienne Diver, the best agent and friend you can have on your side.

Thanks to John Hartness and the fantastic people at Falstaff Books for making their excitement, professionalism, and passion for publishing culminate in the book that you are holding.

To Roger Zelazny, for Princes, and shadows, and Lords of Light, To Grant Morrison, and Brian K. Vaughan for Barbelith and rocketship forests. To Douglas Adams for the towel and the potted petunia.

To my readers, who have become part of my family. Your unwavering support and friendship makes this the best job ever. Thank you!

# ABOUT THE AUTHOR

R.S. (Rod) Belcher is an award-winning newspaper and magazine editor and journalist, as well as an author of short and long fiction in a number of genres.

Rod has been a private investigator, a DJ, a comic book store owner and has degrees in criminal law, psychology and justice and risk administration, from Virginia Commonwealth University. He's done Masters work in Forensic Science at The George Washington University and worked with the Occult Crime Taskforce for the Virginia General Assembly.

The Grand Prize winner of the Star Trek: Strange New Worlds Anthology contest, Rod's short story "Orphans" was published in *Star Trek: Strange New Worlds 9* published by Simon and Schuster in 2006. It was his first professional fiction sale.

Rod's first novel, *The Six-Gun Tarot*, was published by Tor Books in 2013. The sequel, *The Shotgun Arcana*, was published in 2014 and the third book in the Golgotha series, *The Queen of Swords* was published in 2017. The fourth book in the series, *The Ghost Dance Judgement*, was published by Falstaff Books in June of 2020.

His novel, *Nightwise*, was released in August 2015, and was reissued with additional material in January of 2018. The sequel to *Nightwise*, *The Night Dahlia* was published in April of 2018. Rod hopes to begin work on the third Nightwise book, *Mother of Night*, in 2021.

Rod's novel, *The Brotherhood of the Wheel* was published by Tor in March of 2016. It was a Locus Awards finalist for Horror in 2017 and is currently in development as a television series. The sequel to Brotherhood, *The King of the Road*, was released by Tor in December 2018.

He will begin work on the third Brotherhood novel, *The Zodiac Lodge*, in early 2021.

His novel adaptation of the film,MiB International was published by Titan Books in the Summer of 2019 and he is writing an original audiobook space opera series for Audible with the first novel, *The Queen's Road*, released in December of 2019.

Rod has spoken at numerous schools, colleges, and universities on the subject of being a full-time working writer and the craft of writing.

He is represented by Lucienne Diver of The Knight Agency.

He lives in Roanoke, Virginia with his children, Jonathan and Emily.

# FRIENDS OF FALSTAFF

Thank You to All our Falstaff Books Patrons, who get extra digital content each month! To be featured here and see what other great rewards we offer, go to www.patreon.com/falstaffbooks.

## PATRONS

Dino Hicks
John Hooks
John Kilgallon
Larissa Lichty
Travis & Casey Schilling
Staci-Leigh Santore
Sheryl R. Hayes
Scott Norris
Samuel Montgomery-Blinn
Junkle

CPSIA information can be obtained
at www.ICGtesting.com
Printed in the USA
BVHW031141251120
594206BV00014B/75

9 781645 540533